Pra

The Refusal, The Outcast, The **shortlisted for EIGHTY- … and are outright winners in THIRTY-TWO book awards.**

—

The Refusal and *The Outcast* were gold medalists in The Global Book Award, also winning both the Pinnacle Book Award and the NYC Big Book Award. *The Refusal* also won the National Indie Excellence Award and The National Excellence in Romance Fiction Award for best first book. *The Outcast* was also a finalist in the Foreword Indies Book of the Year and has also won a silver IPPY award. *The Secret* won the Independent Press Award and was the runner up in Pencraft's overall annual award, as well as winning the Firebird Book Award, the New York Book Festival, and the Pinnacle Book Achievement Award. More recently, *The Photograph* has been named the winner in no less than THREE LGBTQ fiction awards.

—

The Refusal:

"From start to finish I couldn't put it down. Any required adulting went out the window and instead I lived and breathed Janus and Jo's world."

– Geraldine Brookhorn, Romance Writer

"The Refusal is guaranteed to be your next bingeable romance."

– Indies Today, Book Awards

"The thrill of the chase was intoxicating, and I didn't want it to end. The Refusal by Eve Riley is an exhilarating read, and I recommend it to those who love a good steamy romance."

– Literary Titan, Book Awards

"Inhaled this book! Smart. Fresh. Nerdy and hilarious rolled into one! This isn't your typical romance: It's smart, edgy, with well-written suspense that also happens to be romantic! Loved every page of this book! Can't wait for more!"

– CK, Amazon Review

"The Refusal is overall one of the best romance novels I have read in a long time. I can't wait to read the next in series."

– T.S. Simons, Author

The Outcast:

"I couldn't put it down and it kept me guessing till the very end. The Outcast was a joy to read!"

– BookishThespian, Book Blogger

"If you love modern love stories dripping with passion, you don't want to miss out on this. The Outcast is a stand-out romance novel with a dark twist. I cannot wait to get my hands on more books by this author!"

– Readers' Views, Book Awards

"If you're looking for something that's compelling, heartfelt, and steamy, but also tender, uplifting, and inspiring, you'll love Fabian and Kate's story. Perfectly crafted, evocative, and enchanting, you won't want to miss this."

– Bookaddict, Book Blogger

The Secret:

"I can't get enough of Eve's books. She makes it so easy to feel like you know the characters and are living the story right along with them. It's steamy in all the right ways and pulls at your heart strings."

– Annie Adams, Amazon Reviewer

"This book is an example of how good a contemporary romance novel can be. What makes this novel stand out is that it's about much more than romance, it's about flawed people, forged friendships, and life's ups and downs."

– Readers' Views, Book Awards

"This book was great. Eve knocked another book out of the park. I cannot recommend this book enough."

– Lisa, Goodreads Reviewer

The Photograph:

"Des and Alex are one of the most lovable couples I've ever come across and I can't remember the last time I rooted for a couple this hard. If you don't read this book, you are an absolute fool, stop reading this review and get over to Amazon already!"

– Flirtyquill, Book Blogger

"This book is lovely on so many levels. The plot is not predictable. So many times, I thought I knew where it was going, and it surprised me. And the writing? It's breathtakingly first rate, and astonishingly inviting. I simply couldn't wait to read the next paragraph." – **Readers' Views, Book Awards**

THE GAME

EVE M. RILEY

THE TECHBOYS *SERIES*

EVEMRILEY.COM

Published by Eve M. Riley.

ISBN: 978-1-0687177-2-7

Ordering and Enquiries Information:
Quantity sales. Special discounts are available on quantity purchases by corporations, associations, and others.
For details, contact the author at www.evemriley.com

Cover design and interior formatting:
Mark Thomas / Coverness.com

NOTE TO THE READER

For those of you who have read the whole series, the timeline for this novel occurs before Book 4—in two short months, November and December 2019, immediately after Fabian gets together with Kate, and before Des meets Alex.

The events portrayed here are thus set before the Russo-Ukrainian War.

Adam and Anna's story was supposed to be the focus of Book 3, but it took me a little longer (too long!) to wrestle their book into shape.

To Andy and Caroline, for being the very best of friends.

CHAPTER 1

Anna

When I click play on the video Mila has sent me, the roar of the music, conversation, and clinking glasses makes me hold the volume button down with a wince. The camera pans over a sea of people partying, a view from a balcony and lights in a valley, before turning back to show a room and the people behind. As I pick out Arty's black curls, I suck in a sharp breath. He's tucked into a couch making out with a girl, his hands on her large breasts as she grinds all over his lap.

My phone vibrates with a message:

Just thought you'd want to know.

I text back:

Where are you?

Spain. But this is from a party in Moscow.

I roll my lips together. Someone must have sent this to Mila. Why is my main competition on the tennis circuit sending me a video in the middle of her day? Shouldn't she be practicing? Every tournament, I tease her about the fact she's turned up again like a bad penny and she does the same to me. A cold Manhattan winter sun streams past outside the window. Mila and I live on different continents now, but we both clawed our way out of Russia through competing and share the terror of something forcing us to go back. Neither of us wants to remember what we did to escape. We may be rivals on court, but all the time we're not playing, we look out for each other.

My boyfriend of six months with a girl in his lap. Arty was in Moscow over the weekend, some business deal his father insisted he was involved in, he said. He flew into JFK today, and I'm meeting him after practice. Arty's a typical guy, I guess: a bit full of himself, but solicitous toward me. *Not like my previous one.* I thought an athlete would be better, and downhill skiing is a winter sport, so completely different from tennis and well out of the small, incestuous circle I live in. How wrong can you be? My hand shakes as I tap out a reply:

How did you get hold of it?

You know I have spies everywhere.

I pull my protein oats out of the fridge. The way Mila keeps her ear to the ground is nothing short of astonishing, and for good reason: You never know when something or someone in Russia is going to come back and bite you in the ass.

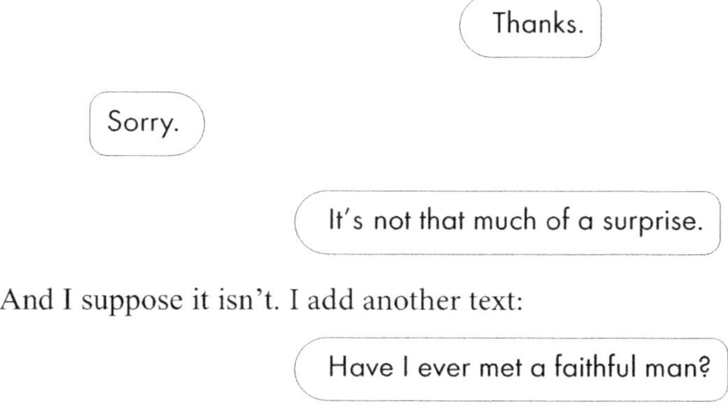

And I suppose it isn't. I add another text:

Have I ever met a faithful man?

Not even my father was faithful.

> You could always try women.

Interesting. Is Mila queer or bisexual? We've never had that conversation because we're Russian, and nobody tells the truth: They tell you what they think you want to hear. No one throws off the threat of being thrown into jail, either. Paranoia is my middle name.

I say yes or no to guys who ask me out without any deep thought, and perhaps that's why I end up dating assholes. Moving around tennis camps when I was younger helped me learn how to approach people, to laugh in all the right places, and be understanding and warm. Then I would lose people as they dropped out and have to start again, over and over. A profound wariness has settled inside me. Deep connections don't sit well with me: Things are going to end at some point and stab me in the heart. I sigh as I place my phone on the counter and scoop up a spoonful of oats. The tub in my hand has a label that says eight hundred calories and divides it into protein, carbs, and fat. *Moë telo khram*—my body is a temple, as my mother would say.

And I've got more important things to think about than Arty Maroz: like eight hours of tennis practice, like the twinge that's been bothering my right shoulder all week, like how well Katarina Yenko is doing. Like the fact I played the worst tennis of my life at the Billie Jean Cup. But if I keep working hard enough, keep pushing, it'll all come out all right—right?

*

Arty's face is flat as his eyes flicker over the video on my phone. He hands it back to me, eyes narrowed as he lifts his chin.

"Who took this?" he says in Russian.

"I don't know."

"But you got it from that bitch, Mila," he adds, waving his hand at the screen.

Fuck, that wasn't very cautious of me. "She didn't take it. She's in Spain."

He grunts and my eyes drift over his dark hair and eyes. I thought he was so handsome when I met him. But a creeping sensation runs down my spine as I watch him digging for who found him out. Will he make trouble in Russia through his father's connections, and here? What he doesn't care about is that he was with someone else, and presumably slept with her. The last time he stayed with me, he said, "Condoms are a pain, baby. Let's move on." *Jesus.* How much risk would I have been putting myself in if I'd said yes to that?

I pocket my phone. "Who is she?"

"I have no idea. Who cares?" A muscle ticks in his jaw. "Were we supposed to be exclusive?"

Oh, Christ. He's gaslighting me now?

I grimace. "You're right. We never had that conversation." I nod my head. "Of course, I should know better than to assume that a man who asks me on a date, and is with me for six months, is looking for something just with me."

His eyes fix on mine. "If you want exclusive, I can do that."

"Didn't we discuss not using condoms?"

"Yes. But I use them with everyone else, Anna, so you would always be safe! I would never put you at risk. You know that." He leans forward as if he's going to cup my cheek or kiss me. I jerk backward, and his eyebrows shoot up. "What is this about, Anna?"

God, I hate men. *All men.* We never had that conversation, my ass. But he's asked a valid question: What is this about? "I think it's about disrespect. About being a grown-up. Consideration for other people and their feelings, maybe?"

He frowns, jerking his hand out. "And what about my feelings, Anna? We aren't together all the time. You go away to tournaments for months. How did you think this would work?"

Once. Just once I'd like a man who thinks with something other than his dick. Don't my needs count for something, too? Okay, I go away a lot, but he knew that going in. This was *one weekend* apart! I need something better than a manipulative conversation where everything is couched in terms of something *he* did wrong being *my* fault.

But also, why am I even annoyed? We haven't been together for long enough for me to really care, except for a bit of wounded pride maybe, and this is the kind of guy I date. I don't think I could go out with someone who wasn't Russian, although technically Arty was born in Belarus.

"Did you fuck her?"

He frowns again. "Is it important?"

"Probably not." A familiar sadness I can never quite put my finger on grips my chest. I drink the rest of my coffee. "I need to be heading back. I've got a physio appointment and an interview and …"

He spreads his hands. "How do you expect to ever have a relationship when you commit so little time to other people? It's all about you, Anna. *Your* career, *your* success. You could have come with me to Moscow. I could have fucked *you* at this party."

This gets under my skin because it's partly true. I *am* always away, and the terror of trying to stay in the top tennis rankings throbs under my skin like a sore. Does he not understand the sacrifice it takes to do this? And *why* doesn't he? He's a downhill skier, albeit an injured one right now, but he competes.

"I had to train all this weekend" is all I say.

"*I had to train. I had to train*," he repeats in a singsong voice. "You're always training, Anna."

"It's my job!" Maybe he can afford to attend parties and live it up, what with his father bankrolling his sport and business interests, but I've never had that luxury.

I stand up. "Bye, Arty."

He sighs. "Anna, don't play games."

Who's playing games? Do women never turn him down in Russia because of who his father is? "It's not a game. I don't want to be with someone who fucks other people."

He shrugs. "Suit yourself. Call me when you've sorted your head out. Good luck finding somebody who doesn't mind the fact you're never in the same country as them."

If it wasn't all so bad, I'd laugh. My mom is going to kill me. His father runs Pteroka, the largest oil business in Russia. She practically ordered me to date him when I made the mistake of telling her he'd sent me a flirty message which basically said, "As two Russians in a foreign land, we should go for dinner." I think it was the culmination of her life dreams. My dad was the tennis guy.

"And don't think I'm coming to this fancy-ass event tonight to keep your sponsor happy," Arty adds as his parting shot.

Goddammit. I'd forgotten all about that. I groan internally. The press will eat me alive if I go on my own.

CHAPTER 2

Adam

I tap the final formula into the Excel spreadsheet on the screen in front of me and take in the sea of red. If these weren't the figures for my own business, I would be laughing. I have not only cut to the bone; I've taken on a load of debt, too. Unsecured, high-interest loans. *Stupid. Stupid, Adam.* I'm like a frog that's being slowly boiled in water, each year a little worse, a little more red on this spreadsheet. I haven't moved anywhere near fast enough, and the bottom line is a disaster. *Ten years!* Ten years since I started this company and nurtured the ideas I first had in college.

I swing around in my chair and stare out the window at the brick wall of the cheap below-ground space we rent in Brooklyn. We're intimate friends, this wall and I. Staring at it has solved many an electronics problem. Every crack in it is familiar. How long can I string my business out? Borrowed money and borrowed time.

My phone vibrates, and I turn back to my desk, flipping it over to find the words *Janus Phillips* across the top of the screen, and a small sigh seeps out, even as my mouth curls up. I press to answer.

"Adam! How's it going?" he says.

Janus is one of my best friends and runs one of the most successful tech startups in New York. Am I envious? Yeah, a little, but he's also loyal to a fault. He has everything figured out, and I'm never sure how or what I'm doing that's so different from him.

"All right. Still soldiering on."

"Yeah. All I remember is the constant terror that it was all going to implode."

I laugh. Janus raised a lot of money and played a high-stakes game with his company, which has paid off spectacularly. Mine's not in the same league at all. Selling small electronic components and kits via a website to people who want to prototype and experiment hasn't taken off like cloud computing has over the last ten years.

But I couldn't bring myself to go down that risky road. I've seen plenty of startups struggle because of the funds they've raised, and the pressure applied by banks and VCs. I like making things and working on them with my own hands, not shifting numbers on a screen. My parents and sister Victoria are all accountants, and their belief in the finance industry and my opposition to it has led to a somewhat strained relationship.

Victoria used to make fun of me having a startup, and I ribbed her in return about being a corporate drone, but as she's progressed in her company and her salary has increased, the jokes have been replaced by a deafening silence. She's bought a house and goes on fancy vacations. She's not exactly mean, my sister, but we're both competitive and I'm sure she's secretly pleased she's doing better than me, given that she's three years younger. My parents, on the other hand, don't even try and conceal their frowns and pursed lips whenever the subject of my business comes up, and it's become more and more difficult to hide how much I'm struggling.

"I'm calling because I got an unusual request," Janus hums, dragging me back to the phone in my hand. "I mean it's a bit late now …"

"What is it?"

"Anna Talanova's agent called my PA, Jenny, and asked if I'd be amenable to going to an awards event with her tonight."

Before Janus found Jo, he attended a lot of red-carpet events with gorgeous women on his arm, and the resultant publicity gave his business a huge leg-up.

"She's a tennis player, right? Does she know about Jo?"

"Yes, the tennis player, and yes, she does know about Jo. But she's really stuck. I've helped her out in the past. She's got some problem with the guy who was supposed to accompany her."

"What's this got to do with me?"

"Well, I suggested you go in my place."

"You did *what*?"

"I sent Anna a link to that interview you did with *Electronics Today*, and she said you looked 'cute.' Her words, not mine, buddy."

I glance down at my old T-shirt and faded jeans and laugh. That would not be the word she'd use if she could see me now. They tidied me up for the photo shoot for that magazine article. No one would ever describe me as "cute." Sensible, yes. Boring, possibly. OCD, for sure. I'm not interested in anything beyond technology and getting this goddamn company to survive. Oh, and money! I'm always interested in that.

"Isn't it a bit odd that …"

Janus sighs. "This is what they do."

"They eye up guys in the paper and ask their agents to call their offices?"

"Pretty much."

"That's ridiculous. I can't go to some high-profile thing with a tennis player, Janus! What the hell would we talk about?"

He chuckles. "She's gorgeous by the way, and probably earns a ton of money."

That sounds far too close to echoes of the past. "Who are you—my mother? Are you trying to find me a woman?"

"Well, you have to admit you don't get out much."

"And we all know why that is. I don't do women anymore—you know this."

The long pregnant silence on the line makes sweat break out on my neck.

"Did you ever go out when your business was small and struggling to survive?" I add, deflecting. Damn, I'm giving more away than I want to here—though, of anyone, Janus would understand a company being on the edge. *But for ten years, Adam?*

Goddammit, is it possible to surgically remove my mother's voice from my head?

"She's good people, and she hasn't had an easy time of late."

And that's a hard no. A needy woman who's messed up? Absolutely not.

"Please. As a favor to me. I'd like to help her out," he says.

Oh! Goddamn Janus and his ability to lean on people.

"I'm sending you a link," he adds into my stony silence.

My phone vibrates, and when I click the link, a beautiful dark-haired woman fills the screen.

"Whoa! That's her?"

Janus laughs. "Go on, it will get you out of the office, and if you're anything like me, I'm betting you slept on the couch there for the last three nights."

Damn, he has a terrible habit of being right. "I'm not dressed for an awards thing, and I'll fall asleep in my soup."

Clearly sensing I'm weakening, he says, "If I can find you a suit, will you go?"

"You're not spending your time finding me a suit."

"Jenny will organize it."

Jesus Christ. I glower at the on-screen circuit board I was designing before he called. My plan for the evening was to finish it. "What time?"

"7:30 p.m., but you'll have to be at her apartment two hours beforehand."

Fuck that. "Two hours!" I glance at my watch—it's 2:30 p.m. now. How's Jenny going to drum up a suit that fast?

"Thanks, man. I really appreciate it. I'll get Anna's agent to give you a call." And he hangs up.

I stare at the phone in my hand.

"Why do I have to be there two hours earlier?" I say to my empty office.

I look at the design on my screen again. Is finishing this going to make the difference between success and failure? No, no it isn't. But as I'm studying it, my phone vibrates again.

"Hey, Mr. Miller, Barbara Levy, Anna Talanova's agent. Thanks so much for helping Anna out tonight. Can I call you Adam? And you've got to call me

Barb." Her words rattle out in a strong New York accent.

That fast? I want to groan and bury my head in my hands, but all that spills out is: "I'm happy to help, but I'm the dullest man on the planet and I can't do small talk."

She chuckles. "Anna has dated several athletes. You can't be worse than them, trust me."

What's wrong with athletes? Do I want to know? Probably, yes. "What did they talk about?"

"Stats. Competitors. How they were three tenths of a second off a gold medal. I think Anna has enough of that in her life already."

I laugh. They have no idea how boring tech is. "I can talk a good game about voltage differentials across a resistor."

"Sounds fascinating."

"What do I need to wear?"

"A suit of some description. Janus said his PA was going to courier a few options over to you."

Holy shit. I'm struggling to make the rent on this little unit in Brooklyn and people are couriering designer suits around New York. But "Great!" is all that comes out.

"They want you at Anna's apartment at 5:30 p.m. sharp to get you ready and give you a briefing. Is that okay?"

They? Who are *they*? And *get me ready*? What are they planning to do to me? Jesus. I still haven't got my head around that two hours. No way can I afford that kind of time.

"Is two hours really necessary?" I say. Am I sounding like a diva here?

The phone goes muffled on the other end—voices in the background—and I chew my lip. This is probably a pain in the ass for Anna, and they don't need some guy who runs a small tech startup throwing his weight around.

Barb comes back on the line. "I'm afraid there's too much media interest in Anna, Adam. The whole thing will be scrutinized, and we don't want to put you in a position where you're unprepared for it."

What can I say? I'm in this now, for Janus, and I'm not the kind of person who'd let someone down. "No problem, I'll be there at five-thirty." Boy, am I going to get something good out of him for this!

"We'll make sure it goes smoothly, Adam. That's what I'm here for."

"Thanks, Barb. And I appreciate you inviting me. I'm excited to meet Anna." I smile at the wall to try and make myself sound genuine.

"She's excited to meet you, too." *Suurrre.* "See you later." And she hangs up.

I turn my phone over in my hand. I spent most of my college years bailing Janus and Fabian out of one problem or another. This doesn't feel too different. I pull up the texting app.

Is this going to be a load of hassle?

Janus responds instantly:

Get over yourself. It'll be an amazing experience, and I'm quite liking my new role as your social secretary.

I chuckle.

Smallest job role in history.

But he's right. I *should* be flattered. Janus told me a tale or two when he first started dating famous women, but it didn't seem like something that would happen in real life. But here we are.

Jenny's sending you a briefing on Anna.

I laugh. Of course she is. Damn, I'd love to have a PA who helped me out like that. I can hardly afford the admin person we've got these days.

Good. I need to know more about this woman who's getting her agent to phone around eligible bachelors in New York.

Eligible. Ha! I grin at my phone. Well, at least this has stopped me thinking for a night about how my business might be going under in two months if I don't pull a rabbit out of the hat.

CHAPTER 3

Adam

I step out of the car that Anna's ... agent? manager? someone anyway ... sent for me and shiver with the cold. I stare up at the steel-and-glass building rising like a transformer from the sidewalk in front of me. *Probably makes a ton of money. Riiiight.* More than a ton, I'd say.

My gut is bubbling away. What am I doing here? I avoid women most of the time, apart from the ones who work with me. Why did I let Janus persuade me into this? He ribs me sometimes that I'm going to be a lonely old man, but I like my own company. I don't need a woman who I've got to look out for; it's bad enough looking out for myself. Me and a couple of cats—that would be perfect. Why should old cat ladies have all the fun? Let's make a pitch for little old cat men.

When I enter the building, a man with floppy brown hair, a perfectly tailored pair of pants that finish at his ankles, shiny pointed shoes, and a tight white shirt is waiting for me. He's holding a sheaf of papers in his right hand. His brilliant smile is blinding.

Is he wearing makeup?

He scans me up and down. "Perfect suit," he says, as he starts to walk around me, lifting my jacket at the back. "At least that's one problem solved," he adds under his breath.

What?

His eyes drift up to the top of my head, and he sucks on his lower lip. "We're going to have to cut it," he mutters, "and change the shirt. Come," he says, beckoning to me with his hand.

I'm almost too scared to ask what's wrong with my hair, never mind my shirt, but not totally.

I run my hand over my short, tawny-colored waves. "Is something up with my hair?"

The guy eyes me over his shoulder as we head toward the elevators. "Have you ever been to a red-carpet event before?"

I shake my head as we step into the elevator, and he scans a card and presses a button that says penthouse. Janus is having a laugh about that money thing. He knew. Of course, he did. *Perhaps one day I'll own something like this*. The idea makes me want to chuckle. I resell Chinese electronics to the American market and design little electronic kits. How would that ever make me rich?

Mr. Floppy Hair types frantically into his phone. "Well, let me tell you …" He puffs out his cheeks and taps on his screen a few more times. "They will dissect *everything*." His eyes veer toward my crotch. "Including whether your boxers are visible through your pants. It's my job to make sure they concentrate on Anna, the awards, the movie, the sport …" He waves a hand. "Whatever it is, not some faux pas we could have seen coming."

"Doesn't that make it all a bit boring?" Personally, I love all those stories where someone shows some sideboob by mistake, or the dress is see-through.

He rolls his eyes at me. "You want the outline of your penis to be discussed on prime-time television?"

Okay, maybe I get it.

"There are celebrity bulge sites, if you get my drift."

"Are you serious?"

He raises his eyebrows at me and then holds out the sheaf of papers. "Before I forget, I need you to sign this NDA. There's some instructions on protocol in there, too."

I take the papers from him and start reading. No pictures, no posting, no discussion of anything that happens in the penthouse or at the event. *Okaaaay.* I feel like I'm running behind the curve: Everyone is taking this seriously except me. I turn my phone over in my hand and type in my text thread to Janus:

An NDA is required for drinks and dinner?

When the doors of the elevator open, another man in form-fitting pants, heels, pink hair, and red glasses is standing waiting.

"Serge," my companion says tightly with a nod, and the air crackles. Hmmm, interesting vibe—what's going on between these two? And Mr. Floppy Hair never gave me his name.

"Julio," Serge replies, glancing at his watch. "It's going to be tight."

"But you're a genius, darling," Julio murmurs, before gesturing at my hair. "What do you think?"

Serge stares at my head. "Turn around," he says, moving his hand in a circular motion.

I obey. Because, hey, with these two guys I wouldn't dare do anything else.

"I think it would be fabulous with those instant highlights you did on Matt," Julio says. "More blond, for sure."

Serge's eyes widen. "Yes. Oh yes!" Then he scowls. "But we'll have to do his makeup at the same time."

"Makeup?" I say.

Julio sighs and leans into Serge, saying in a low voice, "He's very straight."

Serge gestures down my body. "He actually doesn't look that bad for a straight guy."

Julio's eyes bug out, and Serge claps a hand over his mouth, but I laugh as they both stare at me wide-eyed.

"Trust me, I'm very flattered that you think I look even halfway decent," I say.

Julio rolls his shoulders as his eyes flick to Serge. "Don't say *too* many inappropriate things to him. You know what happened last time," he says, and then he gives me a wave and heads off down the corridor.

Serge beckons me in the opposite direction. "What happened last time?" I lean in to whisper.

He shakes his head and makes a zipping motion over his lips, and now it's become my mission to find out what he said and who he said it to.

Half an hour in and I like Serge so much that, if I had any money at all, I'd ask him to come and work for me. He'd be an amazing additional marketing person. He has gossiped nonstop about actors, actresses, and the jobs he's worked on. Matt, apparently, is Matt Damon, and I can't believe I've got Matt Damon's hairstylist doing something to my short locks. He won't tell me what happened *last time*, but it wasn't Matt who is "the cutest." It turns out that someone complained about Serge coming on to him. "In all fairness, darling, all the indications were he was gay, and he didn't give me the vibe he was going to be offended, like *at all*, if you understand what I'm saying."

He tells me all this while slapping some paste on various parts of my hair, and I take in his leather pants, tight white vest, and dark chest fur with an interesting necklace dangling over his pecs.

"I like your outfit."

He blinks at me and laughs. "Why thank you!" He leans forward and whispers, "I'm starting to think that you're less straight than you're letting on."

I chuckle. "I'm sorry to say I'm definitely straight. I've just never been that good with putting clothes together. I'm more of a faded tee and jeans type of guy."

He purses his lips. "I have a friend, a stylist to the stars. I could put you in touch with her."

I laugh. "I don't think I've got that kind of profile … or money."

"Are you kidding me? You're red-carpeting with Anna! If you didn't have any visibility before, you will after this."

"Is she that big of a deal?" I don't mean this in the insulting way it probably comes across. "I don't know much about tennis," I add. "I've heard of her but …"

He rolls his eyes at me. "Do you live under a rock, darling?"

"Very possibly," I mutter.

"My friend will cut you a deal. She's brilliant at finding inexpensive classics. She likes working with people who are up and coming."

Up and coming? I can't help the snort that escapes from my mouth.

"I'm just a nerd, really. Look ..." I pull out my phone and drag up pictures of me in my office surrounded by electronic components and kits and dressed in an old T-shirt and jeans.

Serge's eyes go round. "You're in tech?" When I nod, he takes the phone from my hand and zooms in. "You scrub up well, though, and once we've finished with you today, there'll be no holding the ladies back." He squeezes my arm. "It can't be all sitting behind a desk. You look pretty fit to me."

I'm not offended by his upfront assessment, not at all. "I do jujitsu to keep in shape."

I don't want to tell him I started it so I could defend myself at school. I was a skinny, small guy. I'm still not that big, but I fight better now. And once the bullies found out I could go head-to-head with them, they left me alone. More or less.

He blinks.

"I was part of my college team. I used to compete," I say. "I still do a bit." I scratch my cheek. Something about Serge makes me want to reveal all my secrets. "You know what I really worry about is whether I smell like burning rubber. It's the solder."

"The solder?"

"We melt it to connect wires on electronic boards."

He bends down and sniffs, then squeezes my shoulder. "You smell fine to me."

Before I can say any more, a sharp-faced woman appears in the doorway, nods at Serge, and holds out her hand to me.

"I'm Anita. I'm here to do your makeup." Her voice is slightly accented.

She unravels a large roll of brushes on the counter and unzips a multi-compartmented padded bag. The array of small pots and colors is dizzying.

"Do I honestly need makeup?" I say. I'll look like a dick, surely.

She nods. "The way they light up the red carpet for the photographers and the cameras? It's actually like a stage. You'll look strange in photos if you're *not* wearing any. Don't worry—you won't be able to tell."

"Really?"

She smiles. "Trust me. I've done hundreds of guys." Serge meets my eyes in the mirror and bobs his head in agreement.

I watch her and my reflection as she rubs various creams followed by things with tints over my face. I can't quite believe what's happening to my skin: brighter, smoother, clearer. God, it's impressive. This is why celebrities always look so polished.

At some point, Serge whips me off to wash whatever coloring thing he's been doing out of my hair, and Anita threatens to cut his balls off if he messes with her work on my face. And then I'm back, being snipped and blow-dried and numerous products applied to my hair as Serge scrunches it.

A woman comes in with four shirts on hangers, all in slightly varying shades of dark plum.

"Ooh, nice," Serge says, nodding. "Definitely his color."

I have a color?

And in a final flurry, I stand up and the shirts are tried on and Serge and Anita do some extra things to my face. I think maybe they've finished.

Julio appears suddenly in the doorway. He raises his eyebrows when he spots me, giving me an approving nod. "Much better," he says.

"How are they doing with Anna?" Anita turns to him to ask.

"She's out of the shower," Julio says, waving his hand in front of his face. "We're running late. Stressful!" He does jazz hands.

"What do you think?" Anita asks.

The three of them gather together by the door and scan me up and down.

Julio smiles. "Masterful, you guys." Then he gestures at my hair. "There's some stray strands near his crown."

If they're worrying about the odd hair now, I'm not going to be able to touch anything on my body all night. Serge does something to the top of my head and turns me to a full-length mirror and I take in the total effect. I almost don't recognize the guy staring back at me: Ostensibly it's me, but at the same time everything has changed. My hair's been transformed into a tousled mess, and somehow it works. The color doesn't look fake at all; it's like he's just given my hair some natural variation by adding a bit of … interest, depth? Jesus, I've never thought about my appearance this much. The plum shirt with my dark blue suit is perfect. Who knew? I would never have put those colors together.

"Thank you, guys. This is perfect."

They all beam, and Serge presses his hand to his chest.

Julio claps his hands. "Okay, I need you in Anna's suite, pronto."

As they go out the door, I hear Serge say, "He is literally the easiest guy I've ever worked with. I think I'm in love."

And I laugh at my reflection in the mirror.

What do I do now? A woman with a headpiece appears and directs me down a long corridor to a seating area. And I'm just settling into a chair when another woman, this one wrapped in a huge fluffy bathrobe and with dark wet hair curling right down over her shoulders, slides out of a door that looks like it is part of a wall. With a start, I realize it's Anna Talanova. She's small, and her hands are clutched together in a deathlike grip. She's nothing like the smiling, confident woman in the picture Janus sent me, or the player in her post-match interviews where she glowed with energy and drive.

"Adam! Hello!" She holds out a hand, and flustered, I take it. Her hand is surprisingly big, firm, and warm. "They told me they'd finished with you, and I wanted to come out and thank you for stepping in at such short notice and also to apologize for all the fuss. They employ professional teams for these events and then …" She waves her hand around.

I smile at her. "It's been fun. I've had a lovely chat with Serge."

She blinks at me. "Seriously? Oh! Okay. That's great." Her voice has a slight accent, but her English is perfect.

I grin. "It's all good. No need to apologize. Just relax and we'll have a fun evening, yeah?"

She frowns for a second and then a wide smile lights her face. "Yes, fun. I think I remember how to do that from third grade."

I laugh. "I don't have much fun myself these days, either."

"Your business sounds amazing. You'll have to tell me all about it." She turns with a wave of her hand and disappears into the door she came out of.

Women always say that, but none of them really want that conversation. It's as boring and as incomprehensible as you might expect.

*

When I settle down in the living room, the security lady brings me a coffee and a plate decorated with some tiny canapes, which only serves to remind me how hungry I am. Did I have lunch? I don't remember it. And I've only been sitting there a couple of minutes when there's the sound of feet scrabbling on the marble floor and an odd-looking brown-and-white fluffy dog with big ears comes barreling into the seating area.

I instantly put my hand down and click my fingers. "Hello there. Who are you?"

He or she charges up to my hand, nudges my fingers, and then licks them. I give her a body rub as I bend down to subtly check the sex. *Okay. Lady dog.* She jumps up and her tongue swipes across my face.

"Oh Jesus, don't do that. We'll be in trouble with Anita."

She cocks her head at me and races over the room to pick up something in her mouth, before trotting back and dropping it by my feet. It's a … pink rabbit?

A very chewed pink rabbit.

Her big brown eyes stare up at me expectantly.

Hmm. I grab the rabbit as she circles around a few times and then crouches down, tail wagging, before I throw it across the room.

In a flurry of scrabbling claws and bouncing fur, she dives over and fetches it and drops it again at my feet. *Okay then.*

I put my hand out and ruffle her head.

"You're a cutie, aren't you?" I stroke her chin, and she whines a bit. Grabbing my phone, I snap a couple of quick pictures, even though I'm not supposed to. I'd like some pictures of tonight. Perhaps I can chat to Anna about it.

So, we play a game of fetch for I don't know how long until a voice says, "Ah, you've met Pepper."

As I raise my head, my jaw drops. Anna is standing at the entrance to the corridor in a red dress that clings everywhere, her chocolate-colored hair piled in heaped curls on her head, and her makeup dark and sultry. She looks nothing like the woman who said hello to me earlier.

"Fuck. You look *amazing*!"

She laughs. "I like you, Adam. You can come back."

I grin at her. "Wow, what a dress!"

And what a person in it, I don't say.

"Whenever you need a plus one, I'd be very happy to step in," I add.

I wince. Am I coming across a bit strong? I've never been smooth, and my woman radar is a little broken.

She raises her eyebrows. "I might hold you to that." Her eyes drift down my body. "That's a very smart suit."

I wish I'd thought to bring something for her. Some flowers, a gift, something that would make this ... *nicer*, less transactional maybe. *Next time.* Ha. Like there's going to be a next time for Mr. Awkward with a woman like this.

In times like this, I always think of channeling Fabian. But the problem is that, with his tattoos and long hair, he looks the part. So, he sits and broods and women fall all over him. I'm more like Pepper, sensible and loyal, and trying to appear cute so someone will play with me. The double meaning makes heat climb up my neck. It's years since I've been with anybody, and there's a good reason for that, I remind myself. I'm happy with my life the way it is, and I am never going back down that path.

CHAPTER 4

Anna

I gaze in the mirror, not registering my reflection, while Serge works on my hair. *Adam Miller*. What a cute guy! So laid back. He doesn't have a problem with being here, getting primped for an event, or anything really.

Adam was a boring computer electronics guy, Janus said, so I was expecting a beard and sandals, not some good-looking tousled man in a sharp suit. Was that Serge and Julio's doing?

Serge flicks a glance at me. "He's nice, eh? I could ravish him myself if he swung both ways."

I laugh. Serge and Julio are a blast. "Did he turn up with a beard and sandals?"

Serge frowns. "Not at all! He came in the suit, and I added a bit of va-va-voom to his hair. But that body is all his own work." He winks at me in the mirror, then leans forward. "I think Julio decided to change his shirt color just so he could admire him shirtless."

He's wiry, certainly. But there's something attractive about that. Not my usual type at all.

"Oh God! Please don't tell me that. I need plausible deniability for anything even vaguely inappropriate."

He bites his lip, then grins. “Me? Inappropriate?” He gestures down his torso. “He had lovely blond chest hair, and a very sexy trail.” He winks.

Christ, he needs to stop talking about Adam’s body. Adam’s a total stranger, doing me a favor.

“He’s like a small powerful animal,” I say. Am I making this any better?

“Like a dung beetle?”

I lean forward with a snort, bending my head toward my knees as I struggle to breathe, wheezing as I straighten up.

“What?” he says, grinning wildly at me in the mirror. “They are nature’s strongest animal! They can move balls of poop 1,141 times their own weight.”

“I don’t think he’d thank you for being compared to a dung beetle,” I choke out. “Anyway, how do you know all this stuff?”

“I studied Animal Science in college.”

“You did *what*?”

He waves his hand. “It’s a long story. But suffice to say, gay men are a bit of an exception on those types of courses in certain parts of this wonderful country.” He gestures down his body again. “Especially ones dressed like me. It’s like spotting a leopard in the Serengeti.”

My eyes meet his. “I’m calling him DB from now on.”

He snorts into my hair. “Don’t you dare, missy.”

“I was actually thinking of something sleeker, more fast-moving.”

“Like a ferret.” He sticks his top teeth over his bottom lip and screws up his face.

And I can’t hold my laughter back now. Serge grins and shakes his head as I tip my head back and tears stream down my face.

“Okay then, a cheetah,” he says.

I gulp in a few sharp breaths. “That’s much better,” I gasp out.

He hums as he parts a strand of my hair and runs a flattening iron down it. “Hmmm, yes. A cheetah. All high-speed grace and long soft fur,” Serge says, running his fingers through my hair.

“Stop talking about fur!”

He giggles and waves a hand over my head. “It is literally my job, darling! I am paid to notice hair of all kinds, no matter where it is on the body." He winks at me in the mirror. "Let's make you look amazing, so DB falls head over heels for you."

"Don't call him that!"

And some guy falling head over heels for me? That's something that's never happened. They discover the tennis schedule and run for the hills. Plus, I've just wriggled out of Arty's clutches, although whether I've actually escaped him or not remains to be seen … and Pietr … God, how little I understood when I was with him. I need to message Mila and warn her that Arty spotted her account name on the video she sent me.

"Oh, but you're dating that sexy downhill skier, Arty Maroz, aren't you? Where's he tonight?"

"We split up. Today actually. But please don't say anything until I've had a chance to agree all the media announcements with his PR person."

"I am the soul of discretion," Serge says, placing a hand over his heart, and I laugh again. "I'm sorry you broke up, darling. You were a cute couple. All that wonderful dark hair, yours and his." He flourishes a hand over my head.

"Don't be sorry. He cheated."

"He *what*? He cheated on *you*? Honestly, men are so fucking useless. They don't know when they've got it good."

"Tell me about it. You want to see?" I shouldn't show him the video, but sometimes you want someone to have your back and Serge loves the gossip.

He peers over my shoulder as I pull up the clip.

"Wow." He purses his lips as it gets to the part with Arty on the couch. "Jesus, look at them go. You've got the right kind of friends watching out for you like that."

Mila's small face peering out of her bunk bed in tennis camp swims in front of my face. We were always stuck in some place miles from anywhere and terrified. Terrified of not making it; terrified of not hitting the standards required by the men who ran the camps and getting sent back home; terrified of not escaping what our lives would otherwise have been.

As Serge starts twisting my hair into tendrils with a heated brush, my phone vibrates on my desk. I stretch forward and pick it up. It's a message from Arty.

Check your inbox, bitch.

Oh, Jesus. Maybe I spoke too soon about being free from him.

I open the app and don't spot anything, but there is an email from a legal firm. When I scan through it, it's a deposition concerning the ownership of Pepper, bought by a Mr. Artyom Maroz.

He's suing me for custody of Pepper?

She was a birthday present! He doesn't even want a dog: He never bothered to walk her or even play with her. He just wants revenge, the asshole. And, goddammit, I can't respond because it will all be used in evidence against me, no doubt. I type back:

I've forwarded it to my lawyer.

See you in court.

His reply is followed by a string of celebration emojis. *Shit.* I close my eyes. I love tennis, but this is a huge pile of crap. I'd do well to remember that, no matter how cute men are, there's always some sting in the tail. I know nothing about Adam. As a friend of Janus's, he's probably okay, but I've always known I can't trust people, and that's only gotten worse over the last couple of years as my profile has grown. I'm like a matryoshka doll: shell after shell until I don't know who the person is inside anymore. It's as lonely as hell.

Perhaps I'm always going to be asking myself that question now: Are they with me for me, or for Anna Talanova, tennis player?

CHAPTER 5

Adam

When we're settled in the limousine, I glance sideways at Anna. "Where are you from originally? Do you live in New York?" That accent is …

She shakes her head. "I grew up in Russia. Honestly, I'm not sure I belong anywhere. I'm on the road a lot." She gives a small, forced laugh. "But I keep the apartment here, so I have somewhere to come back to. My visa allows me to come and go, and I'll apply for a green card once I'm not traveling so much."

"That sounds …" I want to say lonely, but what do I know? Her life could be crammed with good people, and she might have lots of friends in New York and on the tennis circuit. However, if that was the case, why did she invite *me* to this?

As if she can read my mind, she says, "Yeah, I don't think tennis is conducive to steady relationships."

I chew my lip. I know nothing about steady relationships. Although at one time I would have called myself a relationship guy, my trust was torched. So, what am I now? I don't know how men can do one-night stands, and I don't understand women at all. I'm like an odd creature that lives under a rock and comes out blinking into the sunlight once a year. There's no way I would ever be on the radar of a woman like Anna Talanova, gorgeous as she is. The thought almost makes me laugh out loud. "Are you in town for anything in particular this time?"

She turns to me with a small smile. "A break before Christmas. I've been competing on the international tennis circuit for seven years. I've just come back from the Billie Jean Cup. I'm gathering that you're not a tennis fan?"

A cup, huh? That sounds impressive. "Sorry, I'm so out of touch. Did anyone pass on to you that …"

"You're a very boring computer guy?"

I chuckle through my wince, and Anna laughs. "Don't worry. I understand the obsession with the thing you're doing. I'm fairly nerdy about tennis. The problem with my line of work is, when you spend eight hours on court every day practicing, and the rest of the time traveling, some people take exception to that."

By *some people* does she mean men?

"Anyway," she adds, "the Billie Jean Cup is the main international team competition in women's tennis."

My eyes go round. God, half the world must be watching her play. "It's finished? Crap. I'm sorry, I didn't know that. That's incredible. Holy shit, Anna, playing in something like that. Congratulations!"

She makes a face at me. "I sort of messed it up. We lost spectacularly badly."

Oh! *Damn.* I rub my hands together. "Well, I think I'd take a gold medal in messing things up myself."

She laughs. "Really? Why's that?"

"I don't want to get into how bad things are with my company right now."

She raises her eyebrows. "I looked your business up. It looks amazing. Super complicated."

The idea that she looked at my nerdy electronics website makes my heart ache. She turns in her seat. "Tell me about what you do."

Oh dear. "There's these things called printed circuit boards that connect together all the components used in electronic devices." I wave my hand around the car, then fish the PCB out that I dropped into my pocket earlier as I was leaving the office and hand it to her. She turns it over in her palm. "I design these and then write the code that makes them do something interesting. We sell these alongside components for people who want to learn, experiment, or prototype. It's a nice community, and we do online tutorials, too. It's as nerdy as all get-out."

She laughs. "Wow, Adam. You must be very smart."

"Not so smart in business, I think." Why am I telling her this? "But my marketing manager, Susie, bends over backward to make what we do sound exciting."

She blows out a long breath. "I have a good marketing team, too. Sometimes the expectations are a bit much, aren't they? The technicalities of tennis … how hard I have to work. I'm expected to do well, so they try and knock me down a little. My team is good at handling all that for me."

They knock her down? Jesus. "How on earth do you cope?"

"I keep my head down and ignore it. I'm lucky enough to have had success in the past and sponsorship so I can pay for people to take some of the heat. At one time, my parents did a lot for me. Sometimes I have to do these things …" She waves her hand around the car. "… but mostly I just practice and play."

I stare out of the window. "Yeah. Gloss over the shit bits, right?"

Her eyes widen. "I didn't mean to imply that going out with you isn't enjoyable, I …"

I shake my head. "I didn't take it that way at all. There are parts of my job I dislike, too."

She laughs. "Yes! Losing. Doing deals, like sponsorship. I hate that. I have an agent, so that makes it less …" She waggles her hand back and forward. "… Like I'm selling my soul."

I laugh. "What's this event tonight?"

"A sports personality award."

"Are you up for it?"

She shakes her head. "I haven't even been shortlisted. But one of the brands that sponsor me sponsors this event, so …"

"Anything I need to be aware of? People you want to stab, dicks we're avoiding, that kind of thing?"

She bursts out laughing. "Interesting question. It would be sensible to chat about it."

And we're off as she fills me in on all the people who will be at the awards and the various rivalries going on between them. It's riveting.

In no time at all, the limousine pulls up at the American Museum of Natural History, cameras flashing outside the car's tinted windows. A man in a tuxedo opens Anna's door, and she steps out onto a red carpet. Everything slows like molasses, my breath a strange rasp in my head as my shoe lands on a strangely synthetic sea of red, and I pull myself upright, blinking like a mole as lights flicker and pulse and people shout from all sides.

And then we have to stand and pose. People shout questions at Anna about who's accompanying her tonight—I realize with a start they mean me—and about where someone named Arty Maroz is, but she only smiles back. When we get inside, the main hall is like a coral sea, multicolored lights panning across the ceiling with a huge blue whale suspended over the space, beautiful yellow flowers on every table. Everything shimmers: the people, the lights, the dresses.

And the evening morphs into a whirlwind of faces and names. At some point, Anna's fingers curl around my arm and I keep her tucked up under my elbow, my eyes fixed on her as she transforms into the confident chatty person I saw in the post-match interviews. Thank God I don't have to be on like this in my work, it would be exhausting, and I'm warm and light inside as I stand and watch her talk and smile and nod. No one is interested in me. I'm just the arm candy. I chuckle to myself: I wonder whether Janus had these exact same thoughts when he did this. If only my business could follow in his footsteps so easily.

And later, when the car pulls up to take us home, a man and a woman I don't recognize climb into the back seats with us.

"Adam, this is June and Damian. They work on my social media and PR."

June nods at me and smacks gum. Damian's gaze tracks down my body and smirks. *Okay.* I nod at them as though having two marketing people in a limousine with me at midnight happens every night of the week. As soon as we're settled, they start scrolling through their phones and talking to Anna about the coverage that's appearing, comments about her hair, her dress, my suit, who I am. It sounds terrifying. As we drop them both off in Harlem, June blows Anna a kiss and promises a full report tomorrow. When the door shuts, Anna leans back on her headrest and closes her eyes. I study her pale face. The last thing she needs is to feel she has to talk to me, too. I turn my head and examine my reflection in the car window as the lights of the store windows zip past.

"Thank you for tonight. You've been very easy and supportive and that's made everything so simple for me," she says quietly, and when I twist my head toward her, her eyes are still closed.

I have? I provided my support to another lady once. Unease spreads across my shoulders.

"My pleasure. It was good to meet you. I was happy to help out."

"Janus is a godsend." A smile curls over her lips. "He's completely smitten with his fiancée. God, I followed all the comments about that relationship so closely. When he did that thing with the *Wall Street Journal* …" She waves her hand. "That was so romantic."

The hairs on the back of my neck prickle. Was she ever in a relationship with *Janus*? Perhaps that's why he was insistent about this favor, and it was nothing to do with encouraging me to get out more.

"Did you and Janus ever …"

But she shakes her head before I finish. "No. He's an amazing guy but energetic and impatient and completely subsumed in his company. Don't get me wrong, I really recognize the drive and admire him for it, but I don't think either of us would have thought we were right for each other." She laughs. "And there's the small matter that I travel for ten months of the year." She stares out of the window. "All the girls adored him, though."

"The girls?"

She turns her head on the back of the seat with a quirky grin. "The women he accompanied to events."

"I still can't believe this happens."

"Word gets around about the jackasses. It's actually kind of essential."

Yeah, that makes sense. A frown drifts across her face, so I shift the conversation back to Janus. "Women loved him at college, too … once he lost the weight."

"Lost the weight?"

"Yeah, he was in bad shape when he started at NYU. Our friend Fabian forced him through a daily gym routine and a strict diet. The soundtrack of college for me was him grumbling about eating rabbit food."

"Wow. I can't imagine him like that, big, I mean."

I smile at her. "I think we've all changed a bit since college."

She nods and closes her eyes again as she says, "What were you like in college?"

An idiot? Sucked in by a woman and unable to see the reality?

"Quiet."

"The silent brooding type, huh?" Her eyes pop open, twinkling at me, and I laugh.

Her eyes drift shut again as we weave our way through the cross streets and past gleaming store windows. After twenty minutes or so, the car pulls up outside my apartment building. Thank God she can't see the tiny space I inhabit here, one I can only afford because I took it when nobody wanted to live in the Meatpacking District. The place was full of drug addicts, and pedophiles used to prey on young girls in the park across the road. I think the guy I rent it from has sort of forgotten I'm here. But I'm also a reliable tenant: I sort stuff out for him, so he's let me keep living here, despite the way the area has gentrified over the last ten years.

Her eyes blink open. She must have dozed off a while ago.

"God, I'm sorry. Did I fall asleep? Is this your building?"

I nod. "It was great to meet you, Anna."

She reaches out her hand and squeezes mine. "Thank you."

I step out of the car and stand on the sidewalk. As the driver pulls away, she gives me a little wave.

And I'm not sure why I feel so unbearably sad, like I missed something important in that whole conversation.

CHAPTER 6

Adam

Susie bounces into my office, dreadlocks pulled back from her face and bright yellow overalls slouching around her small frame. Susie used to sit on the corner of the main street near our building with her cat, playing her guitar for money. When I talked to her, she told me that Bandit was a talking point because other street performers typically had dogs and he gave her an angle and an ability to charge for photos. I liked the way she thought, so I always found some change for her. Turned out she'd worked as a street artist since she was sixteen, followed by a job in an industrial print studio, but was adamant she didn't want to work in a company anymore. I wasn't sure why.

One day, I was flustered and pissed and she asked me what was wrong. We'd had one of our worst months ever, and when I told her about it, she offered to help, and I realized she had a real flare for marketing. So, she ended up taking over not only the visual stuff we do, but everything else as well. I can only pay her peanuts but I'm so grateful she's here and helping me. We have this conversation a lot: She says she'd still be on the streets if I didn't put up with her crazy, and I tell her the company would be nowhere without her. She slaps a pile of newspapers down in front of me, and I look up from the printed circuit board I'm fiddling with to glower at her. She grins.

"I'd say you're a hit."

"A hit?"

"WHO IS ANNA TALANOVA'S NEW MAN?" the first headline screams at me from the papers strewn across my desk.

Oh fuck!

I shuffle them around as Susie slumps into the seat opposite me and holds up her hand ticking things off on her fingers as she talks. "I've had four calls from journalists this morning wanting an interview. Three conference organizers have been in touch to ask you to speak, and, get this, two calls from agents asking whether you're interested in attending other events. With. Other. Women." She taps the words out with her finger on the desk.

I stare at her. Shit. I didn't brief her on this weird-ass thing that famous women do. "Ah yes, I got an invite via Janus from Anna Talanova's agent. This is apparently something women in the public eye do. They look for men to accompany them to …" I wave my hand. "… things they have to go to."

"Are you kidding me? It's like … *organized*?" She rolls her lips together. Then she leans forward and whispers, "One of the agents said she'd been told you 'understood exactly how to behave' and were—and I quote—'nonpredatory.'"

I frown at her. "What the fuck does that mean?"

"It means you weren't handsy … or anything worse." She chews her cheek.

I think back to Anna's slight … what would I call it? Nervousness? I wouldn't dream of doing something like that to a woman.

"God, is that what happens?" I say.

Anna has so much on her plate, imagine if something upset her game?

"I'll bet my ass it does."

She's a world-class tennis player for Christ's sake. What kind of man does that? But when I glance down at the papers again, I'm conflicted about the calls and the conferences. We struggle for coverage a lot of the time—who wants to talk to another startup these days? But this interest in me … it could help the business. Is that taking advantage in another way? My stomach churns. Julio's comment about my penis on prime-time television echoes in my head. What do I know about how this works? It's clearly a high-wire act, and I don't want my company to be roasted for some faux pas I didn't see coming. Maybe Serge's suggestion of a stylist makes sense: I don't want to be papped wearing old sweats with bed-hair at the supermarket. *You never wear old sweats, Adam.* Yeah, Mom had strict rules about that kind of thing.

I groan. My compulsive overthinking is the bane of my life. And am I that vain already? One night out and a few photos and press articles and I'm worrying about my wardrobe? *You have no money, you maniac.*

"Sounds like we could pick up some coverage. What do you think? Am I setting myself up for a nightmare here?"

She laughs. "To be honest, I don't care if it is a nightmare. All publicity is good publicity, right? This is a marketing dream. I've fixed two of the interviews for tomorrow, but you don't have to do them."

"Do you think we need a PR company to handle it?"

"Well, that would be wonderful, but we can't afford that, can we?"

"No."

She grins. "I can manage it for now if you're happy to talk to the journalists." She waves her rainbow-colored nails at me. "It'll die down in a few days. The press is terrible. It's all flavor-of-the-month stuff."

She's right. We should take the opportunity while it's here. "Sign me up for everything."

She stands to head back to her desk. "By the way, I also set up personal social media accounts for you this morning. You've already got thirty thousand followers on Instagram."

"*What?*" I grab my phone as Susie comes around the desk to show me the account. She's posted a photo of Anna and me outside the event on the red carpet.

"Shit. I signed an NDA."

"Oh, don't worry, it's one of their pictures."

I nod my head and start to scroll down, and she sticks her tongue in her cheek.

"What?" I say.

"Don't read the comments."

"What? Why?" I flick down further.

OMG hot!

I'd let him do me on a red carpet.

"Oh, Jesus."

Susie sniggers. "I was tempted to post a picture of you in your old jeans and your high-magnification glasses you use for fiddling with electronics, but decided I shouldn't ruin the illusion."

"Probably best if I don't look at any more of that."

She smiles. "You polish up well, boss."

"Thank you. They certainly did a job on me."

Her gaze roams over my hair. "Did they … color it?"

Laughing, I say, "They did." I fill her in on my crazy evening.

"It sounds amazing," she says eventually. "Did you take any photos?"

"I did. I shouldn't have, given the NDA." I turn my phone toward her as she leans over the desk and flicks through some pictures and videos. Serge doing my hair, Pepper with her rabbit, a couple of shots out the window of the car and at the event.

"Adam, these are fab! We could do a behind-the-scenes."

I study her over my glasses. "You do realize I did them for myself."

"But social media would love them. That video of Anna's dog is the cutest." She chews her lip. "I could talk to Anna's people about it."

I love that Susie is always bursting with ideas. I wave my hand. "Knock yourself out. Lord knows I'm not going to be posting on this account myself."

Susie eyes me balefully. "Are you saying this stuff you do"—she waves at the board I'm designing on the screen—"isn't riveting?"

"Put some of your art on there. That'd be way more interesting."

"If I post as you, I'm going to have to sound like you."

"Yeah. Yeah. I understand how this works. Just make me sound like I'm a fascinating person."

What am I agreeing to? And a *personal* account? But yeah, Susie is right.

I'll be a one-week wonder, and then everyone will move on to the next story. Most companies have armies of people spending their time trying to create a buzz about what they're doing. No way is the interest in me going to carry on. *The guy who once went to a red-carpet do with Anna Talanova*. Big fucking deal. This is my fifteen minutes of fame.

Susie bustles off to talk to whoever she needs to, and I forward her the photos and videos from my phone before swinging my chair around to look out at my brick wall. It's less like a dead end and more like a protective fort this morning. I thought this event thing was a bit of fun, but capitalizing on it could be very useful. Invitations to speak … wow. That's never happened to me before. I need to thank Anna.

I do a quick search for flowers, and in a few clicks, I've set up a same-day delivery to the apartment I went to last night. In the message box, I type:

I had a wonderful evening. Thanks, Adam.

Christ, could I sound any more boring? I type in a few more equally terrible attempts, go back to what I wrote in the first place, and then click through all the payment stuff.

I did have a nice time. She did talk a lot about tennis, but it was interesting and for once I stopped trying to design boards in my head, which is my usual go-to for keeping myself entertained.

I lift up a newspaper from my desk and a picture catches my eye. The text underneath it describes me as *dashing*. Heat warms my cheeks as I shake my head, lips turning up in a grin. As I read down, I find several references to the business. No wonder people called Susie. My gaze snags on a line: "Adam Miller runs a fast-growing electronics company and has experienced meteoric success."

I let out a howl of laughter. I've only just stopped laughing when my phone buzzes, and when I pick it up, there's a text:

Handsome, dashing, charming.

Followed by some GIF of a man in a tuxedo throwing champagne over himself. Fuck. Fabian.

Three dots appear:

Anna Talanova, man. She is HOT.

I scowl at the screen. No wonder she's nervous. Fabian's a solid guy, but how many men make comments about her all the time? Ignoring the fact she's worked her ass off to reach the top of her sport, and reducing her to *hot*.

But Fabian hasn't finished:

Liked the plum shirt, good call.

Not my decision. I had an hour and a half of hair and makeup.

My phone rings in my hand.

"Are you shitting me?" Fabian rumbles in my ear.

So, I fill him in on the whole thing: the call from Janus, the people, the primping. "They'd have a field day with your long hair and tattoos," I say. In fact, why didn't Janus call *Fabian*? The press would have gone wild over his bad-boy vibe.

He laughs. "A low profile is kind of essential for hacking. But never mind that. Her agent called Janus?"

"It's insane. But get this, my marketing manager, Susie, has had two *more* calls this morning from women who'd like plus ones. Apparently I've been described as *nonpredatory*."

"As in you didn't hit on her? That's the deal? That's what they're all trying to avoid? Beautiful, successful women and guys just …"

"Seems like it."

"Who are these assholes? Find out from Anna who's screwed her over and I'll hack into some systems for her and give her enough dirt on them to last her a lifetime."

I start to laugh. I know he's done the odd bit of work for celebrities in the past. "I could suggest you as another nonpredatory companion … Looking like you do, I'm sure you'd get a lot of takers."

"Yeah. I'm sure Kate would love that." He chuckles. "Imagine the headline: 'Famous hacker Fabian Adramovich wanted by the Russians and several other Eastern European states …'"

Fuck. "Wanted by the Russians?"

He clicks his tongue. "Not seriously."

What the hell does that mean? There are serious and nonserious levels of being on someone's watchlist? Actually, that doesn't sound so unlikely. But still …

"Chill. They don't know who or where I am."

I'm never going to relax about Fabian and the crazy stuff he does.

"How are you doing?" My constant worry with Fabian is his lifestyle, the drug experimentation, the dangerous sports, the hacking. Safe to say he lives a *very* different life from mine.

I glance out the glass partition in the office at Susie waving her hands as she talks on the phone. Perhaps mine's about to become crazy in a different way. Not sure I can deal with that.

"I'm good," Fabian says in my ear. "Kate's keeping an eye on me."

"You eating enough?"

Why did I ask that? Am I his mom? And he just survived an attempt on his life. I should be asking him about that. "You all healed from that stabbing now?"

He chuckles. "I'm good. Cool your heels. Coming back to the food question, you offering to take me out and feed me?"

Is he changing the subject? Yes. Gah, I can check him out if we meet up. "I will, if you'll let me pay."

"You're on."

Shit. It'll have to be somewhere super cheap.

*

Four hours later, Susie sticks her head around the door.

"These pictures and the video you took are terrific, boss."

I raise my head from the board I'm designing. "Yeah?"

She brings my phone in and clicks on the reel she's put together, and my jaw drops. It starts with a picture of Serge fixing my hair, followed by Pepper bringing me her rabbit, then a red swish of a dress and shoes in front of me moving across the sidewalk, a pan across the inside of the venue, and finally a selfie I took of Anna and me smiling at the end.

"Her team has cleared it. I'm going to post that with something like 'I had a great night' and tag Anna."

I watch the video again. It feels so foreign to put stuff out on social media about a night out when I'm running a serious electronics company.

Susie pats my arm. "It can't hurt to be better known, Adam."

So, I give her a thumbs-up.

CHAPTER 7

Anna

Damian whirls into my apartment at 10 a.m. with a bag over his shoulder and two coffees in a cardboard tray in one hand, and a plastic box in the other. He leans in to plant a kiss on each cheek.

"June's fighting fires, so I'm doing the update today."

"Fighting fires?"

He shakes his head. "Nothing bad. Talking to journalists. Making sure we get the correct story out there." He waves the tub at me. "Pastries from Steve."

His boyfriend, Steve, is the patisserie chef at an upscale restaurant. I take the tub and unclip it, peering in at some amazing-looking pastry creations.

"Oh my God, you are the best. And can I just say I could offer Steve a very nice life?" I sweep my hand around my apartment.

Damian rolls his eyes. "I'm sorry to say you really don't have the right parts for him."

I grin at him as he slides past me into the kitchen. "I'm under strict instructions to heat these up for five minutes." He fiddles with the dial on my oven and pops the pastries on a tray. My stomach growls.

"He's decided you need feeding up."

"Feeding up?"

Damian tuts. "Or at least a treat or two after that asshole …"

I hold up my hand. "Don't mention his name."

"Arty the Asshole. It could be a comic strip. Dennis the Menace. Arty the Asshole."

I sip my coffee. "Can we fix on that nickname for all future correspondence? I like it." But I really don't want to talk about Arty. I suspect I've got no choice this morning, though. "So, what have you got for me?"

"It's like fucking magic," he crows. "Damn, I love my job."

"Why? What happened?"

He props his shoulder against the end unit by the built-in oven. "No one is the least bit interested in the fact you've 'split up' with Arty." He makes air quotes around the words. "June and I talked to a lot of journalists last night and early this morning, and all they wanted was information about Adam."

"Oh shit! Is Adam okay with that?"

"He's fine with it. I've been liaising with his marketing lady, Susie—who's awesome by the way—and she's keeping him up to speed with everything. It's moving so fast we've hardly been able to keep a hold on the stories."

"I ought to touch base with him."

Damian leans in. "I don't think we even need to issue a statement about you and Arty splitting up or waste time agreeing on the wording with his awful PR people. It was a master stroke taking a cute guy to that event, Anna. Honestly."

"I did it in a panic!"

Damian waves his hand. "Many an excellent decision comes out of a flailing panic. That's how I met Steve. I kissed him when I caught an ex of mine making out with someone else. But enough of me. We've had loads of questions from the media: Who's this new man? etc., etc. So, June and I did a straightforward press briefing: Anna and Arty have split up, Anna's just dating now. But get this, several of the female journos were *delighted*. One said, 'Why did she go out with Arty Maroz in the first place? He's an opportunist and an angry one at that.'"

"He has a reputation for having a temper, but I never saw it. Until I dumped him for cheating, that is."

Damian chews his cheek, leans forward, and whispers, "He's a real revenge queen, so I'm told."

The buzzer sounds, and he grabs the oven mitt and lifts the tray out, placing it on the stovetop.

"Ugh. Revenge." I say, prodding the toffee-colored top of a hot pastry, and the smell of honey and warm raisins drifts up.

"Yeah. He goes after his exes like you wouldn't believe. I don't know how much you shared with him, but you might need to talk to your lawyers."

"I've already had to."

"*What?* Why?"

"He sent me some legal papers about the ownership of Pepper."

"Are you *kidding*? Pepper? And that fast? He split up with you *yesterday*. He gave you that dog for your birthday! We built her Instagram on the back of that little gem. Didn't love the man, but that was an outstanding gift."

"Yeah. I love her to bits, even though it's impractical when I'm away so much. Thank God for my adopted family." I squeeze his arm and take a bite of flaky pastry that dissolves on my tongue in an explosion of sweetness. "Sure I can't ask Steve to marry me?"

Damian smirks. "I'll pass the message on."

"Why would Arty bother with all this?" I mumble, still chewing. "He doesn't like dogs. Can you even take back a present?"

"I'll bet it's because she's got her own Instagram. He'll be seeing dollar signs." He purses his lips. "I'll talk to your lawyer about what we can and can't say to journalists about the fact he's going after Pepper. What a jerk."

He makes a note on his phone and picks up a hot pastry and nearly drops it. I reach up and pull two plates out of the cupboard.

"Anyway, babe, not one journalist cared," he carries on. "Didn't want the deets on why you guys had split up. Didn't want to write about Arty Maroz. They just wanted to know all about the very sexy Adam Miller." He winks at me.

"Oh stop! You're incorrigible."

"It's excellent news, though. We've buried the Arty-being-a-jerk story before it's even started. I don't want to get into some argument and mudslinging in the press about his cheating video. It's nasty, and he'd get publicity from that, too. Also," he says, wiping his hands on his pants, "let me show you this."

He pulls up a clip that starts with Adam laughing with Serge while he's having his hair done, then he's standing next to Serge and Julio with Anita behind him looking at himself in the mirror in his plum shirt. It cuts to Pepper bringing her pink rabbit to him, and a picture of the back of my red dress and shoes. Then his face appears in front of the camera, grinning. It's wobbly, unguarded, and so goddamn cute—not like a made-for-social-media reel at all.

"It's on his Instagram, and it's now on yours and Pepper's and it's racking up the hits." Damian scrolls through his phone. "Over two hundred thousand views on Adam's account alone and he's only got ... Oh man, he's got sixty thousand followers already! His marketing lady told me she only set up his account this morning. *Holy shit.*" He waves his hand. "But also, Rolex called me at 7 a.m. and they are *delighted*. Look at this."

He rewinds the video, and, at the end of my swinging arm, my watch is glinting on my wrist.

"You are the master, lady. Their marketing guy was practically wetting himself. Talking about how this was going to land him a promotion." He laughs. "I'm going to let them reuse the footage. The dress people, too. See whether Adam took any more."

I don't feel like a master: My team just lost one of the biggest tournaments in tennis. But it's fascinating how easily that, too, has been buried under everything around last night's event.

"Could we get a Rolex for Adam?"

"I'm sure they'd gift him anything. I can ask them if you like."

"Yeah. It'd be lovely to give him something. It was so kind of him to step in at the last minute. And thanks, Damian, you're doing an incredible job. Just dealing with this and ... I'm so grateful."

He presses his hand to his chest. "Thank you. I love working here with you. But we haven't even started talking about what I *really* came to talk about, which is this." He pulls a stack of newspapers out of his bag and spreads them over the kitchen countertop: They're full of pictures of Adam and me, which is no doubt going to make Arty furious. One headline screams:

WHO IS ANNA TALANOVA'S NEW MAN?

"Oh my God, why are they all so interested?"

"Because you're a successful tennis player?" Damian says, smiling down at the headlines fanned out over my countertop.

Am I going to be that successful tennis player when I head out to the Australian Open in January, though? Ugh. I hate the way that losing eats into me.

"It's an interesting idea this," he adds, waving his hand over the papers.

"What is?"

"Taking some new guy to an event. Deflecting bad news by giving the press something else to sink their teeth into."

"That's not really why I did it."

Damian squeezes my arm. "I know, but your instincts are golden."

"I hope Adam's okay. I don't want to be some asshole quasi-famous person who exploits a situation … who ends up using someone for their own gain."

"I'm sure he doesn't think that at all. Give him a call. If he's amenable, we could definitely squeeze more publicity out of this."

My only thought was that I didn't want to annoy the sponsors of the awards event who provide all my tennis gear. And I'm delighted that Rolex is happy. It was touch and go when Barb, my agent, finally landed me the contract with them, and they negotiated me down hard. They didn't want to sign a Russian athlete; there were rumblings that it wasn't quite their image. Some of the tension in the back of my neck starts to lift.

My relationships never last. I'm away too much of the year, and my past history in Russia is awful, but I've had to accept that that's my reality. I like Adam—he's cute—and perhaps Damian is right. For the next seven weeks, before I head off to Australia, maybe we could have some fun, and a bit of positive publicity could help all round.

CHAPTER 8

Adam

Later that day, a text appears on my phone:

So, we're dating now?

I laugh. I like Anna. We live in very different worlds, and I thought we wouldn't have a lot in common, but it's scary how much everything she said last night resonated with me. And who wouldn't be flattered? She's clearly amazing.

Apparently.

Is all this okay? Some guys don't like the scrutiny.

Some guys, huh? *Interesting.*

Something about being confronted with Anna's drive and determination last night forced me to do more work on my spreadsheet, despite how late I got back. Once I dove into more of the detail, I could see that things were even worse than I thought. There is no stringing it out: If I can't make the figures improve, I'll have to give the business up. Ten years of my life down the drain. My mind keeps shying away from the reality of that, and the sheer effort of pretending everything is fine is making me nauseous. I look down at my phone again and tap out a reply to Anna:

> I've had a few calls from journalists wanting to interview me about my company, so it's all positive from my end.

> That's great!

> Thanks, Anna. I really appreciate the invite and I had a wonderful night.

A picture drops into the chat, followed by another message:

> Thank you for my beautiful flowers.

> My pleasure.

> I'm happy to go to some more events together if it's useful for you. It was useful for me, too. Sponsors like the publicity and that's less pressure for me.

Huh, that's an amazing offer. The dots are still appearing though, so she's still typing:

> If I'm seen out and about, the speculation about my tennis reduces and there's fewer questions about my game, if you can believe that. God that sounds terrible.

> No, no it doesn't. I totally get that.

I don't want to think too long about this. This could help the both of us. Where's the harm if we're both on board? All Susie's efforts with the new account and posting a reel seem positive—surely the extra publicity would be good for the business? At least I'd be going out to things with someone whose company I enjoy, and that's been a rarity over the last … well … I don't want to think about how many years it's been. It'll have the added bonus of keeping Janus off my back, too.

I'd love to meet up again, Anna.

Then I type:

My marketing manager, Susie, is talking to your marketing people about social media. She's clearing content with them that we might want to post to my personal account.

I saw your video! It was great.

If there's anything you don't like or want to take down, let me know.

I think you're a TikTok ninja.

I'm not sure how to respond to that apart from with hysterical laughter. I start typing again:

I'll tell Susie to send you a picture of me in my normal nerd gear.

Nerd gear? Is that code for some dubious accessories?

Code for something?

Oh God, I'm making bad tech jokes without even realizing it.

I'm nerdy enough to think that was an awesome joke.

Stop buttering up us poor technophobes. How about a coffee tomorrow to chat?

You're on.

*

As I'm about to leave the office for the evening, my phone lights up with a call and I pick it up, then raise my eyes to the heavens.

"Adam!" my mom says. "How are you?"

In my mind's eye, she's standing in the hall of the bungalow I grew up in, landline receiver pressed to her ear, the same swirly patterned carpets and embossed wallpaper that have been there all my life. Sometimes I think that, when my parents die, we'll discover they are closet millionaires from all the money they've stashed away. If it was left up to Dad, they'd still be watching a black-and-white television. I settle back in my chair. Has she called to persuade me to come home for Thanksgiving? With the state of the business, I just don't see how that's possible. I'll be working here every weekend.

"Hey, Mom, I'm doing okay."

"I'm calling to find out when you're coming home," she says.

Before I can answer, I'm momentarily distracted when Susie shouts goodbye as she leaves.

My mother adds, "Are you still in the office?" My dad is as quiet as the grave, but my mom is like a restless ferret. She worries all the time and then asks pointed questions.

I glance at my watch: 9 p.m. "Yes, I'm still here." I don't want to tell her how bad things are with the business. "I'm not sure. It's a very busy time for us fulfilling orders." Although God knows what the runup to Christmas will be like this year. "I've got some jujitsu stuff going on, too."

"Oh! That silly fighting thing! And really, Adam! How can some website take precedence over coming home to see your parents?"

It's a familiar conversation. I always struggle to get home at this time of year, and she always refers to my business as a website. If what I do interferes with some idea of hers, it's a useless endeavor. But, surprisingly, she doesn't pause for an answer but launches instead into an update on all the people we know locally and what their children are doing. I place the phone on my desk and sink back down in my seat, pulling up the PCB I was designing.

"I've got some news for you, Adam!" she says eventually.

"Mmm," I say as I trace out a connection on the board.

"I don't know if you've heard, but Jennifer is getting married. Her parents have kindly invited us to the wedding, despite everything."

Despite everything? And *Jennifer.* A girl I went out with in my final year of school, over thirteen years ago. Nonetheless, my chest warms. She's the quietest person on the planet, and I never thought we had a long-term future together, but she was lovely and we loved each other in the way you do when you're seventeen. Jennifer wasn't even upset when I left for NYU and told her gently that it wasn't going to work anymore. She just nodded and gave me a hug.

"I'll reach out and congratulate her," I say.

"Now, Adam, you don't need to go upsetting *that* apple cart again," my mom says, and my jaw drops.

"What apple cart?" I say, but she tuts at me.

Over the years, it's become clear my parents expected me to come home after college and settle down in the small town I grew up in, and I never know whether to be amused or exasperated by this. I couldn't wait to leave the endless gossip, the lack of career opportunities, and how everybody knew everyone else. The anonymity of New York—where so many different people live so many different lives and make things happen—makes me happy. For all I envy Janus, I love his go-getting attitude and the business he's created from scratch.

"You could have been married by now, too," my mom says.

My gut roils. "Who to?"

My mother tuts again. "To Jennifer, of course! That girl was head over heels for you and she's lovely. It was a real mistake to let her slip through your fingers."

She's almost humming with suppressed energy on the other end of the line, and too late I realize *this* was the reason she called. She's been stewing on some nonsense of *it should have been Adam* ever since she found out that Jennifer was engaged.

Heat creeps up my neck. "She wasn't the right girl for me, Mom," I say as firmly as I can.

But there's no stopping her. "Honestly, young people today, what do they expect marriage to be? It's all some big romantic ideal …"

Can Dad hear this conversation?

"… spending all this money on weddings. They don't realize that it's a lifelong commitment and you need to be with someone solid, not be swept up in some romantic nonsense …"

And suddenly, just like that, laughter starts to bubble up in my throat. "What about Dad?" I say, grinning at the wall in my office. "Was he ever swept up in some romantic nonsense?"

"Of course, he wasn't," my mom snaps. "We married each other because it was the most sensible option available."

"And here I was thinking you two loved one another," I mutter, trying to stop the enormous grin that's threatening to take over my face. "You married him because he was the most sensible man available?" I repeat.

"Of course I did, as he did me," my mom says breezily. "That's what you should be doing, Adam. I don't know why you're in New York City. You should be back here building a solid career and married to that girl, not messing around in New York."

My dad's take on this would be amazing, but getting him on the phone will never happen. But then I hear a cough followed by a noise in the background.

"You should marry for love like I clearly did," says a voice coming from somewhere in the distance behind my mom, and my heart clenches as a sharp thrill runs through me. It's times like this, when his dry sense of humor comes out, that I love Dad so intensely it's difficult to breathe. He's so quiet. Does he approve of what I'm doing? Probably not. But he notices everything and has always been this dependable, solid presence in my life. Even if he doesn't agree with most of my decisions, I could always go to him for advice and he'd help me.

I grin. I'm not even annoyed at my mom's reference to my business as *messing around*. "Tell Dad I'll let him know when I've found someone as wonderful as you, Mom," I say, almost giddy with this whole conversation.

"Oh, you two!" my mom says. "Call me when you know what you're doing, Adam." And she hangs up.

I breathe a sigh of relief. I'm not stupid enough to think it's gone away; my mom is like a dog with a bone, but I've dodged the Thanksgiving problem for now.

*

When I meet Anna two days later at the entrance to Central Park, her gloved hands are clutching two coffees, breath white in the cold November air. She looks like any other person on the streets of Manhattan, long dark hair flowing out from beneath a wool cap. She holds out a coffee, and I lean in and kiss her cheek.

"In case anyone's taking photographs," I wink at her.

She laughs as Pepper jumps up at my legs.

"She's your number-one fan."

"What kind of dog is she?"

"A Papillon. Big ears, big attitude."

"She's a sweetheart," I say, but Anna wrinkles her nose.

"She pooped on a very expensive rug this morning."

This makes me laugh. Even high-powered famous athletes have to clean up their pet's poop. I bend down and give Pepper a full-body rub, and she wriggles and tries to lick my face.

"Were you a naughty girl this morning, hmmm?" I ask.

I glance up to find Anna watching me. She bites her lip as her eyes flutter away and she gestures toward the entrance to the park with her cup.

"Thanks for meeting up and doing this. After I won my first Grand Slam title, photographs of me cropped up everywhere and I got paranoid for a while. I stopped going out at all."

The sadness I felt after I left her white face in the car two days ago settles into my chest. You think these people have amazing lives and then you realize that they're on a treadmill just like the rest of us, albeit a bit more of a glamorous one. Or maybe it just appears glamorous because they win competitions and fly around the world. But I'll bet that hours of hard tennis practice a day and endless flight delays aren't exciting at all.

"So now I try and make sure I go out and do normal, everyday things with someone else as a buffer," Anna adds, then pauses and swallows. "Oh God, that sounds terrible, I don't mean that …"

I laugh. "I'm more than happy to be described as a buffer."

Her cheeks pink up. "I'm so sorry! I'm such an awkward nerd sometimes! That came out all wrong."

I shake my head, laughing. Surely, I'm the awkward nerd here?

"The pressure around tennis is pretty intense. Who's beating who, rankings, rivalries. I like to concentrate on the game, but the press always asks me all these stupid-ass questions. Was Parakova favoring her right side after her injury earlier this year? Last time you met, Mila beat you in three straight sets—is she going to do that this time? The same things over and over, things you can't answer."

God yes, I would be so annoyed if someone watched me write code and critiqued it all the time. *Jesus, that would be terrible.*

"Anyway, if they take pictures of me with a man, and quiz me about him, somehow that is so much easier."

I laugh at this. "I always thought people hated speculation about their personal lives. I remember Janus went through hell with Jo because she loathed the media attention."

She shakes her head. "Not me. It's part and parcel of being a successful athlete, I think. I have a short career window, and I have to make the most of it. Sponsorship is about how I perform, but it's also about having a high profile, too. I've made my peace with it to a certain extent. They're going to print stories, whether you like it or not, and I fought for this life." She shrugs. "It's also so easy to answer those kinds of questions."

"I presume you don't want me to be your real boyfriend?" I blurt out without thinking. Fuck, now why did I say that? There's no way she'd be interested in me.

She narrows her eyes at me. "Correct me if I'm wrong, but I didn't get that vibe from you."

Heat creeps up my neck. She's an amazing woman. Am I really standoffish like that? Yeah, okay, but the very idea I'm behaving like that with someone like Anna Talanova … I'm cautious, I get that. Memories of Celine are never far from my mind, even though it's been over ten years. Sometimes when I close my eyes, I can see her earnest face imploring me to do something. Half the time I can't remember what it was. I shake my head.

Anna waves a hand, misinterpreting my silence. "I understand, Adam. Don't sweat it. I'm not here for ten months of the year, and I'm off to the Australian Open in seven weeks. I'm also coming out of a bad breakup, so something easy and platonic was exactly what I was thinking."

"I'm down with that." But unease winds through my gut again, as though I've misstepped somehow.

The sun sparkles through the avenue of trees, orange leaves providing a soft carpet underfoot as Pepper sniffs at anything she can find.

"Is this breakup something I should know about if we're going to attend some more events together?" There was speculation in the press about a man named Arty Maroz, and I remember that name from the red carpet, too.

She rolls her lips together. "Arty Maroz. Olympic athlete, downhill skier. He's turned out to be quite the asshole. And before that I was with a guy …" She trails off, and her small, neat teeth work their way over her bottom lip. "He insisted I did everything the way he wanted, down to the last detail. My outfits, my hair. Lots of gaslighting. Praise if I did the right thing. I was young and didn't realize how bad that was. He was good to me for big chunks of time and supported my career … at least initially." She shakes her head.

Now I'm all sorts of curious. "Wow, that sounds like a nightmare." But God, do I get it. For the last ten years, I've tortured myself with what-ifs and felt that gullible was my middle name. I can never tell Anna that, though.

"It was." Her breath shudders out. "I'm glad I'm out of it. The control got worse and worse the more successful I got. He would turn up unexpectedly, raging, and message me over and over again if I was anywhere without him. Arty was supposed to be my attempt to have a more normal relationship, whatever that means. Now all I'm thinking is I'm done with men forever."

A slight tremor runs through her hand as she lifts her coffee cup to her lips and takes a sip. "I don't believe in love anymore," she adds, then laughs. "If I ever did. I think I'm destined to be on my own."

That's a crime for a woman as lovely as Anna. But, God, how does this whole conversation mirror my own experience in the scariest ways? "Don't beat yourself up or think you were gullible. People can be so convincing."

She eyes me for a second, then says, "Somehow I need to get …" She hesitates. "… Back to my normal self. Does that make sense?"

"Absolutely. I dated a woman at college who was very difficult. Demanding." I stare off down the path snaking through the trees, the noise of the city distant and buried. "I don't think I've ever sorted out what was real and what wasn't from that relationship."

Anna smiles up at me. "Sounds complicated."

"Yeah. Yeah, it was." God, I don't want to talk to Anna about how fooled I was. "I've got a company that's struggling, so I am totally down with uncomplicated."

I've kept my head down and focused on my business for the last ten years. I wouldn't say I was lonely exactly. I have great friends and an amazing team, but I'm aware I'm on my own, in every sense of that phrase.

She gives me a big, genuine smile and holds out her hand. "Friends?"

She doesn't seem to mind that I haven't explained more, and the warmth of the space she's giving me to breathe percolates through my body.

I take her small warm fingers in my hand. "Definitely."

CHAPTER 9

Adam

Two days later a video of Pepper in what appears to be a wind tunnel drops into WhatsApp. Her eyes are shut, and her furry little head is tipped back like she's in ecstasy. I stop working on the board I'm designing as a laugh barrels up my throat. She closed her eyes like that every time I gave her a rubdown. One word from Anna follows the video:

Blow-dry!

I like a woman who's easy to please. Where are you?

A fancy-ass dog salon on Lexington.

Sounds like fun.

Yes! The pinnacle of a woman's existence is a bespoke wash and dry.

A bespoke wash and dry? I could make some cheeky comment here, but that would be treading over a line, right? Adam, don't be an ass. Who in their right mind makes jokes like that to a world-class tennis player? The dots stop and start again:

It's perfect, actually. No wonder Pepper's so happy. Much better than all this tennis business.

That is one pampered pooch.

I love her expression! It's like the When Dogs Drive cartoon.

She knows who Gary Larson is? I press the call icon on her message.

"You like Gary Larson?" I say.

Anna laughs. "Oh God yes. I'm a huge fan of *The Far Side*!"

I raise my eyebrows. She's Russian—how does she know who Gary Larson even is? Shut up, Adam, with your assumptions. She probably has eclectic interests, and why not? Not everyone is my mother.

"You like cartoons?"

"You'd be surprised what you do for a bit of light relief when you're resting after eight hours of training a day."

Eight hours? No wonder she's such a superstar. Maybe we have more in common than I thought. I could suggest a book festival or a comic con. I want to laugh at myself. Look at the nerd talking—he wants to take a famous tennis player to a *book* festival.

"I was wondering," she says, as though she's read my mind, "whether we could schedule another event together?"

"Only if it's a dog show," I say. Much better idea than books, Adam.

"Oh my God, that would be my dream date."

Now I *am* laughing. She's so easy to please. I thought people like her were all divas. Perhaps I could find some tickets? I'd be down for that. I start scrolling on my phone.

"I could get some blow-drying tips," she adds.

“I think we could discover all sorts of exotic dog-pampering techniques.”

She laughs. “That sounds like fun.”

“Okay, there’s something called the American Kennel Club National Championship but that’s in Florida. Let’s park that thought, and I’ll investigate some others. Did you have any other ideas?”

“I’ve got loads of invites for November and December. You could take your pick.”

My jaw drops. “What kinds of things?”

“Oh, gallery openings, parties, promotional events run by sponsors. Some of those I have to attend. They’re usually boring as hell. Movie premieres.”

Movie premieres? “Would you like to see me fight?” God, will the open-your-mouth-and-come-out-with-an-awful-idea never end?

“What?”

“I’ve got a jujitsu competition this weekend. It’s nothing special, nothing like …”

“You do jujitsu? God, I’d *love* to watch that.”

“It’s very amateur. Not professional or anything.”

She gives a delighted laugh. “It sounds amazing. You’re an unusual man, Adam Miller.”

Voices reach me from the background. “Oh! Fans. Hang on.” Her voice muffles.

I wait on the line, catching some faint laughter, conversation, and a dog bark.

“Sorry, I just needed to sign some autographs. Let me get out of this salon.” Her voice mutes again.

When she comes back on, she says, “The worst thing about Pepper is that she was a present from Arty.”

“She was a gift from an awful boyfriend? Ugh.”

“Exactly.”

“I could say something trite here like sometimes the best things come from the worst things, but honestly, that’s bullshit and it sucks that Pepper was a present from him.”

"Yeah, it does. Most of the time I forget about it, because otherwise every time I looked at her it would remind me." Her breath whispers in my ear. "He's trying to take her away from me."

"Oh, fuck. Are you *kidding* me?"

"It's going to cost in the region of two hundred thousand dollars in legal fees, or so my lawyers tell me. Arty's determined to go to court."

"What?"

"When you reach the top of something, people file lawsuits against you all the time." She tuts. "I'm sorry, I must sound like some whiny diva to you."

"God, Anna, no. You're a professional tennis player. It's not like you're on *Dancing with the Stars* or something. What the hell do people take you to court for?"

"Copyright infringement, mistreatment of staff, employment law, abuse. Sometimes, like this, it's for the publicity. You name it, people do it."

"What do they get out of it?"

"Money, usually. But mostly it's a raised profile. That's why Arty is going after Pepper. He was always doing shit like this, plotting his next move to generate press coverage. I think he was delighted when we split up. Perhaps he even engineered it deliberately so he could milk it for all it was worth. Sponsors pay for column inches. Performance can be secondary."

It's a clear reminder that our relationship might end up being measured in column inches, too. The thought tastes a little sour. Anna is a nice person, and fun, too. I'm glad we agreed on friends: It gives this a relaxed vibe I wasn't expecting, and we both seem to be thinking this will be a bit of fun. But, given her profile, there's bound to be speculation, too. Will we have to go through some dramatic breakup for the sake of column inches? A shiver runs down my spine.

"I don't want to be a disappointment, but I am not the guy for creating a drama that gets publicity."

She hoots in my ear. "God, no, Adam, you have no idea how little I want that. It can mushroom out of control so fast. I want to keep the comments about my tennis where they belong, before and after games, and damp down all the speculation about fitness and performance and who's a rival of who, to allow me to relax into my game. Is that selfish? Believe me, after the last two years, the last thing I want is drama. I'm delighted you're a no-drama kind of guy."

After seeing all the remarks about the event and me afterward, I get it now. "That doesn't sound selfish to me; it sounds sensible."

"Anyway, send me the details for the jujitsu. I'd love to come along."

I'm ridiculously flattered by this, who wouldn't be when a gorgeous woman wants to come and see you fight? I'm getting attached to Anna, I can tell I am, and warmth is washing through my bloodstream. She's a delightful person, fun and a total surprise. But it's not like I'm interested in stepping into another relationship or anything. I can keep this about being friends. Easy-peasy.

CHAPTER 10

Anna

My chest fills like a balloon when I see the arena and all the mats on the central floor. I'm attending a sporting event that I'm not competing in, and even better, one I know nothing about. A carousel of images from when I used to compete on the nonprofessional circuit flood my mind: my dad … my Russian tennis coach, Konstantin. A shiver runs down my spine. I didn't give Adam an honest explanation about my relationship with Konstantin's friend Pietr, but how could I?

As I head up into the stands, I pull my ball cap down over my head and slide my sunglasses up my nose. But the small stadium is filled with parents watching their kids fight: Who's interested in some random woman weaving her way through the crowd? How many tennis fans would even be here? They'll all be martial arts people who don't know who I am. *Get over yourself, Anna!* Settling into my seat, I avoid eye contact and focus on the central floor. Adam is standing off to the side in a white suit in a line of other competitors. God, how familiar that is—the waiting. After I've been sitting there for ten minutes without anybody asking for an autograph, my spine starts to unwind.

They all walk toward their respective mats, and the first person Adam's competing against is a stocky, burly-looking guy, considerably bigger than

Adam. *Ugh. I don't love that.* Adam bows to his opponent, the *A. Miller* clear on the back of his top, the referee raises his hand, and they launch at one another. And whoa! My heart leaps into my throat at how fast and aggressive the other fighter is. His leg sweeps out, and in seconds they're grappling on the floor, hands white-knuckled on the edge of each other's tops. Mr. Burly flips Adam over, and Adam twists him straight back. The muscles in his legs and forearms strain as he struggles to grip on to his opponent's jacket, and they're flipping and grappling, flipping and grappling … Damn! Adam gets the guy into some kind of lock that he's trying to wriggle out of and break Adam's hold. Sweat is already making Adam's hair darken and stick to the side of his head. The crowd's noise builds, as the other guy does something with his leg again until the referee makes some kind of signal, breaking them apart. Some points go up on the board for Adam.

This is riveting!

They both stand, and Adam lifts the corner of his jacket to wipe the sweat off his brow giving everyone a flash of some very toned abs. Good Lord, he's this quiet easy guy, but he does … this! It's like there's a rod of steel running right through him.

They circle again, batting their hands at each other. Mr. Burly gets hold of Adam's jacket, bending over with his arms down around Adam's leg as he drives Adam backward. Adam tries to twist out of his grip, and they careen off the edge of the mat and the referee raises his hand.

As the fight carries on, Adam's skill is clearly winning him the match. I thought he said he wasn't very good? The jujitsu videos yesterday didn't prepare me for this. It's neck-and-neck, hard-fought, and the burly guy is leaning in all the time with his weight. *Ispol'zuyte vse svoi preimushchestva!*—use all your advantages! The voices in my head from whenever I was losing never go away.

Eventually, the match draws to a close and Adam has more points than his opponent, but his face is red and his hair is plastered to his temples—it's taken everything he's got. God, is this what it's like to be a coach? … My dad? Sitting on the sidelines, stewing? I'm not sure I could do it. I'm going to breed puppies and work in Adam's business when I retire. *What the hell, Anna?* You're not *with* Adam … Martina Navratilova played senior tennis for years after she retired: That's what I'm going to do. I want to stay in the USA. I love training here. Coming back here every year between tournaments has eased all the fear and uncertainty I've had about being coerced into going back to Russia. I'd do anything to keep it that way.

Watching Adam's second match I feel a wave of nausea creeping up my throat. He's getting annihilated—held down in so many positions. God! *Losing!* I clench my fists in my lap.

The older man sitting beside me leans toward me and says softly, "Who are you here supporting?"

"A. Miller, mat 4."

He nods. "He's had some hard matches. That's my grandson on mat 3."

I study the blond guy on mat 3 who looks impossibly young. "How old is he?"

"Sixteen. He's an excellent fighter but …" He chews his lip. "Professional sport takes its toll."

"You sound like you're speaking from experience."

"Competed myself for a long time, won a few things decades ago. It was very different then. I used to grapple with him when he was younger, but he's much better than I ever was."

Oh boy, this man is my dad. "Is it torture watching?"

He huffs. "Always."

Two girls appear at the end of the row, notebooks and pencils at hand. *Ah, shit.*

"Could we have your autograph?" they say shyly.

I'm about to take the books when the man's hand comes across me. They're talking to him? I stare at the side of his face. Who is he?

"'Scuse me," he says. "It happens once or twice every tournament."

He starts writing on one of the pages, and when I glance over at what he's doing, he's written a header that says *Rules for Life*. I read his list over his shoulder. *Don't drink*, the first one says, followed by … *and definitely don't do drugs.*

What a cool idea!

He writes the same recommendations in both exercise books and signs them with a flourish, handing them back to the two waiting girls.

"Brainwash 'em young, that's what I say." He chuckles with a wink.

My eyes drift back to the mats. Adam and his grandson have finished their matches.

"Who won?"

"They both lost, but he's skilled, that man of yours." I open my mouth to say Adam's not my man but he's looking at his watch. "We've got a bit of a break now, thank God. I need to go for a smoke." He holds up a hand. "It's a vice, I know—but I'm no hypocrite, so I never write *Don't smoke*." He grimaces and then drifts off like a mirage.

I follow him out, find myself a ginger tea from the stand serving hot drinks, and try and calm down. As I'm standing waiting for my order, a text buzzes on my phone.

It's a picture of Arty's receipt from the dog breeder, accompanied by a picture of him and the breeder holding Pepper who's looking up at him adoringly. I roll my eyes. That must have been the only time he ever cuddled her. What a jerk. I tap two buttons to forward it on to my lawyer.

When I come back scowling, I'm immediately sucked back into Adam's third match. My heart bleeds for him. He's such a fighter, the way he puts a loss behind him and carries on. It's impressive, and it's one of the hardest mentalities to learn in sports, too.

My friend reappears beside me, sucking on a coffee and eating a donut. *Yum*. He breaks some off and gives it to me then grunts and nods toward the mats. "That man your fella's fighting, don't like him, never have."

The guy launches himself at Adam, who's immediately got his hands up batting him away, trying to block his attempts to get a hold on him.

"Far too aggressive, hurt my grandson last time 'e fought 'im."

Shit. I don't think I needed to know that. My throat tightens.

The other fighter takes Adam down to the mat in a hold, but he manages to wriggle out of it and the guy is scowling. But a takedown will get him points,

I'm sure. My new friend grunts next to me.

"How's your grandson doing?" I ask.

"Okay. He's going to give me a heart attack."

Tell me about it, I don't say.

"My name's Dean, by the way," he says, bright blue eyes locking with mine.

"Nice to meet you, Dean."

He nods and leans back into me and starts explaining some of the holds and the strategies, and I forget whether Adam is winning or losing and try to understand the technicalities instead. Two other girls appear at the end of the row, and this time they want *my* autograph, so I sign their programs as unobtrusively as possible as Dean peers over my shoulder.

"Anna Talanova, eh?" he says, a smile creeping over his face. "Kept that quiet."

I grin back at him. "Yeah, trying to fly under the radar."

He pats my hand. "You'll get a real kick out of it when people remember you when you're older." He winks at me again.

Adam wins all but his second fight, even beating Mr. Aggressive, and after it's all finished, I thank Dean and we laugh as we sign each other's programs and I head out of the stadium keeping my head down, but I'm giddy with the idea I've been out and about and only two people have recognized me. I send Adam a quick text:

> That was amazing! Congrats.
> Where should I meet you?

Three dots immediately appear, disappear and appear again:

> Meet me around the left-hand side of the stadium. There's a battered blue door. It's the competitors' entrance, and there'll be a load of parents waiting.

When I reach the side of the building, sure enough, the entrance is teeming with parents and children, chatting and celebrating or commiserating. My dad always stood and waited for me, too, smoking a cigarette with either a neutral expression or a scowl, depending on whether I'd won or lost. He never said a lot. He'd take the bag with my rackets from me, and we'd head to the parking lot. My gut burns. I wanted to please him so much. He played when he was younger and understood only too well how difficult it was to win, to be better than everyone else, the impossibility of winning *every* game. He never blamed me and was frequently generous when I messed up, but his competitiveness was like a black cloud, like a third person in the back seat heading home, looming in the darkness. I escaped his moods when I got old enough to go away to train at camps, often in Spain, where the weather was warmer. And it got so much worse because of Konstantin. After I met Mila, he used to pick one or the other of us to "coach." A shudder rolls down my spine.

"Are you Anna Talanova?" A small, awed voice comes from beside me, and dammit, I didn't put my shades back on. I turn to find a girl of about ten years old with a dark plait hanging down her back standing next to me.

I smile. "I am, but shh," I say, pressing my finger to my lips. "Don't tell anyone." I slide my sunglasses back over my eyes.

"Can I get your autograph?"

She holds up a pen and a piece of paper, and I lift my head and quickly scan the crowd, eyes snagging on a woman who must be her mom because she beams and shuffles forward.

"Of course, what's your name?"

"Christie," she says.

"Are you a jujitsu expert?"

She nods sharply up and down, her brown hair bouncing.

Her confidence makes my mouth curl up. "Did you win today?"

"Yes! All my fights!" She grins.

I press my hand to my chest, but I'm aware that people are turning to look at us in my peripheral vision and my heart sinks. I don't want Adam to come out and find me surrounded. This was about me watching him, not about tennis. I write:

Congrats on winning all your matches, Christie! Go conquer the world.
Love, Anna Talanova

This is a blip in time. Someday, no one will want my autograph or remember who I am, and I will be coaching ten-year-old girls like Christie, or even have my own ten-year-old. Something lodges in my throat.

Two more boys appear and hover in the background, and people drift forward and suddenly I'm surrounded by people wanting autographs and asking me about tennis. Everyone is friendly, not pushy, and form an orderly queue, and I manage to work my way through all the people who want to talk to me. As I sign the last few autographs, I'm aware of someone else off to my right-hand side, and I turn to catch Adam's amused hazel eyes. He grins at me, and it's so little boyish that my heart climbs up into my mouth. I still can't get used to how easygoing he is. No doubt Arty would have been fuming by now. *Anna, Adam is not your boyfriend—of course he's going to be relaxed about this.*

"Congratulations!" I say, stepping into him and giving him a hug as I inhale some amazing smell of pine and sweat. He laughs. "You won all but one of your fights!" I add, moving back quickly before I do something embarrassing like sniff his neck.

"Still annoyed about the one I lost." He gives me a lopsided smile. "A bit of a different standard from what you're used to, I'm guessing."

"Oh, but it was so exciting to watch! So much better than tennis."

His lips curl up farther, and he shakes his head.

"It reminded me of the tournaments I played when I was younger." I swing my arm around to encompass all the kids that are now drifting off. "If that doesn't sound patronizing or insulting or anything."

"Not at all."

"I'd forgotten what a slog it all was. How there was no reward for any of it, year after year, competition after competition. How I knew who I had to beat and exactly how talented they were, how much better they'd got in the last year, how much better I had to be."

Adam gestures forward, and we start walking away from the stadium as he tilts his head at me. "That sounds hard. What kept you going?"

I tuck my hand into his arm. "My dad really. It was his dream, not mine. He played but had to give up tennis to take care of his younger brother, who had muscular dystrophy and died when he was twenty-one. He never got over giving up his dream. He tried to go back to it, but he couldn't catch up and eventually stopped playing when he was twenty-seven, I think."

"That sounds rough."

"It was tough on him, but I was happy to do it, to carry on his dream, you know? I wanted to do it for him so badly. He isn't an ogre, and I always loved the game and going to competitions with him. It was something we shared."

"He must be over the moon with how successful you've been."

I eye him sideways. "He is, but underneath it all there's anger in him, too. Tennis was his life. He could have made it. He was a terrific player when he was younger."

"God, I'm sorry, Anna. That's such a sad story."

I squeeze his arm. "Why are we talking about me when you just won so many fights? What are we doing to celebrate?"

"Well, I need to eat, if that's something you'd be up for?"

I grin up at him. "Definitely."

*

Later on, when I'm back alone in my apartment, full of delicious food, and watching jujitsu videos like my life depends upon it, a text drops into my phone from Damian:

Nice!

It's a picture of Adam and me in the little Chinese place we went to, and I laugh. He's got his head on one side, listening intently. I was explaining to him about how to develop a killer backhand and offering to play tennis with him.

I zoom in on the earnest expression on his face. God, he's such a good person. What was Damian saying about my instincts? Maybe my instinct to be friends with Adam is a smart one.

God knows, I need some better men in my life.

CHAPTER 11

Adam

When I'm back at my desk at 8 a.m. on Monday morning, a call lights up my phone.

"Hey, Ted, how's it going?" It must be something urgent if he's calling this early.

Ted and I have been friends for years. He runs an electronics company we supply components to when they need something fast.

"Adam, I'm not going to beat around the bush. I've got some bad news. We're closing the business."

"Closing what business? *Your* business?" My heart takes a dive off the edge of a cliff without a support rope.

"Yes. I'm so sorry, Adam. We made the decision last night. I wanted you to be one of the first to know. You've helped us out a great deal, but we can't make any profit from being middlemen for the Chinese market anymore."

"But I thought you did a lot of bespoke work? Design and build?"

"Yeah, we do, but we've been losing money for years and ..." He breaks off with a long sigh. "You know how it is, Adam. Hardware is tough. Staff are difficult to find and expensive, contracts are impossible, and no one wants to pay what they really cost to deliver. They can do more and more of this bespoke work in China now."

"Tell me about it."

"I'm so sorry, Adam. You've been a great guy to work with over the years. Decent. Fair. I hate to do this to you."

"I understand, Ted. It's business. You think the last order you did is your final one?"

"Probably. We might have a few bits and pieces as we wind down, but it won't be much."

"Shit, I'm sorry. You've been running almost as long as we have."

A sigh whispers over the line. "I'm in debt up to my eyeballs, to tell you the truth."

I huff out a laugh. "Me too."

"It's not worth it, Adam. You can't fight a rising tide."

God, I can't think like that. "Yeah, I can see that."

"Keep in touch, okay?"

"You got it."

After he's hung up, I stare out the window at my wall again. No sunshine beaming down into the little courtyard area today. I chew the end of my thumb as I plug the numbers into the spreadsheet and my heart sinks. We were in a bad position before, but now … Ted's business was at least ten percent of what we sell. It doesn't sound like much, but I've already cut to the bone. Even if sales pick up with more publicity, it's still not enough. We can survive a couple of months at best, and that's if I really stretch it. I'm going to have to say goodbye to my wall and this little space. My throat tightens. *Fuck.*

I push up from my desk and tell Susie I'm going for a walk, and as I press down through the streets, past coffee shops and cafés, I study the faces of the people sitting and talking. A well-dressed guy with glasses is working on his laptop. Some of these people are no doubt techies who get paid top salaries in New York companies. I find a bench on the edge of a park eight blocks away. *Ten years.* To get nowhere. In fact, worse than that, I could have been saving thousands of dollars from a high-flying job. Is my mom right? Have I been messing around here? I set up this business because I love electronics, love designing and building things. I never thought Ted's business would go down. I should talk to Janus; he's the one person who would understand this. He's been on the brink many times himself, but I can't bear the idea. Not because he'll say I told you so, but because he'll be sympathetic and insist on lending me money. I've resisted that for years, too. It's one of the reasons I haven't talked to him about my company's problems. Well, I'll sleep on it tonight and check over all the figures with a fine-tooth comb tomorrow. But I'm definitely going to have to close the business down. I close my eyes as ice sheets across my skin. There's no point in prolonging the inevitable, Adam. The newspaper references to my flourishing electronics company feel like a wasp sting.

I think about Anna and her dad and what she said about her competition getting stronger every year. How does anybody fight their way to the top? Is it luck? It's not even that there's some mythical pinnacle I'm trying to reach. I just want my business to thrive. Maybe Anna would understand that better than anyone.

*

The next day, I pull the team into my office and run through Ted's call. Keith's face is white, and Chris stares at the floor. In the past, I've shared the numbers and the fact that we're not doing too well, but now I fill them in on what it all means. Susie's eyes are glassy and she won't meet my eyes.

"I wanted you all to be prepared, to give you some time to start looking for jobs." I clear my throat. "I think we can keep the company going for a couple of months. Does anybody have any questions?"

"Is it really that bad?" Keith says.

"Yes. I've stretched to all the debt I can persuade anyone to lend to me. Would you guys like to go through it in detail?"

Everyone nods, so I pull up the spreadsheet I was poring over last night, and as their eyes scan over the sea of red numbers, and I talk through the issues, the mood in the room gets more and more subdued.

"We're not selling enough," José says as he peers at the figures.

Susie is looking at her hands. "We've also been spending more. It's been getting more and more difficult to sell online. This is my fault."

"No, Susie, it's not," I say. "You work damn hard, and I've always been impressed with what you do and how tenacious you are in stretching what little marketing budget we do have."

"We have to make the right things to sell, too," Keith adds.

Chris clears his throat. "We'll all put our thinking caps on, Adam. We've got two months. The warning is appreciated. We can do a good job here at the same time as we're looking for work."

Everyone murmurs in agreement, and my eyes prickle.

"Thanks, guys. I appreciate it. I'm happy to give you time off for interviews when you need it." I have the best team here, and my gut is tight at what's coming down the line. I'll have to get a job, too.

About an hour later, I glance up to see Susie leaning on my door jamb.

"With your increased profile, boss, we might have a chance of improving things. I've just been digging into the data, and sales have been up on the website over the last couple of weeks."

I don't know how we're going to get ten percent extra out of that, but the guys are great, and I'm not going to let them down if they come up with ideas.

"What were you thinking?"

She sits down in the chair on the other side of my desk, and Chris appears in the doorway and raises his hand in greeting.

"I was talking to Chris about animal videos on TikTok and how much I liked them," Susie starts.

"My girlfriend's got a craaazzy dog," Chris interjects.

"I know the core of people who buy from us are hobbyists with good technical skills, but I was thinking we could design some simple dog-themed electronics kits that ordinary people could make, maybe kids, like Rover's Robot or The Beagle Bot, and use Chris's girlfriend's dog to promote them. We could put together some fun videos."

I laugh. It's so far away from a serious electronics company, but it would get us eyeballs. "I actually love that idea."

"People could share their dogs as well as the kits they've made. We could run competitions to have a kit named after their pet. I'm sure I could come up with lots of things."

Susie's brain runs at a mile a minute. "These are all good ideas," I say, smiling at her and Chris. I have no clue if it will get us anywhere, but where's the harm?

She beams at me. "We'll make a start on it.'

"I'll check on Salty's availability," Chris chips in.

"Salty?"

"That's the name of my girlfriend's dog," Chris says. "He's a real grump."

I laugh again, but also … "God, Anna's dog is named Pepper."

Susie's eyes widen. "Of course she is! Salty and Pepper! That's ridiculous. We could do a video of them together. Does Pepper have an Instagram or TikTok account?"

"I've no idea."

She pulls out her phone and starts scrolling. "Oh, amazing!"

"What?"

"Half a million followers, Adam, that's what."

"For a dog?"

She raises her eyebrows. "Where have you been for the last ten years?"

I gesture at my desk, and she rolls her eyes.

"She probably charges a fortune for a post. Do you think she'd let us use Pepper?"

I purse my lips. That's a big favor, but whatever, might as well go all out. "I can ask. Two secs."

> Would Pepper be up for trying some dog-tech toys?

"Okay. I've asked the question. I'll give you a shout when Anna gets back to me."

But my phone buzzes almost immediately in my hand:

Absolutely! Do you want me to bring her over later?

My eyes scan over the office, taking in the stained carpet and the old desks I took out of a skip. "Shit. She wants to come over here with Pepper."

"Who? Anna Talanova? Are you shitting me?" Chris says, eyes bugging out as he follows my gaze around the room, lingering on the carpet stains and the scuffed walls. Our vibe is more bad seventies throwback than exciting tech startup.

"No way," I say. "This office …"

Susie chews her lip. "Could we sort this place out today?"

"Today?" Chris's eyebrows shoot into his hairline.

"What, before Anna gets here?" I glance around again.

"I've got a friend that does graffiti—we could make it really cool with a funky wall," Chris says, hands flapping.

"That would be an amazing video backdrop."

"We don't have to do it all today, necessarily," Susie adds. "But we do have to move quickly on it for it to help the business."

"We've also got to design the kits," Chris adds.

"Day after tomorrow?"

"Let me text Anna."

We might have to sort one or two things at our end. How about the day after tomorrow?

I can come after practice.

Sounds good.

I wave at Susie and Chris. "Okay, guys, we've got until the day after tomorrow to do something here. Do whatever you need to do. Let's see what we can organize in two days."

Susie grins. "I'm on it, boss. And a dog influencer? That's a sensible backup plan for when Anna quits professional tennis. She's a smart lady."

I grin. "Yeah, I think she is."

God, I'd never even thought of that. How long can you compete in professional tennis, and what happens afterward? All that work to reach the top, and then you have to give up what you love and find something else, or take a back seat and lose the thrill of the fight, of winning.

It certainly puts my business problems into perspective.

CHAPTER 12

Anna

When my driver drops me off next to a warehouse in Red Hook, I stare up at the old building with its black shutters as surprise burns through me. When I imagined Adam's company, it was in some hi-tech business park, not this. It's quiet, with beautiful views out across the water and so deserted I don't think the paparazzi would ever find it.

How does all this work for him? His office and his staff? We've had so little time to talk about any of it, but I'd love to help his business out if I can. He's said a couple of times that it's struggling. I'm beginning to understand him a bit better, but I'm totally adrift with his business and what it takes to be successful in his line of work. Perhaps I should talk to Janus.

I head into the entranceway to the building to find a large open area with brick walls surrounding a gray-painted staircase winding upward. There's no reception and no front desk. Pepper trots along by my feet on her leash, and I eye up an old steel elevator in the corner before heading over and pressing the button. Unit five, Adam said, in the basement.

When I step out of the elevator, Adam is standing in the corridor, an unchecked smile on his face, and Pepper shoots forward as he bends down to give her a tummy rub.

"Welcome to Electronic Man," he says, long fingers sifting through her fur as I watch his graceful hands.

My eyes dart to his face to find him smiling up at me. "I hope we can help," I stutter out.

He straightens and gestures to his left, and we head down the corridor past neon light sculptures hanging on the walls between a series of black doors.

"Are you sure you're okay with doing this?" he says.

"Absolutely. You were so great coming along to that event at the last minute, it's the least I can do."

"I've realized we haven't been very organized about this being a shoot: things like makeup, etcetera. Although we've got a photographer and some lighting. Susie thinks we can do casual stuff as well as some more official shots."

"I'm happy with something more informal: Behind the scenes always works well," I say, stopping by one of the illuminated signs. "Or so they tell me. In fact, we could take a picture here."

"What?" he says as I grab his arm and hold up my phone to take a selfie in front of the sign.

"Smile!" I say, and as he starts laughing, I take a few shots.

Adam looks at my phone as I flick through the pictures. The fluorescent lighting gives it an interesting vibe, but something's missing … I pick up Pepper and smush her near our faces as she wriggles about and I snap more photos, then she licks Adam right up his face.

"Ugh!" He wipes his sleeve over his cheek, and I snatch some more shots. "Can you tell I'm not an influencer?"

It makes me laugh, but oh, the images are gold! A fantastic one of Pepper licking Adam: his face is all scrunched up as her tongue swipes across his nose.

So, I pull up Instagram and post the picture to my account, Pepper's too, adding the caption "Looking forward to a day trying out some exciting new electronic toys!", and I tag Adam and his business and several big dog accounts in the hope they'll share it, and dump some hashtags in for good measure.

Adam peers over my shoulder as I do it, and he smells of something like …

burning rubber? It's strangely appealing. I turn my head after I've posted the shot, and his face is right there, smiling.

"You're good at this."

A smattering of freckles run straight across his nose. Small black lines in his hazel eyes. Warmth starts in my chest and seeps downward. *You're staring, Anna.* His eyes catch mine for a beat before he takes a step back.

I look down at my phone and clear my throat. "Damian, my social media manager, taught me to keep filming and shooting until you capture something that works."

"Look at the sign behind us on the wall in the picture," he says, not meeting my eyes but leaning in again and tapping the screen as a smile curves over his lips.

LET'S PRETEND THIS NEVER HAPPENED says the neon right behind Adam's left shoulder, and we both turn to look at it.

I start to laugh.

"Serendipity," Adam says.

I'm not sure if he means me and him, or Pepper licking him or something else.

"Damian will be in touch if it's bad," I say as my phone buzzes in my hand. "Uh-oh."

I pull up our marketing WhatsApp channel. The words …

Fabulous, Anna!

are followed by a few heart-eye emojis.

"Wow, he's on it, isn't he?" Adam grins as he reads the message, and I sneak a quick look at his freckles again. "Come on, let's go and meet the team," he adds.

Farther down the corridor, we stop by a black door with a huge white *five* written on it, and he turns the handle to reveal six people standing nervously in the center of a large room. Two guys with long hair are setting up lights in front of a mural of two dogs that takes up the whole wall at the far end of the room. Pepper starts jumping up, nearly strangling herself with her leash in the process, desperate to say hello to everyone. I turn to Adam.

"Can I let her off her leash?"

"Go for it," he says.

Tail going like a propeller, she races around, and Adam's staff crowd in. Dogs just remove all awkwardness in any social situation. Adam is laughing at Pepper, so I study the office. The walls are whitewashed, and the ceiling has all its old beams on display. A squishy red couch and Persian carpets adorn the concrete floor. Brown wood desks spill out across the space at jaunty angles, and there's some tall cupboards and a separate room at the back. It's so Adam—warm, relaxed, welcoming.

"What a lovely place."

Everyone looks up from where they're fussing over Pepper and stares at me. God, did I say something off? It is a nice office, isn't it? Sometimes my lack of depth with people screws with my radar, I think. I swing around to focus on the mural. "And I love this!"

One of the guys with dreadlocks and painty fingers beams at me from where he's setting up the lights.

"Are you the artist?" I add.

He nods as a girl in pink pants and red boots steps forward. "I'm Susie. Adam's marketing manager. It's great to meet you, Anna."

I instantly like her offbeat vibe. "Likewise."

She gives me a crooked smile. "You posted something on the way in!"

"Yes! Was it okay? I realized I should have brought Damian with me to video me arriving and ..."

She shakes her head. "It's a brilliant shot. I've reposted it to Adam's personal account. Maybe we could shoot some more behind-the-scenes footage. I've got some of the guys putting the kits together."

"I should have brought Damian to meet you."

"What even is all this social-media stuff?" Adam says, waving his arm around.

"None of us understand TikTok, boss," says a man with a beard standing to my right.

"This is Keith," Adam says, "and Sean, and Chris, Don, José." He points to each member of his team in turn.

"I'm the only woman in the office," Susie adds.

"Yeah, but you do the work of six people," Don mumbles with a grin.

"You're basically our mascot," the guy next to him says. Sean, I think.

I open my mouth, but Susie gets in before me, "Not sure we should be talking about women being mascots in a professional company, Sean."

Sean flushes and starts stammering an apology, but Susie rolls her eyes at me. "Welcome to my life working with a bunch of engineers."

"Don't be engineerist," Don mutters, and Susie punches him in the arm. He howls. "Workplace abuse!"

"Guys. Can we try and look at least semiprofessional for Anna?" Adam says, swinging around as a grin splits my face. These people are adorable.

"This is Chico, who did the graffiti mural, and Andy who's going to do the photos for us today," Adam adds. Chico waves, but Andy blushes to the roots of his hair, steps back, and crashes into a light.

"He's a bit of a tennis fan," Sean whispers.

"If you have all finished being lunatics, maybe we could do some test shots?" Chico says.

Susie directs Pepper and me over to the mural, and I bend down to fuss over the dog while Andy takes a few pictures. Keith has his phone up, filming everything.

"Looking good," Andy says. "Sean, can you bring over some of the toys?"

Sean brings over a small dog made of electronics and metal parts and sets it on the floor, and Adam comes to stand next to me as Pepper sniffs it. When it starts to move, she stares at it for a couple of seconds, tilting her head quizzically to one side, and then she barks.

The dog does a backflip, and Pepper goes berserk, down on her haunches, growling and barking like mad, circling around and around. Everyone begins to laugh: Chico, Andy, and Susie all double up. I put my hand on Adam's forearm as I start giggling. The solid muscle flexes under my fingers, and when I glance up at him, his head is tipped back and he's laughing uproariously, too, and all the noise makes Pepper bark more and more. I stare at the joy on his handsome face. He hunches over, and when he straightens, water is leaking out of the corner of his eyes. He puts his hand over mine on his arm and squeezes.

"This is priceless," he says, wiping his eyes with his other hand.

What a lovely guy he is.

"Can I turn it off?" Keith says, stepping forward, and still grinning himself as Pepper carries on growling.

"Was that a success or a failure?"

"Who cares?" says Susie. "I got some amazing footage. Never mind people making this themselves as a kit, I think we should put it up, ready-made, as dog entertainment and find out if it sells."

"More like human entertainment," Keith says as he bends down to switch it off, and Pepper comes back to me and hides between my legs, looking uncertain. I don't want to move my hand from where it is under Adam's, but I have to give her a stroke and a fuss.

"You silly," I say, bending down to ruffle her fur. "It's stopped moving now."

Adam crouches down, too, fondling her soft ears, still grinning. "Well, that's the most fun I've had in about a decade," he says drily, but an odd expression flits across his face.

What? What has he been doing for the last ten years of his life? Surely his business hasn't been in trouble all that time? And he has close friends, like Janus. The people in his company also seem lovely. Why has he not been having any fun?

*

My solitary car ride home does nothing but fuel more questions, so when I get back, I call Janus, but before I can get anything out, he wades right in:

"So, you and Adam, eh? He's been typically tight-lipped about it."

Really? Janus has talked to him? Does Adam play his cards close to his chest, even with good friends? I mean he's self-contained, almost stoic. Maybe especially with guys who might rib him about things.

"What did he say?"

"He told Fabian and me to mind our own business."

I chuckle. "Adam and I are just friends. I don't think either of us has the space for a relationship right now."

There's a long silence on the other end of the line. "I think it's about time Adam made space for a relationship."

Oh, interesting. "Really? He mentioned something about a woman at college ..."

But Janus is too smart to fall for a leading question and barrels on. "I worry about Adam's business. Hardware is difficult, especially consumer stuff, and all this stuff in the press ... Do you know whether he's got a PR person?"

"I think he's got a marketing lady, Susie, but no agency."

"He needs somebody to handle stuff like this or it could all blow up in his face."

"Yeah, he does."

"I'll talk to him."

I roll my lips together. Is Adam's business the reason he's not been having any fun? Or is it his past? "This woman he went out with in college ... can you tell me any more about her?"

There's a long silence. "It's not really my story to tell." He pauses. "Why are you asking?"

That's the fifty-million-dollar question, isn't it? "Adam's a nice person. I like him. He's never tried or suggested anything with me. I guess I'm curious." Is that *all* I am? Ugh. "I'm trying to be his friend."

"He's a great guy. Be careful with him, Anna. It's not my place to tell you about his relationship in college, because it's his story to tell. But he was deeply bruised by it. On the surface he's fine, but underneath ... I don't know. I can understand why he hasn't had another relationship. He thought she was the one, and she turned on him in the worst possible way."

What? Now I'm all kinds of curious.

CHAPTER 13

Adam

It's funny how surreal the first awards event I attended with Anna felt and how this one feels almost normal, like I've acclimatized to this whole thing. Several women are standing farther up the red carpet in long dresses, talking to journalists, and Anna's silver dress glitters in front of me as she steps out of the car and smiles at me over her shoulder as we move up toward the entrance, back straight and strong, brown curls piled on her head. When I reach her side she leans into me, red lips curling up as she whispers, "My mother isn't speaking to me," as we approach a waiting line of journalists.

"What? Why not?"

"She thinks splitting up with Arty Maroz was the biggest mistake I ever made."

Before I can answer, the man in front of us moves on, we step forward, and the waiting journalist sticks a microphone in Anna's face. Before either the journalist or she can speak, however, a voice comes from behind me:

"That bitch stole my dog!"

I turn as if in slow motion, cameras flashing and calls of "Over here!" echoing from my right. I step forward instinctively, putting myself between the voice and Anna, as a man with short dark hair and broad shoulders barrels toward us. *Arty Maroz*. Before I can even jerk back, his arm is up and I stagger sideways as a blow blooms hot and sharp across my cheek.

Shit. *Anna*. My response to an attack is instinctive now. It's what I used to do with Fabian when he was on a bender. *Take them down. Immobilize.* I jump on Arty, and he goes down on his knees. *Not a trained fighter, then*. In seconds I have him pinned on his back. The frantic clicking of cameras and shouts wash in and out as his arms flail at me, catching me on the face again, so I wrestle, trying to pin his wrists down. *Definitely strong*.

Suddenly, three huge guys in SWAT vests loom over me. One of them grabs my shoulders and hauls me off Arty like I weigh nothing, and I let myself be pulled up. As I take in the three security guards, one of them draws me away and guides me down the red carpet toward the street and a waiting line of photographer lenses behind a barrier. When I glance back to the entrance, Anna has disappeared.

"I need to find Anna Talanova and …"

"We have to move away from the building, Sir." The guy taps his ear.

"Where did Anna go?"

His two colleagues are pinning down a struggling Arty Maroz, and the cameras are going berserk, people shouting questions at him.

"I've been instructed to escort you away from the venue." He fiddles with his headset. "I hear you," he says.

"What?"

"You can't attend the event now, Sir. Our security policy is that anyone involved in a fight has to leave."

"He punched me! I was restraining him, not fighting with him."

"I can't make a judgment about who started what, Sir. All guests who are part of an altercation are ejected immediately."

"But I was restraining him! He tried to attack Anna Talanova!"

"That's not our concern, Sir. You need to leave."

A subtle whirring right behind his shoulder catches my attention, and a man with a video camera is recording our whole conversation. Is that a good or a bad thing? Arty Maroz is now on his feet and surrounded by more security guards, who he's trying to shove past to get into the venue.

I take a deep breath and pull out my phone, and the guard's hand shoots out. Presumably to stop me filming anything.

"I need to text Anna to tell her you're throwing me out!" I gesture around at all the photographers. "I was her plus one. You think this whole incident hasn't been recorded in great detail? There'll be a slow-motion replay on the news." What an asshole.

He doesn't respond, just stares back at me. I shake my head and drop a message to Anna:

They're saying they aren't going to let me in. That I've got to leave.

What? Why?

Apparently, anyone who's involved in an altercation is ejected. No exceptions. No discussion.

Hang on.

"What's going on?" The voice comes from behind me, a man with a microphone leaning right over the barrier and trying to catch my attention. Maybe this is an opportunity to set the record straight at least.

So, I move his way and gesture at where Arty Maroz is standing now, shouting toward the venue.

"They won't let me into the building because I tried to stop him attacking Anna Talanova," I say.

"Don't worry, Adam, we got it all on video," the guy says, eyes flicking to the security guard who has followed me as I moved to the railings.

He knows my name? Yes, Adam, of course he does, you've been plastered all over the papers.

The journalist, or whoever he is, turns his microphone to the guard. "Adam Miller, Anna Talanova's boyfriend, was blatantly attacked here. Why are you throwing *him* out?"

The security guard completely ignores him.

"Do you know who this man is?" I ask him as I gesture to where Arty is still arguing with a man in a security vest.

His eyes narrow. "Arty Maroz. Belarusian downhill skier. Anna Talanova's ex."

This journalist is surely getting the best footage and interview from this whole event!

My phone buzzes in my hand.

Now they won't let me out!

Anna. I show the security guard my screen.

"Are you going to be responsible for Anna Talanova being imprisoned at your event?"

"They've shut her in?" the journalist says, hardly able to contain his glee.

"Hold on, Sir. Yes," the security guard says, pressing his headset into his ear. "Yes. Yes."

He takes my arm. "You need to come with me."

The journalist grabs my hand and presses a card into it as the security guard drags me away from the barrier. When the journalist tries to follow us, two other guards appear from nowhere and start talking to him as I'm pulled away from the crowd on the red carpet.

"Call me!" he shouts after me. "We've got footage of the whole incident. I'll tell your version of the story!" But the guard tightens his grip on my elbow and manhandles me around the corner of the building and down an alley.

"Where are you taking me? I need to …"

Ahead of us, a door on the side of the building opens to reveal an older man with a shaved head and popping muscles like a veteran Navy SEAL. He gestures at me impatiently. Are they letting me in now? As soon I'm over the threshold the first guy disappears, and the older man points me down a corridor, then places his feet wide and crosses his arms on his chest. God, these *idiots*, they like to look so hard. A white-hot fizz ignites in my chest.

He's twice my size, widthwise anyway, but I trained to fight men like this, the guys who think they're tough and that a gun will get them what they want. Often they aren't all that, and Fabian taught me some of the dirtiest tricks I know, although I can't use them in jujitsu. I'm being a jerk here, but *fuck this, I learned to fight for a reason.* It gives me a sense of power and control against exactly this kind of male assholery. Before he can react, I lash out with my leg and he goes down like a sack of potatoes, and I have his headset off and his Taser out of its holster in seconds as I immobilize him with his arms behind his back.

"What the hell?" he bellows into the glossy marble floor of the corridor.

"You tell your buddies to be more alert at events. I wouldn't have had to do anything if you'd all been doing your job properly," I hiss at him.

"Fuck off!" he shouts. "What the fuck?"

"I hope your teammates got footage of me taking you down, asshole," I say. "Stop manhandling guests like you have the right to do it. You don't. So don't be surprised if one of them retaliates."

I lever off him and walk off up the corridor, hands shaking. When I turn the corner, I lean against the wall for a couple of seconds and suck in a deep breath. It's been so long since anything like this has happened to me that the floor tips up at me for a second. *Come on, Adam. You're fine. That was easier than most of the jujitsu competitions you've been in.* I close my eyes and a flash of a laughing face and blonde hair whips through my mind. *No, Adam. Why am I remembering that now?* I glance down at my suit and dust off the knees of my pants, running a hand across my hair. A white corridor leads off to my right toward a roar of chattering voices and clinking glasses, and I head down it toward the noise.

The corridor brings me out into the main hall and a sea of guests. Everyone has champagne in their hand, and I draw in a deep breath, trying to dampen down the adrenaline as I scan for Anna's silver dress. Where is she? I pull my phone out of my pocket. Breathe in, breathe out.

I'm inside now. Where are you?

A guy in a tuxedo appears at my elbow with a tray, and I give him a tight smile as I take a glass, staring down at my screen as the seconds tick past. Nothing. A woman in a group close to me laughs loudly, red lips pulled back over her white teeth, the men all with slicked-back hair and in dark suits. I start forward, weaving in and out of the crowd, scanning over the chandeliers and made-up faces. Ten minutes later, I could swear I've swept the entire floor and there's no text and no sign of Anna. I chew my lip. What's going on? Perhaps she's in the bathroom? Or maybe they took her somewhere? Arty didn't reach her, but she could have been shaken up by the whole thing. As I take a sip of champagne, I spy another security guard talking into his headpiece by a door at the back of the venue, so I head over to him.

"I'm the person who was attacked outside by Anna Talanova's ex-boyfriend," I start, as he narrows his eyes at me. Shit, maybe he knows I took his teammate down? "I'm trying to find Ms. Talanova, but I've swept the place and there's no sign of her. She said they weren't going to let her out."

He holds up a hand and talks into an earpiece, then makes a beckoning motion with his hand. We head down a corridor at the back of the event to a room that contains three other security guards and a bank of screens. They all turn and eye me curiously.

"Is this the guy that took Jock down?" one of the men asks with a chuckle. Another man shakes his head.

"Any idea what happened to Anna Talanova?" my security guard says.

"The tennis player?"

"Yeah."

"I think I saw her leave about fifteen minutes ago," another man says. He starts doing something on one of the screens, rewinding video, and eventually I see a flash of silver.

"That's her," I say.

He slows the footage down and runs it forward again. Anna exits the side door to the venue into a waiting limousine. *She's gone home?* The man peers up at me.

"That's her, right?" he says.

I nod. She's left me here? My heart clenches. Why would she go without texting me? Maybe she thought they weren't going to let me in. Either way, I guess I need to try to find her. I take a deep breath.

"Okay, thanks, guys. What's the best way out of here?"

"I'll take you, Sir."

At least they're being more helpful now. No doubt worried about blowback or the way I took down that Jock guy. I shouldn't have done that really, but I was so goddamn mad.

When I'm out on the sidewalk, I squint down at my phone. Anna's apartment is about twenty blocks from here. Would it be a huge intrusion to go to her place? I want to check she's all right. I could walk? Not fast enough. I pull up the Uber app and order a cab.

As I'm waiting, my phone vibrates in my hand:

> I left! Arggh, Adam. I'm so sorry! I came out to find you, but my security said I couldn't stay outside the venue, so they got me a car. I'm at home.

The tightness in my chest eases. She sounds okay. The thought of someone getting to her … That jerk almost did.

> No worries. I'm on my way.

In no time, I'm sliding into the back of my Uber. It takes me forty minutes in solid traffic to reach Anna's building, and I have no idea how to get in. But the doorman nods at me and calls up to the penthouse before sending me up.

When I arrive at the apartment, there's a scampering of feet and Pepper appears, pink rabbit dangling from her mouth. I crouch down, and she jumps up at me, losing her rabbit in the process. Anna is right behind her, looking much like she did the first time I met her: wet hair and a makeup-less face.

"Adam." Her face melts with relief. "God, I'm so sorry! I can't thank you enough for what you did. They hustled me inside and wouldn't let me out. When I got your message about not being able to get in, they got all weird with me and said I couldn't leave. I threatened to sue them, and at that point I think they were happy to see the back of me!"

"Are you all right?" she adds, eyes flicking down and landing on my hands. When I look down, my breath catches at the scrapes and red marks all across my knuckles, the skin broken and bleeding.

"Oh, God, your hands! We need to get them cleaned up."

I grunt. *I'm fine.* She's the one who has to put up with Arty. My grazes are a minor inconvenience compared to that. "Don't worry about it. I just wanted to check and make sure you were okay."

But she's already turning and beckoning me down a corridor, and she pushes through a door into a marble bathroom, opening and closing cupboards. She pulls out hydrogen peroxide, cotton balls, and antibiotic ointment, and so I sink down on the toilet seat.

"I've had so many injuries diving for tennis balls, I'm an expert on scrapes and bruises at this point." She gives me a half smile. "Let's have a look." She takes my hand and examines my knuckles, and her fingers are warm and comforting. Where her dark head is bent toward me, her hair is falling forward, so I reach up and push it over her shoulder without thinking. But she raises her head and her wide eyes meet mine, warm pink lips only inches away.

She licks them, and I can't help but follow the path of her tongue.

"God, I'm so sorry you got hurt like this," she says, voice hoarse in sympathy or something else ... I'm not sure.

I look down, cheeks heating, and shake my head. "Anyone who fights as a hobby is always messing up their hands."

Fortunately, she laughs. "I'm sorry I missed your messages. My phone started blowing up." She bites her lip. "I wasn't sure what to do. I thought Arty might persuade them to let him in. It seemed sensible to leave."

I reach out and touch her elbow. "It's no problem. Not my usual Friday night out, but at least the jujitsu came in useful." I grin at her. "It's a long time since I used it for *actual* fighting."

But she doesn't smile back. "It will be all over the news sites tomorrow, Adam. Ugh. I'm so sorry to drag you into this nonsense."

"I'm fine. I talked to a journalist outside." I fill her in on the guy with the microphone. "He said he'd videoed it all."

She nods, chewing her lip as she turns back to the sink and turns on the tap. "We might need that footage. I should talk to my lawyer, and I'll let the PR team know. We could get ahead of this whole thing if we feed them the true story. Find out how much they videoed."

She adds some soap to the water and dips cotton wool into it. The pants of her tracksuit are molded to her ass, and God, I should *not* be checking her out but … I don't think I can ever tell her how much I like her tracksuits. She turns around and dabs at the wounds on my hands as I try not to stare at her lips again. It takes a second before the sting kicks in. I wince.

"One of the guys I was in college with, Fabian, got himself into trouble all the time. I quickly realized that, if I was going to hang around with him, I needed better defense skills. I've done jujitsu for years, but I also fought with Fabian, and he lived on the street at one time, so he taught me some mean tricks." I laugh. "I competed while I was at college until other things got in the way."

She grins at me. "You're a man of many talents."

I smile, shaking my head. "Concentrating on one thing is a more fruitful idea, I think, and I'm better at defense than attack. I feel like that's the story of my life."

She tips her head. "Defense is an underrated skill. Have you ever heard of the loser's game?"

"No."

She squeezes out the cotton wool in the sink and turns back to dab at some more cuts on my hands.

"It's a concept from a research paper on strategies for winning games. In some games you can increase your chances if you simply try not to *lose*. You don't have to go on the offensive; you basically wait for the other side to make a mistake. Unless they're very good, people always make mistakes."

God, this woman. "Wow. Is tennis like that?"

She reaches around and picks up the antibiotic ointment, smearing some on her fingers.

"Until you reach the highest levels, yes. Then you get to the point that people make so few mistakes that you need to switch strategies." She gives me a crooked smile. "There I go, being a nerd about tennis again." She starts rubbing the ointment over my cuts, and I stare down at her hands. It's such a long time since anyone touched me like this.

"There. That's not too bad now, I think. Would you like a drink? I feel like I've turned your life upside down. Like we started with something that was useful for a bit of publicity, and it's taken a sharp right turn into crazy town."

I like Anna—she's good company. For some reason I don't want her to think whatever we're doing here doesn't work for me. It's surprising in so many ways.

"A glass of wine would be very welcome," I say, as I stand up and we head out of the bathroom and down the corridor into a beautiful high-ceilinged kitchen. "And don't worry about me, I'm used to insanity. If you ever meet Fabian, I think you'll probably understand."

She laughs. "That sounds like fun."

"Are *you* okay? That asshole appeared out of nowhere."

"I'm a bit shaken up, to tell you the truth. I haven't ever really needed security in the USA, although I've employed some people in Russia in the past, but tonight …" She blows out a long breath as she retrieves a bottle from the fridge. "I've only had one or two incidents where people got persistent. Most people are really nice. That's the first time someone has tried to do something more serious." She shakes her head. "I mean it was Arty, not some fan, so to some extent it's my fault. I don't know what would have happened if you hadn't been there."

She pulls two glasses from the cupboard and pours the wine.

"God knows, it's not your fault, Anna. You should have punched him with that amazing right arm of yours."

Fortunately, she laughs as she passes a glass to me and raises hers to her lips.

"I could teach you jujitsu if you like?" I add.

"Ha! That would be great. I did do some martial arts when I was younger, judo and things like that." She laughs again. "I was too competitive and got into a bit of trouble about fighting too hard. I thumped a girl in the face … sort of by accident?"

Now I start to laugh. "Sort of by accident?"

She smirks. "Well, she was a real bully, and all through our fight she was smack-talking me and cheating, trying to pull illegal moves. I got an opportunity to put her in a choke hold, and my hand slipped and I ended up punching her in the jaw. Of course, it was a foul, but she went down like a felled tree, howling."

I'm still laughing. "You're scaring me now. What would happen if I taught you jujitsu?"

She grins back at me. "But you took him down so fast, Adam! You're like this self-contained, mild-mannered guy but then, bang! He was on the floor in seconds. You're much more ruthless than you look."

"Martial arts are excellent for defense. You learn a lot of restraint techniques."

She eyes me with raised eyebrows. "Don't think I didn't notice that you avoided the *more ruthless than you look* comment."

The buzzer echoes suddenly in the quiet of the apartment.

"I wonder who that can be?" With a frown, she disappears out of the kitchen to the intercom and I follow her.

"Ms. Talanova, Arty Maroz is in the lobby …" the doorman starts, and Anna's face goes white, and even from where I'm standing, I can hear shouting coming out of the speaker. She presses her hand to her lips.

I lean into the intercom. "Mr. Maroz attacked Ms. Talanova at an event earlier tonight. Can you keep him busy while I call the cops?" I pull my phone out of my pocket and press 911 as I'm talking.

"I don't know, Sir, I …"

"Sir?" The shout echoes in the background, and there's a loud crash.

I hand my phone to Anna. "Talk to the police. I'm going down to the lobby."

Her eyes go wide. "You can't do that, Adam! He could be dangerous." She runs a hand through her hair. "God, why is he here? I thought what he did was just some stupid publicity stunt, that he was just trying to get attention."

"I can't leave that poor guy on the door to deal with it," I say, and before she can stop me, I walk down the hallway and mercifully the elevator is still on the penthouse floor. I step inside, push the button for the lobby, and the doors slide closed.

As soon as I walk out into the lobby, Arty launches himself at me, but I'm ready for him, neatly sidestepping and managing to kick his legs out from under him. When he falls over, I jump on him and pin his hands down. But I'd forgotten how fucking strong he is. He kicks his legs, trying to buck me off and my knees slide against the polished marble floor.

"*Kozol!*" he shouts.

He wrestles a hand out of my grip, and I manage to deflect another blow to my face just before it connects. *Come on, Adam, he's all action and no skill.* I jump off him. I need to get him on his front, and I circle around with my hands out looking for a grab.

"What are you doing, you *mudak*! This is not a martial arts class." He laughs as he watches me, running a hand through his hair, and that's my opportunity.

I launch at his torso, twisting as we fall, and when we hit the floor, I manage to get him on his front and pin him there. *Hallelujah!* This almost never happens in jujitsu: My opponents are all too well trained. I twist his hand up behind his back. He squirms and kicks, but once you've got a hold like this, the person under you is going nowhere. Gah! my knuckles have started bleeding again.

The security guard scurries over, eyes bugging out. "Mr. Miller! Mr. Miller! Oh my God! I didn't know what to do! I'm so sorry. He damaged the desk and the walls." He gestures behind him. "I told him someone was coming down to talk to him."

"It's fine," I grit out. "Can you find out if the cops are on their way?"

But as soon as the words are out of my mouth, the familiar wail of sirens reaches me from the street. Please let these sirens be for this prick. Sure enough, in seconds, three cop cars pull up outside the glass doors of the building and five cops lever out.

"This dickhead attacked me," my friend on the floor shouts as soon as they come through the doors.

Jesus Christ, what is this guy on? But the doorman is outraged.

"What the fuck!" he yells. "This asshole came in here shouting and cursing, and now he's damaged my desk and the walls." He gestures to large gouges in the wood, and wow, that's going to cost a mint to repair. "I'm in so much fuckin' trouble here, man, you get me? I'll have to pay it back 'n' all and … I'm gonna be fired and my old lady will be all up on my ass."

Cops understand that doormen take a lot of shit in buildings like this: People wander in off the street, tenants complain, and they get sacked, and they don't have anything to defend themselves and they don't get hazard pay for dealing with people like Arty Maroz, who's now squirming underneath me. Cops are always on their side. One of them heads over to me, nodding as he takes his cuffs out of his waistband, and he leans over to where I'm holding Arty down on the floor. I maneuver so he can slap them around his wrists. As I shift my weight off him, Arty kicks out, catching me on the ankle.

The cop hauls him up. "Hey, asshole, none of that unless you wanna be tasered for resisting arrest. You want to tell me what all this is about?"

"This is bullshit! I'm an Olympic skier."

"I don't care who you are, buddy."

"He's an ex-boyfriend of Anna Talanova," I say. "He attacked her at an event tonight, I ended up restraining him, and now he's turned up here."

"She shouldn't be out at an event where any crazy can get to her. It's not safe," Arty says. "I would never let her …"

What is this guy on? "What's with the sudden show of concern? You cheated on her, you asswipe. You don't get to dictate what other people do: That's called restricting personal freedom. You're the only one who's putting her in danger," I say.

"And you are?" The officer standing next to me says.

"A friend of Ms. Talanova who accompanied her this evening. It was a big event. If you need evidence, everything I've told you will have been captured on video."

"Camera footage. Sweet. That kind of thing makes my job a helluva lot easier," the officer mutters.

"Is that that cute chick that played in the Billie Jean Cup?" the other cop says, eyebrows raised.

"Yes."

"You're that tech guy who's been dating her, aren't you?"

"Yes."

"Holy shit. Are you an idiot?" he says to Arty, who glowers back at him.

"You got security cameras in here?" the other cop asks the doorman.

"Yes. Yes." The doorman's face relaxes a bit.

"She want to file a complaint?" another officer asks me.

"Let me speak to her."

When I call Anna, she hems and haws about complaining to the police and the potential repercussions with Arty's father, but eventually agrees to speak to her lawyer. One of the officers talks on his walkie-talkie for a while, as two more manhandle Mr. Olympic Skier into the car outside. Two of the cops come up in the elevator with me, and Anna gets her attorney on speakerphone and they all talk to Anna for over an hour. One of the officers encourages her to file for a restraining order, and her lawyer approves.

After they've gone, she blows out a long breath and pads into the kitchen. "You want a soda or some vodka or a whiskey or something?"

"You have these things?"

"I'm not a total killjoy." She smirks at me and heads toward the kitchen, and I rise up from the couch and follow her. She's standing staring out the window at the lights of New York outside. It's past 11 p.m. now.

"Are you okay?"

She turns her head to look at me, and her eyes are faintly pink. "My life is such a mess, Adam"—she spreads her hands—"You're a good guy and I'm connected to a bunch of awful people, and I know we said we'd be friends, but I don't want to drag you into something that puts you in danger."

I walk over to where she's standing by the countertop and reach up and touch a finger to her shoulder and she turns her head. She's so strong and vulnerable all at once. *I don't want to give this up.*

"I think we could both do with a friend we can trust in our lives right now. If you want to make it transactional, I'm helping you and you're helping me, but it doesn't feel transactional to me. I want to help. I enjoy your company, and we have fun together."

She gives a choked little laugh. "Thanks for saying that. I enjoy your company, too. Sometimes I think I've managed to escape my past, and then it comes and bites me in the ass."

"Your past?"

She hesitates, staring out of the window again. "Arty, you know?"

Why do I think she was going to say something else? "Yeah." I give her hand a squeeze. "Would you like me to stay?"

Her eyes widen, and my face heats. I gesture around. "To keep you company, bunk down on your couch or something."

She laughs. "You don't have to sleep on the couch. This place has five bedrooms."

I laugh. "Of course it does. Do you ever use them all?"

"When my parents come to stay, yeah. My sister, sometimes."

"You have a sister?"

"Yes. They're all still in Russia. She's a swimmer. Arty's father might try and make trouble for them." She chews her lip.

These glimpses into her life come out bit by bit, like puzzle pieces she's carefully placing into my hands, one by one.

"We'll sort Arty out." I reach out and squeeze her forearm.

"Thanks for offering to stay. It's nice having someone else around." She blows out a long breath. "Let me show you your bedroom."

She moves across the large open-plan kitchen and living area and heads down a long corridor that appears to have no doors at all. But then she stops and presses on a panel, revealing a room with a thick patterned carpet and textured cream walls.

"This is beautiful," I say.

She grins and gestures to a door on the left-hand wall. "I had an awesome designer. The bathroom's through there."

She studies me for a second before taking a step forward and wrapping her arms around me. I almost jerk away. I haven't been hugged by a woman like this in a long time, and my body stiffens reflexively. I force my hands up and rest them on her strong back, muscles shifting under my fingers.

"Thanks so much for today," she mumbles into my shoulder.

My head brushes against hers as I nod. I breathe in roses and something more, a soft caramelly smell, like she's been eating toffees.

And the sad softness I've been feeling for Anna morphs into something else entirely.

CHAPTER 14

Anna

When I step into Adam, he's so solid and real. Next to my eyeline, a pulse thrums in his neck and I'm seized by a sudden urge to press my lips to it. I breathe in a faint smell of coffee and something metallic and sharp, like lingering wood smoke, as his hand presses between my shoulder blades, every finger strong on my spine. I should move away now, but I take one more inhale, and, as if he can sense me on the edge of retreat, his arms tighten momentarily. My chest is pressing into his hard pecs, and his long legs brush against mine. It's not sexual exactly just …

"It's my pleasure," he rumbles, and his deep tone vibrates through me.

Sighing, I sink into him as his fingers drift down to press into my lower back. But I can't stand here getting sucked into his warmth and how nice it is to just be held, with no expectations or worry that this person could harm me in some way, twist my arm or twist my heart or get me sent back to Russia.

Although I liked Arty when we first started dating—he was sexy, charismatic, and such a good-looking guy—I was wary of his surface charm. A meanness would rise up every so often, and I knew that was always lurking inside him and could rear its head at any time, with me as its target. Adam isn't charming in that obvious way: He's not out to please anyone, but he is full of a genuine quiet appeal.

But I've gotten Adam involved in a fight and with the police. There's helping each other out and then there's dragging someone into some difficulty that they don't need to be involved in. I don't want to bring trouble to Adam's door. I step back and blink up at him and his eyes do a slow circuit of my face and my lips when I lick them. He blinks several times and sucks in a deep breath.

"Let's hope that's the last of the excitement for tonight," he says, and I tilt my head at him, the couple of inches between us snapping like a forcefield.

My hand flutters up. I'm not sure what I'm going to do with it—maybe squeeze his arm—but he steps back and clears his throat, so I step back, too, and wave my hand at him. "Sleep tight, Adam. Thanks again."

I turn and go to my own bedroom, where Pepper, in her usual position curled up on the left side of the bed, greets me with raised ears and a turn of her head. As I take off my lounge gear and slide between the cool sheets, she curls into my waist and I stare at the ceiling and play with her soft ears. She lets out a long, shivering doggy sigh.

Adam has enough on his plate with his business, and possibly with some past relationship history he doesn't want to talk about. I huff and roll onto my side, pulling up my notes app and jotting down things I have to organize. I've employed security once or twice, but I need to think more seriously about it. I talked to Adam about scrutiny, but not about putting himself in physical danger. I should be concentrating on my tennis, on the pain in my elbow and my hip, not that I've got an ex-boyfriend who's a publicity-seeking slimeball and is trying to intimidate me. A text in Russian flashes across the top of my screen as my phone buzzes in my hand:

What's going on?

Kira. Why is my sister texting me so late? Oh God, the videos of tonight must already be online. And my mind skips back to the bedroom we shared for so long in my parents' cozy apartment in St. Petersburg, full of my grandmother's old furniture and patterned quilts.

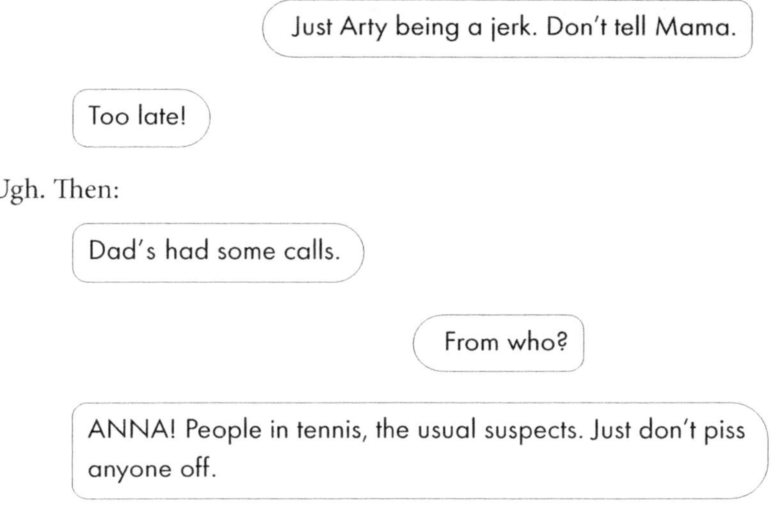

Ugh. Then:

A shiver runs through me. I feel like I'm always pissing someone off. Another message appears on my phone:

She follows it with a winking emoji, and it makes me smile. But who's pressuring them? Calling my dad? Turning over again, I punch my pillow as Pepper shifts beside me. I don't want to give up on my friendship with Adam. It's gone from a fun night when we first met into something deeper and steadier. Something I'd call a real friendship, something I don't feel I've had before. There's not many people I trust. Not even really my sister or my parents. They could so easily be manipulated or blackmailed in Russia. Adam's rapidly become someone I could turn to for help.

But how are we going to navigate this? What seemed like useful media interest has now morphed into something else. The video clips must already be circulating, but I'm too tired to look—the press is going to have a field day and Adam is right in the middle of it. If I were him, I'd be running for the hills.

CHAPTER 15

Anna

Sunlight is filtering through my bedroom blinds when my eyes blink open and my hand stretches down the covers to find … *No Pepper.* Usually, she licks my face to wake me up when she needs to pee. Curious, I get up and use the bathroom, scowl at my phone and throw on my pants and top from last night. As I head down the corridor, a noise reaches me from the kitchen … like beating or grinding? There's an immediate scrabble of feet against the floor and Pepper appears around the corner where the open-plan kitchen sits just off the living room, barreling straight for me at speed. I bend down and scoop her up, and she wriggles as her tail goes round like a windmill. I round the corner into the space between the dark wood island and the cupboards to find Adam in last night's pants and shirt, whisking a pale liquid in a bowl.

"What are you doing?"

He turns and grins at me and … oh, the slight scruff on his chin and bed-tousled hair! My stomach swoops and dives.

"Pancakes," he says. "It was a Saturday tradition in college."

Did a guy ever cook breakfast for me? Oh, God! I have to stop comparing him to boyfriends. He's a *friend.* A friend I want to keep.

"After a wild Friday night?"

"It probably won't surprise you to discover that I always made the pancakes as the least hungover of all of us—I mean Fabian, Janus, and me."

"You're talking to the wrong person about wild nights. My whole life has been about tennis performance. I don't really drink."

"You don't? But you've had champagne at some of the events, a bit of wine …"

"I might hold a glass, but I have a few sips at best."

I step up beside him at the countertop as he frowns as if he's trying to remember, strong fingers whipping the whisk around the bowl.

"Suffice to say, I must be the most boring woman alive," I add.

He turns his head and his eyes twinkle at me. "I prefer thinking about it as being fun in a different way."

I grin at him. "Well, let me know when you work out what that way is."

"Maybe in a comic book and dog show way?"

I laugh, and he gestures at me to move back as he shifts toward where the griddle is warming on the stovetop, so I step around the island, sliding onto one of the bar stools.

"I'm sorry about last night. You didn't need that." I bite my lip, trying to gauge his expression.

He pours the mixture into perfect circles on the pan in front of him and chuckles. "I wasn't expecting how goddamn strong a downhill skier would be, that's for sure."

Does nothing faze him? "God, Adam, we have to stop going to events like this. This must be way more trouble than you ever anticipated. I'm sure you don't want to …"

His head snaps up, eyes narrowed, and he puts the bowl down on the countertop and gestures between us. "We're friends, right? Things just got difficult for you. I'm not leaving you to fend off that scumbag on your own."

I press my hand to my chest. "I've no idea how much of a threat he really is. He's probably doing this for the publicity. That's his modus operandi. Up until his injury, he'd been losing, and brands pay for his bad-boy image. A fight is perfect for getting the media attention he's after." I sweep my hand out, and it catches on some Saturday newspapers on the counter.

"You went out?"

He laughs. "Pepper came to find me, so I took her to relieve herself and decided that pancakes should be the order of the day. Then I saw some of the headlines in the papers, so I bought them all." He tips his head toward where my hand is now resting on the papers.

I drag them over to study them. In one of the photos, Arty's face is in full fury, inches away from Adam's. In another, the photographer has caught me just as I heard the commotion behind me and turned around, mouth open and staring.

I scan down the first article in *The Post*, then push the paper away.

"My lawyer is pressing ahead with a restraining order. He says we can get a temporary order of protection in place today. I've had messages from Arty trying to intimidate me, and he thinks he won't go away unless we escalate." I sigh. "But I just … I don't want to give more oxygen to that asshole, and this is going to generate a whole other round of speculation in the press focused on him. But I guess I've got to roll with it."

"He's texted you?" His voice is sharp, and when I look at him, his eyebrows are drawn together in a hard slash. "I can get rid of him for you if you like," he says suddenly, and my eyes bug out.

"What, like, bump him off?" My voice wobbles.

He laughs. "Hell, no. I'm not a closet member of the mafia. My friend from college, Fabian, can hack into almost anywhere. He'd be able to dig up some dirt on Arty that you could use to deter him from interfering in your life ever again."

Whoa, really? That sounds amazing. But then my stomach plummets—if he could find stuff on Arty, what could he find out about me?

"Arty's been blowing up my phone since 7 a.m. I can't bring myself to read any of the messages."

Adam straightens, the expression on his face no less intense. "Are you serious? Why haven't you blocked him?"

I sigh. "My lawyers thought it was a sensible idea not to, because it's likely he'll incriminate himself, or at the very least it will be evidence of harassment and intimidation."

"Fuck. I hate that you have to do that. I loathe this guy."

"You and me both."

"Let me know if you want me to find something that'll keep him at bay."

"I don't want to do anything illegal."

Adam laughs. "Well, that might be a problem. I'm not sure Fabian does any legal stuff at all."

CHAPTER 16

Adam

Seeing my face in print no longer produces the strange gut drop it did after that first event I attended with Anna, and we both look so comically surprised in the photos of Arty Maroz's assault. Another paper has my face contorted into an angry snarl. It's badass, something I could use in competitions, and *badass* is a word I've never used to describe myself. But God, is this what people are going to find when they do a search on my name? Prospective employers? *Fuck.*

After I leave Anna's, I head to the office. There's still a ton of work to do on the kits: Susie is launching them on the website at the end of the week. As I take in the wonderful weekend quiet and the shadowy desks in the half-dark, my phone rings just as I turn on the lights.

Carly. The PR Janus bullied me into using two days ago. He said he'd talked to Anna, and I "absolutely needed" someone for my personal stuff, or it would "rapidly spiral out of control." I huff out a breath. When I told him I couldn't afford it, he swore at me and said he was going to add it to the Janus Industries contract.

"Hey, Adam, I saw the videos and photos from the event last night and I'm calling to discuss tactics," Carly chirps in my ear.

"Sounds sensible."

"I've spoken to Anna Talanova's PR team …"

Already? On a Saturday? Wow. How much are they charging? "Okkkaayy …"

"And they want to play the angle of harassment … I understand Anna's lawyer is trying to tie down a temporary order of protection for her today. I don't think this is the first time this has happened to her."

Oh really? She didn't mention that. My mind plays back her slight hesitation last night and something hot and sharp bubbles in my chest. "Jesus."

"Exactly."

"We were thinking that we'd push the line of you wanting to do your best by her, etc. Low key."

"That sounds sensible." I blow out a long breath. "The whole thing makes me mad if I'm honest. What women have to put up with. All the bullshit Arty Maroz is dumping on Anna, and all she can do is collect his texts and go after him through some long slow legal process? It sucks."

There's a short pause on the other end of the line. "Would you like to make a more political statement?"

A what? "What kind of political statement?"

"I'm not sure exactly, but along the lines of the idea that he's a predator—a feminist support approach. We'd have to draft up something. I can't guarantee that anyone will be interested, but if you make a statement, some of the press might want to talk to you, and that changes the angle from him to you."

Wow, what a cat-and-mouse game this is. Do I want more media interest? I'm starting to wonder whether it's worth it. But Carly barrels on:

"This is how it works, Adam. You come to the attention of journalists for whatever reason, and you have to make the most of it when it happens."

"Not sure this is happening for legitimate reasons or that I want to take advantage of it."

"But that's where I come in. My job is to build your profile and get the right type of coverage. Trust me, Adam, in situations like this, Arty Maroz's PR company may step in and spin some tale about you to justify his behavior—why he assaulted you or even Anna. The truth is, he's more likely go for you because attacking a woman doesn't look smart. They could easily make some awful stuff up. I've seen it happen."

I bury my head in my hands. This has really spiraled. Like some messy, threatening thing that Janus or Fabian might get sucked into. I need some advice. Fabian never touches the media, but I could talk to Janus.

"Plus, you can push things like pictures of that fight down with something more positive," she adds.

I guess there's no harm in getting Carly to write something as a starting point.

"If you could draft something, that would be amazing."

"Excellent. I'll do that now. It'll need to go out today, Adam."

"I can do that."

"Great. Good to catch up with you." And she hangs up.

I immediately phone Janus.

"Adam!" he says. "To what do I owe the honor of a call on the weekend?"

"I know you're in the office, asshole."

"I'm in the home office, yeah," he says, chuckling.

"And Jo?"

"Korea. Is she ever anywhere else?"

"Didn't you kickstart all this interest in her company?"

"I am not taking any credit for it. It's all her. So what if the people at Samsung are in love with her? Although they're more enamored with Des if I'm being honest."

"Des?"

"Her number two. He's a great tech guy."

"I called for some advice, actually."

"Excellent. No one wants to listen to what I think about things in the business at the moment, so it's a welcome change."

I find that hard to believe. "Well, I got involved in an actual fight last night. Anna's ex-boyfriend went after her at an event we were attending …"

"Wait. Like on the street? What the hell, Adam?" His fingers tap away on his keyboard.

A sigh seeps out while he searches online. He lets out a low whistle. "These pictures are … hang on, I've got a video."

Oh dear, I couldn't bring myself to watch the whole thing.

He starts to laugh. "He didn't stand a chance! The rage on your face is priceless. He went down like a sack of potatoes."

I growl down the phone. I don't want to be praised for decking some guy. I can just imagine my mother's views if she thought I was involved in an *actual* fight. And God, I hope this little gem doesn't reach the far corners of bumfuck nowhere. I clench and unclench my fist. It was strangely satisfying taking Arty Maroz down.

"I sounded off to Carly about what Anna puts up with, and she's suggested she could try and spin the media a bit. Talk about predators and widen it out into how women are treated more generally, how they're subjected to more abuse online than men … all that stuff."

"Are you comfortable with that?" Janus says. His chair rolls back and footsteps echo across the floor.

"What are you doing?"

"Getting a double espresso. This feels like a caffeine kind of conversation." I hear the clinking of cups and beans being ground in the background. "Jo would love you forever."

"What? Why?"

"She's vitriolic about how women are judged in business. You can imagine what it was like for her starting out. A petite redhead in kickass clothing? No one treated her seriously. She had to dress completely differently." He chuckles.

"What's funny about that?"

"When I first met her, she was all dressed up in an executive suit. I made some assumptions and, as you can probably guess, that didn't go well for me. When I met her later in what she normally wears, it kind of blew me away."

My mind swings back to Susie in her dungarees with dreadlocks begging on the street. How adamant she was that she was never working for another company. Did no one take her seriously, either? Or maybe something worse? Goddammit. This stuff is terrible …

“It makes me furious that anyone has to put up with this kind of bullshit.”

“I could never step out that far,” Janus says ruefully. “That’s a terrible thing to say, but my board of investors would flip … They’re all super cautious … they don’t want anything that would rock the boat with the company or its valuation. But you could certainly do it …”

“It could all blow up in my face.”

“Carly will make sure it doesn’t. She’s the best.”

“Yeah. I like her. Thanks for that, by the way. She’s going to put together a statement for me. Will you look it over? It has to go out today if I do it.” I chew my lip. I’ve never asked him for help.

“Of course!” he says, something light lifting his voice. “I’d be delighted.”

Even with my small brushes with the media so far, I’m starting to understand how all this works, how a reputation can be manipulated so easily. And later, after Carly and I have gone back and forth getting the wording right, the statement goes out and all I can do is cross my fingers and hope this doesn’t come back to haunt me.

CHAPTER 17

Anna

When I pick up my buzzing phone from the counter, the words *Arty the Asshole* flash across the screen and I grimace at it as it vibrates then goes to voicemail. He's moved from messages to calling. I sigh as I take in the silvery dampness of the Monday dawn beyond the window. My body aches, but it's nothing out of the ordinary, nothing a deep massage won't iron out. Working on my backhand is the top priority today, given it fell apart during the Billie Jean Cup. I text my coach, Ilov, to say I'm on my way, then screw the lid back on my water bottle, pull my coat up around my neck, and head down in the elevator.

When I step outside the door, I don't see the arm that flashes out and grabs mine. My bottle slips out of my hand, bounces across the sidewalk, and rolls into the gutter.

My mouth drops open as I gaze up into Arty's angry face. "You're not supposed to be here!" The Russian words erupt out of me, hot and fast. "You're not allowed to come within a hundred yards of me. I got a restraining order against you yesterday, you prick."

The wet winter streets are empty at this time in the morning: only a solitary car swishing down the street and pulling to a stop at a red light.

CHAPTER 18

Adam

I could have gone to Janus's or Fabian's to escape the press attention at my apartment but for some reason, I'm here. And how could I inflict this media nonsense on them? Fabian refuses to get on anyone's radar, and at least Anna's in this with me. I'm telling myself that staying here also allows me to keep an eye on her, but that's bullshit, clearly. This is a woman who travels around the world on her own. The shiny elevator doors wink at me as I wait, and I turn to study the lobby. Nevertheless, she's here by herself, and what security does she have apart from a guy on the front desk? It would actually be so easy for somebody to get in.

Being here a couple of nights ago and waking up knowing someone else was in the same apartment made my chest ache in an unfamiliar way. I've gotten so used to living on my own. And when I took Pepper out to do her business, the idea of buying stuff for pancakes hit me. *There was another person to do it for.* When did I last make pancakes? A fuck of a long time ago. I don't do it for myself, and I haven't invited any friends over for breakfast in ages. I think Janus and Jo have been to my place once for brunch.

And why is that, Adam?

It's the same reason I don't ask Janus for help. I'm embarrassed. I'm thirty-two, living in a tiny, rented apartment, and my business is going under. I studied electronics and computer science. I could be on a fat salary working for a bank, squirreling money away, and already sitting on a tidy sum. Am I such a sad sack that making breakfast for someone else is a thrill?

When did I become a hermit? In the conversation about the first event I attended with Anna, Janus told me I should get out more. But as my company has struggled, I've put more and more time into it and less and less time into anything else. It's been a long slow slide. I haven't even seen Janus and Fabian much over the last couple of years. Although Fab does turn up every so often to check on me.

When I arrive at Anna's floor, she's in a gap between interviews and I lean in to kiss her cheek inhaling the familiar smell of roses. I dump my bag on the floor and follow her into the kitchen.

"You went home for your clothes?" she says, smiling at me.

"Susie went to my apartment and got a load of stuff for me and brought it to the office. She told the wolves I was going away for a few days to avoid their bullshit doorstepping tactics." I laugh. "Those were her actual words."

Anna takes a beer from the fridge, hands it to me, and starts making herself a ginger tea.

"So … you're stocking beer now?" I grin at her, and she flaps a hand at me.

I gesture back toward the elevator. "Have you thought any more about getting a bodyguard for yourself, Anna?"

She makes a face as she fills her mug with boiling water. "It restricts your life quite a lot because you have to decide if you want twenty-four-hour security, and then whether you're ever going out without them." She grimaces again.

I can see that, and I don't want to push her. I don't feel like I have the right to do that. A book is sitting on the counter next to her tea: *Anna Karenina.*

"A bit of light reading?" I say, picking it up, and she flashes me a grin.

"I've never read it, and Tolstoy is kind of compulsory in Russia. I never had the time."

Her yoga pants and a soft top are draped over all her tight muscles. I've watched some videos of her matches, my jaw slack at the power behind her thumping shots over the net and the hundred-and-thirty-mile-an-hour serves. How strong is she? *I said I'd teach her jujitsu.*

"How about I take you to a jujitsu class while I'm here?"

"Oh! I'd love that!" She swings around beaming, then wrinkles her nose. "A class? Do you think that would work?"

I think of the club where I train in Midtown. Yeah, she's right: It would be a shit show if the two of us went there.

"Perhaps you can give me a private lesson? I've got a gym here."

I laugh. Of course she has. Hidden behind the myriad of doors.

I rub my hands together. "I can do that." I'm not sure why the idea of throwing her around appeals so much, but I haven't had the chance to work out for a few days. "What's happening with your tennis training at the club? Is the press there, too?"

"Yeah. It's a hassle. The paparazzi have been here and there every morning. Fortunately, the tennis facility is fairly impregnable, and the management has been very accommodating. I've given them some money for extra security." She shrugs. "We could employ some security for your place, too, you know."

I blow out a breath. "The security is poor, but I don't know how it would work at the building I live in. There's no lobby space, nowhere where a security guard could sit or stand, apart from outside the door."

Part of me doesn't want to talk about what my apartment in the Meatpacking District is like, and I certainly don't want her funding security for me. It's bad enough that Janus is paying for my PR, although Carly has been an absolute godsend. What would I have done without her?

"Someone got into the building yesterday. They tried to jimmy my front door open. Fortunately, the guy who lives next door caught them and called the police."

She swings around, eyes wide. "Oh God, Adam, why didn't you tell me?"

"I didn't want to worry you. Susie sorted it out. She got some man in to put better locks on my door. She's talked to all the neighbors, who are pissed off, but more with the press than with me. I've been a good neighbor to a lot of them. I've lived there a long time."

"I'm so pleased I persuaded you to stay here now. I'm sure I'm sounding like a broken record, but I'm so sorry."

I reach out, curling my fingers over her arm, just stopping myself from jerking back at the hard muscles and smooth skin under my hand. "We both went into it with the best of intentions. It seemed logical to me after that first event. Neither of us could have foreseen what's happened since."

She nods. "I know. Doesn't always feel like that when you're in the thick of it, though."

"True. Have you eaten?"

"Okay, this is going to sound a little strange. You made me pancakes on Saturday morning, but in the normal run of things, I have five very specific meals every day, developed by my nutritionist. I got her to double them up while you're here." She peeks at me. "Is that okay?"

I laugh. "That sounds amazing. Eating like an athlete. Are they weird?"

"Not at all. They're just designed to give me the right balance of nutrients and fuel my training and muscle mass appropriately."

"Then I'm down. I'm not fussy about food."

She smiles. "How about a jujitsu lesson before we eat?"

"Sounds good to me."

Anna gives me a little tour of the apartment this time and shows me to the same bedroom I stayed in three nights ago. She also does a detour via her study and tells me to make free use of it. Heading back to my room, I shrug into a top and shorts and come out to find her waiting for me in the living room in her yoga pants from earlier and a form-fitting sports vest that leaves her shoulders bare. We head up one floor in her penthouse to another living room and a gym with a bathroom off to one side, overlooking a beautifully manicured outdoor space on the roof. It's got all sorts of equipment, including a huge soft black mat. Perfect.

"This is gorgeous."

"I bought this apartment when I got my first competition check. It felt important to have a home outside Russia. The building was new at the time, and I got a good deal. Sometimes they want somebody with a name in the building; it supposedly gives them cachet. They're not supposed to let on who lives here, but people know."

Interesting. "You said you'd done some martial arts in the past?"

"Judo. At school. I learned some of the basics."

"Before you decked someone." I grin at her, and she laughs. "I'm quite nervous about what you might do to me," I say, but she shakes her head at me.

I rub my hands together. "Okay, let's talk jujitsu. It's a ground-based martial art, so initiating and defending takedowns is a large part of the skillset. The idea is to collect points and, if possible, make your opponent submit. Most of the sport is about defense, certain holds, submissions, and learning to escape." I wink at her, and she smiles at me.

"Could be useful for tennis," she says. "Submissions? I'm starting to understand why you like it." She winks back at me.

I raise my eyes to the ceiling. "Are you going to be a troublesome student?" I say, my gaze dropping to her grinning face, and I have to stop myself from focusing on her mouth. "I'm going to run through some basic moves and holds, okay? The first thing to learn is a takedown. Your job in jujitsu is to avoid positions where your opponent can score points."

I put my hand on her warm shoulder, and even just in gripping her the muscle and power is so evident. That shouldn't be sexy, but it is. I close my eyes. It's getting hard to ignore all the things I notice about Anna that I shouldn't. The way her dark hair catches the light, the curve of her lips when she finds something funny. I hope staying here isn't going to be a mistake.

"So, the aim of this session is for you to take me down."

She steps forward, and in about a nanosecond her leg has wrapped around the back of mine and I'm on the mat. I blink up at her. It's such a basic move, and I didn't even see it coming. I'd forgotten what a competitor she is.

"Like that?" she says, a broad grin stretching her mouth. Then she laughs. "It's a takedown in judo, too."

"That's the one and only time you'll take me by surprise." Seeing her wild grin makes my chest hot, my pulse too fast like I've been running. She's ballsy,

Anna, in all the best ways. When I see her like this, I realize I haven't seen a lot of joy on her face.

"Ooh, smack talk now." She fakes a boxer dancing on the balls of her feet and punches her fists into midair. "Come on, Adam, fight me."

I smile up at her. "You're a joker."

I hold out my hand for her to help me up, and as soon as she takes it, I take her down and pin her to the mat on her front. She lands with a surprised *oof*, all her muscles tensed under mine. *I mustn't get turned on—that would be a disaster.* Fuck, what was I doing offering to teach her something like this? You were thinking you were her friend, you idiot.

"Lesson number one," I say, inhaling the rose scent that I like so much, "don't give an inch to your opponent. If he or she spots an advantage, they'll exploit it."

"I asked for that, didn't I?" she grumbles underneath me, sounding a bit breathless.

I lift back off her before I do anything embarrassing, like kiss her neck, which is right under my chin.

"Did I wind you?"

"Crushed a few ribs I think," she says, pressing her fingers along her side.

I narrow my eyes at her. "Do I trust what the lady is telling me? You just took me down."

She grins. "Maybe not. I've had a lot of injuries over the years, so go gentle on me."

I wave a hand at her. "Yeah, yeah. Spin me another one. This is worse than fighting with Fabian."

"Your friend from college? The hacker? What did he do?"

"He tried to gouge my eyes out."

She laughs.

"No, he actually did. It wasn't funny at all. I had to knee him in the balls. He said that, if I got attacked on the street, that's what they'd try and do. Said it had to feel real or I wouldn't fight hard enough. He taught me to fight dirty." I laugh. "It's been surprisingly useful. I hope you're not going to knee me in the balls." I raise my eyebrows at her, and she grins.

"Can't promise anything," she says.

"I've changed my mind. I'm not teaching you. I value my balls."

She suddenly lunges for me, and the tips of her fingers whisper over my crotch before I smack her hand away as my jaw drops. *Whoa!* She's not giving an inch. And fuck, I love it. I haven't been surprised like this in a very long time. But my cock is way too interested in what just happened; it hasn't been handled by a woman in a very long time, either, and I'm dangerously close to getting an erection. Her foot swipes out as she tries to take me down, and I make a grab for it, but she's so fucking strong she's out of my grip before I can get a hold of her. It's like sparring with a guy. I use a more complicated maneuver and pin her under me again, hips just off her backside this time. *Jesus.*

"Anna. Jesus. What are you doing?"

"Fighting. Isn't that the aim?" she pants.

"I thought the idea was that I was teaching you?" And there's that scent that makes me want to sink my teeth into her neck. Where are these thoughts coming from? Most of the time when I'm with her I've got total control over it. And I want to groan: what an admission!

"It's a competition, isn't it?"

I chuckle. "Not while you're training. We need to warm up, and I want to teach you the basic moves."

"Okay, get off me. I'll behave."

"Promise?"

"Yeah."

"Can I trust you?"

She laughs.

I lever off her and stand up. "Let's do some warm-ups. Just follow me."

Lying on my back, I start rolling around on the floor. She instantly follows what I'm doing. I use one leg to push myself around in arcs, back still on the mat.

"A lot of floor work, eh?" she says.

"Yeah. Now bridge up and twist."

We do a few more of those, then I say, "I'm going to teach you how to shrimp."

"Shrimp?"

"Yeah, watch me." She sits up, and I turn onto my side and bend my legs, one behind the other, pushing myself backward in circles again, pivoting on my shoulder while Anna grins at me.

"I'm liking all this new terminology I'm learning." Lying down, she copies me. "I saw you do a move similar to this in one of your matches."

I roll to my back and start egg-beating my feet. "Okay?"

"Yeah, this is excellent for hips." She laughs. "My coach would kill me if he could see me right now."

"Seriously?" I sit up.

"It's fine, Adam, yeesh. Sometimes I want to do things that aren't part of the treadmill of what's right for tennis."

"Let's do some guarding exercises." I cross my legs at the ankle, bring them to my chest and extend them out again. "This move is your friend. It's the core of jujitsu."

I sit up and study her form as she copies me. She's picking this up so fast.

"Okay, basics first," I say. "We're going to practice some defensive moves."

Anna sits up and rubs her hands together. "I'm looking forward to this."

"I'm going to teach you a trap and roll. You're on your back on the floor, and I'm on top of you like this." I climb over her and straddle her hips.

She's warm between my thighs, smiling up at me. *Fuck.* I'm teaching her in a quiet apartment, all amped up for a fight.

"Reach up," I say.

"Like this?" She stretches her arm up toward my face, and I stretch down and tap the side of her face. Something about the position and her earnest expression … I'm starting to get hard. I adjust my pelvis.

"My hand is nowhere near your face," she says.

"Exactly. That's why this is such a dangerous position with anyone whose reach is greater than yours."

And I can't help it, all this rolling around with her. It's so long since I had sex, and it's *her*! My body won't calm down ... won't respond the way I want it to.

"I need a minute to ..."

But at the same time that I shift slightly away from her, she rolls her hips up into mine. Sound wooshes out like I'm underwater, and all I can see are her rose-colored lips and clear brown eyes. I fall forward onto one hand, which lands on the floor just above her shoulder, and I close my eyes, grappling for control as a groan rumbles up my throat.

When I open my eyes again, hers are closed. "Anna," I whisper, and her eyes open, meeting mine, and I don't know what I'm seeing there, but it's not reluctance. Not at all. Her tongue slips out to wet her lips and that's it. I can't ... I can't ... Her eyes flicker over every inch of my face as I lower myself toward her, pink lips getting closer and closer, slowly parting. What am I doing? When I touch my lips to hers, they're soft ... so soft ... like clouds. I brush my mouth across hers, and heat ignites in my chest and streams down my body.

She touches my lips with her tongue, and I slant my mouth as her lips part, tongue tangling with mine. Any hope of restraint is gone, gone, gone. I tilt farther forward, and her hand comes up to invade my hair. She tastes of ginger and smells like toffee, and *my fucking God*, I'm on fire.

I can't do this. I can't. *Where is my self-control?*

But her hand in my hair pulls me closer and I shift down onto her, pressing my chest into her toned body, my erection trapped against her stomach. A shiver runs through her, and she shifts under me, rolling her torso into mine and my eyes roll into the back of my head with how it rubs against my cock. *Holy shit.*

My hips move back of their own accord as her legs flatten to the floor, and I stretch out along her, my cock suddenly right at the notch at the top of her thighs. She gasps into my mouth as she pushes her pelvis up into mine, seeking friction, and I'm only too happy to oblige. My cock has never been happier as I grind all over her, pressing and titling as she moans, and her legs part as they come up, wrapping around my hips, feet locking at the base of my spine, reversing our earlier position. And God, now I can rub all over her properly, and she arches her whole body as I trail my mouth down her neck, goosebumps rising up on her skin.

Then her hand at my waist steals under my T-shirt, pushing it up as she explores up my back. Her rough fingers make me want to arch into her touch like a cat.

She lets out another moan and shamelessly presses against my erection, and a warning tingle ignites in my balls. Shit, I'm on the brink, embarrassingly fast.

"Oh God … Oh God …" she whispers, right into my ear.

Holy shit. She's … what? … she's close? Her body tenses as she rubs all over me. She's wet too, the fabric between us is sliding over her, and I grind my hips a couple of more times over her.

"Oh yes …" she gasps, fingers creeping down and tightening on my ass. "Oh I'm … oh Jesus …"

My skin flashes hot as she moans underneath me, and I keep the pressure up, watching as she gasps for air and curls into me, her body shuddering under mine.

Holy shit. I think she …

Holy shit.

But my cock has not got with the program. The warning tingle has morphed into a full-on ache, and my hips have a mind of their own. I'm still moving against her, my whole body tightening as my orgasm goes from hovering in the background to outright certainty. Even as I pull my pelvis back, my cock starts to jerk.

Fuck. Fuck. I'm on my knees and then my feet in an instant. Anna is lying on the floor, her eyes closed, cheeks pink. In one second, I'm in the bathroom, slamming the door as I shudder and shudder against it, coming in my boxers.

Shit.

Shit.

Shit.

What did I just *do*?

I close my eyes and try and breathe through my nose. How did I let that happen? Five minutes. Five minutes of rubbing off on a woman who's probably been abused by more than one man, and I'm supposed to be her *friend*. I'm helping her out. Ostensibly, I'm *protecting her*. Teaching her fight moves. Not rubbing all over her like a creeper.

The man in the mirror opposite me is red-faced and has a damp patch on his dark shorts, and my whole body flashes hot, burning up my cheeks. Fuck, I need to apologize. That was out of order. How am I going to say sorry to her? How am I going to leave the room, looking like this?

A soft rap at the door behind me makes me jump.

"Adam?"

Fuck.

"Are you okay?"

"I'm fine." My voice sounds like gravel. I clear my throat. "I'm just ..."

I'm just what? What are you doing in here, exactly, Adam? My breathing is heavy in the silence.

"I'll see you downstairs," she says.

Jesus, is she okay? I wrestle with the door, wrenching it open just as her dark head disappears around the bend in the stairs. *Fuck*. But maybe this is better, and I can calm down and give her a proper apology. I count to ten, then twenty. I grab some tissues and clean myself up the best I can. When I open the door again, I peer through the gap like a thief, but Lord knows who I'm expecting to see there. As I pad down the staircase, the sound of a shower running is coming from a distant room down the corridor.

My bag is still sitting on the bed in my room where I left it. Anna Talanova is a top-five tennis player and I ... I rutted on her and came in my pants like a schoolboy. Why did I decide to stay here? The friends idea has been a fraying rope for a while, but I can't go there again. It devastated me.

I should have gone to stay with Fabian or Janus. Standing in the corridor, I chew my lip and glance down at my gym shorts, which are drying now. I should talk to Anna and explain. She must think I'm a lunatic. At the very least, somewhere else to stay might be sensible, if this gets awkward. *What do you mean,* if, *Adam? It's already awkward!*

Sinking down on the couch, I pull my phone out of my pocket and type a quick text to Janus:

> The press are hassling me at my apartment. Any chance I could crash with you for a couple of days if I need to?

In seconds, a message buzzes back:

> Are you kidding? That sounds like the best news I've had all week! Jo's still away, and I need saving from myself. This is awesome!

Then:

> Plus, I'm stuck with some code, and another head on it would be incredible.

Okay, okay. But as I sit with the night skyline shimmering like jewels out of the window, five minutes roll past, then ten, and there's no sign of Anna. What is she doing? Should I get washed, changed? I pace over the floor. I don't want to miss her if she comes out. God, she must be pissed with me to not even come out and say anything. I walk down the corridor to where I thought I heard the shower going ten minutes ago. As I lift my hand to tap, her voice reaches me through the door.

"In what way am I bullying Arty Maroz? I think the video for that event is self-evident, don't you?"

Her feet scud across the floor. I take an instinctive step back, but her words recede again.

"Adam Miller was protecting me."

Ugh. *Protecting her.* Look where that ended up. Am I any better than Arty Maroz here? I got turned on from teaching her fight moves. What if everyone who coached her did something like that? Horror burns through me.

I head back to the living room and stare at the perfect gray couch and warm sidelights. Goddammit, she told me she had media interviews set up tonight. Now I've got Janus amped up about the fact I might come and stay with him. I groan to myself. Patience, Adam. I sink down as another ten minutes tick past, then a half hour, and there's still no sign of her. Texts from Janus keep dropping in:

> Are you coming? Your help would be invaluable.

Followed by:

> I'm sending you some screenshots of what I'm stuck on.

She could be on calls for ages. *The rest of the evening?* I tap my fingers on my thigh. Perhaps I should go to Janus's. It's not the best thing to leave, and I'm being a coward, but giving us both a bit of space might help, and I'll call her and apologize when I get there.

Before I can overthink it, I pull on my coat, grab my bag and slip out of the apartment, and in minutes I'm out on the street. All the journalists have gone home for the night and the street is quiet, an icy wind sifting through my hair. The lights on the buildings are like a computer array, reaching up into an inky sky. Darkness presses in around me, and the smell of garbage and the strawberry scent of an e-cigarette hit my nose as I walk past a man under the awning of a building. A solitary car swishes over the asphalt, speeding past all the people lurking in the shadows.

When I reach the corner, I pull up the Uber app and order a cab, and two minutes later I'm in the warmth of the back seat, watching the stores and businesses fly past. I'm sick to my stomach: I liked my friendship with Anna, and I can't shake the feeling I've just destroyed it for good.

CHAPTER 19

Anna

When I finish my conversation with the horrible combative journalist from *The Enquirer*, I pad through the apartment to the kitchen as Pepper skitters after me. I could die a happy woman if I never had to speak to that man again. I peer up the corridor, but Adam's bedroom door is shut. That interview was terribly timed and far too long: I hope he's not annoyed with me. I turn the tap to put boiling water into a mug and stand at the counter staring as the pale color of the ginger infuses through the liquid. Images flash through my head: Adam's face as he propped himself over me, screwed up as if he were in pain; his taut muscles under my hands; his cock pressing into me; *how I arched up into him …* A red-hot flush engulfs my body.

Mortification swamps me. I've struggled with sex for years, unable to wrestle my mind away from playing shots over and over in my head when I close my eyes. A fact Arty frequently reminded me of. But the ache when Adam pressed into me. *I can still feel it now. It was minutes.* Jesus. I dragged him into my crazy-ass life to the extent that he can no longer go *home*, and then I rubbed myself all over him in the gym.

The hot tea burns down my throat as Pepper chews her pink rabbit at my feet. I stare out of the window over the lights of the city. This apartment is so peaceful and quiet. Frowning, I move into the hallway, hand gripping my mug, and tilt my head.

"Adam?" I call.

Pepper has followed me into the hall. "Where's Adam, Pepper?" I say, but she just cocks her head and wags her tail.

I pad up the corridor to his room and listen outside the door. Nothing. Not even shuffling steps.

I tap on the wood. "Adam?"

It's like the silence of a crowd before you serve. I chew my lip as I stare down at Pepper, still wagging her tail next to me. She's not jumping up, scrabbling at the door, is she?

"Adam?" I rap on the door again.

Turning the handle, I step inside. And my stomach drops: There's no bag, nothing but a small imprint on the cover of the bed. When I peek into the bathroom, it's empty.

He's gone?

I tap my phone to wake it up and the message icon winks at me, so I click on it:

> Hi, Anna, I'm so, so sorry about what happened. There's no way I should have taken advantage of you like that. It's been a long time for me, and I lost it a bit. I thought it might be best if I got out of your hair. I've gone to stay with Janus, so I'm safe from the press hordes. Love Adam

… followed by two heart emojis. I clutch my phone in my hand and stare unseeing at the trendy piece of art on the wall above the bed, with no idea of what it's of. Doesn't Adam remember me rubbing myself all over him like I was short of water and he was a long cool drink? I think I was the more desperate one in this scenario.

"Why did he leave, Pepper?"

She cocks her ears at me. I can't imagine leaving this and seeing him tomorrow or the next day and saying … What? What would I say? Thanks for giving me the fastest orgasm I've ever had? What do I know about normal relationships, about how to interact with someone I like? Someone you just did *that* with, Anna … He didn't take advantage at all! And I want to do it again. Perhaps he doesn't? Although *losing it a bit* is … good, right?

Pepper whines when I stare down at her. Goddammit. My best friend is a dog that can't give me any useful advice.

"Well, fuck it, I'll just have to go and find out."

Pepper barks at me like that's totally the right decision. Perhaps I can use a one-sided conversation with a dog to justify anything.

CHAPTER 20

Adam

When I arrive at Janus's apartment block, there's a towering Christmas tree in his foyer and I admire it for a couple of minutes while the doorman calls up. A few moments later, I'm staring at my reflection in the glass walls of the elevator, heading to Janus's penthouse. Two amazing apartments in one day. I don't think I ever expected to be rich with my business, but I'd like to live somewhere a bit better than a tiny studio in an old rundown building where half the time the heating is off and the water system doesn't work properly. But then Janus opens the door with his crazy mop of hair, wearing some nerdy glasses, sweats, and an old T-shirt, and my heart lifts. Perhaps we're not so different: Reassuringly, he looks just like he did in college, minus the weight.

"Don't let the press catch you dressed like that," I crack.

He glances down at himself. "This goddamn code," he grumbles, turning back toward the huge space that houses his open-plan kitchen and living room. "I've been stuck in the weeds for days. Sorry, I probably also smell at this point. Not that you'll find that at all unusual. Come on in. I am so fucking pleased to see you."

There's no awkwardness that I've turned up to stay with him, no probing questions. I release a long breath I didn't know I was holding.

"Beer?" he says, diving into his fridge, as I take in the warm yellow lamps and beige couches that someone's added some cushions to since I was last here.

He turns and scans down my body. "Why are you in your gym clothes?"

"Long story." *And one I don't want to get into.* "Mind if I take a shower?"

"Be my guest. Come and join me in the study when you're done." He gestures down the corridor on the far side of the kitchen. "You can take the blue room, third door on the left."

I've always liked how Janus doesn't sweat the small stuff. He's always on a mission with his business or with Jo and sometimes pushing you along too, if you let him. If I told him about all the media speculation and Arty Maroz, he'd probably just say, "Idiots. Forget them, Adam."

I dump my bag down in a gorgeous bedroom, all fluffy rugs and navy walls. Stripping off, I dive into the shower and, as the hot water rains down on me, I soap up and wash off the remnants of the last few hours. I wish I could rid myself as easily of the shame. *I dry-humped Anna Talanova in her gym.* You know, the international tennis star. *Smooth, Adam.* What would Janus say if I told him? Good for you? I laugh for the first time since this whole thing started.

As I pull on some jeans and a fresh shirt, my stomach grumbles from a lack of food. I walk through to the kitchen to track down Janus, and the lights of New York glitter beyond the long windows on the far side of the space. I've been here before to do stuff with him, so I make my way to the study, tucked away in the farthest corner of the apartment. Two cats are nestled together on a beanbag beside a desk that runs all the way down one wall with two chairs and a bank of screens. A window at the end frames the roof of the old warehouse building next to his. I smile.

"Every time I've been here, I'm always struck by how this is a den for two techies … even before Jo moved in."

Janus laughs as he spins around in his office chair, the screen behind him covered in code that makes my fingers itch.

"We have this huge, beautiful apartment, and Jo and I spend ninety percent of our time holed up in the tiniest space in it with two cats."

"They look pretty cozy."

"Yeah, they have their moments. Just like Jo and I. They don't argue as much as we do, though. That's what I get for shacking up with a woman who's smarter than me." He winks at me.

"And she puts up with you," I say, with a grin. "The press was so much fun while you were dating."

"Not sure I'd call it fun," Janus grumbles. "She thinks I'm a lightweight. She likes talking to Fabian about security stuff. I struggle to keep up with them most of the time." A wry smile twists his mouth as he looks down at his keyboard. "I still can't believe how lucky I am to have found her."

And that's all you'd want, isn't it? To feel lucky? I feel incredibly lucky to know Anna … if I haven't messed the whole thing up.

Janus raises an eyebrow at me. "Pull up a chair and tell me what's wrong with this code," he adds, gesturing at his computer.

"Take me through what it does."

And all the thoughts of being hungry, the shame of what I've just done, drift away in the clarity of functions and algorithms. We've just got on to discussing the problems with relational databases when the apartment buzzer goes.

"Are you expecting anyone?"

"It'll be a delivery," Janus says.

"Get some more beers, would you?" I add as he heads out the door, and he gives me the finger. I lean closer to the screen and examine a routine he's written, but in seconds he's back.

"Apparently, Anna Talanova is here," he says, glancing at his wrist and narrowing his eyes at me. "I'm assuming she's here for you, since internationally renowned tennis players don't usually spontaneously drop by my apartment."

My stomach sinks as I nod. "Probably."

"She's running around after my buddy, huh?" He winks. "She's on her way up. I'll shut myself in here while you two do your thing, whatever that is." He grins a shit-eating grin, and I roll my eyes at him.

But as he heads toward the front door, I'm right on his heels, coming to a halt behind him when he opens it up. Something sour turns over in my gut at the way she aims her big smile straight at him and how he envelops her in a warm hug. But then I feel small paws pressing against my leg, and I peer down to find Pepper, wagging her tail like a maniac. I bend down to give her a rubdown.

"Hey, Janus," Anna says.

When I look up, Janus is giving her his casual lady-killer grin, and I want to punch my fist through a wall. How did I ever snag a girlfriend in college standing next to Janus, all golden, cute-boy charm, and Fabian, Mr. Bad Boy personified with a hint of dangerous and fucked up thrown in for good measure? The memory of the girlfriend I did get, and how lucky I thought I was and how wrong I was, makes me light-headed for a second.

"I presume you're here to see this idiot," Janus says, jerking his thumb toward me, and oh, for once, he doesn't know just how right he is.

"Come in and have a drink," he adds. "What would you like?"

Her eyes skim over me, and my face heats, but hers dart away, a hint of pink hitting her cheeks, and something warm ripples through in my groin. *For fuck's sake.*

"Do you have an herbal tea?"

Janus rolls his eyes. "Athletes! Not even a glass of wine?"

Her eyes sparkle as she shakes her head and says something in Russian that I don't quite catch.

I haven't heard her speak Russian before, and a shiver runs from my head to my toes. She's sexy in these unconscious little ways, Anna. But my head is like a runaway train. Now I know her face and the sound she makes when she comes, I'll never put the genie back in the bottle.

"What was that?" I say, taken aback by the growl in my voice.

She grins at me, and it's almost shy, and that does nothing to persuade the possessive asshole who's suddenly seized my body to step down. Her eyes meet mine, and in seconds, I'm back over her watching her eyelashes flutter against her cheeks and the red building under her gym top, feeling the tingling in my pelvis. My cock doesn't seem to want to forget being pressed into her. The idea of just being friends flew right out of the window the minute I sat on her and started talking about jujitsu. *Fuck.*

"My body is a temple," she says.

I'm less like a temple and more like a raging inferno.

Janus pulls a sad assortment of teas out of his cupboard, and Anna manages to dig out a mint one. He putters around in the kitchen making her a mug then turns to the fridge, pulls out a six pack of beer, and hands me one, raising his eyebrows and smirking. He waves his hand in the direction of the den.

"I'm in the middle of some software, so I'm going to leave you guys to it." And he pivots on his heel and exits the kitchen.

Pepper is sniffing along the kickplate under the cabinets. Anna rolls her lips together and takes a sip of her drink, not meeting my eyes. "Adam, I'm so sorry," she says.

My mouth falls open. "What? Why?"

She runs a hand over her hair. "I'm so embarrassed! I rolled my hips up into you, and then I …" She stops abruptly.

Then you came all over me and it was the hottest thing I've ever seen? What is she apologizing for? Without a second thought, I step forward and wrap my arms around her, and, because I'm an idiot, I kiss her forehead. I made her come and then shot off like my ass was on fire. I think *I'm* the one who needs to apologize here.

"It's me who should be sorry. I feel like a creeper."

Her head tilts back, and her wide eyes meet mine. "What? Why?" She bites her lip. "I can't believe I did that. You left so suddenly, and I've co-opted you into this crazy shit and turned everything upside down for you. You can't even go home! Two minutes in contact with your body and I'm rubbing all over you like a cat in heat."

Two minutes in contact with my body … I tip my head back and examine the ceiling. "I left because I was embarrassed, Anna. I couldn't control myself. I rubbed all over *you* and lost it completely and …" I can't say that I came in my pants like a teenager. I tighten my arms and whisper in her ear. "I came, too."

"Oh!" Her face flushes, but her eyes are bright when she tips back to look at me. "I'm glad it wasn't just me."

"No. Fuck, Anna. No." I groan. "That whole thing was as hot as hell."

Her body relaxes into mine.

"You've been messed around by all these guys behaving like jerks and then I offer to teach you self-defense, and once I've got you on the floor I'm all over you because I couldn't control myself. I am the *worst* kind of guy."

Her breath is a warm puff over my neck as she laughs quietly. "Do you think we could stop apologizing to each other? Stop debating who rubbed off on who?"

I squeeze her closer and kiss her temple again. "Okay." But being this close to her, my body is amped up. "It was amazing."

She groans into my shoulder. "I can't stop thinking about it."

Me neither, I don't say. The tight antsy feeling in my chest starts to ease for the first time this evening.

"I don't think that's a training session I'm going to forget in a hurry," she adds, laughing quietly again.

"Tell me about it." I start chuckling. "I think you've ruined jujitsu for me." I pull back to look at her. "It's been a long time for me, Anna. I know that probably sounds weird, but the woman I was with in college, I don't want to get into what happened with her, but I've found it difficult to trust anyone since. Even for a hookup. That's why I lost it."

She rests her head on my shoulder. "I don't mind you losing it, Adam." Her face turns pink again. "Are we okay?"

Anna's fast becoming my favorite person, but I've fallen hard and fast before and I need to keep a guard on myself.

"We're good."

When I look down at her, her lips are right there, and all I can think is how soft and warm they were under mine, the taste of ginger and toffee. I lean down and brush my mouth over hers and her lips part, our tongues tangling. The whole thing goes from a lip touch to a scorching kiss in three seconds flat. My cock hardens in a heartbeat. "Oh, this one!" it seems to be saying. "I remember her. That was a good time." The sex bit of my brain, now it's woken up, doesn't want to go back to sleep.

"Do you want to stay over?" I say, pulling back, and fuck, my restraint has taken a long dive off the top of a cliff.

"With you?"

"If you want to, although I'm sure Janus has other bedrooms." I glance at my wrist. "It's late. Have you eaten?"

She shakes her head.

"If you stayed, I could rustle us something up and you could avoid the paparazzi in the morning."

"I have practice."

I smile at her. "How early?"

"7 a.m. I'd like to stay, but I have nothing with me and I'd need to get up at the crack of dawn. Will Janus be happy with having Pepper? He has cats, doesn't he?"

"You can sleep in my T-shirt. I'll talk to Janus. I'm certain the cats will survive for one night." Am I railroading her? *Maybe.* "Let me show you where I'm sleeping."

When I tap on the study door, Janus peers over his shoulder with that grin on his face again.

"Enough already," I say before he opens his mouth.

"My lips are sealed. What do you need?"

"Anna's going to stay tonight. Is it okay if Pepper's here? I wasn't sure about the cats and ..."

"They'll be fine."

"Have you eaten? Is it okay if I raid your fridge?"

"Yeah, I've had something. Feel free to raid anything you like."

"Have you got a spare toothbrush?"

"Of course, anything else?"

"Just that, I think."

He stands, smiling. "Guess my tech help got a better offer, huh?" He heads off to hunt out a toothbrush.

Janus turns up with a toothbrush just as I'm raiding his fridge, and I cook some toast and eggs and we chat with him as we eat at his kitchen island. Then we bid him goodnight and head into the bedroom.

After Anna showers, she appears in the T-shirt I've given her and slides into bed. Seeing a woman in my tee … it makes my chest tight in an unexpected way. It's been a long time. I take another quick shower and pull on my boxers, examining my face and the inky smudges beneath my eyes as I brush my teeth. Nothing's happening tonight, Adam. We're sharing a bed, that's all.

The room's dark when I open the bathroom door, so I pad across the floor and climb under the covers, settling on my back and tucking my hands behind my head. Anna doesn't move or say anything. I close my eyes and take a deep breath as I listen to her breathing. Did she fall asleep that fast?

"Anna?" I whisper. Nothing.

I guess she did.

When I wake again in the middle of the night, I'm wrapped around something warm, something else pressing into the hollow of my back. It's such a foreign feeling. I live alone. When did I even last touch someone out of affection? I peer over my shoulder and can dimly make out the shape of Pepper curled up. My nose is surrounded by a cloud of tickling hair, and I'm inhaling rose and mint. My arm is tucked over Anna's waist, every fingertip resting on abs that are firm under my palm, her bottom snug against my crotch. Her lungs move against my torso, the steady in out, in out of the deeply asleep. Protectiveness roars through me, and I curl in a bit more, wanting to absorb her. The warmth surrounding me seeps in everywhere, stirring something deep in my body, like a peace and light I haven't felt for a long time. Perhaps not ever.

We had a cat when I was younger, and my mom didn't let it any farther into the house than the kitchen, but sometimes it snuck into my room and hid under the covers down by my legs. When my mom asked whether I'd seen it, I said I hadn't, so the cat got to spend the night in the warmth with me, like a furry hot-water bottle. I'd sneak him outside early in the morning to do his business so my mom wouldn't find him in the house, and in this way the cat and I avoided the trouble that that would bring. He always seemed to understand. He would look back at me as he headed off down the path in the backyard as if to say: We know what we're doing, you and I.

For the last eight years, I've always thought I enjoyed the peace of my apartment. A quiet little space where I can sit and think and do my own thing, nobody needing me or asking me to do anything. After Celine and realizing what she'd done, having the apartment was like throwing off a huge weight, like I'd dodged a bullet and cheated life, and I'll forever be grateful to Fabian for what he made me understand about how Celine behaved. Living alone without the oppressiveness of first my mother and then her, I was giddy. But now all this with Anna is making me wonder. Has it been peace or avoidance? Have I buried myself away? My eyes drift shut. The heat, the comfort of a shared experience, holding on to something and being held in return. I loved that old cat at home. He was my best friend.

When I wake later, Pepper and Anna have gone, and when I turn, blinking at the clock, it says 8 a.m. Light is seeping around the edges of the blinds and casting lines across the ceiling. I can't believe we slept curled together like we've been sharing a bed forever.

You don't have to head into the office today.

Would Janus be up for working with me this morning? We haven't done that in a long time. I fling back the covers. I want to sit next to an old friend and chat about software. But first, *coffee.*

I whisk through the shower and head through to the kitchen to find the machine has already brewed a pot of coffee, so I pour myself a mug and make my way to the study where Janus is peering at his screen, dressed in jeans and a sweatshirt. He turns to me with a smile.

"Have you been here all night?" I say.

He shakes his head. "Bed at about 1 a.m. I heard Anna leave around six, so I got up about 7 a.m. and put the coffee on, came and sat down, and now you've appeared."

"You want a refill?" I nod at the mug on his desk.

"Yeah, please. Good night?" he adds, smiling.

He didn't give me shit last night, but I think I'm going to get it today.

"Thanks for letting Anna stay." I sink into the seat next to him and pick at my hands. "We're in a funny place, I guess."

"Funny place?"

"Friends, maybe more?"

"You want more?"

I laugh. "Sounds crazy, doesn't it? Why would she be interested in a guy like me?"

"That's not what I meant, buddy."

"I have nothing to offer a woman like Anna Talanova."

"You have everything to offer her, Adam! Loyalty, kindness, commitment, honesty, friendship, other talents that I don't know about and wouldn't want to know." He winks at me then sighs. "It's no surprise you're in an odd place. She's had a bad time of it, and so have you. People took advantage, but you're both amazing people, and if it becomes more … then I couldn't be more delighted for you."

"Thank you." I chew my lip as I stare at the code on his screen. "I don't think I've ever really gotten over what she did."

He understands immediately who I'm talking about, of course he does. "It's been a long time, Adam, and if you still feel like that, then you should get some help, some therapy. It was abuse."

"It was." I take in the concerned frown on his face, and I know that expression only too well: the Janus-is-about-to-wade-in look. I tap his arm and pick up his mug. "I'll think about it, okay?" I nod at his computer. "Same issue as last night?"

He studies me for a beat, as if he's not going to accept the subject change, then he huffs and turns back to his screen. "Yeah. Wanna help?"

"Let me get your coffee."

*

Five hours later, I think we've broken the back of his problem, and Janus is bouncing around talking about how this is going to solve lots of issues with his company's software.

"Lunch?" he says.

I pick up my phone to find pictures of Anna, looking like she's arriving at the place where she practices tennis. When I click on the link, it takes me to some gossip site:

ANNA TALANOVA DEFENDS DECISION TO TAKE OUT RESTRAINING ORDER AGAINST ARTY MAROZ

Fuck! Was she doorstepped this morning? The article has today's date on it, but they could be using old shots and regurgitating old news.

I glance at the time: 3 p.m. I shoot her a text:

> Got fed something from a news website. Were you ambushed today?

There's no immediate reply: She's probably still playing. I pad through to the kitchen where Janus is brewing some fresh coffee.

"Looks like Anna was ambushed by the press this morning," I say.

"Really?"

I hand him my phone.

"Goddammit, I hope she's okay."

"I sent her a message. She's a tough cookie. Seems to think it goes with the territory."

Janus nods at this. "Yeah, you can't raise your profile and benefit from that in terms of business or sponsorship or whatever the fuck it is, and then expect them to back off when there's some more juicy stories around. That's why Carly is so invaluable: She manages to spin it to your advantage most of the time."

"She's been a godsend. Even in such a short time, I don't know what I'd do without her. I can't thank you enough for insisting I use her. Are you sure that …"

"Adam, I don't know what you think happened with my business, but I didn't make it on my own. I had investors and loads of advice and help. Success is a team effort."

I nod at this. I don't think I'm bad at being a team player exactly; I just know my role and it's not being a leader. I'm more the one who keeps everything on track.

About an hour later, my phone buzzes with a message:

Bit of a nightmare day.

Then:

My dog walker picked up Pepper from the practice facility at 7 a.m. this morning and the press gave her a bunch of hassle. One of them even tried to grab Pepper. The walker was freaked and ran, then bailed into a cab. She took Pepper to her mother's house in Queens.

Crap. I tap in a reply:

Can I do anything? Come and pick you up from somewhere?

I've got Pepper back now, but the media are still outside my apartment building according to the doorman. Making a real nuisance of themselves. Where are you?

Still at Janus's. Come here. We can have dinner here and chill.

"Is it okay if Anna comes here again?" I say to Janus. I turn my phone around and show him the texts.

"Goddamn it," he growls. "Tell her to come and stay. Why don't both of you crash here for a few days? It'll take them a while to work out where you are, and you could do with a break from all this hassle, yeah? Tell her to bring Pepper. The cats will survive having a dog here. It'll be good for them to have some more excitement in their lives. Plus, it's Thanksgiving on Thursday, and I'd be on my own otherwise, so let's do a proper dinner, the whole works."

Janus says to come and stay for a couple of days. By then, hopefully things will have died down a bit. He said to bring Pepper, and that having a dog would be good for the cats. Hahaha.

Sounds amazing. Is he sure? He must have lost his mind.

He never had any sense to begin with. But his place is as cavernous as yours. We can put Pepper at one end and the cats at the other. He says we can do a Thanksgiving dinner together on Thursday.

I add a winky-eyed emoji. Then I type:

We can sort something with Pepper if it's a problem.

Thanksgiving! I always forget that.

I guess we've both been a little distracted.

Let me organize some stuff. Give Janus a big hug from me.

You can give it to him yourself when you get here. And me!

I'm an equal opportunities hugger.

When Anna arrives an hour later, she has Pepper on a leash and is still wearing what I presume to be her practice gear. I take in her tight shorts and top and drag my eyes away, stepping forward and pulling her into my own hug. *So warm and solid.*

"You found some workout clothes," I mumble.

"Yeah, I keep some stuff in my locker. It's surprising when it comes in useful, and, despite everything, I had a decent practice. Mainly fueled by anger at all this bullshit."

"I know the feeling," Janus says from right behind us. "All the speculation in the press Jo and I dealt with drove us mad. Come and have a drink."

"Is the glass of wine from yesterday still available? It's rest day tomorrow. I might as well celebrate with half a glass."

Janus grins. "Absolutely. Let's go wild. Adam?"

"I'll have whatever Anna's having, thanks. Make mine a full glass." I wink at him.

Anna claps her hands like an excited child. "I've none of my nutritionist's food! Can we do a takeout? Oh, this is like a holiday!"

Janus starts to laugh. "I'm up for that. What do you want?"

"Indian. The full works—tandoori chicken, korma, samosas, rice, naan. I'm starved. All I had was an energy bar because I didn't have my prepped meal and we couldn't buy a sandwich without being hassled."

"Sounds like a nightmare," Janus says.

"Gah, I wouldn't have got anywhere if I buckled under a bit of media aggravation."

She absorbs pressure like a sponge. She doesn't take any bullshit from anyone. She reminds me of Jo. Perhaps you have to be like that when people are snapping at your heels all the time.

Janus winks at her. "So, what are you doing hiding out here then?"

"Someone else is here," she says, cheeks going a bit pink as her eyes dart to mine and away again.

And my whole body roars. *She likes me?* We were friends, and she was okay with the jujitsu debacle, but this feels like a deeper admission. An admission that she wants to be with *me*. That this is good for her. This remarkable woman who is made of titanium. And for the first time it occurs to me that perhaps she was as eager as I was for what we did on the floor of her gym and I didn't cross some boundary I shouldn't have crossed. I want to smack my head. I'm always two steps behind, like I'm so rusty I can't keep up with how this works. I made her come, and I ran away like an idiot. I should have lifted her over my shoulder and taken her to bed. I want to push Janus to one side and pin her against the kitchen cupboards.

Now *I'm* turning into an antsy, aggressive guy.

"Let's order Indian," Janus says, like I'm not exploding inside.

*

I can hardly manage sitting quietly nursing a glass of wine while Janus and Anna chat about their days. I am mute.

"So, you're going to stay for a few days, right?" Janus says, after the food has arrived and containers are spread out across his dining table. I can almost see the cogs in his brain whirring, how he's sliding into the role of matchmaker. He's invested after he persuaded me to go to that event. He's never been Mr. Subtle.

Anna's eyes dart from him to me, and I smile at her because, dammit, I was already down for staying at her apartment. As far as I'm concerned, we've just switched venues.

"To be honest, you'd be doing me a favor," Janus adds. "We can do Thanksgiving together. It's shit on my own when Jo's away, and you can't leave me with this guy." He jerks his thumb toward me.

Manipulative bastard.

Anna forks some rice into her mouth. "I'm sure you guys would have an amazing time being geeks together."

She's not buying his smokescreen. A laugh bubbles up.

"It'd be good to escape the media attention, though, wouldn't it?" Janus counters with a smile.

She shakes her head. "I can't believe I thought it was a sensible idea to encourage it."

He shrugs. "It's difficult to make publicity work how you want, especially when you've got assholes working against you."

For a hot flash I think he means me, but then I realize he's talking about Arty Maroz.

"Why did I get involved with Arty the Asshole?" Anna says with a deep sigh. "I'd love to stay, Janus. I'll ask someone to bring my stuff over here."

*

Later on, we all veg out on the couch in front of a soccer game. Anna's case arrives, and soon after, at about 9 p.m., she declares she's tired and is going to bed. Janus decides he's got some more work to do on his software, so I chat with him for about ten minutes and then follow Anna into the bedroom. She's sitting on the bedcovers in the T-shirt of mine she wore last night, her long bare legs crossed as she studies her phone.

Somehow this is more loaded than yesterday. "Are you okay with sharing a room?"

She raises her head, smiling. "That's a question?"

I walk around to lie down on the other side of the bed from her and prop my hands behind my head. She turns to study me, and I stretch out my hand and beckon her closer, and she shuffles up, placing her phone on the nightstand. Her head settles into my shoulder, and her hand lands on my stomach, which my libido finds far too interesting.

"I'm sorry I left you lying on the gym floor after what we did," I say. "I can't believe I bolted. It seemed logical at the time, but …"

She chuckles. "The whole thing was a bit of a surprise if I'm honest." She squeezes my middle. "A *good* surprise."

She lifts her head to look at me, and my gaze roams over her lips, cheeks, and deep-brown eyes. My hand invades the back of her hair, loosening her ponytail, the strands like silk against my fingers as I lean in to brush my lips across hers. Her mouth chases mine, and my body tightens as her hand moves from my abs up my chest.

She pulls back. "You said it was really hot. It was for me, too. Clearly!"

I groan. "Don't say things like that. I'm about to share a bed with you, and I won't be able to keep my hands to myself."

"You don't have to keep your hands to yourself! And I'd do another jujitsu lesson with you any time."

I laugh, rolling her onto her back and nuzzling into her, and that smell of ginger and toffee fills my nose again. I kiss up her throat, and she tilts her head to give me better access. Fuck, I've missed this. Touching. Being touched. Warm skin under my fingertips. I trail my mouth over her cheek and find her lips. I'm hard already, and I don't want a repeat of the gym where my control went out the window, so I ease off a little, rolling onto my side beside her. She turns her head on the pillow to look at me, reaching out to stroke her thumb across my lips.

I can't quite rid myself of the thought that she's this megastar and I'm a random guy who hasn't had sex in a really long time. "So, what are we now, friends with benefits?" I blurt out. *Can I not be smooth for one second?* Open mouth, engage brain later.

She shrugs. "I don't want to label it at all to tell you the truth. Perhaps we're doing what feels good, what we'd both like to explore. God knows, the boyfriend/girlfriend thing hasn't worked for either of us."

I reach up and capture her hand, squeezing her fingers. "I like you, Anna."

This gets me a beaming smile. "I really like you, too, but I want to be cautious. I've dragged you into a mess of my own making—rather selfishly, I'm thinking now."

"Maroz created the mess, not you."

She nods, and her pink lips are right there, so I lean in and touch my mouth to hers. It's like my body has woken up from some deep slumber, like I have no say anymore in where this goes. But she's just as eager, opening her mouth as our tongues meet in a heated tangle. Perhaps resisting whatever this is is an impossible dream right now.

Kissing down her neck, I move the T-shirt with my nose, and her palms trail down the front of my shirt across all the buttons, so I shift over her propping myself up on both hands as she fumbles and starts to pop them open, strong fingers working their way down from my chest to my waist. Holy hell, I want them somewhere else. My hips tilt forward into her of their own accord, and she wriggles against me, eyes meeting mine with a smile.

"Are you rubbing all over me again, Anna?" I say, grinning.

"I hope so. I went off like a bomb last time." Her answering smirk makes me laugh.

But her questing fingers have reached my zipper, and she trails a thumb down the front of my jeans. Vibrations spread out from where she's touching me, and I close my eyes, heart thumping.

"Anna." My eyes pop open to fix on hers. "I haven't … I haven't done this in a while." Shit, I don't want to admit how long it's been. I've been celibate, sort of by choice, for the best part of ten years. It wasn't even a conscious decision—my business just sort of took over my life.

Her eyes are fixed on mine. "How long?" she whispers, and I shake my head. "What have you been doing instead? I mean …"

"My hand has been my friend if I'm being honest here."

"But why?"

I rest down on my elbows. Maybe I don't need to tell her the whole story. "The relationship that blew up in my face in college broke something in me. At first, I didn't want to be anywhere near a woman, and somehow I let that feeling carry on and I buried myself in my business. The idea of doing this …" I swallow thickly. "You're the first woman I've wanted to be with in years. That's what happened in the gym: I had a mini freak-out."

She squeezes my waist. "Just to reiterate, I liked what we did in the gym."

I grin down at her. "Despite me disappearing into the bathroom like my ass was on fire?"

She laughs. "Despite that. I enjoyed being sat on and ground against."

"That sounds good." I tilt my hips into her.

"Actually, I just liked seeing the pain on your face."

"Oh, so you're a masochist? No, that's not right: a sadist. You like torturing men."

She laughs. “Perhaps it’s my new kink.”

I raise an eyebrow. “So, it’s not just men you like to torture; it’s this particular man right here?”

She hums a little. “Well … men like to dominate in bed, or at least the ones I’ve been with have. You didn’t do that with me. It was all push and pull.” She bites her lip. “It was … hot, Adam.” She goes a bit pink.

“Here and now … best-case scenario, my control will be terrible. Worst-case scenario, I won’t even be able to do it.”

“We don’t have to do *anything*.”

Do *nothing*? When she clearly wants to? I chuckle and run my nose across her cheek and nibble her earlobe. “Oh, yes we do.”

She shifts her pelvis, rubbing against me, then wraps her legs around my waist and rolls me. And I don’t even think about it: I shift my hips to the side and lock a leg over her thigh and roll her straight back.

“Fight moves,” she says with a grin.

“Oh really? You want to fight me?” I groan and close my eyes. “I’ve never had so little control as I did on the floor of your gym.” I laugh. “Perhaps we both discovered a new kink on that mat.”

But in the heat of being over her again, I’ve forgotten how strong and competitive she is. She rolls me again, putting herself back on top, shifting backward an inch into just the right place, and all my fight moves fly out the window as my pelvis tightens. The only thing stopping me from pushing inside are two flimsy little bits of fabric. I can’t help but push up and rub my erection against her, and the warmth and the ease of movement tells me she’s slick and ready. I run a palm up her leg and tease my thumb over the crease at the top of her thigh.

She blinks down, lips parting, so I burrow under the elastic of her panties, and oh yes, this is so much better. Concentrating on her instead of me. *That’s how this works.* My finger brushes along the edge of the smooth skin there, all soft and warm. A shudder rolls through her body.

“You’re so good at this,” she whispers.

I am?

Emboldened, I dive deeper, my thumb stretching farther across her skin, into the wetness that makes everything slide around. She gasps and grinds down on my erection, widening her legs, and I'm embarrassingly close all of a sudden. Maybe that's just how it's going to be. Maybe it's her.

With both hands planted on my chest, she rubs against me in earnest, eyes roaming my face and a slight crease between her eyebrows. Warning tingles travel from my balls and up my cock. *Oh, fuck.*

"Adam! I need ..."

"Yeah, me too, baby, hold on. I need my wallet."

"Did your condoms expire in 2009?" She grins.

"No, smart-ass."

She laughs. "Where is it? I'll get it."

I nod toward the bureau, and she levers off my legs, my T-shirt sliding over her strong thighs, her dark ponytail cascading down her back, all mussed up from my grip. When she comes back with a condom, I place it on the comforter next to us and urge her back over me. My hands drift over her hips, up into the T-shirt, and when I reach her ribs she arches back, so I rub my thumbs along the underside of her breasts. She grabs the top and pulls it over her head.

I am not prepared for the muscle definition of her torso and naked breasts. They're toned, full, and round, a perfect handful, and I slide my palms over her, thumbing her nipples as her thighs tighten around me.

"You're so gorgeous," I whisper.

With a half smile, she shuffles back, her gaze snagging on my open shirt, her hand coming out to stroke the trail of blond hair down the center of my stomach, and my abs flex under her questing fingers. She's too close to my erection pressing against my fly. But there's no hesitation as she undoes my top button, fingers exploring where I'm hard. A groan rumbles up my throat as she parts the fabric and my hips lift almost of their own accord. She drags my jeans down, feeling the shape of me through the front of my boxers, touching my balls when she gets to the base. Goosebumps ripple over my arms and chest.

Sitting up, I press my body into hers as I twist to shrug out of my shirt, finding her lips as she pushes the cotton off my shoulders. My hand steals up to take the tie out of her ponytail, hair spilling around her face and over her collarbone, and I grasp huge greedy handfuls of it, as I rub my chest against hers and trail my lips from her mouth down her neck, skin warm and damp. My hand slides up to cup her breast, bending my head to suck on a rosy nipple, lapping at it with my tongue and then testing my teeth on it. It tightens in response, so I roll the hard nub between my lips.

"I want these off," she gasps, hands scrabbling at the elastic of my boxers as she pushes them down, and my cock springs free. She wraps a tight hand around it.

"Oh, this is so sexy," she whispers as a long groan shudders out of me. I can't take her hot hand on me, not if she carries on exploring the way she's doing now, her thumb rubbing over my tip and down, finding the sensitive area at the base and playing, playing, playing. And I must be leaking because the movement of her finger is easier and slicker with every passing second. She's swiping back and forward as shivers run down my back and my legs.

"Anna!" I gasp. "Stop. Stop. Too good." I take her mouth in a bruising kiss. I'm burning up, heat radiating off my body, sweat breaking out across my skin. She leans sideways and grabs the condom, tearing at the wrapper with her teeth, swiftly examining it, and rolling it down over me. The whisper of her fingers on my cock makes me jerk.

She shifts over me, and I press into her and *fuck*… I'd forgotten this: a tightness along my length like I've never felt before.

"Christ, you feel good."

Can I remember how to do this? I give an experimental push forward, and my eyes roll into the back of my head. Christ, how long am I going to be able to last? But I don't think she needs me to. She's already gasping, hands on my shoulders and grinding down into me like she can't hold back, like she wants what I gave her on the floor of the gym.

Okay then.

I roll her over.

"Adam," she exhales on a gasp, her long dark strands splaying like a spider's web across the pillow.

I prop myself up on my hands, and her fingers tickle down my side and over my abs, exploring where I disappear inside her. A trailing hand drifts back up to play with the hair on my chest. It's ticklish but sexy how much she likes *touching*. All my nerve endings are on fire. Everywhere her fingers land sets up an answering call in me, electricity snaking through my torso and pulsing in my cock.

"This is so good," she gasps.

Damn right it is. I reach down and run my thumb over the soft skin between her legs, finding her nub and playing gently. I want to do everything here. I want my mouth all over this sweetness. She's so wet and tight, making the slide in and out easy but so fucking good. Fit and strong, she's rising up to meet my hips on every stroke; she's *active* under me. It's missionary position but like something else entirely. I'm watching her abdomen contract and the muscles in her arms move as she trails her long fingers all over my torso, tangling in the hair on my chest and my stomach.

I lean down into her and trail my lips across hers. "How are you doing, sexy girl?"

"Oh God, Adam, it's just … I never want to come." She lifts her knees and locks her feet around my ass and she's lost the friction of me against her, but some memory of how this works makes me push deeper, playing with her between her legs.

"Oh … Oh … Oh. *More, Adam.*" Her torso arches off the bed.

"More what?"

"I don't know!" she gasps. "More everything."

"So demanding."

"Sorry … I …"

"Shh. I like the demands, Anna."

I firm up how I'm rubbing against her and thrust harder. How am I holding on here? It's like a tag team of her losing it then me losing it. The tingling in my balls started so long ago, but if I concentrate on her, on giving her pleasure, somehow I can override the pressure that's building at the base of my cock like a huge dark cloud on the horizon.

I like strong women, I realize now. I think Janus and I have that in common. Celine turned out to be needy in the worst possible ways, though she appeared strong when I met her. There's something so hot to me in a woman challenging me and not having a problem with me challenging her back. Not shying away from anything, *even rolling me during sex.*

I start to laugh, and my hips falter as Anna's eyes widen on mine. "What?" she whispers.

I lean down to kiss her, still laughing. "I'm sorry," I mumble. "I thought the fight moves were funny."

She growls at me and rolls me again, and I'm weak with laughter as she widens her knees and sinks deeper, hands on my chest as she leans forward and moves her hips.

"Yes," I gasp, trying to grasp onto the last threads of the rope that's rapidly unraveling. "Take what you need."

My thumb finds her nub again, rubbing softly. I've no hope of holding off now, her wetness is all over my fingers and the sight of her breasts moving and the muscles of her strong arms and shoulders is too much.

"Anna, I'm going to …" The tingling races up my legs and into my balls.

"Yes," she hisses, forehead dropping down to meet mine, and I tilt my chin for a sloppy kiss as she starts to contract around me. My whole body locks, my cock jerking inside her, and I roll her fast, thrusting, once, twice, and empty myself into the condom as I grind all over her. Her eyes widen, unseeing, fluttering shut as her head goes back and she jerks and shudders under me.

I bury my head in her throat, my length still twitching as I inhale her sweet smell, now mixed with sweat and sex. "That's called a power move," I gulp out. "The final killer roll."

She snorts, then blows a raspberry into my neck.

CHAPTER 21

Adam

I think the next three days must be the most perfect I've ever spent. Anna and I hang around Janus's apartment, and when she goes off to practice, Janus and I hole up in his den. When I ask him why he's not in his office downtown, he says, "You're here, buddy, and we never hang out together anymore. And if you think I'm not taking this opportunity to get help with my code, you're off your rocker." When I protest that I can come round anytime, he waves his hand, grumbling, "I can work remotely, and they can get used to me not being there and making their own goddamn decisions for a change."

So, we both do meetings online and take calls, but it still makes my heart sing to fill the time in between with getting things done and sharing tech ideas, scarfing down homemade sandwiches and drinking too much coffee. I sketch out concepts for electronic kits and send them to Keith and Sean, and because I'm not there being sucked into day-to-day tech problems, I have more time to talk to Susie and give her more support. Janus and I walk Pepper and buy a fabulous flat white from the café downstairs in his building. After the first walk, Janus starts talking about buying a dog because he never walks around his neighborhood, and if he had one, he'd "get out more."

I tell him what he needs is a kid in a stroller, and he tells me there's nothing he'd like better than having a little Jo in miniature. He talks about how his parents are already dropping not-so-subtle hints about grandchildren and about a guy who's got involved in Jo's company whom he hates. And I tell him he has to make me the godfather of at least one of the children or I might never speak to him again.

Each day, Anna comes home and we take Pepper for another stroll through the neighborhood. The paparazzi haven't caught on yet, so it's a peaceful walk through quiet streets and a detour along the Hudson, and I talk to Anna about the ambitions I once had for my business and how I always wanted to buy a brownstone, and she tells me about fighting her way up through the Russian tennis system. When I listen to her stories about the pressure to take performance-enhancing drugs and the abuse from coaches, I understand why she doesn't worry too much about a few press people with cameras on street corners, irritating though they are.

Most evenings, Janus, Anna and I do a Google Meet with Jo, who, it turns out, has never met Anna because Anna's on the road so much. Jo claps her hands when we tell her we're keeping Janus company, and Janus rolls his eyes at the lot of us. She fills us in on Samsung and all the big business politics she and her number two, Des, are dealing with, and I'm hit with a renewed enthusiasm for my little startup. Susie calls with figures for the last month and they're better. We're not setting the world on fire, but the dog kits are slowly ramping up, so I do a revised budget and it pushes the time I'm going to have to close the company out by a month. I tell Susie that, if she can keep the sales creeping up, any extra we make she can spend on advertising the dog kits.

On Wednesday night, a grocery delivery arrives with turkey and all the trimmings, and I wake up on Thanksgiving morning to find I'm alone in bed with two cats and Pepper sleeping in a row all along Anna's side, like they're all BFFs, and I snort into the bedsheets. I never want to leave the peace of this place, and when I tell Janus this while we're cooking, he says I should move in, that "he loves having friends living here" and has plenty of space. When Anna comes back from practice, we've got a veritable feast on the table and we stuff ourselves and then lie around groaning.

If I thought my lack of control with Anna was due to a long dry spell, I'm starting to think I'm mistaken. Every night in the wide bed in Janus's beautiful spare room, we sweat and fight and pin each other down, heat swirling around our bodies. I become more and more insatiable, and Anna gets braver and more adventurous. And I know this because she tells me she feels she can do anything she likes to me, that she's never been like this in bed with a guy. And good Lord, letting her do things to me sets my skin on fire. She says she has nowhere and no part of her life where she can let loose, but now she's found it, and I close my eyes and suck in a deep breath and ache. I can't contemplate stopping living together and sharing a bed with Pepper. The idea of me going back to my place or her going back to hers turns my gut sour.

And lying there, on what will turn out to be the last day I stay in Janus's apartment, I fondle Pepper's ears and hope in my heart of hearts that she feels the same way.

CHAPTER 22

Adam

After three days, the fact I have a team to run forces me back into the office. And after some resistance from me about the cost, Anna has persuaded me to let her pay for some extra security for our little space out in Brooklyn. The building manager spluttered at me on the phone when I tried to explain to her why we needed it, but eventually agreed to having more people on site, muttering something about famous people and their agendas. If it had been Janus's building downtown, I'm sure they wouldn't have batted an eyelid. Even to me, it's all ridiculously over the top, but after the paparazzi tried to break into my apartment, I have to admit that I need to protect my staff. So, on Friday, I pull them into a meeting and give them a briefing, and stress that the best defense if anyone accosts them is to pretend they don't understand what they're talking about.

Now Susie is looking at me across my desk, her phone held to her ear and her eyebrows raised, as the building manager squawks on the other end of the line.

"Arty Maroz is in reception and says he wants to speak to you," Susie whispers, her hand over the microphone. "He grabbed someone from another business in the lobby and slammed him against the wall before security pulled him off. They called me instead of calling the cops."

I bury my head in my palms. Maroz has turned up here? Why? God, I hope Anna's all right. "I'll go and talk to him."

Her eyes go wide. "You can't do that, boss."

I wave my hand. "We've got security now; I'll have backup."

She gives me a dubious smile. "I can watch your back. I learned to fight dirty on the streets."

She and Fabian both. "I'll be okay. I'm a ninja." I make a chopping movement with my hands like an idiot, and she grimaces. *Not convincing then.* Whatever, I've taken him down before.

One of the security guys stops me when I step out of the elevator, concern creased across his face. "It's that guy who's been in the papers. He's not armed. He said it's important, and he just needs to talk to you." He glances back over his shoulder. "But I'm not sure you should be down here at all," he adds.

"Let me find out what he wants. Maybe I can persuade him to leave quietly. Just cover my back."

He makes a face, but he's right behind me as I head down the corridor to the lobby where I discover Arty Maroz pacing red-faced across the floor.

"Finally!" he says, like I'm some minion who's kept him waiting.

"Do I know you?" I say.

He scoffs as I widen my stance and fold my arms over my chest. If he comes at me, I want to be ready. "Why are you here?"

"You need to stay away from Anna."

"That's it?"

"You can't just say, 'that's it,' like it's easy. Things are never simple. You don't understand."

He's like some kid who can never put aside high-school rivalries. What is his agenda? He's mightily persistent. If I can work out what he's doing and why, we'd have more leverage with him.

"What don't I understand?"

"Russia. The whole thing. Have you asked Anna about her tennis coaches? The deal she did."

"The deal?"

"You don't get out of Russia without making a deal."

"What sort of deal?"

Maroz paces across the floor, scowling. "She never talked to me about the deal she did or who she did it with, but *everyone* makes a deal." He waves his arm around. "No one talks about it. If you come from Russia, you're looking over your shoulder all your life. You never escape, and that's the end of it. People want things from you, and you have to do what they ask, because you won't be alive in twelve months if you don't."

Is this true? "How about you, Arty? Did you do a deal, too?" Is he, I suddenly wonder, doing something someone asked him to do, right now?

He stops pacing and says nothing as he stares up at the ceiling, face screwed up, and runs a distracted hand through his hair. "Yes, I made a deal, and that's all I'm going to say to you."

Is this the reason he's being such a nuisance? *Maybe his deal has something to do with Anna.*

Suddenly I lose patience. I step forward and grab his arm, twisting it behind his back and slamming him up against the wall. Defense tends to be my default—wait it out and let them make the mistake—but I can do offense when it's warranted.

Maroz yelps, perhaps more in surprise than anything. "What the hell are you doing?" he grunts out from where his cheek is pushed into the concrete.

"Why are you so interested in her business? Does your deal involve Anna?" I growl.

"What? Fuck, no!"

"So why are you pestering her?" I twist his arm a little tighter, and he cries out again.

"How the fuck are you so strong?"

"Answer the question."

"She owes me."

"She *owes* you?"

"My father negotiated all her first sponsorship deals in tennis. She fucked him over and switched to a US agent. It cost him millions, and he lost a lot of face. Ask her. Ask her about the stupid games she plays with the people who support her career. She uses people."

"Don't athletes switch agents all the time?" I'm sure I read something about this.

"Not in Russia."

"We're not in Russia."

He glowers, even though his face is still hard against the concrete.

"Is your father the person she made this supposed deal with?"

"I already told you I have no idea what she agreed or who with."

Christ, I'm starting to believe some crazy deal-making system exists. It's dangerous to talk to a guy like Arty Maroz. Is this the whole reason for all his bullshit? Some problem with his father losing money and face? Is Maroz the attack dog that oligarchs like his father set on people they can't reach themselves?

I put a bit more weight and an extra little twist into his arm, and he howls. "What are you doing, you fucker!"

"Leave Anna the fuck alone. I don't care about you or your stupid stories about deals. I don't want to see your face anywhere near her." He grunts at me, and I lean in a little more, making him yowl again. "I didn't hear your agreement."

"Yeah, okay! Okay! Motherfucker."

I step back and blow out a long breath.

"You'll regret this," he says, straightening his jacket. "My father is friends with a lot of powerful people. You're the idiot here. Try asking her a few more questions before being so eager to defend her. You have no idea who she is and what she's done. Ask her about what happened in Russia."

He gives me one last scowl then turns on his heel and heads out onto the street.

*

Later on that evening, when I talk to Anna, we talk about how Christmas is only four weeks away now, how she's trying to persuade her parents to come over for the holidays, and how I'll have to go back home and see mine. And it feels wrong to think about leaving New York, even for a few days. The urgency to sort out Arty Maroz throbs in my veins.

I don't tell her about Arty's visit or the stuff he spouted about some deal. Everything he told me about Anna and "making a deal" is likely bullshit, but something is going on here and I want to understand what it is and why he's hanging around, *before* I speak to Anna. My best way forward has to be Fabian. Anna didn't want to do anything illegal when I first mentioned it to her, but that's not such an issue for me. Fabian won't do something that will land me in trouble, and what option do I have? Maybe Anna didn't want me digging into her past, but the questions Maroz has placed in my head mean I've got to do something. It turns my stomach. Hopefully, Fabian will find some stuff that will force Maroz to stay the fuck away from the both of us and we can nail this stuff for good.

CHAPTER 23

Fabian

Kate has long since disappeared to her medical work at the hospital when my phone vibrates on my desk. I glance down at the screen at a picture I took of Adam at college giving me the finger.

"Hey, Adam, how's the world at the forefront of celebrity gossip? I hear via the grapevine you and Anna babysat Janus for a few days."

"Yeah, he was so demanding."

"How are things with Ms. Talanova?"

"Oh, you know, the usual: being chased around by the media and violent ex-boyfriends."

Morning sunlight is glancing across the shelves of hardware along one wall of my bedroom, and I tip back in my office chair and examine the stains on the ornate ceiling far above my head. I can't believe Adam was punched by that jerk, and don't get me started on a guy coming after a woman like that. "Fights and dodging the press—that doesn't sound like you at all, buddy."

He laughs because he knows just how true that is.

"But with Anna? It's going okay?" I say, stomach bubbling. He's been so closed off over the last ten years. Hell, I'd love for him to …

"We'll see."

Ugh. *So goddamn cautious.* "Be careful you don't lose her."

Though I'm hardly one to talk. Adam dealt with Janus and my excitability in college, plus all the crap we managed to land ourselves in, with admirable calm. What's his deal with Anna? He's always played his cards close to his chest, but if this were Kate, I'd be apoplectic with the idea she'd been out with assholes in the past. I groan. She actually did do that. That guy David … *No. Nope.* Not thinking about that.

"Why are you and Janus so invested in my love life? You're like a couple of old busybodies. Just because you guys have settled down, it doesn't mean I want to."

Gah, the man doth protest too much, methinks. From what Janus told me when they were staying at his place, they're both smitten. Out of the three of us in college, Adam was the only one you would have bet money on to settle down, the only one who wanted it. Then he got sideswiped by Celine and has avoided romantic entanglements ever since—until now. I've tried to persuade him it was a one-off, a very fucking unusual situation, but every time I say something, he doesn't talk to me for weeks. He won't thank me for saying anything now.

"Talking of violent ex-boyfriends," he carries on, oblivious, "I'm calling because I wondered if you could do me a favor—dig into Anna's ex, Arty Maroz, for me?"

Oh, interesting. "Yeah sure, why?"

"He came to Electronic Man this morning, and given this is a guy I fought with, I was surprised. He spun some yarn about how everyone who's left Russia has done some deal they spend their whole life repaying. In fact, he said they could never escape from it. It's likely all bullshit, but I got curious. Why did he come out to a middle-of-nowhere office in Brooklyn to tell me this face-to-face? Is it true?"

"Is that all he said?"

"He also said Anna had shafted his father on her sponsorship deals. He told me to stay away from her, that she couldn't be trusted."

"She doesn't seem like a devious, double-dealing character to me."

"Yeah, me neither, but I've been wrong before."

Jesus. "A long fucking time ago. Why don't you ask her about it?"

"Because he's a stirrer and a prick, and I want to find out some stuff about him first. I suggested digging into him a while ago to Anna, and she was reluctant to do anything illegal. I got the impression she thought it might make the situation worse, and I know nothing about the criminal aspects at work in Russia. I'm feeling my way around this. Digging into him could be the worst idea ever."

"Yeah, you're right to be concerned. I wasn't joking when I said I was wanted by the Russians. But it's only a problem if they find out, and that's more about what you do with the information than looking for it. They won't know I've been in there; you understand that. Anyway, I'm up for the challenge. You know me, Adam, I love a hacking project, especially when it's helping a friend. You want me to look into Anna as well?"

"Ugh. Who wants to investigate someone they're in a relationship with?"

Oh, *interesting.* He's admitting to a relationship, at least.

"Have you ever looked into Kate?" he adds.

I laugh. "She's so straitlaced, it's never occurred to me. Although I did look into her family once, and what a can of worms that opened up! Let me check out Maroz. Anna will certainly come up, and I'll see if any surprising connections get thrown up. I've broken into plenty of Russian networks for one reason or another. Russia's a funny place. What he told you doesn't sound all that odd, to be honest. There's an obligation-to-the-motherland vibe with a lot of Russians: It's them against the world because the West has betrayed them. But that could just be the hacking world. The FSB has tentacles everywhere and a real propensity to threaten people and carry it through, too."

"The FSB?"

"The Federal Security Service, successor to the KGB."

"Jesus Christ, Fabian, what the hell are you doing digging around in Russia? I don't want to put either you or Anna in any danger."

"If she's on the FSB's radar, she's already at risk. You finding out about it just means you're better informed, and her, too. I'll be careful."

"Fuck, that sounds bad."

"You've seen some of those hacking boards, though. They *are* bad. Full of maniacs and conspiracy theorists. If they knew how disorganized most Western organizations are, they'd realize there's no way they'd have the wherewithal to organize a conspiracy."

He laughs. "Too right. And thanks, Fab, I really appreciate it."

"My pleasure."

After he hangs up, I start wading through all the online press for Arty Maroz, and there's a huge raft of stuff about Anna, too. I come across information about her previous boyfriend, Pietr Petrov, going back a number of years. When I find the pictures, my gut drops: He's *decades* older than her. Her face is pale, his arm always tight around her waist. What's the story there? Anna's split with Pietr hit the news about a year ago, and all the gossip about her has moved on to our friend Arty over the last six months. There's so little in the press about her breakup with Arty: It all just transitions to stuff about Adam. It looks like Maroz was supposed to go to that event Adam attended with her.

I fire off a text to Adam:

> Do you know why Arty Maroz and Anna broke up?

Adam replies immediately:

> He cheated. A friend sent her a video of him at a party with another girl.

Interesting. There's nothing online about that.

> The name of the friend might be useful.

> Mila, I think she said. No surname. She's a competitor from the tennis circuit.

Ah yes, Mila Sokolova. I've come across her already.

Did Anna say anything to you about her boyfriend before Maroz? Pietr Petrov?

Not much. She talked about a bad relationship. Someone who was very controlling.

I fire off some links to him.

Let me know if you want me to dig into him, too.

I carry on exploring. I go through Maroz's LinkedIn connections, which throws up a bunch of interesting characters, and I make a list of names. A quick search turns up bank accounts for him in the US. Adam messages me back and gives me the thumbs-up to investigate Petrov, too. I put that on the back burner while I continue diving into Arty. Soon I've got addresses for him in three countries: Russia, Italy, and the US. He lives in the Italian Alps in winter and trains in Chile in the off-season. More recently, he's been spending a lot of time in Manhattan: to be with Anna or for some other reason?

His name comes up as a board member of several companies. Many with Russian links and some with outstanding court cases against him. There's another legal case concerning Pepper. Then another one related to an investment company. I have backend access to the court's database, and when I search, I'm stunned at the number of lawsuits he's involved in. Some are ex-neighbors of his; some involve media sites, a couple of which have paid him off. Two further ones relate to two women, which, when I do a bit more research, turn out to be girlfriends he dated before Anna. *Fuck, this guy!* He must be lawyered to the hilt. I delve into legal cases in Italy and Russia, and there are more cases with his name on that I translate using an online translator. He appears to be using no-win-no-fee people all over the place. Wow. Who would willingly do that? Those guys are sharks.

All this paints a pretty disturbing picture, but there's nothing we could use against him yet, and that's always my favorite thing to find.

There'll be a ton of dirt on this guy if I could get into his email and his bank account. I spend the rest of the day setting up some spam emails I've used before, taking some of the information I've managed to dig up from the court cases. If I can encourage him to click on something that appears legit, that's an easier way to get into his accounts. I set it up to send every few days and notify me if he clicks on anything.

In two days, I'm in. When I start scrolling through his inbox, my jaw drops. All his emails are loud, shouty versions of something someone would say, not write, littered with swear words. In one or two he plays nice, but the remainder are abusive, aggressive, threatening. There are messages from porn sites, too; others he's sent to women offering to take them to dinner or to parties and on trips, a few in Russia, one particular woman in Italy going back several years. *And over the same time period he was seeing Anna!* At least half of the other emails are demands for money he owes—bills he hasn't paid. Many of them are shared with or directed to a georgiy.maroz@pteroka.com—who turns out to be his father—asking him to pay for things around skiing. When I look up his dad, he heads up one of Russia's biggest oil and gas companies. And before you can say Jack Robinson, I'm deep-diving into a sprawling network of business interests in Russia and, surprisingly, Italy. I map it all out on a piece of paper.

I need to fill Adam in on all this. I pick up my phone to find a message from him,

> She did say the guys she'd dated were assholes.

Too right.

I hack into Maroz's US bank account through a file he keeps on his system with all his passwords, and I want to roll my eyes at how easy people make this stuff. But his account is a real eye-opener. He's half a million dollars in the red and racking up fees like nobody's business. I thought my finances were in bad shape. When I delve in deeper, there are large payments from his dad and a settlement from a court case. None of this is incriminating, although I guess Anna would find the emails to other women pretty interesting. He's just a tool. It's like standing in the wreckage of somebody's life or having a ringside seat while it implodes.

So why is he so interested in Anna? And why did he go and say everything he did to Adam? I think I'm going to need to get a little more up close and personal with Mr. Maroz … I fire off a text.

CHAPTER 24

Fabian

I jump down off the bridge, landing a hundred yards from where Hejay is standing, tapping an impatient finger on his leg. He goes for his pocket, shoulders tight, but then his face clears and he jerks his chin. When I reach him, he bumps my fist with his.

"What's up?" he says.

"How are you doing? How's your mom?"

His face morphs into a deep frown. "You relentless fuck," he says. "Stop hassling me. I'm okay. She's better. I got those diabetes drugs your woman recommended, and things are picking up with her, so get off my back."

"Good. You still dealing?"

He looks to the side, and shakes his head, which I'm presuming is a yes. That's how I met Hejay—he sold me some stuff. It didn't take me long to catch on to the fact that he not only dealt drugs but also did other freelance jobs as well and was supporting two sick parents and four siblings. His dad was disabled in an industrial accident and his mom has diabetes and they have no healthcare. His life is shit. He's been trying to escape the drug-dealing world for years, but some crisis or other always hits and he needs the money. He's smart. Motivated. I want to get him to college, but every time I suggest it, he says he can teach himself and that it's impossible right now. At least I can pay him to do jobs for me.

"I've got a job for you."

He jerks his chin at me, still annoyed. I bump his shoulder.

"Don't be pissed, man. It's my mission to get you out of this shit." I wave my arm around, and he scowls more. "You know Anna Talanova?"

The mid-afternoon sun makes him squint as his eyes come to mine. "The tennis player?"

"Yeah, she's got an ex-boyfriend, a volatile guy named Arty Maroz." I pull up a picture of him on my phone. "I need him followed. Photographed. The usual deal."

He nods. "Send me the link. You got any more information? Where he lives, his schedule?"

I run through what little I know about the history of Anna and Arty.

Hejay pulls out a cigarette and lights it. "Why am I tracking him?"

I have to give him some version of the truth here; he's too smart not to. He'll connect all the dots anyway.

"Anna Talanova is seeing a friend of mine, Adam Miller, and Arty Maroz has been making a nuisance of himself. Adam has got into a couple of scraps with him when Arty's tried to hassle Anna. I'd like to understand what we're dealing with here, and what his gig is. I'd like to make him go away."

"I saw something on my phone about a fight at some red-carpet event. How volatile is he? Do I need …?"

I shake my head. "He fights, but it's not with guns or knives as far as I'm aware. Just make sure he never notices you."

Hejay gives a little hiccupping laugh. "I hate it when people say no guns or knives. There's always some weapon."

I lift my hands. "If you want to protect yourself, that's up to you."

He laughs again. "I always do. Easy-peasy, then. Usual rate?"

I nod, and he grins. I don't know whether he thinks he's ripping off the poor white guy who doesn't understand how the street works, or if he's just pleased to have the work. I get it: I lived on the street for a while, but I'm happy to pay him well and I make enough money now to do that. Now Kate's sorted out my finances and what I charge people.

"You wanna parkour sometime?" he says.

"I haven't seen you out much," I reply.

He snorts. "Like I've got time. Fucking homework with the kids."

The images of my brother Zach bent over a textbook, scowling and shouting, bloom hot and sharp, and I still couldn't save him from his relentless decline. I miss the crazy little shit.

"Some nights it's better if I get out, you know?" Hejay adds.

Seven people in a two-bedroom apartment, I'll bet. "Count me in," I say.

CHAPTER 25

Anna

Arty is leaning against a railing, head down, a beanie rammed over his ears and his finger hammering on his phone as I head along the waterfront. We agreed on East River Park as a meeting place so I would feel safe with people around but I wasn't likely to be recognized. A runner jogs past me along the path, hardly sparing me a glance. I'm not sure why I'm here, but Arty was very persistent—more than you'd expect from a disgruntled ex-boyfriend. I know it's incautious, but something about the way things work in Russia and what might be happening behind the scenes always exerts a pressure I can't quite escape.

As soon as Pepper spots him, she goes berserk, the traitorous dog. Does she not pick up on the fact he's a jerk? Perhaps the dog view of the world where everyone is a potential friend is the better approach. I huff out a breath: I've been badly treated too often for that. Arty straightens and then bends over to give Pepper's ears a fondle as she strains on her leash. My neck prickles. Will I have to bathe her afterward?

"Glad you finally agreed to meet me," he says in Russian, glancing up.

I sigh. "Why am I here? You're not supposed to be within a hundred yards of me."

"You think a piece of paper will keep you safe?"

"I wasn't aware I was in danger. Should I be worried?"

He shoves his hands in the pocket of his down jacket and looks away, scowling. The steelwork of the Williamsburg Bridge stretches across the water beyond his shoulder like intricate gray crochet.

"What's all this about, Arty? Why all the fighting and the court case and …" I wave my hand around.

He shrugs. "Got to keep the attention hounds happy, Anna—you know that."

"It seems like a lot of trouble for a limited return."

He laughs. "Oh, there's an excellent return."

I tilt my head at him. What does he mean by that? He stares out across the water, so I gesture along the path to encourage him to walk. At least I can give Pepper some exercise if he's hell-bent on wasting my time.

"Why did you come to the apartment and mention Pietr?"

"I thought you might need the reminder."

"Reminder about what? That I dated him once?"

He shrugs, and I take a sip of my coffee. I'm not sure how much he knows, who he's working for, if anyone. Someone in Russia? His father?

"If you pay me a million dollars, I'll leave you alone," he says suddenly, and I laugh.

"So, this is about money?"

"It's always about money, Anna. Why do you play tennis? For money."

He takes his sunglasses off and his dark brown eyes for a moment appear almost earnest. "They own us, Anna."

"Who?"

He rolls his eyes. "The people who got us out of Russia."

I shake my head. Was he tasked to keep an eye on me by people back home? *Home.* Damn, Anna, don't call it that.

My relationship with Arty shimmers in front of my face. Was he with me for some reason other than the obvious *let's date*? Why did he reach out in the first place? His father? … No one in Russia is just a straightforward businessperson.

Perhaps his father has connections I'm not aware of. How would I even find out?

He jerks his chin. "Who's this Adam Miller guy, anyway?" he says, and oh God, that question! Coming right after a conversation about people in Russia. Ugh.

"A friend of a friend. He agreed to step in when you conveniently told me you weren't accompanying me to my 'fancy-ass event.'"

"He's been on social media with you a lot."

"And?" I gesture down at Pepper. "She's on social media with me a lot."

His brown eyes continue to flicker over my face. "It's not a smart idea to get attached, Anna."

"Attached to my dog?"

"Don't play games. You know exactly what I mean."

"What are you talking about?"

"You should be careful around him, Anna. I don't think he can be trusted."

"Are you saying Adam Miller can't be trusted?"

He scowls at me again. "Do you know what his connections are? Anyone can be bought."

"Why are you so interested?" Why would Arty say that? The gray green of the river behind him is as murky as this conversation. Is Adam on their radar? Have they offered him money? I bat these far-fetched thoughts aside. It's obvious Arty is fishing. But for whom? I don't think Arty himself would care. He wasn't with me because he cared; he was with me for some other reason I can't quite put my finger on.

He gives me an oily smile. "Just looking out for you, Anna."

Like hell. I can't quite shake the idea that I've brought Adam Miller to the attention of some people in Russia. And I don't like that. I don't like it at all.

CHAPTER 26

Adam

Two days after chatting with Fabian a text drops into my phone from an unknown number. It's a picture of Arty Maroz and Anna walking along some waterfront. I examine the skyscrapers behind them—*the East River?* Anna is carrying a coffee, and they don't look friendly exactly, but I don't see a great deal of animosity either.

> Of interest?

is all the message says. Followed by:

> This guy is a tool. He trains for most of the day and gets into arguments with people all the time.

Fabian. I tap in a reply:

> Sounds about right.

I press the button to call him.

"Hey," I say. "What's this picture? How did you get it?"

"Ah … I might have omitted to tell you I put a tail on Arty Maroz."

"Because that's something normal people do."

"Well, yeah. His life is a car crash, but hacking into his life didn't give me anything to explain why he's hassling Anna and why he visited you, so I thought I'd go old school."

"So … when was this taken?"

"Yesterday."

My whole body locks up.

"What the hell? Anna met with Maroz *yesterday*?" I can't suck enough oxygen into my lungs. "Are you *certain*?"

"It's timestamped, so yes, I'm sure."

"She has a restraining order against him." They're talking. She's walking her dog. "Why the fuck is she on some waterfront with Maroz? With Pepper?"

"Yeah, it's pretty odd."

"Fuck. I haven't told her you're looking into Maroz." What *is* she doing? He tried to attack her at an event and … "Perhaps she's trying to persuade him to back off. He's still suing her for ownership of Pepper." A long groan seeps out before I can stop it. "How do I always end up with women who say one thing and do another?"

"Adam. You got unlucky one time; this is nothing like that. You don't know what's going on here. It's one photograph. Nobody knows we're digging into him, okay? He could have something on her that she doesn't want made public. He might have forced this meeting."

"Blackmail? You always did like the conspiracy theories. Sounds likely, though, given what you said about his finances."

"You'd be surprised how often *something*'s going on. Blackmail's more common than you'd think."

"Did you find anything on Pietr Petrov?"

"I've been concentrating on Maroz, but I'll dig into Petrov a bit more."

"I need to talk to her about this picture. What the hell am I going to say?"

"Just tell her you were worried about her and thought looking into Maroz might help. Simple enough."

"Yeah. Can't help feeling I went behind her back, though."

"It came from a genuine place of concern. She's not going to be unhappy with that."

"Yeah, I suppose so. Thanks, Fab."

"Should I say it's my pleasure? I'm not sure. I'll keep digging."

*

When I head over to Anna's later on, unease is still burning through me. What is she doing, and why didn't she say anything? But I guess I didn't tell her I was enlisting Fabian to dig into Arty, did I?

When I reach her building, the street is empty apart from a few pedestrians. No men with cameras. Maybe she met with Maroz to calm things down. That would make sense: If he stops creating a media storm, all the hassle goes away.

Anna meets me at the door, her hair down around her shoulders and soft-looking lounge gear clinging to every muscle. I can't resist pulling her in for a kiss, and she smiles against my lips.

"I have a confession to make," I say, as I follow her from the door to the kitchen island.

She swings around and blinks at me. "Something bad?"

I shake my head. "Arty Maroz visited me. So, I asked my hacker friend Fabian to do a little digging into him."

She turns away toward the sink, silky hair falling forward. "What do you mean, he visited you? He came to your *office*?" When I nod, she says, "That asshole. He doesn't know when to stop interfering."

"He told me to stay away from you. Like a warning. It was odd, to be honest." I scroll to the picture on my phone and hand it over to her. "But Fabian had him followed, and this photo was taken yesterday. I ..."

Her eyes are wide on the phone when I place it on the countertop in front of her and my stomach sinks into my shoes. No famous person wants someone she's sleeping with to set a tail on them and start taking photographs: There are quite enough paparazzi doing that. It's very stalkerish.

"I wasn't trying to spy on you, Anna. You didn't mention seeing him and ..."

She rolls her lips together. "That's the problem with people that dig for dirt—they always find it." Her voice is sharp, a tone in it I don't think I've ever heard before.

I swallow. "Are you saying there's some dirt on you and Arty? You're entitled to meet with him, I just ... You have a temporary order of protection against him. I wanted to tell you I had this picture. It would be dishonest not to."

Her shoulders relax a bit, and she turns toward me.

"I met up with him to try and stop him from hassling me. You. Us. To see whether I could make him go away. He asked for a million dollars."

"A million dollars!"

"Yeah. Now I wonder whether he's always seen me as a meal ticket and that's why he's being such a pain in the ass. He wants money."

I step into her and wrap my arms around her. "I'm sorry. I didn't want to sound like I was suspicious. You don't need to tell me what you do."

She shakes her head. "I get it, Adam. I know this violates the restraining order, and I shouldn't have met him but ... sometimes I want to knock problems on the head, you know? I don't like sitting around waiting for something bad to happen or think about seeing him in court."

This sounds so like Janus that I almost laugh out loud.

"Did your friend Fabian find anything else useful?" she adds.

"Apart from an email account full of porn sites and gambling debts and a disastrous bank balance, you mean?"

Anna leans back and stares up at me. "He got into his *bank account*?"

"I don't think that's even that difficult these days. He's very good at what he does."

"I guess that explains the demand for money." Anna's eyes dart around, narrowing on the countertop.

"What are you thinking?" I ask.

"Whether Fabian could get me ammunition on people in Russia. People who might want to manipulate me for one reason or another."

"Manipulate you?"

She shakes her head. "It's dog-eat-dog in Russia. In sport. People hold things over other people and blackmail them. Everybody is trying to grab a little bit more than everyone else. You're always looking over your shoulder."

Well, it's not quite the deal Maroz was talking about, but it sounds similar. I slump into her. I need to remember that Anna is as tough as old boots. "You could talk to Fabian. He's had some dealings with Russian hackers in the past."

"He has? *Wow.* Let me think about it. Some of these people are ones you wouldn't want to cross. Who knows what they'd do if they found out you or I had some dirt on them?"

One day, I hope she'll tell me more about all this. It's odd the relationship I have with Anna. We've agreed we're not boyfriend/girlfriend and we're exploring this, but she's a famous person: Do I have the right to ask questions? I'd rather she spontaneously shared things. She's been badly burned in the past, and who am I? Some random stranger she met about a month ago. But I want to be more than that. I want to be her person. She's the most remarkable woman I've ever met.

My body is reminding me of the unfortunate consequences of standing next to Anna while I'm trying to have a serious conversation with her. When I'm close to her, my mind replays the nights we're in bed together like they're on a permanent reel. And she must sense some shift in my mood because she lifts her head and gives me a small smile.

"I'm sorry. I don't want you to think that ..." I start.

"It's fine, Adam. You're honest about what you're doing, and it means a lot. It's rarer than you'd think."

Sliding my hand into her hair, I trail my lips over hers, and she grabs my neck and pulls me right into her body. I push her against the wall, mouth greedy as I harden in my jeans. Her other hand reaches into my back pocket, strong fingers squeezing, so I hoist her up and she winds her legs around my waist as I carry her down the corridor. And fuck, she's as eager as I am because, as soon as I set her feet on the floor of the bedroom, she yanks my shirt out of my pants with unsteady hands, grabbing the collar and trying to wrestle it over my head. Breath saws in and out of my chest. When I take over getting my shirt off, her questing fingers run all over my torso, mapping my muscles, and it makes me grateful for all those long years of jujitsu training. I'm pulling her top over her head when she undoes the first button on my waistband and then pops several more.

"Oh God," she says, on a gulp, fingertips brushing my erection. "I need ..."

I swallow her words with my mouth; she doesn't have to say it. I want this, too: the hot tightness of her down my length. My years of abstinence have made me insatiable. I pull my wallet out of my pocket, fumbling for the condom before handing it over to her, throwing the wallet to the floor, followed by my jeans and boxers that I step out of and kick away. As I peel her soft gym pants over her hips, she shimmies her panties down and I shuffle forward until the backs of her knees hit the bed, and she falls onto the covers and I follow her down, shifting so we're fully on the mattress. She takes me in her hand and plays with the base of my cock and, as her fingers drift down to my balls, all the muscles in my pelvis lock tight.

"I love you doing that," I whisper. "It feels so good."

She winds a strong leg around my thigh as I press into her, bringing her other knee to my hip and adjusting herself to get me right where she wants me. I rut against her. Fuck, can I not take anything slow with this woman? *Maybe one day.*

But she's pressing on my chest insistently, so I lift up onto my hands, taking in her flushed cheeks and dark, stormy eyes. *Turned-on Anna.* Her fingers trail down my body and find my length again, rubbing her thumb tantalizingly over the tip and my hips move, pushing into her hand. But she brings her other hand up to her mouth and rips open the condom packet with her teeth before rolling the latex down. Then she wriggles closer and guides me to her entrance. As I push forward, she gives around me, all tightness and heat as I press slowly inside and her muscles clamp down. *Holy shit.* My cock twitches, and I groan as I bury my head in her neck. *This is always so good.*

"Anna," I mumble into her damp skin, trailing hot kisses over her collarbone.

Goosebumps follow the path of my mouth, and she rocks her hips up, pulling me farther in, undulating all around me. So I reach between us and play gently with her clit as she gasps, her legs widening to make more room for my hand and I pull back my hips, thrusting slowly through it, my fingers wandering all over slippery skin.

Her head thunks into my shoulder, and her head turns into my throat, mouth open in a silent plea, wet and warm, and it makes me feel like a king that I can make her come apart like this.

"Adam," she says in a strangled voice.

She's so slick, everything hot and loose, and I roll us onto our sides, deepening my thrusts.

"You're soaked," I say. "I want to taste all this later, get it all over my face," and when I test my teeth on her neck, she twitches around me. *Close.*

"Do you remember," I whisper as I thrust into her, "how wet you got when I put my mouth on you last night? How much you liked my tongue just here?" I slide my hand between us to play, and she moans into my throat. I'm relentless as I push into her. Fuck, I'm on the edge, too, my release tingling in my balls and up my cock.

"Oh God, Adam," she gasps. "Please, you need to ... oh *God* ... please ..."

My stomach knots. We've come at this so fast, yet again. One day I'll be able to savor this for longer, but it feels impossible right now. I don't let up with my fingers and she starts to fall, her head lifting up, hot breath on my neck, a long groan pressing into my skin that sounds like the best sound in the world.

"Yes, Anna," I hiss as my whole crotch tightens, sweet sensations burning through my legs and curling my toes. "Oh, *fuck*."

I'm dimly aware of pushing so hard that I'm moving her across the bed as I tip over the edge, shudders ripping through me as everything shimmers around the periphery of my vision, and an inky blackness curls in at the corners and narrows my focus down to beads of sweat on sweet, pale skin.

Hot.

Hot.

I'm so fucking hot.

The light on the nightstand fades in at the edges of black. My hands are tensed on Anna's ass in a bruising grip, and her head is resting on my shoulder. As I tilt my head trying to look down at her, she's completely motionless, her breath coming in short gasps, so I move back and prop myself up on my elbow, taking in her pale face. I pull back onto my knees and remove the condom, tying a knot in it before disappearing into the bathroom. When I come back, Anna is lying on her back, eyes closed, hands now splayed over her head. Crawling onto the bed, I lie down next to her, and she turns her head, opening her eyes and examining me.

Her lips curve up slowly. "Oh my God," she says, making me laugh.

I shift onto my back, and lightness lifts my chest. *She doesn't think I'm some crazy, desperate guy, then.* Rolling onto her side, she shuffles into me, palm snaking over my ribs and the warmth of how she curls into me all night, and how much I like it, winds its way around me like she's cast a spell. My limbs are like deadweights. It's been a hell of a day and for her, too, it seems. Words bubble up and sink back down again, so I sit forward, pulling the comforter from the bottom of the bed over us, and the world drifts away.

CHAPTER 27

Anna

Arty *visited* Adam—turned up at his office and threatened him. Calm, law-abiding Adam Miller. Hairs lift on the back of my neck. I've been burying my head in the sand for the last week, acting like I'm living someone else's life, but now it's snapped into sharp relief.

There's so much water under the bridge in my life, so many loose cannons like Arty Maroz, and now Adam's asked his friend Fabian to help, and he can get into *bank accounts*! It's only a matter of time before Fabian finds out everything about me, everything that I had to do, and that's not even the least of it: If he finds out more, he'll be putting himself in real danger; Adam, too. Perhaps loneliness isn't the worst thing in the world; perhaps being responsible for somebody else getting hurt is a lot worse. Being on my own is just one of the prices I pay for getting out of Russia, for the success I've been chasing all my life.

How could I put someone like Adam in danger? He's the kind of committed friend who never backs down. To lose his friendship, I'd have to do something awful that would make him think I'd totally betrayed him. I sigh as I study the clay court at my feet. Should I tell him? But if I tell him about Konstantin, then he'd really be in the firing line because he would know … and *nobody* knows. Only the people who've been through it, like me, and we never talk about it. Never. And if I'm honest with myself, I don't want him to find out that Anna Talanova, successful tennis player, is an illusion. Maybe my history means it's inevitable that I'll end up with a man who understands the system I came up through. Somebody like Arty or Pietr who doesn't care about who or what I am, but just wants a trophy, someone they can say won a Grand Slam tournament and looks decorative on their arm.

I bounce the ball a few times on the asphalt and hammer a serve across the net to Ilov. It goes way outside the line.

"*Kontsentriruysya!* What's up with you?" he barks.

Ugh. I don't even want to count the number of double faults today. I shake my head and walk over to the water bottle on the bench by the side of the court. We've lost Mila to a physio today and a consultation about an old knee injury. Thank God she isn't here to watch me screw it all up.

Ilov jogs over to join me and runs a towel over his head, grabbing his own water.

"You okay?" he says more quietly.

I grin at him. "Don't give me sympathy. Barking orders at me is better."

"You've been on fire lately, Anna. Despite our conversation about Arty Maroz, you haven't put a foot wrong these last couple of weeks: I haven't had to bark at you at all. I take my hat off to you. That's the expression, no?" His eyes are kind as he smiles at me.

I nod. I *have* been playing well. I've been pretending to play happy families with a man I can't get attached to. "My concentration is shot today."

"You want to take a break?"

I shake my head. My father's mantra was always to soldier on. "If you can tolerate all the mistakes, let's just hammer through it. Feel free to yell at me and give me grief. I'm just distracted." I shrug. "I'll try to put it aside."

"*Otlichno!*" he says. "That is also good practice. It happens in matches, too."

I nod and he adds, "It's a joy every day to train with you, Anna. That's why, when you make errors, I am surprised."

I laugh. He's a good motivator. "I've got a feeling there's going to be a lot of surprises today."

*

After my tennis practice, I'm still mulling over what to say to Adam and getting nowhere, when a text drops into my messages.

That dog of yours need a walk?

This is immediately followed by:

I'm on my way home from the office and thought I'd take a detour via your place.

I sigh and turn my phone over in my hand. Then I type:

Text me when you're close.

I'm waiting on the street with Pepper on a leash when Adam rounds the building on the corner. The paparazzi have melted away, along with Arty, but I'd be a fool to think Arty's doing anything other than biding his time. Meeting him was a mistake.

Adam's long loping stride eats up the sidewalk, his right hand tucked into his pocket as he moves. There's something so sexy about it that I want to groan out loud. He's hot in all these subtle, unintentional little ways.

His face lights up when he spots me standing on the sidewalk, and now I feel even worse.

He grins and nods down at Pepper, who's going berserk jumping up and wagging her tail. "Was she raring to go? Expecting another blow-dry?"

I laugh.

He takes hold of my hand and tucks it into his elbow. "Where to?"

"Let's just walk."

Halfway up the block, as Pepper sniffs at everything she can stick her nose in, I clear my throat. "Adam, I think we should stop seeing each other."

He turns toward me, frowning. "What? What do you mean?"

"I think we should stop …" I gesture between us as a flush builds on my neck. "Doing this. Getting together, being friends."

"Stop being friends?" He sounds incredulous, and I'm dumbstruck, too. The thought of not even seeing him even as a *friend … That wasn't really what I meant …* I want to groan out loud. Why didn't I plan this better?

"When we first met, I never thought of us getting together." *That's a lie, Anna.* "My life felt like such a mess. I'd just got through two bad relationships, and one of those guys was still harassing me, but now he's also hassling *you*. I said to you at the beginning I didn't want more or anything complicated. I think this is moving toward something I'm not ready for."

Something flashes across his face. Like a wince of pain. Oh, sweet Jesus, I don't want to do that to Adam. A flush is building on his neck, too.

"You also said we shouldn't overthink this, that it was something you wanted to explore," he says.

I close my eyes. *I did say that.*

"Anna."

"That was before people started doorstepping you and Arty Maroz paid you a visit!"

"He's an asshole, Anna. We'll sort Arty Maroz out."

"You don't understand what we're dealing with," I mutter.

He folds his arms over his chest. "Why don't you tell me what we're dealing with?"

No. Nope. I can't do that. Oh God, how am I going to persuade him? Do I have to hurt his feelings? Hot sweat drips down my spine. I'm in this disaster of a conversation now. The only way out is through.

"When we did the jujitsu in my gym, it took me by surprise. It was just friends, and then I did something stupid," I say. "I persuaded you. I rolled my hips into you. And you were right to be cautious."

His fists clench by his side. "It wasn't just you, Anna. I didn't need any persuading in case you've forgotten."

"Whatever, I …"

"It wasn't stupid." He clears his throat. "Am I something stupid to you?" His voice is gruff and angry, and it cuts through my skin like a barbed wire. I've never seen Adam angry before.

"No. No of course not."

"It sounds like it."

"You said you had a bad relationship in college, and I …"

"Don't make this about me. If you want to finish things, fine, but this is not about me."

"I know she turned on you, I …"

He clenches his fists. "Who told you that? Janus? Did he tell you what happened?"

When I shake my head, he says, "Yes, she turned on me, much like you're doing right now." And the barb is like a stab to the heart. *You lose people, Anna, and it always hurts.*

I shake my head at him. "I messed up my practice today," I blurt out.

His head tips back and he closes his eyes, and I watch his throat move as he swallows. When his eyes come back to meet mine, they're wounded and dark like bottomless pools. I wince.

"I'm sorry, Anna, I'm really sorry to hear that," he says, clearing his throat. "I'd never want to be a distraction to you."

As I open my mouth to say that it wasn't him, that it was all my fault, that I'm being a brat, he turns on his heel and heads down the street like he can't bear to be in my presence a moment longer. Pepper's tail droops, and she lets out a soft whine.

Watching him go, still looking as sexy as he did when he was heading toward me, makes my heart somersault in my chest. Well, I fucked that up but good. I want to run after him and tell him he's everything I need, that I've been happy, not lonely, perhaps for the first time ever. That I messed up my practice only because I knew I had to have this conversation, and I've screwed up practices many, many times before and he's made me feel strong, powerful, able to do anything. *Put my bad relationship history behind me.* He'd laugh at that in his cute, self-deprecating way and tell me I was strong and powerful before I met him and it wasn't anything to do with him.

How could I be so unkind to such an amazing guy?

But I have no right to keep him close. It'd be like cursing the best, most loyal person I know. I can't do that. He doesn't deserve to get on their radar. He doesn't deserve Arty and all these other scumbags in his life, being exposed to Russia through association with me. Hiding and dodging the press while his business slowly implodes.

If I was any kind of decent person at all, I would stay well away from Adam Miller. So why does it feel like the worst decision in the world?

CHAPTER 28

Adam

As I walk away from Anna, my hand flaps by my side, heat burning through my body like someone took a torch to my skin. I don't get angry. I don't let it bubble over. I flap my hand as I try and suck in a couple of deep breaths. Did I misread the signs? This seemed good. This *was* good. I want to march back and shake her. But what the hell, that would make me just like Maroz with his violent outbursts.

There was no warning, right?

I'm an idiot. I put myself through this again. I started to open up. I started to *hope.*

Jesus Christ.

What the *fuck* am I going to do now?

Just at the point I thought I was getting over whatever the hell's been wrong with me for the last ten years, fear most probably, another woman pulls the rug out from under my feet.

I just … Fuck. I wanted more. For the first time in a very long time, maybe ever. I shouldn't have compared her to Celine; she's nothing like her. Celine hung on to *me*. I've never been in a situation where a woman has been interested and then said, thanks but no thanks, and God … A sharp pain constricts my chest. What do you even do or say, when someone says something like that?

To me, she didn't seem like she wasn't ready for a relationship. I huff out a laugh. I'm so out of my depth. I understand nothing about relationships or the pressures she's under to perform, to win. Maybe I wasn't what she wanted anymore, was too much of a distraction. *Anna Talanova*. It's like a dream in time, the kind of thing you look back on when you're older and congratulate yourself on being wise enough to have had the experience, to go with something for once. I don't want it to be only that, though. I want to wake up every day into the life I had for three days in Janus's apartment. Curled up in a big bed with Anna and Pepper. My eyes start to tighten.

Restless energy seethes under the surface of my skin, and I want to do something, anything. Like burn the whole house down, and for the first time maybe I understand Fabian's desire to take stupid risks. A sort of jittery, suicidal feeling. I laugh to myself. I was never a risk-taker: I'm way too much of a coward for that. So, I'm going to have to do what I always do, what I did ten years ago, button it up, push it down, pretend I didn't fuck up, didn't miss all the signs.

I tip my head back toward the blue sky between the buildings towering overhead. The thing is, I didn't miss the signs. I knew. Right from the get-go and even recently, I knew that Anna Talanova would never settle for me. I told Janus as much but walked right into it anyway. I let my heart become involved. And the thought makes my chest clench.

Over the next few days, I don't understand what comes over me. Something is raging through me, turning me into a man possessed. It's like anger, at myself, at her, but somehow far worse, and it spills into everything I do.

I ask Keith to have ten more designs of different animals ready by the end of the week and tell Susie to produce marketing campaigns for all of them. I go on long runs up the west side of Manhattan, pushing harder and harder until I can't breathe and exhaustion takes hold of me, and then, only then, does the restless feeling stop because my body is too tired to sustain it.

I wake in the middle of the night and pace around my small living room. I think about getting a dog. I miss Anna, but I miss Pepper, too: her silky ears, her wet snuffly nose, her unbounded joy.

The last ten years have been a retreat into electronics, but that doesn't help anymore. I can't concentrate on the details. I can't work through schemas of boards and understand what all the components are doing.

How do I get over this? The ache in my body is deep and never-ending. And as the days roll by and I don't hear from Anna, the hyped-up restless feeling morphs into white-hot anger looking for release.

CHAPTER 29

Adam

I'm still trying to sit on the anger when I go to meet Fabian in East One Coffee Roasters partway between his place and my office. It's four days since Anna gave me my marching orders. He's looking fidgety and unwashed, and something about it matches my inner turmoil: I can relate to forgetting to shower and exhausting yourself. What does Kate make of it all? She's this incredible, tolerant woman, and I can tell Fabian's so much happier now, despite his appearance. He's lost that gaunt, haunted look he had six or eight months ago. But whenever I see them together it makes my heart ache. Kate's like me in some ways—solid, calm, sensible—and I always hoped I'd find someone who valued those qualities. Now I think I found someone who took advantage of them and made me feel like a fool for thinking it was more.

"How's it going?" I say, sliding into the seat across from Fabian.

He looks up from his coffee and brownie, and my own heartache drops away when I see the expression on his face. "What is it?"

"I've pulled together some stuff I want to share with you. I don't think I've got it all yet, but …"

Wow, we're straight into it. No messing around. "Okay."

"I did some more deep diving into Pietr Petrov. He's a business associate—

and the details are somewhat sketchy—of a man named Konstantin Lebedev, a Russian tennis coach. By all appearances, *the* Russian tennis coach. Certainly, no one from Russia makes it in tennis in the West if they haven't been through one of his academies. Although you'll not find Petrov listed as having any connection with the academies."

"Anna?"

"Yes, she went through the Alliance Tennis Federation's coaching, but it's difficult to tell who her actual trainer was."

"So, this Pietr guy was involved …Is that how Anna met Pietr?"

"Presumably, although I'm not a hundred percent sure. Lebedev and Petrov have a lot of legitimate business concerns in Russia and elsewhere, but I've found some stuff … I think there's something suspect about the academies. My guess is they're running pedophile and prostitution rings, handpicking the teenage kids coming through the academies and"—he swallows—"selling them."

"What do you mean, *selling* them?"

"Getting businesspeople who have a certain set of, let us say, illegal interests involved, who then 'sponsor' a young person of their choosing. On the surface, you could make that seem legitimate, but I think something quite different is going on underneath."

Oh Christ! Did Anna …? "Like what?"

He purses his lips. "They run a lot of weekend camps attended by sponsors, with young people staying in sponsors' apartments. Large organized events as well, which on the face of it are competitions."

"You think it's not legit?"

"Well, it *could* be, and perhaps on one level, it is, but *all* the sponsors attend these events. Religiously. I checked. They have their own place where they hold them, with accommodation, and parents are not allowed. I think they want you to think they're legitimate. They're always done within the academy, too; they're not competing against other academies. It's not open to anyone from outside."

"But that doesn't exactly …"

"Then I hacked into some tennis chats by masquerading as an up-and-coming hopeful who'd had an offer from a Lebedev school and been given access."

"How the hell did you pull that off?"

He waves his hand.

"In *Russian*?" I add.

He eyes me over his coffee. "You ever heard of Google Translate?" He shakes his head. "In any case, I've done a lot of stuff in Russian. A lot of the bad actors in hacking come from there, so you have to understand the language to some degree if you're a hacker. Anyway, the tennis academies are not all Russian nationals. It's an honor to be selected from anywhere in the world. People attend from all over."

"What did you find?"

"Lots of coded conversations."

"How coded?"

"The way things were written. Comments like 'He's my wolf.' References to being taken away for weekends by their sponsors and responses like 'Be safe' and 'Call me if you need me.' Sentences like 'He will give you gifts and you have to accept them.' Quite a lot of chat about 'gift giving.' I didn't get the impression that gifts were actual presents if you get what I'm saying. There were girls complaining that they didn't have a sponsor, that they weren't 'what a sponsor was looking for.' There was also talk about 'demotion,' which I don't think had anything to do with an aptitude for tennis; I think it was about keeping the sponsor happy."

"This … you … you think Anna …"

"I don't know."

Bile burns in the back of my throat. "What do you think they're making them do?"

"You know me, Adam. I saw too many people turning tricks on the street, including Zach. I always think the worst."

"Fuck. Oh, fuck." I bury my hands in my hair, sucking in a jittery breath. "Perhaps it wasn't sexual abuse, maybe it was something else …"

"Whatever it is, Anna certainly did it."

I bristle immediately. "Why would you think that?"

"Because she got out of Russia. She made it. It's rare. That's what they're all aiming for. That's why they want a sponsor. It's the only way out."

"Jesus."

"My guess is Pietr was her sponsor. He was her way out."

The coffee shop is full of people chatting at tables, backpacks and shopping bags clustered around their feet. It's all so Western and normal; we have no idea in this country what goes on elsewhere. How bad it is. How amazing is Anna? How much has she had to fight?

Fabian pops another bit of brownie into his mouth and chews. "The thing is, I think it might involve boys, too."

"Boys … sponsored by male sponsors?"

"Yes."

"So, if it is abuse … then boys being abused by men?"

Fabian nods.

"But homosexuality is banned in Russia, yes?"

"Well, technically it's not illegal, but it's so heavily disapproved of that that's an irrelevance. The pedophilia is obviously illegal. I suspect the tennis academy could be making big money on all of it. Blackmail's a possibility, too."

Is this true? Or does Fabian see shadowy figures and illegal activities everywhere?

"Do you think Maroz …?"

He shakes his head. "I don't know. The interesting thing was, he was a tennis player originally. He didn't meet Anna at the camps; he was older than her, but he made an abrupt switch to skiing. I mean he was a talented skier, obviously, but he suddenly dropped the tennis. I've no idea why. His father is high up in the Russian hierarchy, and it's possible something happened."

Wow. If this is true, then … But does any of this digging matter anymore anyway? I haven't heard from Anna in four days, and having Fabian unearth this information about her feels like a huge intrusion into her fight to the top. She didn't share any of this with me. Some half comments and hints, sure, but nothing more, and perhaps that says it all.

But Christ, I didn't tell her anything about my past either. Despite how good it was, maybe neither of us wanted to sully it with the awful things we lived through.

"If Pietr was her sponsor, I'd say it's slightly odd that she was publicly with him for years and then somehow escaped from him and stopped being his girlfriend," Fabian muses, frowning.

"She did tell me that he was controlling, that the relationship was abusive." Hell, the hints were all there, now I come to think of it.

"Yeah, well, it's not going to be sunshine and roses, is it?" Fabian's eyes roam over my face and he frowns. "What's up with you anyway?"

"What do you mean?"

"You don't seem like your normal solid self. You're looking a bit wild-eyed, if I'm being frank."

I shrug. "I guess none of it matters anymore. She said she didn't want us to …" I wave an arm around. "… Continue with whatever it was we were doing."

"What? She split up with you?"

I frown at this. *Yes, yes she did, Adam.* But God … "We were friends, Fabian."

"Are you still friends?"

I guess that's the fifty-million-dollar question. And in all my anger this week, I haven't really asked myself this question. I've been too agitated to think about being friends. But if there was an argument for friends at the beginning, maybe that rationale still exists. The anger is all about me, the pain that constricts my lungs, stopping my breathing. I wonder how Anna feels?

"What were you guys doing, exactly?"

Another excellent question. I still don't know, despite four days of chewing it all over. Getting over our pasts?

"Friends with benefits," I say, but the words curl up inside me like burned paper. "God, what is it with me and women? I know how to pick them, that's for sure."

"I think they pick you, Adam. Because you're this amazing, dependable, organized guy."

I start to laugh. I don't think women see me that way, only Fabian with his crazy unbalanced life would see something positive in that. "Yeah, I don't think those are killer traits with the ladies."

"I think you'd be surprised. When your life's a mess, or when you can't rely on those closest to you to tell the truth, what do you want? Someone calm and capable and honest, that's what."

Yeah, his home life was a real car crash before he met Kate. "Like Kate," I say, smiling.

He grunts. "She's all that, and about twenty-six other things besides. I'll never keep up with her."

Doesn't he realize he's like this incredible hacker, at the top of his game, even if no one recognizes it?

Maybe Anna still needs somebody who is calm, capable, and honest. The waves of loneliness that radiated from her when I first met her haven't gone away, have they? Perhaps she still needs someone who's on her side. Something wild takes a grip on my chest. It's hope, and fuck, how could I be hopeful in a situation like this? But something is driving me on, like seeing a mirage in the desert. I've had a taste of the life I want, something I never thought I'd find. I was settled in my little underground office, not exactly happy, like a forgotten book that's unread and covered in dust, and then she came in and flicked through all my pages, stirring it all up. Ten years ago, I lost part of myself. I don't know what bit it was: trust, belief, an inherent feeling that your life is going to go forward, not backward. It disappeared after Celine, and then Anna opened Pandora's box.

"She kicked me to the curb," I say. "How would I get over that?"

"Blackmail."

"*What?*"

"Blackmail. Make her feel guilty for abandoning you. Lean on her a little."

"What are you talking about?"

He narrows his eyes at me. "You want her?"

"What kind of question is that? She's Anna Talanova!"

"Well, you need to be devious."

“Like slash my arm in the ER, you mean?”

He has the good grace to shift a little in his seat. “I wasn’t in the best frame of mind when I did that.”

“No kidding. Jesus Christ. You’re a lunatic. I’m not manipulating Anna into … into … whatever.”

“I’m not saying that. Just manipulate her a little into spending time with you. Be a friend. Someone she can’t do without. I couldn’t do that: No woman has ever viewed me as a reliable friend. I’m not that guy, but you are.”

“Yeah, because that’s so sexy.”

He laughs. “It fucking is! Good friends are like gold dust, and most men can’t do it. You’re incredible at it. You’ve kept the three of us together for years. Talk to her, send her pictures, invite her to things, and offer to help. No one fucking does that. I can’t believe I’m the one talking about shit like this.” He starts laughing.

Maybe he’s on to something.

“You provide her with everything she can’t find anywhere else. She needed you for events, didn’t she? How about offering to be her plus one again?”

I open my mouth and close it. I’m not sure that worked out so well for us. But perhaps I know something she’d like better.

CHAPTER 30

Anna

The text arrives while I'm running way beyond my normal pace on the treadmill in my gym, sweat dripping onto the belt. Because eight hours of shit tennis is not enough in a day, apparently. Am I so angry about the terrible practice today that I have to punish myself more? Ilov is being so patient with me, and I've got to leave for Australia in three weeks for the buildup to the Australian Open, like a big fat dead end to this whole car crash.

The evening ahead yawns in front of me, with a nutritionist-designed meal and ... *and what, Anna?* What are you doing tonight to take your mind off the awful men and the competition and the tournaments and all the other shit ricocheting around your head on a never-ending loop?

I sigh and press the message icon on my phone:

> How's Pepper for walks today?

What? This is what he texts me? After I told him what a distraction he was and after I made an ill-judged comment about our relationship being stupid and he stormed off—that's what he comes back with? No rage or disparaging comments or arguing, just a question about my dog?

I haven't walked Pepper today, apart from a short visit outside this morning to do her business. I'm exhausted. *And who's fault is that, Anna?* I slow the belt down to a walking pace, and as if she has some sixth sense Adam has texted, Pepper whines and scratches at the door. She heard the treadmill, you lunatic; she's not psychic.

Adam's always so calm, about everything. If he's going to be a grown-up, perhaps I can be one, too. My fingers fly over the screen:

Are you offering?

His response is almost immediate:

I'd love to. Should I pop over and pick her up now?

Is that it? So, he's presuming I'm not going on this walk with him? *Huh.*

Give me thirty minutes.

I can't meet him looking red-faced, sweaty, and frustrated. This might be some ruse to talk, to revisit the conversation we had on the street.

But when Adam turns up, he doesn't take off his coat or make himself at home or even throw questions at me. No, he stands in the hallway, looking ridiculously cute in a puffer jacket and a woolen cap, which he proceeds to take off for a moment to run a hand through his toffee-colored curls. Gah. I don't need to be thinking about his curls, his soft hair, or anything else.

Pepper goes berserk, jumping up at him and wagging her tail like a maniac as his long fingers rub all down her body. I don't want to think about that either. As I stand with the leash and poop bags in my hand, part of me wants to jump all over him, too. I haven't seen him for a week, and dammit I'm hollowed out all over again seeing his thoughtfulness and the way his eyes narrow on you when he listens.

"How are you doing?" he asks, looking up from where he's crouched down on the floor.

I can't help myself: I make a face. When he raises his eyebrows, I say, "Practice isn't going so well at the moment." He nods and doesn't say anything more. "It's always ups and downs to tell you the truth," I add. "I'm sorry that I implied that you ..."

God, I'm the one that's going there. He shakes his head and holds up his hand.

"It's fine, Anna. I get it. We veered way off our original agreement, and neither of us wanted that. I'm over it. I'd like to think we can still be friends, though."

He's *over* it? Something red hot shoots through me. *Men.* I swear you have sex with them and the only thing that's engaged is their libido, whereas for you ... Nope. Not going there. I'm not thinking about emotions or how his body ground me into the floor of the gym and the bed and ... *Goddammit.*

He takes the leash from my fingers and leans in and squeezes my shoulder. I inhale his burned, woodsy smell and almost keel over. I'm so light-headed. No doubt because I haven't eaten.

"You'll get there, Anna."

I stare up at him, and his eyes pinch a bit at the corners.

I press my lips together. "Thanks for coming here and offering to walk Pepper. I'd like us to still be friends, too, but I don't think we should be seen in public together. The press interest caused so many problems."

He nods. "That makes sense." Then he smiles and studies Pepper who's still wagging her tail at our feet. "Come on, Missy," he says, "let's head out and rock a New York evening."

Suddenly, I want to be out with him rocking a New York evening. I want to tuck my hand into his elbow and hear everything he has to say about selling online, small electronic boards, and Tom Gauld's latest cartoon. He disappears into the elevator, turning around and giving me a salute as the doors close. *The dork.* A smile curves over my lips. I'm not sure what the empty feeling in my stomach is, but I don't like it. I head into the kitchen, wrench open the fridge door and stare at the row of plastic boxes left there by my nutritionist.

Hunger. That's what the empty feeling is.

CHAPTER 31

Anna

Two days later, an email drops into my inbox as I'm sorting paperwork and messages from my team. It's something from Adam that he's forwarded on from … *the Westminster Kennel Club Dog Show*?

I can get tickets for this!

I take in the picture of a cute poodle and a smile curves over my lips. *Dammit.* I would love to go to this. I stare at the pot of pens on the back of my desk. But … but … I told him we shouldn't be seen out with each other.

I pick up my phone.

Thanks for the invite to the Westminster Kennel Club Show.

Looks amazing, huh?

We'd be out in public together, though, wouldn't we?

I should be relieved at the excuse to get out of it, but all I feel is twisty inside. The fun we had discussing doing something like this when we agreed to be friends. And that first night when he came to the apartment and let the team do his hair then stood patiently by my side, like some incredible right-hand man, letting me hang on to him … All that feels like so long ago. I pay people to support me; it's never freely given. The dots start and stop again, and again … and then go quiet. I sit in my office chair for five minutes, and nothing more comes through.

Fuck. Sometimes those decisions you're forced into when you give up something that means a lot to you are the most painful. Like leaving my parents' house when I was fourteen to train in Spain—I was so lonely. Tennis got less solitary only when I won the money to build a team around me. But, in the end, I pay them. They're employees, not friends. Adam was a friend.

I really wanted to go to that show. I kick my seat back from my desk and head to the kitchen, wrenching open the door to the fridge as I glance at the clock on the wall. Could I have my snack early?

I pull out the food tray and scowl down at the protein bars and prepared fruit. *Do I ever have any fun?*

My phone vibrates in my pocket.

Leave it with me.

My mouth drops open. *What?* What is he going to do now? I clench my fist. Goddamn all men. He disrupts my rest day, and now I won't be able to stop thinking about having a day out. *A day off. A break.* What are you talking about, Anna? You have *never* wanted a break. I fling myself on the couch and turn on the television, but it's set to the sports channel and watching other people be good at their sport right now is more than I can bear. I flick through the channels as my shoulders droop, and I chew on an apple before flinging the core in the trash and heading back to my computer.

*

Two days later, after practice, another text from Adam lands in my messages:

I've managed to arrange a VIP tour at the dog show. You might have to talk to staff who are tennis fans and sign some photographs.

Oh God! He's arranged a tour? How ungrateful would I be to refuse when he's gone to so much trouble?

That sounds amazing!

I'll see you on Monday at 6 p.m. Should we meet at Madison Square Garden?

Sounds good.

I pick up a pot of fruit and open it up, popping a bit of pineapple in my mouth. When did someone last treat me to a surprise? I've had beautiful gifts from fans, drawings, things they've made, but no friend has ever done anything like this for me. It's so generous of him. *Why is he doing this?* I press my hand into my chest. At least I'm not the most boring athlete in the world anymore.

Pepper appears at my feet with her pink rabbit in her jaws.

"Mommy's going to a dog show. I'm sorry but I don't think you can come," I say, grinning down at her. "Should I see if I can find you a cute boyfriend while I'm there?"

The idea of adorable little miniature Peppers blooms in my head. I wolf down the pineapple and grab a protein bar and an herbal tea. Am I mad? I could never take care of anything like a litter of puppies. And the thought makes me stomp back to my bedroom.

*

When I meet Adam at the side gate to the venue, he's chatting with a dark-haired man in an official-looking blue suit. His hair is being buffeted by the wind, and he's laughing as he talks. My eyes track down his body in a pair of tight jeans and a fitted Henley with a smart jacket over the top. He looks like a model. *I've seen him naked.* His taut abs and his …

Stop, Anna!

I force myself to think about him finding another woman, and it hollows me out. But it's not like I'll be around; I'll be in Australia for the Open after Christmas … which is two weeks away now. The grumpiness of the last few days returns with a vengeance. The man in the suit's eyes widen slightly as I approach.

"Ms. Talanova!"

"Please, call me Anna."

He inclines his head with a smile. "Anna. I'm Kevin. I'm honored to meet you. We're so delighted that you decided to come to the Kennel Club today. I'm going to be your host for the event."

My eyes flick to Adam. Wow, the VIP tours here are good.

"Everyone's really looking forward to meeting you."

My eyebrows rise into my hairline, and Adam takes my elbow like he thinks I might bolt.

"As I mentioned on the phone, Anna doesn't want any publicity for this visit," he says as I examine the side of his face. "Being in the stands would be difficult. We really appreciate you accommodating us."

Goddammit, do they normally do tours like this? Did he specifically request some kind of private thing for me? When did he become so demanding? He's better than my PR team. Speaking of which, I should warn Damian. Autographs mean photographs, which inevitably end up online. I just need to keep Adam out of them.

"Not at all! Not at all!" Kevin says. "There's only three of us in the loop about Anna's visit today, so it's all very hush-hush." He makes a zipping movement across his lips, and I immediately want to giggle. "Though I'm sure when the dog owners see you, they'll want autographs, maybe pictures. I hope that's all right. Please tell me if anything isn't acceptable and I can smooth it over." He wrings his hands. "Do we need a secret signal?" he adds like it's only just occurred to him, and I want to laugh again.

"I can let you know quietly, Kevin, if you're with us all day," Adam says.

"Good, good," he says, rubbing his hands together.

Adam's eyes tip down toward me. "Are photographs okay?"

"I'm happy to do a few selfies with people and sign some autographs. But I'm going to have to touch base with my PR team and tell them that some pictures might appear online."

Kevin beams. "Of course! Let's head inside, and you can call them."

He turns and heads into the venue, and I squeeze Adam's arm and lean in.

"Do they usually do VIP tours?" I mumble into Adam's ear.

He shakes his head.

"What the hell did you say to him to get him to agree to a private tour?"

"I might have said that you were concerned about being harassed given recent events. He said the security was high here because of the large number of valuable dogs, and he was only too happy to oblige. He's a huge tennis fan, apparently. He nearly had a conniption when I told him you wanted to visit. I didn't have to do any persuading at all." He winks at me.

I roll my eyes at him. "Glad to know I'm classed in the same category as a valuable dog."

I sound like a grumpy old bear at best and, at worst, a diva, but when my eyes slide toward Adam, he's laughing quietly.

"I've always thought of you that way," he says, eyes twinkling, and the way they crease around the corners makes my chest go tight.

But he just pats my hand and draws me inside the venue, and we head down some white corridors into the bowels of the building. *Madison Square Garden.* Wow. I've always dreamed of doing an exhibition tennis event here. *Maybe one day.*

We head into a little area that's set out with muffins, cookies, and a tea and coffee maker. Two women are standing chatting, both fidgeting, but they break out into beaming smiles as soon as we enter.

"Would you like a tea or coffee, Anna?" Kevin says.

"If you have any herbal tea, that would be lovely."

"I'll have a coffee," Adam rumbles beside me. He's dropped into his role of second wheel. A quiet solid presence by my side.

"No problem. Can I introduce you to Belle Brown and Amanda Davis, both part of our team running this event?" Kevin adds.

"Oh! Ms. Talanova. I'm a huge tennis fan," Belle gushes as she darts forward, clasping my hands in hers. "I couldn't believe you were coming to visit us today. It's like a dream come true."

Amanda nods along at her side, still beaming.

"To be honest, I think you have the dream job here," I say. "All these beautiful dogs!"

They both laugh, and my shoulders ease. I haven't been out and met any real fans for a while. I forget that most people are polite and nice … I *easily* forget it.

"Would you two ladies like a photograph?" I say.

Belle presses her hand to her chest. "Oh yes! That would be amazing!" she squeaks, scrabbling for her phone.

"And me!" Kevin interjects, waving his own phone.

"I'll take it," Adam says, stepping forward and taking Belle's phone out of her hand, then smiling and nodding and directing people into position, his long fingers gripping the edges of her phone. He ends up taking photographs for everyone, and Kevin keeps saying he can't believe he now has a picture of Anna Talanova on his phone, making me laugh. Then Kevin beavers around sorting all the drinks, and I turn to Amanda and Belle.

"Tell me about the dogs."

Amanda claps her hands. "Well, I don't know about you, Anna, but I'm a woman of action. How about we go and *see* some dogs instead? We thought you might like a trip to the benching area where all the competitors are groomed and prepped. Belle and I can take you through some of the breeds and features, and you can talk to some owners."

Belle narrows her eyes. "And maybe see some Papillons, too?"

"I would die on a hill for that," I say, laughing.

My eyes meet Adam's, and he's looking at me with such warmth that my heart stutters in my chest.

"Pepper, isn't it?" Belle says, and I nod, delight spreading through me. "I follow her Instagram. I've been enjoying the dog toys recently." She gestures at Adam, and he raises his eyebrows as my lips curl up.

When we head into the grooming tent, it's stacked high with crates and crammed with tables. Dog owners brushing, trimming, and spraying in preparation for their turn in the show. It's a hive of activity and what appears to be some very bored dogs.

Adam leans into me. "I'm sure there's a Gary Larson cartoon in here somewhere."

"When dogs primp, you mean," I say.

My stomach wobbles when he grins down at me. Goddamn him, he needs to stop being so fucking charming all the time.

CHAPTER 32

Adam

Anna visibly relaxes as we wander around the benching area and meet the dog owners, and despite Fabian's 'manipulate her' advice, the tight bubbling feeling I've been sitting on for days morphs into warm water flowing through my veins. I've given her this, and they've been kind enough to accommodate her. Maybe that makes me an idiot after she unceremoniously dumped me. *She didn't dump you, Adam, remember!* You were friends. Hopefully, you're still friends.

She signs autographs and poses for selfies and answers questions about tennis, before subtly moving the conversation on to dogs. These people can talk about their dogs forever once they've started: the history, the breed, the coat conditioners. It's a masterclass. Anna grins from ear to ear. *She is a nerd.* A smile curves over my lips.

But the more I watch, the more annoyed I get on her behalf. Arty Maroz unleashed the worst aspects of the media and made her nervous, whereas her real fans are so nice, so genuinely excited to see her. She doesn't deserve to be hounded; she works so damn hard. Why isn't she angry about all the intrusion and disruption to her life? Perhaps she is and is trying to keep a lid on it. Lord knows, I can identify with that. *Maybe she was also helping you,*

Adam? Shame burns through me.

"It's lovely not to have the press around," I say. "No drama."

Perhaps if today is relaxed and easy, over time she might recognize that we could have a different relationship that didn't eat into her concentration. If Arty Maroz stopped hounding her and dropped his stupid court case about Pepper, this whole thing could be manageable. I'm a patient guy. I've hung on to my business for ten years, after all.

When I called the Kennel Club earlier in the week and said Anna Talanova wanted to visit, I was expecting all sorts of conditions. But dog people aren't like that, seemingly. They were excited and said they'd never been asked for something like this before. Seriously? There are no celebrities with pets who want to hang around backstage at a dog show? They don't know what they're missing. It's a blast. The dogs are as cute as hell and happy to be fussed over, although Anna and I learn quickly not to touch them if they're about to go out into the ring and be judged.

As we're talking to a lady about her Schnauzer, two small boys appear at my elbow.

"You're that guy!" one of them says as the other one holds up one of my kit dogs.

"The Electronic Man!" the second boy says, waving the kit around. They must be what, ten, eleven years old?

I squat down, grinning. Is this how Anna feels when she's accosted by kids? "Did you like making it?"

He nods, then kneels down and places the kit on the floor. And of course it's the Beagle Bot, Susie's favorite.

"Don't start that running in here!" A woman suddenly looms over his shoulder, looking flustered. "You'll set all the dogs off!" Her eyes catch mine, and they widen.

"Oh, you're that man!" She pats her hair absently. "On the videos."

"I am indeed," I say, standing up and holding out a hand. "Adam Miller."

"It's so lovely to meet you! We just love all your silly jokes on camera, and we adore your kits in our house. The boys spend so much time making the dogs and then ages playing with them after. It's a godsend if I'm honest."

"That's nice to hear."

"Can I have your autograph?" the first boy says, and it makes me laugh.

"Of course!" I say.

I glance at Anna, and she's grinning at me. "YouTube star," she mutters under her breath.

"Stop it," I say with a shake of my head as I sign the boy's exhibition program.

"Are you here exhibiting?" the woman asks. "We'll come by the stand later. It would keep these two occupied."

"I'm afraid not." Why didn't this occur to me? "Perhaps next year."

When we move on, Anna waves a hand around the tent. "Don't let me keep you from your public," she says, still grinning. I roll my eyes at her.

But after an hour of answering questions and talking, Anna's smile is a little brittle.

"Maybe we need coffee, cake, and a rest," I suggest.

"I'm not sure I'm allowed cake," she mumbles.

"Everyone's allowed cake." My lips curve up, and her eyes roam all over my face. I groan to myself. Every time she looks at me like I mean something to her, I want to kiss her. It's one thing to hatch a plan with Fabian, but another thing entirely to execute it.

Kevin turns around from where he's talking to one of the competitors. "Did someone mention a rest? We have a private box where you can watch the show and have refreshments if you like."

I raise my eyebrows at Anna, and she stretches her back, nodding. "I am tired if I'm honest," she says. "But I'd love to see what the dogs do out on the floor."

Kevin gestures back to where we came in and then takes us through a whole series of long corridors through the bowels of the building. We go up a few escalators to a suite with a perfect view of the center of the stadium, and Kevin disappears to fetch tea and coffee and sort out some cake.

"Look at that Pekinese!" Anna says, flapping her hands as it bounds through tunnels and jumps over several obstacles. I grab a program from the table as we settle into a couple of seats. There are so many kinds of competition. Some are about breeds, but others are trials of sorts—obedience, agility, even something they call "dock diving." It's mind-blowing.

She slips her hand into my elbow, and I'm ridiculously thrilled to have her hand back tucked into my side. "I could take them all home," she whispers.

"Some of them are very valuable, more valuable than Pepper. You might have to take out a mortgage on that penthouse of yours."

She laughs. "Perhaps Pepper would like a friend? That Pekinese was *very* cute."

"Are you kidding me? Share all the glorious fuss and attention she gets? She'd be so grumpy."

I squeeze her hand where it's resting on my arm, and she sighs then rests her head on my shoulder, and I have to fight to stop myself from turning to kiss her hair.

"Maybe she'd like a nice boyfriend." She says this so quietly that I almost don't catch her words, but my heart thumps in my chest when I do.

"Doesn't every woman want a nice boyfriend?" I say.

CHAPTER 33

Anna

The Russian voice on the other end of the phone is one I haven't heard for a year, possibly longer.

"Hello, my little one."

My breath lodges in my chest. "Konstantin." I try to keep my tone level but it cracks nonetheless.

"You are doing well, *lyubov moya*?"

I press my lips together at the endearment. "Can't complain."

"You bring credit to the whole academy, Anna. You were always a good girl for Uncle Konstantin."

Cold fingers of ice creep down my neck. "Can I help you with something?"

"It is kind of you to offer," I can almost see his head incline as he says it. I wasn't offering, and he's well aware of that, of course.

"We have an event planned this Saturday," he carries on, "coaching, a tournament. For the hopefuls, you understand. I thought it would be …" He pauses. "… *beneficial* if you came here and coached. To have someone with your profile there, a member of the academy, would be most favorably received, I think."

Go to *Russia*? "This weekend? That's … that's … very short notice." I stammer out. It's Wednesday now.

Silence. *Oh God.* What is his game here? And what does he mean, *favorably received*?

"You have a gap in your schedule at the moment, no?"

Crap, what do I say to that? "Well, I have a lot of preparation and practice to do for the Australian Open. I leave after Christmas in two weeks. I've got a set program that I …"

"But you can train here, and this will be an opportunity to visit your parents. I will send a jet for you."

I've finally persuaded my parents to come to the US for Christmas, but I don't want to tell him that in case he interferes somehow.

"I wasn't planning on coming to Russia. I don't normally come back for …"

He clears his throat. It's a sound of annoyance that I know only too well that in the past would lead to … My chest constricts.

"There's some people you want to impress?" I hurry on.

"Some influential people will be there. It would be beneficial to you to make the connections. It is time you came home and saw your Uncle Konstantin. We will talk. You have people making trouble for you, I think. Arty Maroz. His father causes problems for me also."

I let out a brittle little laugh. *Home.* Interesting word choice. "Arty's a publicity hound. The media are always diving into my business these days. I think Arty has sponsors he needs to keep happy. As have I."

Breathing in my ear, hot and tight. "I hope that wasn't a threat, little one?" His voice has a familiar mean tilt to it.

"A threat? What do you mean?"

"The press, Anna. You wouldn't want to get on the wrong side of Uncle Konstantin, would you?"

"Why would the press be a threat? Building a higher profile for your academies could be amazing. My PR team would be delighted." Perhaps the media provides more of a buffer than I thought.

"I took your parents out to dinner last time I was in St. Petersburg. They were pleased with how well your tennis is going, Anna."

My parents? My father wasn't impressed at how I played in the Billie Jean Cup, and he wouldn't say anything to Konstantin even if he was thrilled. If they went out to eat with him, he must have threatened them.

"It is a shame he had to give up his game," he adds.

Why is he talking about my dad's tennis career? Shit. This is a typical Konstantin conversation. He just wants to remind me he could go after my parents. Dammit, I would love to get them permanently out of Russia. But the reality is, I'm probably going to have to suck this up.

"When would I need to be there?" I say.

"Friday."

Two days away. *Christ.* "Let me think about it."

And he explodes, spitting fury about how I need to watch my step. Eventually, I manage to get off the phone but it's clear that not going is not really an option. I'm shaking when I hang up. I've seen him do this before. It starts with the threats, then someone returns bruised or has some strange, unexplained accident. My stomach turns over. *Russia.* Every time I go, I have a gut wrench that I might never get out again.

I pace around the apartment, staring out of the window across the rooftops of the other tower blocks close to mine. How far does Konstantin's reach extend? Is this building being watched? Adam talked to me about my getting some personal security and I haven't bitten the bullet. I should have listened to him. The only thing between me and someone getting in here is the doorman downstairs. *Stupid, Anna.*

I pad over to the system and lock the elevator.

Then I walk over to the cupboard and grab some tea. Ginseng and chamomile. Perhaps watching a movie tonight would be a good distraction. Something light and fluffy. I pull up Netflix and browse through the options, choosing a romantic comedy and settling in. But ten minutes in, the male character has already knocked a gorgeous woman off her bike and sworn to his guy friends that he's not interested because he's committed to being single forever. It's so unrealistic it makes my eyes roll.

I pause the movie, head back to the kitchen, and take my snacks out of the fridge. Konstantin keeps an eye on what I do, but he hasn't called me in such a long time. I was hoping I'd thrown off that period of my life, but how naive is that? From thirteen to twenty-five—haven't I given them enough of me? My gut is churning with the idea I might never leave it behind.

I want company and a chat, something to take my mind off that call, but who do I have who'd understand? My parents would worry if they knew. Mila? At least she'll get it.

I press her number on my phone, and her throaty voice answers: "*Privet*."

"Hey, Mila. It's Anna." I say, dropping into Russian.

"Hey. You okay?"

"Konstantin just called me. He wants me to go to Russia this weekend to coach." No point in beating around the bush.

"Eh, he's dragged me back a few times. Is it a problem?"

Yes, it's a problem, Mila! He's a monster. But she's always been more involved with Konstantin than I have, and feels she has a duty to him in some twisted way.

"Was it okay when you went back?"

"It was fine." Her voice is flat.

She never talks about anything between her and Konstantin. Maybe ...

"Did he ...?"

"Anna!" she interrupts. "Enough! We don't talk about it!"

Ugh. Maybe we should.

"You're thinking of not going?" she hurries on.

I sigh. "He always makes these threats."

She huffs. "Control is his thing. He will put you in your place, for sure. I wouldn't cross him, Anna. Just don't, okay? He's a difficult man but he's okay if you keep him happy. And we owe him, remember? He gave us this life."

Ugh. We've never seen eye to eye on this. I shouldn't have called her. She's not going to be sympathetic, and if I tried to brainstorm ways to wriggle out of this, I think she'd rat on me.

"We can't ever let it come out, Anna. Remember that," she says. "How great we were at tennis will be forgotten. All our accomplishments will go down the drain; we'll just be victims. Every achievement we make forever will have that tacked onto the end of it. Do you want that? I don't. I am great at tennis—that is what I want my legacy to be."

God, is she right? I say the only thing I can. "Yeah, you're right."

"Let me know if you need anything. I'm happy to help, Anna, always."

"Thanks, Mila. I appreciate it."

And she hangs up. Ugh. That was *not* the conversation I was hoping for.

There's always Adam? A little voice worms into my head. I chew my lip as I stare at the dark windows and the city lights beyond. I should explain to him how it all works in Russia. It might help him understand and make him more cautious about both the friends-with-benefits thing and whatever he's trying to do now. *Be your friend, Anna?* My heart sinks. I want us to be friends, but even as my friend he'd be in the line of fire, completely negating the purpose of ending things with him. I don't want him sucked into the life Mila and I have, forever looking over our shoulders. I glance at my wrist. 7 p.m.

I chew my lip as I tap out:

Are you busy tonight?

My finger hovers over the button before I close my eyes and press send. There's no response for a full ten minutes, and I'm just giving up on the whole idea when a message pops up:

You feel like going out? Dog walk? Pizza? Skydiving?

I snort into my tea.

Not sure my insurance would cover skydiving.

Then I add:

Is the press still hanging around your place?

Only one or two during the day.

Can I come over?

For some reason, I want to escape this apartment and the idea that I'm being watched, and I want to see Adam's Meatpacking place. Nothing comes back for another five minutes.

My apartment is tiny and rundown.

I don't mind if you don't.

Another extended pause, during which I second-guess myself and what I'm doing about sixteen times.

Come over then.

See you in thirty minutes.

I grab all the things I might want—treats for Pepper, a bottle of wine—shove them in a shoulder bag, and put Pepper in her coat. Then I call the car service, and ten minutes later my doorman buzzes up and I'm out the door and into the car breathing a sigh of relief. When did I stop feeling safe here? *Arty Maroz.* I make a face. *And the paparazzi.*

I text Adam when I'm close, and he's right, his building *is* old and dilapidated. He appears in the lobby and holds the front door open as I step out of the car. He's wearing jeans and an old soft flannel shirt, as well as some glasses I've never seen before.

I gesture at them as I walk into the small area by the elevator. "Very nice."

"Oh!" he says, touching his face. "I forgot I had them on."

"I'm surprised I haven't seen you in them before, at Janus's or …"

"They've got high-magnification lenses. Sometimes I wear them if I've been doing a lot of close work, I need them to be able to see electronic components.

They're tiny these days." He takes them off and folds them into his hand.

As the rickety old elevator creaks up past several floors, he says, "You'll have to excuse the state of this building"—he makes a face and gives me a rueful smile—"*and* my apartment."

I flap my hand at him. I understand he's embarrassed, but I lived in some terrible places myself as I was fighting my way around the tennis circuit. I know how hard it is. And he's trying to build a business. None of this stuff is easy.

We shudder to a halt and step out into a corridor with scuffed walls and a badly worn wooden floor. I follow Adam to a door at the far end which he unlocks to reveal a tiny foyer.

I toe off my shoes, he hangs my coat up in a hidden closet, and we head into the main room, which houses a small gray kitchen of four or five cupboards against one wall, a couch, and two armchairs perpendicular to two large windows that look out over the building behind. There's a thick rug on the floor and fluffy blankets on each of the chairs. Two warm lamps cast a golden glow over the whole space. A staircase spirals down from a platform above.

"That's my bedroom up there," Adam says, gesturing upward and shifting from one foot to another. "The bathroom is here." He indicates a door tucked in behind the winding staircase. It's all immaculate.

I grin at him. "It's lovely and cozy," I say, and he laughs. "You're very tidy."

"Janus thinks I have OCD," he says, shaking his head.

I put my bag on his kitchen counter and pull out the wine. "I thought I might have a glass."

He bends sideways and says in a low rumble, "Who are you and what have you done with Anna Talanova?"

I shove his shoulder, fingers connecting into hard muscle, and I'm not sure I needed the reminder of his body or his ability to pin me down.

"Have you eaten?" he adds, and I shake my head and he raises his eyebrows. "No preprepared meal?"

I give him another small push. "Don't give me the sarcasm. They're not that bad."

He pulls his phone out of his pocket. "Let's order something. If I remember correctly, you have a bit of an obsession with Indian?"

"Oh, that sounds like the *best* idea."

Once we've chosen our dishes and ordered our food, Adam finds a bottle opener in a drawer and starts cutting the foil off the top of the wine. "What's got you drinking alcohol tonight?"

"I had a call."

He glances at me as I rest against the countertop next to him.

"A bad call," I add.

"Ah," he says. "Work related?"

A long sigh seeps out. "When I was a young hopeful in Russia, I attended a lot of tennis camps. It's a strange situation. All the training in Russia is run by this guy named …"

"Konstantin Lebedev," he says, and my mouth drops open as I stare up at him.

"How do you know that?" My hand flaps. He's been looking into me? Into this? *Jesus Christ.* My veins turn to ice. What does he know?

"Fabian came across him when he was digging into Maroz," he says, pursing his lips, oblivious to my internal meltdown.

Okay. Okay. I let out a long, controlled breath, but my heart is still thumping in my chest. How thorough is this Fabian guy? How much did he find out? I pace over to look out of the window. Adam or this Fabian guy could blackmail me. *No. No, Anna. Don't be a lunatic.*

When I turn around, Adam is watching me quietly with a soft expression on his face. "Anna. There's no obligation to say anything about your life or your past, to anyone."

"How much do you know?"

"Very little for certain. Fabian had some questions about it, but I didn't ask him to dig any deeper."

I sink down on the couch and put my head in my hands.

The seat indents beside me as Adam sits down. He places a warm arm over my shoulders and pulls me into him, kissing the top of my head. "You're safe with me. You know that, right?"

"Konstantin has asked me to go to Russia to coach," I mumble, and when I say it out loud it sounds so innocuous.

"What, permanently?"

I shake my head. "This weekend. He's invited some of his associates"—I shiver at the word—"to a tennis tournament. They'll be important people he wants to impress. VIPs in Russia."

Adam doesn't say anything, but just runs his hand up and down my back, and I turn my head toward him.

"We don't talk about this ever."

"Talk about what?"

"What happened to us."

He inclines his head. "You don't have to tell me about it if you don't want to, but I'm happy to listen." His hand is still running up and down my back.

How fast has Adam Miller become my safe port in a storm? There's no one else I trust like him, and as soon as the thought flits through my mind, my stomach drops out. My whole life and so few trustworthy friends. But if he's found out some of it, I should tell him all of it. I don't know what to do about this supposed invite, or what it all means, but perhaps he or Fabian could help. I suck in a deep breath.

"Konstantin Lebedev has legitimate business interests in Russia, but he has illegitimate ones, too. The tennis clubs are real but also a front. He uses the young people who come into his academies in other ways, especially if they're not going to make it in tennis. Or maybe it's so rare to make it to the top, that it's all a pretense anyway. A lot of shady characters act as so-called sponsors in his tennis clubs."

"Is Pietr Petrov one of those characters?"

Of course he knows Pietr by name. I talked about that relationship, but I never told Adam the whole story, but I guess it's easy enough to put two and two together. "Yes. But …" I sigh. "For me, he was a better option than Konstantin to be close to." I pick some hard skin off the finger where it fits around my racket. "I thought he was looking out for me," I whisper.

"Christ, Anna. What did he do? How did he look out for you, exactly?" Adam stands and walks across the small space to the windows.

And I don't want to answer those questions. "I'm not sure why Konstantin let Pietr have me. There was something between them that I never understood."

"Have you?" His shoulders hunch as he stares out of the window, his face reflected in the glass.

For a second, I can hardly breathe or open my mouth. "It was all consensual." It comes out choked, and I have to cough to clear my throat. "That's what makes it worse. It's implicit that, if you want to progress in the tennis academy, sponsors are a part of it. The worst of it is that the young girls are eager. They know that, if they want to get out of Russia, have any kind of opportunities, then they have to have a sponsor and keep him happy." My hand shakes as I bring it to my lips. How can I say the next words I need to say? "I was a prostitute, basically."

He turns around and walks back to where I'm sitting, settling back down and putting his arm around me again. "It's appalling that these men think they can 'have you,' Anna, but please don't think of it as prostitution. You were coerced at best. You did what you had to do. You muddled through in a desperate situation. You should congratulate yourself on being brave enough to do it. To make a difficult choice when all the choices were bad."

I snort. "Yeah, but if it happened in this country, something would be done about it."

"Maybe. But there are scandals in sport here, too." He squeezes my shoulder. "Anna, you got out."

How is he so calm? I think it's Adam Miller's superpower. He'd be unruffled during a nuclear holocaust: dealing with problems, working out solutions.

Adam blows out a long breath. "Maybe I should tell you something about my own history, too. Would it help if I shared as well?" He gives me a small smile. When I nod, he takes hold of my hand and weaves his fingers through mine. "When you broke up with me, I accused you of turning on me like someone else once did, and I want to apologize for that before I tell you the full story. It wasn't true. You're nothing like Celine."

"Okay."

"Anyway …" He purses his lips. "You know that thing about boiling a frog?"

"Boiling a frog?"

"Well, if you drop a frog into boiling water, it will leap straight out. Whereas if you put the frog in water and heat the water up slowly, it doesn't jump out and boils to death. That's what happened to me."

"I don't understand."

He sighs. "You of all people probably get how relationships can appear to be so good in the beginning." He gives me a wry smile. "I sat next to Celine in one of my first math classes. Janus and Fabian had taken the last two seats in the row behind her, so I took the seat in front of them. Then I realized I was sitting next to a beautiful woman." He huffs. "Even now I hesitate to say that because she wasn't beautiful, not in all the ways that matter."

He turns to look at me, and his eyes are sad and crimped.

"Celine seemed lovely and kind, and she did lots of things for me. My family isn't like that: My mom is judgmental, my father as quiet as the grave. I can't count the number of times I've had to make stuff happen for myself. If that sounds like I'm whining, it isn't meant to; it made me resilient, but perhaps it explains why I got so sucked in." He sighs. "I've spent ten years trying to justify this."

Oh Jesus. I squeeze his forearm.

"After a while, I felt like I'd hit the jackpot with Celine, and I was all in. I could see my future with her mapped out, and would have done anything to protect it and make it work. But looking back now, there were signs even at the beginning that something wasn't right. Celine would become agitated, and I would calm her down. She was angry sometimes. But everyone has stuff that pushes their buttons, right? So, I didn't think much of it.

"As I got to know her better, the times when she was troubled became more frequent. She'd freak out about random stuff, often other people's behavior. Not mine at first. The oddest thing was that she'd be bent on getting revenge, and I …" Adam runs his long fingers through his hair. "I thought it was silly, you know? The incidents were trivial. They weren't things people had done deliberately; they were just someone being busy or thoughtless. But she took them as a personal slight, and I would reason with her, explain a different point of view, and she responded to that. But then there were a few occurrences …"

"Like what?"

"Her roommate, Ali, turned up one evening at my dorm saying Celine had killed her cat. She was in floods of tears. She told me that Celine was dangerous, and I'm ashamed to say, I laughed. I thought it was some stupid fight they'd had. No one kills someone else's cat, right? Afterward, I realized some people are capable of that, and Ali had been trying to warn me."

"She killed her cat?"

Adam runs his hand through his hair again. "Given what happened later, I'm almost sure she did. After we broke up, I had a conversation with people she'd mistreated in the past." He examines his hands. "Boy, I wish I'd done that sooner."

"God, killing an animal … That's just …"

"I know." He reaches out and squeezes my hand. "So, I asked Celine about it, and she said Ali was crazy and obsessed with her cat. She said it was always catching rodents and eating bad stuff from the trash can outside and she assumed that's what had killed it." He gives me a wan smile. "I feel like such an idiot telling this story."

"Don't. Really. Don't. I understand. People can be so convincing."

"After the cat incident, things took an even more unsettling turn. Increasingly, she wanted me by her side and to spend every evening with her. I even accompanied her to her classes sometimes, and she'd show up for *my* classes too, even though they were for courses she wasn't taking. It was like some weird reverse kind of stalking with my consent. When I tried to talk to her about it, she said she was anxious and kept dreaming I'd be killed if she didn't keep an eye on me. It's one of the reasons I stopped competing in jujitsu. She was agitated whenever I had a match and then … one time when someone defeated me, she squeezed my arm and said, 'Don't worry, Adam, I'll get them back. They don't beat you and get away with it.' I laughed it off at first, but I caught a glimpse of fury in her face and I … I didn't know what to make of it."

"Did something happen to them?"

"No, thank fuck. After we split up, I went back to people because I wanted to check. You must understand that, at first, I didn't think the incidents were anything to do with her. She was always as surprised and as horrified as I was."

"What do you mean by *incidents*? What else did she do?"

"Sometimes it was a small thing like letting the air out of the tires on somebody's car. She also spray-painted *bitch* on someone's parents' front door."

"She did that?"

He nods. "There was a pattern. She'd complain about a person, or I would, and the next time I saw them something would have happened to them or their family. Sometimes they got sick. I just didn't connect the dots." He tips his head back. "I can never forgive myself for how long it took me to see it."

"Adam, it wasn't your fault."

He just shrugs and studies his hands again.

"People got sick! Jesus. What kinds of things?"

"Stomach upsets, joint pains. Something they'd attribute to a virus or an allergy. I've no idea where it would have ended up, but then I started to feel sick, too."

My whole body locks up. I don't know what the expression on my face is saying, but Adam's is ashen. "Oh my God, Adam."

"I still didn't put two and two together. I mean when friends tell you they're unwell and then you get sick, you just think there's a bug going around. And she looked after me when I was sick. She was kind and caring. I didn't think she was *doing* these things. She seemed like a lovely person. She was always helping her neighbors and friends.

"I was sick for months, off and on. I'd have bad pains and feel lethargic and then it would clear up. Just for long enough to convince myself it was nothing to worry about. But Celine kept telling me it was odd and that I should see a doctor!" He lets out a harsh laugh. "I was raised in a household where you didn't complain, you soldiered on through if things weren't too awful."

"I can't believe this."

"Then I found some pills in her purse—it was on the kitchen counter, and

I saw a white packet in there. When I pulled them out, the label said digoxin. I was immediately concerned. Was she sick? Was this why she was anxious all the time? But she was so sensitive, so liable to fly off the handle, that I couldn't ask her before I knew what I was dealing with. So, I took a photograph and asked a friend who was a med student what they were. She said they were a treatment for heart problems, and they had some difficult side effects depending on how you responded to the medication and the dose, and then she described them, and they were exactly my own symptoms.

"I thought this explained everything. Celine had a heart complaint, and I'd somehow ingested her medicine by mistake, like she'd mixed it with food or a drink and I'd unwittingly picked up *her* food or drink. She was sick, and she hadn't said anything." Adam laughs. "I *still* thought it was a mistake."

"Adam, this is horrific."

"Can you understand why I don't talk about it?"

"Absolutely. God."

"Anyway, I talked to Fabian. Best thing I ever did. He immediately saw what I couldn't admit to myself. His brother was a drug addict, and he's come across a lot of strange behavior and paranoid people. He told me he always thought something wasn't quite right about Celine. He said she set all his alarm bells clanging, but he could never put his finger on what was off. This behavior made all kinds of sense to him. Control. Power." Adam laughs. "I was dubious. I'd never met anyone who'd do such a thing, and Celine didn't seem unbalanced at all, just a little overwrought.

"Fabian being Fabian, he hacked into her computer and found nothing except a few encrypted files he couldn't access, which was odd. He can get into most things. But there was also no search history and oddly little personal stuff. He wondered whether she might have other records or another PC.

"I decided it was all ridiculous, so I asked her about the pills, and she flew right off the handle. She said they were for problems she'd had for a long time, and it was nothing to worry about. But something seemed off about her explanation. It lacked detail, a medical history. So, I accepted it, but I told her, if anything was troubling her, she could always talk to me and that I'd understand. Perhaps she knew that I was starting to wonder what was going on.

"And that seemed to be it. Nothing happened for weeks. I stopped feeling sick. Fabian couldn't let it rest, though; he was worried she'd flip and do something more dangerous, administer a more potent drug. He said people like this always escalate things because they need a bigger and bigger buzz from what they're doing and it plays on their mind. I told him not to be so stupid, but his suspicions about her made me more wary. He and I argued: I hated that he'd placed these doubts in my head. Then Fabian got into her phone one day when she'd left it on his kitchen counter and downloaded all her contacts. He painstakingly went through all the people on the list and went to talk to the people she knew. He put together everything they said to him. When he decides to do something, Fabian's thorough.

"When I looked at it, the pattern was so obvious. Dead pets, odd illnesses, anonymous threatening letters, random acts of vandalism. There were even people who had suspected her and taken out a restraining order. I didn't know what to do with what he'd found. And then she took the decision right out of my hands."

"Oh God," I say, but he shakes his head.

"She split up with me. She said it wasn't working out and that she didn't think I trusted her, and she wasn't wrong. Perhaps it got back to her that Fabian was asking around and she was spooked. I didn't know how I felt, but by now I was convinced that she was doing these things and there was something wrong with her. I thought Fabian had threatened her or told her to leave me alone, but he swore he hadn't." Adam gives a half smile. "And I believed him. We have a pact of honesty between us, Fabian, Janus, and me, ever since Fabian got admitted to the ER and lied about what he'd taken. They gave him the wrong drug and he nearly died. Janus lost his shit. But that's another story." He lets out a long sigh.

"What happened then? Did you talk to the police?"

"Janus had a lawyer because he was already working on his business, and he took a look at it and said it was complicated given the number of people and what legal action I might be able to take against her. He said I'd need solid evidence. Everything we had was circumstantial, and the best he felt we could do was to file for a restraining order, like some of the other people she'd known."

"So, she's still out there? Holy shit, Adam, that's insane. Where did she go?"

"I've no idea. She disappeared. She left college without finishing her degree, and I never heard from her again. I sometimes wonder whether she changed her name."

"Christ, I can't believe it."

He laughs roughly. "So perhaps that explains all my strange behavior when we met. I'm pretty broken now, I think. It has played on my mind over the years, conversations we had, how slow I was to realize, why I didn't do something sooner, all the signs I ignored, and her friend Ali and the dead cat." He shakes his head. "It left me deeply wary of relationships with women."

My heart aches for him. How can he still feel he was somehow at fault? One thing is for sure: He isn't broken. "I take back what I said when we were arguing about how you don't understand."

He screws up his face. "It's very different from your situation, I think."

"Not so different."

He laughs at this. "I think the idea of closure is a fallacy. Some things are too bad for that."

"Have you ever thought of trying to find her?" He makes a face, and then I laugh. "Yeah, I can see why you wouldn't want to do that."

"I wanted to put it behind me. Maybe that was wrong. It took me years to feel right in myself, and I couldn't bring myself to rake over it again. I've felt so ashamed."

"Oh God, me too." I suck in a deep breath.

"Do you want to talk now about what happened to you?"

And somehow now I do. "Konstantin had his favorites in the tennis camps. No one ever talked about it. You got taken to places, you met people. I was one, and Mila was another. He liked bestowing favors on the young girls who worked hard. I'm not sure when I became aware that something worse was going on. He'd touch you, you know? A hand around your waist, a finger on your arm.

"One night Mila disappeared from a camp. She came back pale and shaking, and even though we were competitors, we were friends of a kind. She wouldn't tell me what had happened, but she did tell me not to go anywhere with him on my own."

He presses his fingers to his lips. "God, Anna."

"I was fifteen when I was invited on a trip, one of Konstantin's yachts that he liked to take people out on as a treat, as he put it. But as soon as I stepped onto that boat, I realized what was coming my way was anything but a treat. It was full of older men—some sponsors I recognized, some I hadn't come across before—and the atmosphere was creepy. One of those men was Pietr. I hadn't met him before, but he said he wanted to talk to me, and when I look back now, I think he was staking a claim. But I asked him questions and he talked, and he didn't do anything else, and it seemed better than the other options I had, so I kept on talking—as much as I could. I was terrified. Trapped and scared about what was happening on that boat, what I might have to do. People had disappeared, I suspected into the cabins below, though I wasn't sure. Pietr looked at me at one point and said, 'You are frightened I think, little one?' And I nodded. He leaned forward and smiled and said, 'You don't need to be scared with me. Uncle Pietr will look after you.'

"Oh, fucking hell, Anna."

"I was ballsy enough to ask him what that protection would cost me, and he laughed and laughed. He told me how much he liked my spirit and how he would hate to see it broken. He said he thought the reason they'd not had a champion from the academy was because what happened there broke young people's spirit and he was tired of it.

"He said that, if I kept him happy, then I wouldn't have to do anything I didn't want to, and after what Mila had said, that seemed amazing. So, I grabbed at it with both hands and we even shook on it, and to keep him happy I slept with him—not immediately, but later. I still think I got unbelievably lucky. How twisted is that? In many ways, he's an awful man, but he also probably rescued me from something much worse, so my feelings about him are complicated."

"Did you love him?"

"What? Christ, no."

Adam squeezes my hand. "Sorry to ask, I …"

I shake my head. "He liked getting one up on people, particularly Konstantin. That was a large part of his motivation. It was all about power and control. He was obsessed with it, with controlling me. I think I talked to you about it that day we met for coffee." That day seems so long ago now.

He nods. "Christ, Anna, this is so much worse than what happened to me. I can hardly believe it."

I huff out a breath. "If Pietr could have kept me locked up in his estate outside St. Petersburg, he would have done. But, of course, I had to go to tournaments. I think he wanted to prove to Konstantin that he could create a champion, and Konstantin couldn't." I shake my head. "He hated seeing the tennis fans; the idea that he didn't own me entirely drove him mad. He'd put me in the public eye and now he couldn't take it back because people would notice and ask questions, and I realized that made me powerful."

"God, that's why you don't mind the publicity—it kept you safe," he says.

"Yes."

"How did you get away from him?"

"I realized something that he kept a secret from everyone. For all that he wanted to control me, he preferred boys. Maybe he was gay, most likely he was bisexual—I mean he slept with me. But it was unacceptable for him to be with men in Russia. So, another reason he came to the junior tournaments with me was because he wanted to watch the boys play tennis."

"How did you find out?"

"He was always so careful, but we came to the US a few times, and New York was … Well, you know what it's like here. It's the gay capital of the world, and it was a revelation for him. So many men who are out and proud when you come from a country like Russia … He fell in love with a young man and, seeing them together, even though he was meticulous about behaving platonically toward him … By then, I could read his moods very well, and he struggled to hide his feelings. There was a real connection there. This man was thirty years younger than him, but something slotted into place inside me. Like a piece of the jigsaw I'd been missing. Why he made that promise to me."

"Did you confront him?"

"Not in so many words. I told him our relationship, such as it was, was over and that I needed to be free, and he should leave Russia and try and be happy himself. He didn't take it well."

"What happened to the young man?"

"He was never going to be with Pietr. Pietr knew it. He was a young tennis player and would never feel that way about a man like Pietr. He viewed him like a father, an older adviser. Not sexually at all."

"Christ, Anna, these men are monsters."

"I know … Part of me has some understanding for Pietr, I guess, but mostly I can't forget what he did to the teenagers from the tennis camps … what an awful man he was and still is."

"Does he keep in touch with you?"

"Occasionally. But he doesn't like that I know what I do about him. He's concerned I could use it against him, and he hates that. He likes to have the upper hand. Always."

Adam studies his hands again. "Although Fabian didn't gather all the hard evidence, he speculated about the camps and what might happen there." He shrugs. "He's an extremely talented hacker. It's rare that there's no digital trail. Almost impossible nowadays, even just locations can give you away … It might be a lot of work to collect all the proof, but I suspect he could do it if you wanted."

I nod. I'm not sure I'm brave enough, but … Adam leans in and pulls me into his side and I slump into him. He kisses my cheek. "I'm so sorry, Anna, so sorry that happened to you. I can't believe you went through all that."

We both jump as the buzzer to Adam's apartment goes, and I press my hand to my chest with a laugh. I forgot about the food ages ago. Adam disappears downstairs to fetch it, and I'm exhausted from all the grand revelations about something I've held close to my chest for far too long. I hate admitting what happened to me, and I feel numb, but undeniably lighter. I hope Adam feels better, too. To be lured into a deceptive relationship like that …

As we tuck into naan bread and tandoori chicken, he turns on the television and Jimmy Fallon is interviewing some actress neither of us have heard of. Pepper sits at our feet, sniffing the air, and I shake my head at her.

“I think she’s in some teen vampire thing,” Adam says, nodding at the screen. “Susie, my marketing lady, is a big vampire reader and watcher.” And the normality of all this—sitting in a warm apartment on the couch with him chatting and watching TV and talking about it—makes my eyes prickle.

“Does she need feeding?” He gestures at Pepper with his fork.

I grunt. “She ate tonight. She’s just being greedy.”

He puts his plate on the coffee table and heads over to the kitchen, opening a cupboard and coming back with … *dog treats*?

I laugh. “I don’t know who spoils her more, you or me.”

He laughs and says, “Pepper, turn,” and does a circular motion with his hand. To my amazement, she does a circle on his rug, and he holds a treat out for her.

“You taught her to do a turn?”

His ears go a bit red. “Is that okay? I’ve got plans to enter her in the next Kennel Club event. She’s way cuter than the dogs that were there.” He winks at me, and I burst out laughing.

“Lie down,” he says, and she goes straight down onto her tummy, wagging her tail as he holds out another reward.

“Roll.”

And she rolls onto her side.

“Still trying to persuade her to go all the way over on that one,” he adds as he gives her another treat.

“Whoa, Adam, that’s amazing! How long have you been training her?”

“Since I met you really. That first event we went to, she brought me her pink rabbit when I was waiting for you, and she was so eager to play fetch, I thought I’d see what else she could do. The Kennel Club just gave me more grandiose ideas.”

I laugh at this, but it turns into a yawn as I glance at my watch. "Oh dear, it's midnight! My practice is going to be shot to pieces tomorrow." Like it hasn't been terrible for a while now.

"Do you want to stay over?"

The thought of going home … Ugh. Could I weather a night with Adam? He's so genuinely good and … that woman, Celine … How could someone do that to him?

But has anything really changed? I'm still putting a target on his back, aren't I? I can't seem to keep away. Even coming here … Oh shit, I shouldn't have come here and told him all that.

I've been silent too long because he says, "Just as friends, Anna."

"Because that always goes so well for us."

He laughs. "I swear. After talking about all that stuff, sex is the last thing on my mind."

Okay, then. "You only have one bed, right?" I gesture up to the top floor above his kitchen.

"I could easily sleep on the couch."

I sweep my eyes over it. "It looks way too short for you."

The thought of sharing a bed with him, and how well I slept, with Pepper curled up either at my back or his, makes my heart ache for the time we spent at Janus's. I want this ordinary life of couch chats and takeouts so badly—where the biggest problem of the evening is getting Pepper to do a full rollover—that my chest aches.

"We can share a bed, can't we?" I say.

"Absolutely. I promise I won't jump you."

"Me, too," I say, crossing my fingers behind my back.

He takes our plates over to the kitchen and puts them on the countertop.

"Let me show you where everything is."

He leads me up the spiral staircase to a large double bed sitting inches off the floor. Two warm sidelights illuminate the space and a row of built-in closets sit along one wall with a door in the middle.

"The bathroom you saw earlier," he says, pointing back down the stairs.

"Have a look in the cabinet above the sink. There should be a toothbrush, makeup remover, cleanser, and other things."

My stomach plummets. He has all this stuff for women in his cabinet? But … but … he said he hadn't had sex in a long time? I tune back into what he's saying.

"… My sister stays over every so often. She's an accountant and occasionally works in the city."

He heads over to the closet and opens a door to perhaps the tidiest set of shelves I've ever seen.

"Wow."

"What?" He turns around with a T-shirt in his hand and then looks back at the shelves. A reluctant smile curls over his mouth.

"Yeah, fighting against the compulsive tidiness and the desire to sort everything is an ongoing struggle."

"All your T-shirts are in color order."

"You see, you say that, but what other way would you arrange them?"

"As a heap at the bottom of the closet?"

He laughs. "I'm sure you don't have them in a heap, do you?"

"No, but only because my housekeeper does all my washing and ironing and tidies everything away."

"That sounds pretty amazing," he says, holding out the T-shirt to me.

I shoot downstairs and do my business in the bathroom, and when I come out again he's puttering around in the kitchen and putting the dishwasher on. As I head back upstairs, Pepper's claws click on the wooden floor, no doubt following him in the hope of another treat. Bribery, ha! Then his steps hit the stairs, and he appears with Pepper tucked under one arm, chuckling when he finds me cocooned under the duvet.

"You look very cozy."

Normally, I fall asleep as soon as my head hits the pillow, and as he puts Pepper down, I let out a huge yawn and he chuckles again before shucking his jeans and T-shirt and folding them neatly on a chair in the corner.

And now he's just in his boxers, and I try very hard, and fail, not to peek at his chest and his abs. *What am I doing here, despite everything?* It's like my head says one thing but my body does another. He slides under the duvet, reaches out and turns off the lamp on his nightstand and plunges us into darkness. I can dimly make out his jaw and his hair on the pillow next to me from the light drifting up from the living-room windows downstairs.

"Is everything okay for you?" I whisper. "I just turned up here in a panic and didn't ask about your company and …"

His fingers wrap around mine, squeezing my hand. "It's all good, Anna. The business is fine. The numbers are ticking up nicely. I might want to borrow Pepper again sometime."

"Anytime."

We're quiet for a little longer, before he rubs his thumb over my knuckles. "What are you going to do about Konstantin?"

"I don't know. He didn't really give me a choice."

He turns on his side, and I can tell he's looking at my face, so I turn my head toward him.

"Is he dangerous?" he asks.

"Probably. He has this way of threatening people that's very effective. I suspect there'd be reprisals of some sort. I just don't know what they would be."

"How about I talk to Fabian?" he says.

"Oh God. I've never gone against Konstantin. I don't know what would happen."

"If I know Fabian, he'll already have been digging into it. I didn't ask him to do that, but he can't stand crooks or people getting away with things. At the very least we could talk to him, then decide."

"Okay."

"Would you rest easier if I called him now?"

"It's late."

Adam laughs. "It's not late for him—he's a night owl. He won't be in bed. Unless he's with Kate—and if that's the case, he'll just tell me."

He rolls over and unplugs his phone from the nightstand, propping himself up on one elbow. I watch all the defined muscles shift in his back.

"Hey," he says, "I've got Anna with me. She turned up tonight, and Konstantin has insisted she goes back to Russia."

I can hear Fabian's raised voice on the other end of the line.

"Let me put you on speaker," Adam says, and he turns toward me and puts the phone on the bedcover between us. Dammit that's worse—now I can see the smattering of blond hair across his chest.

"Don't go, Anna. Seriously, that guy is dangerous. If shit went down, I don't know how we'd get you out," Fabian says.

"I know."

"I've been digging into him," Fabian adds, and Adam meets my eyes with a smirk. "I've gathered a lot of information. We could meet tomorrow and go through it if you like?"

The very idea I might find out more about this, after all these years. My heart flutters in my chest. "How about after practice, at the Billie Jean King National Tennis Center? Does that work?"

"Perfect. I can run there from my place—it's about nine miles," he says.

"I'll come, too," Adam says. "But not on a run."

"You don't have to …" I start but he presses his fingers to my lips just as Fabian says, "Wimp."

Adam laughs. "Thanks, Fab," he says.

"No problem, I'll see you both tomorrow."

Adam plugs his phone back in and settles back down. I shuffle over to him and curl into his side, and he shifts his arm to wrap it around me.

"Thank you," I whisper.

He gives me a squeeze and kisses my hair.

"Let's see if we can make Konstantin Lebedev go away," he says.

CHAPTER 34

Adam

I'm not sure what to make of Anna turning up at my apartment. If I'm honest, it's wrecked me a little. The first time I met her, I felt she was lonely and needed a friend—and despite her curling around me in bed last night, I think I'm now firmly cast in that role with her. I'm only too aware that I've agreed to it, *again*, but the idea of being friend-zoned now … Two weeks ago, I thought we were heading to a different place, and the loss of what might have been is like a yawning cavern in my chest. I hung on so long with Celine and missed so many clues because she seemed like my dream, and I couldn't bring myself to give it up. Is this just another hopeless dream?

Ugh. Can I not have a relationship with a woman where I don't become so attached? I keep coming back to the question of why Anna would want something more with *me*. People are funny about this kind of thing, imagining that, despite some huge mismatch in status, some amazing person will look their way. She's famous. A multimillionaire tennis player. She's going to end up with another celebrity, some gorgeous guy, because that's how this works. My business is just about washing its face now, but I still sit in a back office designing electronic boards with magnifying glasses on my head and wearing old jeans and a sweater when it's cold.

Anna disappeared early for her practice this morning, and I persuaded her to leave Pepper with me. As I head into work with the world's cutest Papillon at my side, I'm having perhaps the best commute I've ever had. Everyone stops to talk to me, well, to talk to Pepper actually, not because they recognize her from TikTok, but because she's just that delightful. I take loads of videos on the way and end up posting one of a girl cooing over Pepper after getting her permission to share it. I tag Pepper's account and put a comment on it:

> I've got a new coworker, and I'm hoping that this one will work harder than all the slackers I've got in the office.

When I arrive, Susie greets me with a big smile. Well, no actually, she greets Pepper with a big smile and fusses over her and then goes off to find a dog treat.

"Don't give her those! I'm training her to do things for them."

"Like what?"

I take the bag of treats from her hand, and Pepper sits on her little butt and gazes up at me, ears cocked, wagging her tail.

"Roll over," I say, moving my hand to the side.

She lies down then collapses sideways on the floor without quite performing the required roll.

"Yeah, we haven't quite mastered that one yet." Still, I hold out her reward.

"That was awesome, though. Can we video you doing some of that with her later?" Susie says. "Speaking of which, that was an excellent post this morning, boss. Look at you rocking the influencer lifestyle."

I shake my head at her.

"I particularly like the comment about the slackers!" Keith shouts from his desk in the corner.

"Get back to work, you layabout!" I shout back, and Susie giggles.

"They reposted it."

"Anna's marketing team?"

"Yeah. Everyone loves it."

I hold up my hand. "Don't tell me."

The very idea that people are invested … But once I'm in my office and Pepper is happily occupied on a dog bed that Susie has produced from somewhere, I can't resist a peek.

Oh, Jesus! the comments.

She needs to put a ring on that guy!

I don't know who's cuter, him or Pepper!

Adam Miller, I have a dog and I will marry you.

They've even created a hashtag for us: *#Adanna*.

"Susie! Do Anna and I have a hashtag?"

She snorts and appears in my doorway. "I knew you'd look at those messages. You've had the *Adanna* hashtag for ages."

"Oh, fuck."

She grins. "Figures are looking really good this month by the way. All the little kits are selling like hotcakes."

"Yeah," Sean shouts from his corner. "We can't keep up with the orders!"

"Slacker!" I shout out, to laughter. "Now that's something I never thought I'd hear in this business. 'We can't keep up with the orders.'"

Sean bounces into my office. "Want to see the new designs?" he says.

Susie steps forward and lays a set of drawings out across my desk. I gape at the pair of them. "What are these?"

"Susie came up with the idea we could turn some of the electronic kits into cartoon characters, so she drew some cartoons for the existing kits …" Sean shuffles the images to show me the dog ones and the cat we've just launched. "She also came up with a whole bunch of other characters, and Keith and I are seeing whether we can make them into kits."

When I examine the pictures, they're really clever. She's drawn components but distorted and bent them so they look like cute animals. Wow.

"I'll have you know we're a serious electronics business," I say, winking at

Susie.

"Not anymore," Susie says with a cackle.

Sean rolls his eyes. "All marketing people are maniacs."

"I like these a lot," I say, shuffling the papers. "Great job, guys. The drawings are amazing, Susie."

She straightens up and smiles at me. "Thanks, boss."

*

I message Anna a couple of times but there's no response, so I assume she's still on court and head to her apartment building at 3 p.m. to take Pepper home. The doorman is the same guy who was on the night Maroz smashed the desk in, so I ask him about the repairs and whether everything is all right while he fusses over Pepper. He nods and tells me that Anna paid for the damage. Somehow, I'm not surprised she's had to fork out for it.

"Are you here to see Mila?" he asks.

Mila? Mila's here? I tilt my head at him. "I'm bringing Pepper back," I say.

"I'll call up," he adds.

I look down at the floor and take a big breath. The doorman chats to Mila on the phone for a bit and then waves me up.

When I reach Anna's apartment, Mila is standing by the elevator, and I give her a small smile which she returns with a grimace.

"Hi Mila, I'm Adam," I say, holding out my hand, which she takes. "It's nice to finally meet you."

"Same. I'm here to look after Pepper," she says.

"Oh, okay." That's odd. Why didn't Anna text me to let me know that Mila would be here?

I bend down to let Pepper off the leash, and she races into the apartment and rushes around sniffing everything as Mila shakes her head. Then Pepper barrels back toward us, racing to Mila and jumping up, tail rotating like a propeller, and she pushes her off.

"Oh! That dog," she grumbles.

I bend down and click my fingers, and Pepper bounces over to me and I give her a rubdown.

Mila's lips are twisted in an amused smirk. "You can always tell a person by how they respond to dogs. That's how you know I am not a nice person. I don't care about the dog, but you, Adam Miller, you clearly do care about the dog."

I instantly like Mila: She's self-deprecating and direct.

"Thanks for dropping her off," she says.

"I'm just off to meet Anna at the training center," I say.

She makes a face and shakes her head.

"What? Why are you shaking your head like that?"

"Anna's not there."

I straighten up. "What? We arranged to meet there later this afternoon. Where is she?"

She shakes her head again.

"What's with the head shake? You're not going to tell me?" That whole conversation last night … "Well, I'll just wait here until she gets back."

"She won't be back tonight. That's why I am here for Pepper."

"What? Where the hell is she?" My stomach drops through the floor.

She shrugs.

"Look, it's pointless you not telling me. I have a friend who can hack into anywhere, so we could work it out. But it would save us both a lot of time if you'd just tell me."

She sighs. "Hang on," she says, and disappears into the kitchen returning with her phone in her hand. Her fingers fly over the screen as she mutters to herself in Russian, and it isn't nearly as hot as when Anna does it. Am I bad for wishing Fabian was here so he could translate.

She grunts. "Anna says she'll message you later."

Message me later? And where the hell is she? Is this why Anna didn't respond to my messages? *Goddammit, Anna.* Perhaps I should try a different tack. "How about a cup of coffee?" I say, still rubbing Pepper who's now wedged between my legs, body vibrating as she wags her tail.

Mila narrows her eyes at me and walks toward the kitchen. The sound of the coffee maker grinding beans starts up, so I follow her, Pepper trotting at my heels.

"You're a tennis player, too, aren't you?" I say, and she nods.

Then she grins. "Anna and I are big rivals." She shrugs. "But we have known each other a long time. We are with one another at all the tournaments, so we are friends, too."

"Are you based in Manhattan?"

"No. I got here from Spain four weeks ago. Anna and I train together when we can, although we are both too competitive. I like the US. It is more tolerant than most places."

"You trained through the academy system in Russia like Anna, didn't you?"

Her face closes off. How much has Anna said to her about what Fabian has found out? Would she expect Anna to have talked to me about the academies? She must know Anna and I are friends and maybe more from all the media coverage. Perhaps Fabian's strategy of a bit of manipulation would help here.

I shake my head. "Still can't believe that happens," I say.

Her eyes narrow. "What happens?"

"Konstantin. The sponsors?"

Her hands ball up at her sides. "Anna told you about that?" She sounds astonished. Angry. But it's also a confirmation of a sort.

But I'm not a liar, and I don't want to lie to Mila. "Where has Anna gone, Mila?" I say more insistently.

She chews her lip as she stares at me. Then she goes to the fridge and takes out the milk.

"Mila …"

"Russia," she says.

And my stomach takes off in panic. *Shit. Shit.* Fabian *explicitly* asked her not to do that. *Fuck, Anna, what are you doing?*

"For any particular reason?" I say through clenched teeth.

"Konstantin asked her to coach at a tennis tournament." She licks her lips. "He's supported us for a long time. We both owe him."

They both *owe* him? Is she mad? He's an extremely dangerous man. She turns and starts another cup of coffee at the machine.

I will myself to calm down. "Is this tournament like all the other competitions the academy organizes?" I say, and even to me my voice sounds strained.

But now she just looks confused. "What do you mean?"

"I thought it was an opportunity for sponsors to be more 'involved' with those they are sponsoring?" I make air quotes around the word.

She rounds on me furiously. "They are proper contests!"

"I'm sure they are."

She huffs out a long breath.

"I guess you're sworn to secrecy," I say, turning the spoon for my coffee over in my hand, and she scowls at me.

"Why the hell did Anna go to Russia? She's putting herself in real danger," I say.

"You are the one who is putting her in danger! The academy takes care of the people it gets to the top. They are not going to harm someone like Anna who brings them a lot of glory. You have no idea who you're dealing with."

"Yes, I do, and they can do all sorts of things to Anna, Mila. Some visible and some less obvious. An accident? A sudden injury? *Rape?*" A hot sick feeling washes through me.

She leans forward, right into my face. "You are here, talking about this. Do you not think they know about you, Adam Miller? That this apartment could be bugged?"

And oh shit! I never thought of that. She's right, I *am* an idiot. Of course they'll be keeping tabs on their academy players. I pick up my phone and text Fabian.

Have you left yet?

Just heading out the door.

I'm at Anna's apartment. Her tennis pal Mila is here. She says Anna's gone to Russia.

There's no response for about a minute, then:

Jesus Christ! I fucking told her not to go there!

Can you sweep her apartment?

You think it's bugged?

No idea. Do you know how to do that?

Child's play. On my way.

Mila's mouth is set in a grim line. "I don't like you, Adam Miller. You and your stupid hacker friend will put us all in danger. You think you are smarter than the people in Russia? You are children."

She leaves the kitchen, disappearing down the long hallway toward the bedrooms. I think I'm revising my earlier opinion of liking her. And one of us is a real expert in this kind of thing, and it's not me. I bury my head in my hands.

Fabian turns up thirty minutes later, and the doorman lets him up.

He pulls a notebook and pen out of a big bag, followed by various pieces of equipment, including his laptop, and starts a piece of software that scans all the devices connected to the router and Wi-Fi signals. He writes something on the pad and gestures to me to read it:

> After I've done this scan, we're going to sweep for different radio frequencies. See if anything else is here trying to communicate out. We'll need to turn off everything that we think has wireless capability.

I nod, and he puts on some plastic gloves and hands me a pair and I start looking for wireless devices, working my way through the open-plan space into the living room.

Mila comes out at some point, makes herself another cup of coffee, and watches us both. I don't introduce her to Fabian. How much can I really trust her?

After about an hour, Fabian writes on the paper:

Why is Mila here?

I take the pen:

To look after Pepper, I think.

Can we trust her? She could be the bug. Or her phone. What made you think the apartment might be bugged?

She did.

Fabian frowns, then walks into the bedroom she disappeared into without knocking.

I hear her say, "Hey! What are you doing in here?" and then, "Give that back!" Fabian reappears with a phone in his hand, and Mila is right behind him. She tries to grab it from him, but he bats her off and pulls a laptop out of his bag, plugging her mobile into it. He loads a program that starts to run through what's on it.

Mila has stopped trying to fight him and is watching the screen, too. Would she do that if she was doing something nefarious?

Several red lines appear as the software churns through the phone, and Fabian grunts.

"What's this?" I ask, gesturing at the alerts, but he shakes his head.

Don't talk until we know they can't hear us.

I nod, and he starts writing again:

You have some additional bits of code stored on your device. I'm not sure what it does: It could be benign or something more sinister.

He turns the pad toward Mila so she can see. She purses her lips, not saying anything.

The program has taken a copy of what it's found, and he scrolls down through it for a few minutes as I examine it over his shoulder. The code is peppered with Russian words in Cyrillic, with keywords in English.

Looks like some kind of tracking software to me.

How can he tell? But he's probably examined a lot of tracking programs. Mila's face goes red. Then she blows out a long breath.

Fabian writes on the pad:

I can fix it. Did you know it was there?

She shakes her head, then takes the pen from him.

How do I know I can trust you?

Fabian laughs.

You don't. But I've got to be better than the other side,
who are the people that sneaked this onto your phone.
But depending on what it's doing, they might realize
something's up if I stop it working.

She purses her lips again, then Fabian writes:

Any idea how it got on there?

She shakes her head. He makes a face and gestures to me.

We spend the next hour sweeping the apartment. Eventually, Fabian writes:

If they like tracking phones, perhaps they've done
something to Anna's too, so they don't need anything
in the apartment.

"Can we talk now?" I say.

"Yeah," he answers. "I'm pretty sure there's nothing here. I'm quite surprised. Perhaps Anna already had it checked."

"That would make sense."

Mila is sitting on the couch. Fabian has put her phone in the bathroom at the other end of the hallway so, if the phone is listening, it won't hear what we say. Maybe Mila was trying to distract us with her suggestion of bugs. Frustration burns down my spine.

"Do you want to tell us why you suggested there might be bugs, and what's on your phone?" I say to her.

"Not particularly. You could be anyone. You, too," she says, waving her hand toward Fabian.

"Fine," I say.

"You want a coffee?" he says to me.

"Sure." I follow him into the kitchen.

Fabian writes on the notepad that's still on the countertop:

We should search Anna's computer while we're here.

I nod. I take Fabian through to the study Anna showed me that first fateful day when I was supposed to stay with her, and he sits down at the computer and sets up his laptop. All this second-guessing and trying to work out what's going on is making the hairs on the back of my neck stand up. It reminds me so much of the Celine fiasco, and something I can't quite grasp flashes across my mind and is gone before I even know what it is. A familiar yawning dread grips my chest: All the endless unanswered questions, the looking for a solution or some clue to the truth. I never would have said I'd become addicted to the truth, but now I am.

Mila appears in the doorway.

"What are you up to?"

"A search. Why? What are you doing?" Fabian asks.

"You're searching her computer? Going through all her private stuff?" She jerks her chin at me. "And you said the other side was worse." Her eyes narrow. "Don't think I won't tell her about this."

"Be my guest," I growl at her. "But when you tell her everything we're doing, feel free to mention the bug on your phone and just be sure you're not putting her in more danger yourself."

CHAPTER 35

Anna

The low, murmured conversation between one of the players and a coach drifts across the icy night air as I head out of the tennis stadium into the darkness. I'm training hard and spending as little time as possible within reach of Konstantin or anyone else he might want to put me in front of.

Fabian told me not to come here at all. But after looking at Adam's tousled toffee hair when I woke in his bed at dawn this morning, I knew I couldn't throw what he and I have away, pretend to be his friend when I want so much more. I have to keep him out of it—this is my problem to solve, not his or Fabian's. I have to fight like I've fought for everything else. My father's words drummed into my head: "Never back down from a fight, Anna!" Konstantin will use every opportunity to remind me that I haven't escaped his clutches, and until I can pry my parents out of Russia, maybe I'll have to put up with his manipulations.

Midmorning, a text message appeared on my phone:

> The chase always makes the prize so much sweeter, don't you think, my beautiful Anna?

So, I've stayed on the indoor courts as long as possible this evening, coaching late into the night, to the delight of all the coaches and the tennis hopefuls. But I'd forgotten the creeping sensation of being watched, the prickle on the back of my neck. Everyone here is on his payroll. What are they doing to these young people? I shouldn't have come back, but ultimately, I'm not sure I had much of a choice.

We're eight hours ahead here, and Adam's messages and calls started at about 2 p.m. today, but I can't bring myself to talk to him. Being back here is making my skin crawl, and I can't face having a normal conversation with a normal person, or even explain to him why I came. I just want it over and done with and to get back home. My New York home. My only real home.

Why did I so willingly accept a relationship with Pietr? It's hard to remember that frightened young girl. Although that word, *accept*: It was never a choice. Chills shiver through me. I was so naive, flattered by what I thought was the attention of a rich older man. Away from home, I had no one to pull me aside and give me advice. I was even grateful for the buffer he provided from Konstantin. Grateful! What a nightmare it was. How controlling Pietr was. He treated me like an immature little girl, and I was, I really was, but Lord knows I lost that naivete fast.

My eyes scan over the teenagers heading toward the buses to take them back to the hotel. The coach wraps an arm around a boy as he talks to him, and I look away. Could I ever do anything about all this? God knows how much danger we'd all be in if I did.

I messaged Pietr before I left, telling him I was coming here and asking whether he would be in St. Petersburg. I don't know why I did that. Because he'd expect it? There's still some part of me that's concerned about his reaction. He's less of a threat than Konstantin because I have ammunition on him, but he's still terrible in his own way.

And Mila. Konstantin's focus on her has never waned, though she's never wanted to talk about it. I think she's always resented that I got Pietr, despite the fact he is his own kind of evil.

I glance at my watch: 10 p.m. What would I be doing if I was home on a Friday evening? Thank God the tournament is tomorrow, and my flight is booked out of here tomorrow night. But as I step onto the bus, my phone buzzes with a message:

> Tomorrow, we are having breakfast together, my little one. In the hotel restaurant overlooking the water. 8 a.m.

Konstantin. I turn and scan the parking lot. Is he watching? I put my hand over my pocket. I brought another phone with me and got an additional SIM at the airport. It's something Mila and I started when our phones were confiscated at an early camp and we felt trapped. Mila got us a couple of small handsets, and after a few years I replaced mine with a tiny Android smartphone I can almost hide in the palm of my hand.

Did one of the coaches tell Konstantin we were finished? What a game of cat and mouse. When I scroll back up the messages on my phone, there's a message Pietr sent earlier saying he's going to be here this evening. I send a text back:

> I'm eating with Konstantin at 8 a.m. tomorrow. Join us?

His answer comes through as I'm settling into my seat:

> Already arranged.

Something cold shivers down my spine. I thought there was some bad blood between them, but they're clearly talking to each other on some level.

*

What with the time difference and the fact I had next to no sleep on the plane over and then went straight into a day's coaching, I wake late, blinking up at the hotel ceiling. I take the fastest shower and clothing change in history and head down to find the restaurant, which turns out is all plush banquette seating and white tablecloths. I've put on a dark suit to appear businesslike, my hair drawn back into a tight bun. When the hostess walks me over the thick brown carpet to a table tucked away in a corner alcove, Konstantin is sitting with two other men. His henchmen, no question. They're always around.

He stands up and leans over, kissing my cheek. "Anna," he murmurs. "I heard the practice went well yesterday."

"Yes, it did. Your academy is doing well I think." I smile. "You have an excellent selection of players. I could barely keep up!"

If I can keep this about the tennis and the coaching, it might not be so bad.

He inclines his head. "I doubt that very much." His cheeks are flushed as he sinks back down into his chair, straightening his cutlery on the table. Has he already been drinking this morning? "I hope your boyfriend is enjoying his night?" he says, as I slide into a seat at the white tablecloth.

I falter a little. It's midnight in the US. Is he referring to Adam? Why would he say that specifically? "Which boyfriend?"

Konstantin smiles, his lip curling. "You have more than one? The one you have been seen everywhere with, the one in all the newspaper articles. Your dynamic young tech entrepreneur, Anna."

Adam would laugh if he could hear this description. But Jesus, hearing it from Konstantin's lips is somehow so much worse. Though I still feel a hot burn of vindication: I was right to be worried. Of course he's on their radar, and I put him there because I didn't think it through. This involvement with me has been anything but positive for Adam. Apart from the fact I've had some of the best times of my life with him, I have led him into nothing but trouble.

I wave my hand. "It is something we do for mutual benefit. He's not a boyfriend, although you know how the media likes a story." I give him a wan smile.

Konstantin purses his lips. "Maybe he is interested in your money so he can support his business. Perhaps these American men will always be after your money, Anna. How would you know?" His puckered lips makes him look like a snake.

My stomach turns over, and I open my mouth to make some retort, but the waiter appears at our table and when I look up, Pietr is right behind him, a tight smile on his face.

"Pietr," I say, standing up as he steps forward. He slides a hand around the back of my neck, and his touch is like an assault. I turn my head at the last minute as he tries to kiss me on the lips, and his mouth grazes across my cheek. He's scowling when he draws back.

Pietr strung me along for such a long time, making me think he was acting in my best interests. But his desire for control eventually got the better of him, and he couldn't hide the rages. I'd been independent for years and didn't understand the expectations he had. If he wanted to contain and dominate my life, he had to travel with me, which often he couldn't do. He was furious about it, but tournaments were vital and the feather in the academy's cap. So, one of his handlers would come along and give me instructions. Pietr hated that compromise and would frequently explode in fury. He's never accepted our separation, and despite my desire to use him as a buffer against Konstantin here, I can see from his tight expression that anger is seething under every action. Damn, why did I message him?

"It's good to see you, Anna," he says.

"Konstantin was kind enough to invite me," I reply.

Konstantin and Pietr exchange a glance. Pietr has houses all over—here, New York, London. He wanted a wife on his arm and told me so repeatedly.

"An invite! What are you talking about? You don't need an invitation! This is your home. Your home with me."

I learned a long time ago to keep quiet when he said something delusional.

"Yes, you will coach here I think, long-term," Konstantin interjects. "When you retire. In our camps. I am pleased how excited everyone is to have you here."

Over my dead body.

"Konstantin and I have your best interests at heart, of course," Pietr says, sitting down in his seat and flapping a napkin over his lap, a dull red mounting at the base of his throat.

I almost want to laugh. They've been biding their time. And *they* is the operative word here, isn't it? Did Pietr do some deal with Konstantin to get his hands on me when I was younger? I wonder whether all the speculation in the papers has prompted this little show of … I don't know what … Control? Strength? A reminder that I belong to them? This is what Konstantin called me back for. Perhaps Pietr is furious about Arty or Adam. Are they watching me? Adam? New York is my home. I have my visa, and my lawyer has told me that a green card should be no problem when I'm ready. I am never coming back to Russia. I roll my lips together.

A smile twists over Konstantin's mouth, and he leans forward and runs a finger down my arm. I will myself not to react. But Pietr's eyes narrow on Konstantin's hand.

"My beautiful Anna, I have waited a long time. I am pleased you have been so successful. You will add a lot to the academy in the future, show all these young hopefuls what's possible, if they work hard and please the people that look after them. Like you." He picks up his glass and toasts me, sipping the viscous brown liquid and watching unblinking like he's ready to strike, fingers twitching on the table. "This speculation in the press about your relationships, it is … perhaps … not the right message to be giving." He tilts his head.

This is about Pietr. When I glance at him, I'm shocked to find his eyes are almost rabid now. I can't believe he still thinks he owns me somehow. *Careful, Anna.* Who knows what they might do here?

I shrug. "I cannot control what they print, and it's all about money, as you know. The more interest there is in my personal life, the more column inches, and the more sponsors pay."

"Are you lying to your Uncle Konstantin now, Anna?"

I take a sip of my water. "Lying? What do you mean?"

His eyes flick to Pietr, whose nostrils flare. "You need to stop messing around with men, Anna!" Pietr barks, and Konstantin places a restraining hand on his arm.

"Adam Miller will be out of the picture soon enough, Pietr," he says quietly.

Cold runs like rabbits down my back. Out of the picture? What does that mean?

I smile at them, as genuinely as I can muster. I want them to think I'm playing their game. "Of course!" I say. "Why would you think otherwise?"

"Well," Konstantin says, perusing the menu. "Let's hope there's no lasting damage."

CHAPTER 36

Adam

Fabian and I got nowhere in Anna's penthouse yesterday with Mila and her sulking and tight-lipped grimace. I pace about my small apartment, looking out at the blank back façade of the building behind mine through my living-room window. Am I destined to spend my life looking at brick walls? No messages from Anna, despite me blowing up her phone. Fuck, what is going on out there? Is she okay? I text Fabian:

Do you think I should go out there?

Where?

Russia?

If you're going, then I'm coming with you.

Then:

No way are you going out there on your own.

I pull up a search engine and examine the flights, but I'm wracked with indecision. My stomach aches, reminding me that I should eat something, but when I examine the contents of the fridge, there's nothing but two lemons, milk, a stick of butter, and three beers. I grab my keys from the kitchen countertop and head out into the cold night air.

Outside, the strings of lights above the stores and across the streets seem almost incongruous. How can Christmas be only five days away? I finally told my mom I'd be home on Christmas Eve, but the idea of going anywhere when Anna might be in trouble makes the acid in my stomach worse.

Once I'm in Chelsea Market, I wind through the central corridor of the building to the food store. A crowd of people are singing and laughing drunkenly up ahead. As a guy comes reeling in my direction waving his arms, I step to one side, but he lurches the same way and careens into me, crushing my arm painfully. Grabbing his shoulder, I try to steady him.

"Careful, buddy." I smile at him, but he has the glazed expression of the truly drunk as he moves past me toward the doors. I twist to watch him go, then turn back to the Christmas revelers in front of me and stretch out my elbow. I'm such a Scrooge. I hope that drunk guy is okay.

In the store, I buy a roast chicken, vegetables, and potatoes and head back to the apartment, sticking it all in the oven on high heat. When it's warmed up, I perch on one of my bar stools in my small kitchen and shovel it down my throat. Gradually, my stomach stops grumbling.

I flip my phone over in my hand. Anna's still not responding, and we can't find out or do anything here. There's no alternative: I have to go to Russia.

But as I sit down at my computer to examine the flights again, the world tips sideways a bit and I almost miss the seat. *Jesus.* I place a steadying hand on the table, blink at the screen, and then stand up again. Maybe that was just something … I walk over to the sink for some water. But sweat is pouring off me, and my hand shakes as I lift the glass to my mouth. My stomach churns. Oh fuck, have I got *food poisoning*? That's all I need. That chicken probably wasn't okay. The countertop swims in my vision as I put the glass down. I've got to lie down. I stagger over and stretch out on my small couch, and the world tips a bit again. *Fuck, this is bad.*

I pick up my phone to tap out a text to Fabian:

Food poisoning.

And that's all I manage to type in because the screen is swimming and my heart is a rapid flutter in my chest.

I rest my arm over my eyes, and the last thing I remember is the clatter of my phone and the pain in my hand as it hits the floor.

CHAPTER 37

Janus

I blink up at … nothing. A dark ceiling: The red numbers of the projector clock show 1:12 a.m. *My phone is vibrating.* The only person who calls me at this time of night is Fabian. I fumble for it on the nightstand and it drops to the floor with a thump. When I rescue it, the screen says *Unknown number.* Fucking Fabian and his burner phones. I swipe up.

"This better be good, asshole," I grunt.

Silence. Then a small voice says, "Janus?"

And I wake right the fuck up. "Anna? Is everything okay?"

"I don't think so. It's about Adam." Her words wobble down the line at me. She doesn't sound like herself at all.

"What? What about him?"

"It's a long story, but I'm in Russia at the moment, and there's a few people I know here …" She trails off. "I can't explain now, but they might have done something to him, Janus. I need you to check on him."

"Of course, of course," I say.

"I don't know what to do, I …" Her voice starts to rise.

"It's fine. I'll go and make sure he's all right."

Beside me, Jo props herself up on her elbow. "What is it?" she whispers.

"It's okay, go back to sleep," I tell her, clearing my throat.

Tucking the phone under my chin, I push out of bed, pull on my boxers from the floor, and grab my clothes off the chair where I threw them last night.

"Where is he? His apartment?" I ask Anna.

"I have no idea." Her voice breaks.

"What made you think these people had done something to him?" I say, buttoning my fly.

"I'm with them now. They said …" Her voice rises again. "They hoped there was no lasting damage …"

"*No lasting damage?*" Oh fuck. *Oh, Jesus Christ.* "What the fuck are you doing with them, Anna? You're in more danger than him. Get the hell out of there."

"I will. Just …"

"I'll find him and fix it, Anna. Promise me you'll leave, right now."

"I'll be fine. Just call me when you find out anything."

Fuck.

"Where are you?"

"St. Petersburg. Please. Just call me when you track him down."

"Goddammit!"

"Janus?"

She doesn't need me to lose my shit, does she? "On this number?"

"Yes. It's just a precaution."

"Yeah, yeah. Get out of there. Now, Anna. You hear me?"

"I will, okay. Just message me as soon as you know." She hangs up on me.

I pull my T-shirt over my head as Jo props herself up in bed.

"What the hell …?"

"That was Anna. There's some problem with Adam. I'm going to go to his apartment to see what I can find out."

"I'll come with you," she says, flinging back the covers.

"No, you stay here. If there's trouble, having you here with access to a computer system or covering things for us might be helpful. They said something to Anna about 'no lasting damage,' as though something had been done to him. Fuck. Do you think it's worth calling around the hospitals?"

She nods. "I'll call Kate. If she pulls the doctor card, she can work through the hospital stuff much faster than I can. Who's *they*?"

"Some bastards in Russia that Anna knows."

"Where is she?"

"In Russia with them."

"Holy shit! Is she okay?"

"I don't know."

"Just be careful if you're going into his apartment."

"Yeah, that's a good call. Perhaps I need Fabian with me."

"I'll tell Kate to send him."

In minutes, an Uber has accepted my trip on the app and I'm on the street waiting, tapping my phone against my leg. Late at night is so blissfully quiet in New York, and a minute later a gray Hyundai appears and we're speeding toward the Meatpacking District.

My phone vibrates in my hand. Fabian.

"Hi, Fab."

"I'm on my way. Don't go in without me," he growls. "I mean it, Janus. Who knows what shit they'll have done if they got to him?"

"Oh, fuck. I should have brought some tools."

"I'm on it," he says, and hangs up.

By some miracle, he arrives at Adam's place not long after me. Kate's with him, talking to someone on the phone.

Fabian surveys the intercom and presses an apartment button. "Come on, come on," he says, pushing it several times.

"What are you doing?"

"Trying to get in."

"Can't you pick the lock?"

"This'll be faster," he says.

I lean forward to examine the name on the buzzer, and it says *JESUS* in bright red lettering.

"What the fuck!" A loud voice suddenly reverberates out of the speaker right next to my ear.

Fabian pushes me out of the way. "Jesus, it's Fabian and Janus. We're friends of Adam's. We think someone might have ..."

"You pricks!" he shouts. "You can't leave him alone even in the middle of the night?"

Fuck.

"No man, look at your camera. It's not the press. It's Fabian. You remember me, we met about five years ago, shared some K I was experimenting with at the time. We wouldn't be here if something wasn't wrong, Jesus. Adam's in danger. Serious danger. Let us in."

There's silence. "What kind of danger?"

"We think some Russians got to him. Let us in, man."

"Fuck. Fuck. Fuck," comes back muttered through the intercom. The door finally clicks as Kate finishes her conversation.

She shakes her head. "No record of an Adam Miller at any of the New York hospitals," she says as Fabian vaults for the stairs, and Kate and I bound up behind him.

By the time we hit the fifth floor none of us can breathe, but we get to Adam's studio apartment, and a guy, who I take to be Jesus, mainly because he's in his pajamas with his hair standing on end and doesn't look like a member of the FSB, is outside the door with a key in his hand.

"Adam gave me the new key," he mutters, scowling at us.

Fabian sets down his backpack and pulls a few things out of it, including a gun. Jesus holds up his hands.

"Holy shit, Fab."

"Just a precaution," he says, waving at Jesus to put his hands down.

He presses a button on a device and gives it to Kate. "Geiger counter to check for radioactivity. Just to cover ourselves."

"I'm going to open the door on a surprise, okay? We need to be wary of it triggering something."

"You wanna look on the fire escape first? You can see right into his living room," Jesus says.

Fab meets my eyes. "Go," he says, and Jesus beckons me into his apartment across the hallway and shows me some rickety ironwork outside his bedroom window. I climb onto his bed and out of the window, testing my foot on the platform that wraps around the corner of the building.

Peering through Adam's windows, I can't see much, but then I spot him. I pull out my phone. "He's on the couch, Fab. Hand dangling down, not moving. I can't see anything else."

"Goddamn it."

A bang ricochets in the distance, and the door bounces open and hits the wall on the far side of the room. Fuck, he's going in.

"Freeze!" Fabian shouts. "Put down your weapons. We are armed and will shoot to kill."

A laugh bubbles up inside me. *It's just nerves.* And shit, I'm the backup! I push on the window trying to break in, but it doesn't budge, so I scrabble back along the fire escape and in through Jesus's window again. When I reach Adam's apartment, Kate is on her knees next to Adam, talking to him but getting no response, pulling up his eyelids and holding his wrist. Fabian is stomping around at the top of his spiral staircase, presumably checking for intruders.

"Is he alive?" I gasp.

"Yes." Kate blows out a long breath. "But his pulse is very thready." She pulls out her phone and dials 911.

I pick up the Geiger counter from where she's dropped it on the floor. There's no reading for radiation. I listen as she talks with the emergency responder.

"Shouldn't we just take him? Wouldn't it be faster?" Fabian says as he hammers down the stairs from the platform that houses Adam's bedroom.

"They'll be here in minutes, Fab, and it's safer. They have all the right equipment. If he arrests on the way, I might not be able to do anything."

I can see Fab doesn't like that answer. He puts his hand on Adam's hair.

"Come on, buddy, I can't lose you," he says.

My whole throat swells up.

"Help me turn him onto his side," Kate says.

It really is only minutes before the paramedics arrive, and of course they know Kate. We manhandle Adam down the stairs—because the elevator in his building won't fit a stretcher—and into the waiting ambulance.

"One person," the paramedic says, and Kate doesn't hesitate—she jumps right on in.

"We'll see you there," Fabian says.

"NYU Langone," the paramedic adds as the doors slam shut and the ambulance takes off, lights flashing.

I've already booked an Uber, which turns the corner minutes later, and Fab and I pile in the back. His leg is bouncing on the seat next to me as the store windows with all their colorful Christmas lights flash past and we speed through the empty streets.

"Those fucking bastards. I'm going to unleash an unholy war on their fucking operations. They won't know what's fucking hit them. They think they can mess with Adam Miller? Think again, amigos."

I reach out and press his shoulder. "Let's just see Adam through this first, all right?"

"If he's even okay after this. If he's not, I …" He leans forward and slams his fist into the seat in front and I grip his arm as the driver glowers in the rearview mirror.

"He's okay," I say.

"Don't thump my motherfucking seats," the cabbie says.

"I knew. I fucking knew Konstantin Lebedev was dangerous as soon as I found out that information about the camps. I fucking told her not to go out there. Why the hell did she go? Fuckity fuck fuck."

What? What the hell's been going on? "You were looking into Anna? And you warned her? Who's Konstantin Lebedev?"

"He runs all the tennis academies in Russia. He's a crook, a pedophile. An extremely creepy guy."

"God, I hope Anna's okay," I start to say, and, oh Christ, I haven't messaged her!

"Fuck knows what they'll do to her if they've done this to Adam," Fabian says, slamming his fist into the seat again.

"Don't hit my fucking seats!" the driver shouts again.

But I'm already fumbling with my phone, and I fire off a message.

> We've got Adam. Found him unconscious, but alive. Thready pulse. We have no idea what's wrong with him. Anything you can find out would be a bonus.

Then for good measure, I add:

> If you need leverage, threaten them with someone hacking into their systems.

"I don't know if she's even with them. They're eight hours ahead, I guess. She said she was getting a flight back tonight."

Just as the words leave my mouth, my phone rings in my hand and Fabian's head snaps around.

"Anna," I say, and Fabian takes the phone right out of my hand.

"Anna. This is Fabian. Put Konstantin on."

How does he know she's *with* this guy?

He listens for a beat. "I don't care. Put him on."

Another pause. "Anna, just put him on."

There's a few seconds of silence while he drums his fingers on his thigh.

"Listen up, asshole. You don't know me and you never will, but I'm someone you don't want to be on the wrong side of," he growls. "I can hack into anywhere, find anything, and Adam Miller is a friend of mine. If he doesn't survive whatever you've done to him, you'll never be able to get any technology to work again without me taking it down. If you touch one hair on Anna Talanova's head, then your organization will go down … for good."

He hangs up.

"Didn't we need to talk to Anna?" I say.

"I don't give a fuck about that."

"Are you going to take his systems down?"

"It's already done."

"*What?*"

"How did you know she was with him?"

"Probability, man. She'd call you as soon as she found out something was wrong, wouldn't she?"

The Christmas tree in Madison Square Park appears over his right shoulder outside the car window.

"Why the hell were you looking into this Konstantin guy?"

Fabian takes me through his conversations with Adam, how he came across Konstantin Lebedev and how he became increasingly suspicious of what he was doing. He also tells me he found links to people he'd come across before in Russia, and about an ex of Anna's called Pietr Petrov. "Anyone who gets to a position of power in Russia … they're as shady as fuck. I managed to hack into Lebedev's systems a couple of days ago. I started a virus running before I even stepped out of the house."

"Christ, didn't you think that would put Anna in even more danger?"

His hand comes down on his thigh in a sharp slap. "She can't be in any more danger than she's already in, Janus! Who knows what those psychopaths might do when she's sitting in front of them? It's my bargaining chip to get her safely out of there … These assholes … they think they can achieve anything by being thugs like this?" He shakes his head. "They are going to burn."

He's a maniac, Fabian, but one I'd always want on my side.

*

When we arrive at the hospital, there's no sign of Kate or Adam. The woman behind the desk says she'll get word to Kate as soon as she can, but Fabian messages her and she appears almost immediately and nods at the nurse, beckoning us through.

"How is he?"

"He's in a coma," she says.

When I make a horrified face, she shakes her head. "He hasn't deteriorated since we brought him in." She glances between Fabian and me. "Has he got any health issues that you're aware of?"

"No. He's pretty fit I'd say. What's wrong with him?"

"We don't know. There was nothing obvious on his CT scan. His heart rate is down, and his blood pressure is low. We've got him on a saline drip, and his blood sugar is very low so we're giving him dextrose. Given the Russian connection, our poisoning specialist is on his way in. We've taken bloods and urine, and we're doing a tox and infection screen. I've been on the phone with the specialist ever since we got here."

"Oh fuck," Fabian says, pacing across the floor. "The Russians have a bad history with polonium."

Kate shakes her head. "There's no trace of radioactivity. We've just got to be optimistic right now. We don't know precisely what it is as yet, but we've probably ruled a few things out given how he's presented. The profound hypoglycemia is very odd," she mutters.

"Does your specialist know anything about Russian poisons?"

"Quite a bit. He treated two polonium cases."

"Holy shit."

"It's going to be a while before we nail it down. Toxic substances are wide-ranging and varied, some take a long time to act, and it can depend on the dose." She pats Fabian's arm. "He's in the best place he can be."

CHAPTER 38

Anna

Konstantin's face is red when he comes off the phone. "You and your little fuckboys. Who are you to threaten me?" he hisses, leaning toward me over plates of food.

Jesus, what did Fabian say to him?

Pietr frowns. "What's going on?"

A man appears at Konstantin's elbow and bends down to whisper something in his ear.

"Yes, yes I know!" he shouts, waving him away. Then the phone at his elbow rings, and Konstantin's face gets redder.

He picks it up, and all I can hear is excitable squawking on the other end.

"I fucking know! What I need from you is how he got into our systems." He hangs up.

He's in some system of Konstantin's? *Holy shit.* Am I elated or terrified? Will Konstantin try and exact revenge? With me, or …

Konstantin blows out a long breath, fingers drumming on the table. I don't think I've ever seen him rattled before. A waiter appears by our alcove with a coffee pot and is waved away by one of Konstantin's henchmen. It's like we're insulated in our own little bubble. I can see people at other tables, but we're too tucked away to even attract their attention. *You're trapped, Anna.*

"Who is this man?" Konstantin barks.

"Who?"

"This man on your phone." He jerks his chin up.

"I don't know."

His eyes narrow. "You called him."

"I rang Janus Phillips, who's a friend of Adam Miller's. I didn't get Janus, I got him. He told me to put you on. I have no idea who he is."

Konstantin clicks his fingers, and the sidekick returns to the table.

"Don't worry, Anna. We will go after him. Find out all known associates of Janus Phillips. If they breathed next to him, I want to know about it."

Fuck. I trust this Fabian guy knows what he's doing. Well, if Konstantin can bluff, maybe I can bluff, too. Adam said Fabian could hack into anywhere, didn't he?

I study Konstantin for a bit. "I hope your technology guys are excellent, Konstantin. I'd make very sure your secrets are out of reach."

His mouth tightens. My eyes flick toward Pietr, whose head is down. When he raises his head, his face is white. Whoa, what's on their system? Something about Pietr?

"Konstantin, that's …" Pietr starts.

"Silence!"

"What the hell is going on?" Pietr asks.

"Some person has taken down our computers. They are trying to blackmail us."

He clicks his fingers at me. "Call him back."

How much leverage do I have here? Possibly very little. I pull out my phone and press Janus's contact details.

"Anna?" Janus says.

"Konstantin wants to talk to whoever he was talking to before."

"Tell him he'll call him back."

We sit for a tense few minutes. Then Konstantin's phone rings on the table.

"How does this snake have this number?" he growls, picking it up and putting it against his ear. "I will tell you what your friend has been given, if you take out of my systems whatever it is you have put in there," he grits out through clenched teeth, eyes flicking over me for a second.

Then he slams his hand on the tablecloth. "You don't threaten me, you worm. You will die quietly one night ..." he starts, and then he takes his phone away from his ear. "He hung up on me."

"Well, gentlemen," I say, with a fake smile, "this has been fun, but I think we have a tournament to run today before I go back to the States."

Pietr snorts. "You don't think you're just going to walk out of here, do you?"

I frown at him. "What else would I do?"

"Stay here in Russia where you belong!"

"I'm competing in the Australian Open in a few weeks, Pietr." I glance down at my watch, and my hand is shaking when I look at it.

Pietr's face goes red, and Konstantin chuckles. Then his hard eyes turn toward me, narrowing.

"You may think you have won this round, little one, but I will make sure you never escape."

CHAPTER 39

Anna

When I board the plane that evening, the crew are in a celebratory mood given it's so close to Christmas, and one of them hands me a pryanik in a little paper bag. When I pop it in my mouth, the spice and ginger takes me right back to my grandmother's house, and for a second it makes my eyes sting. As I'm putting my hand luggage into the overhead locker, a text lands in my phone from Mila:

> Have you seen what's happened to Arty?

A photograph of a newspaper article lands in my phone:

DOWNHILL SKIER CHARGED WITH MONEY LAUNDERING

> I guess he's got bigger fish to fry than tormenting you, girl.

Oh God, no wonder he wanted money. I slide into my seat, pull up the newspaper website, and read the whole article. The implication is that it's been going on for several years, but doesn't seem to be connected to the tennis academy. My skin crawls, but I can't also help the tinge of relief creeping through my veins.

I stare out the window and watch the baggage handlers loading the hold. I'm still half expecting a couple of men to materialize at the front of the plane to slap handcuffs on me, or for an airline official to ask me to follow them back to the terminal, or for me to fall unexpectedly sick halfway across the Atlantic. But all that happens is another text appears on my phone as I'm staring at the flight attendant doing the security demonstration:

You know I can always bring you back, little one.

I close my eyes and offer up a silent prayer, and it's not until I'm in a cab from JFK to NYU Langone that I'm convinced I've escaped.

Before I got on the plane, I spent most of the day texting Janus about Adam's condition instead of concentrating on the tennis tournament. But that doesn't prepare me for how my body swoops when I see Adam through the window in his hospital bed. His face is white, tawny lashes resting against his cheeks. I'm not really a crier. I've had so many injuries and lost so many important matches over the years that something inside me has settled into granite. You can't be emotional when you have to fight tooth and nail for every point, every advantage, but in this moment my throat closes nonetheless. And as I gaze at Adam lying there, I know with a bone-deep conviction that he's my person. There's no one else I want. I want those evenings I keep thinking about with a desperation I've never felt before. It's not sex or how cute he is; it's him. Solid, loyal, everything I need. If he'll even talk to me after this.

When I enter the room, Janus rises from where he's sitting next to Adam's bed alongside a guy with long dark hair and perhaps the most interesting set of tattoos I've ever seen—Fabian, I presume. Unfortunately, he's scowling at me.

"I told you not to fucking go there!" is all he says in greeting, and Janus puts a hand on his forearm.

I step forward and take Adam's pale hand where it's resting against the bedclothes, trying to tamp down the nausea as guilt burns through me. "How is he?"

"Stable," Janus says, putting an arm around my shoulders and pulling me into his side, his warmth seeping into me. "I'm so pleased to see you, Anna. I was worried you wouldn't get out of Russia."

I turn toward him. "They wouldn't do anything serious to a tennis star with a profile like mine. There would be too much publicity."

Fabian lets out a low growl. "They could have done all sorts of stuff to you, Anna—rape, abuse, targeting members of your family. I can do lots of things from here that don't involve putting you or anyone else in personal danger, and I …"

I hold up my hand to stop more words tumbling out of his mouth. "I know. I shouldn't have gone there. I didn't think they'd go as far as they did. I realized far too late that I was putting Adam in danger just by being associated with him." I stare down at his gray face. "I can't apologize enough. I'm …" My throat tightens unbearably again. Maybe I should be staying well away from him, but I had to come here, *touch his hand*. I rub my thumb over his skin.

Fabian's still scowling but says, "Apology accepted."

"They've looked at everything," Janus says, glancing at his watch. "He's been in a coma for eighteen maybe nineteen hours now. It's all a wait-and-see game, and hoping his stats improve."

"Oh God." I sink into a chair by the bed and put my head in my hands.

Janus crouches down next to me and squeezes my knee. "The prognosis isn't bad, Anna. He's not getting worse, and he's had more tests and examinations than you can shake a big stick at. Fabian's other half, Kate, is a doctor, and she's been here since it happened. He's in good hands."

When I headed here from the airport, all I wanted to do was reassure myself that Adam was still alive. Now that doesn't seem like enough. What if he doesn't recover? Or is permanently damaged somehow? How could I ever apologize to him enough?

A woman with blonde hair appears in the glass circle in the door, talking to someone over her shoulder. She smiles tightly as she enters the room.

"Hey, guys," she says as her eyes meet mine, and she holds out her hand. "You're Anna Talanova."

"Yes, more's the pity." I grimace, but she tuts at me.

"I'm Kate Thurman. One of the doctors here and, unfortunately, also this guy's other half." She jerks her hand at Fabian.

"Any news?" Fabian says.

She tilts her head. "We're wondering whether it might be insulin."

"Insulin?" Janus says, looking over at Adam. "Is that bad?"

"It can be terrible if it's administered in the right quantities. It will kill you quite fast if you get a sufficient dose."

The room swims for a second. Kate leans forward and examines one of the machines. "The fact that he's still alive means he wasn't, for some reason or other, given enough to kill him."

Fabian runs a hand over his mouth. "Wow. No shit."

"The strange part is you can only really administer insulin by injection."

We all stare down at where Adam is lying in the bed. "Injection?" I say.

"We found him in his apartment on the couch, so, if it's that, it's a bit of a mystery how such a large quantity got into his bloodstream," Kate says.

"Maybe someone broke in and …" Janus starts.

"There were no signs of a tussle," Fabian says, shaking his head. "He was just lying there."

"How rapidly does it come on if you're injected?"

"It depends on the type of insulin. Some are fast-acting and work within fifteen minutes; others take longer."

"So, he would have had at least a quarter of an hour: Plenty of time to send a text," Fabian says. "What happened to his phone?"

Kate delves under her scrubs and produces a phone from somewhere.

"It was in his hand when we found him. I just put it in my pocket."

Fabian plays with the screen for a second and then groans and hands it to Janus.

"It's in a WhatsApp to you, buddy," he says to Fabian.

When I peer over his shoulder, there's an unsent message to Fabian on Adam's phone:

Food poisoning.

"So, he was on his own, feeling ill," I say.

"He ate something. There were dirty dishes in the sink," Janus adds.

"Delivery driver?"

"Could be."

"He'll have a camera on the apartment, we could look at the footage."

"Good idea," Fabian says, turning back to Kate. "So, what do we do now?"

"We wait," she says, and he lets out a long groan.

"My favorite activity."

She gives him a small smile. "His capillary blood glucose was low when he came in so we gave him a dextrose bolus and an infusion, and we're going to keep doing that and monitor his blood sugar. We don't know for sure it's insulin yet—I'm still waiting on some of the other tests coming back."

"What for?"

"To definitively rule out things like meningitis and other poisons," Kate's eyes narrow. "But we'd expect to see other symptoms if any of these were the case. The fact he thought this was food poisoning is interesting. Let me go and talk to the team."

Fabian follows her across the room. "What can I do?"

She looks back at him. "Do something about the person that did this to him."

"Yeah. Yeah, okay. Better than sitting here brooding." He holds up his hand and turns toward me. "Actually, Anna, we've got stuff to discuss."

A shard of ice rips through me.

"About Konstantin Lebedev," he adds.

Ugh. I don't want Fabian or Janus doing any more crazy shit.

Fabian stretches out his hand. "Give me your phone."

"What? Why?"

"Tracking software. I don't know if Mila told you but there was some on her phone."

*

"So," Fabian says later, shoveling a sandwich in his mouth and talking around it. "Konstantin Lebedev. Tell me everything, Anna."

I eye him and Janus balefully. "He's already done this." I gesture at Adam on the bed. "I don't want you guys any more involved."

"I think you're forgetting I've just taken his systems down," Fabian says, chewing. "I think we're way beyond that. He knows you called Janus. He's spoken to me."

Jo arrived about an hour ago, and her eyebrows rise from where she's sitting next to Janus.

I blow out a long breath and chew my cheek.

"Tell us about Konstantin, Anna," Fabian repeats.

So, I fill him in on everything I told Adam. Unease prickles over the back of my neck. My original idea was just to tell Adam, to help him understand, but we're way past that now—the horse has well and truly bolted. And as Fabian peppers me with questions, I give more and more specific answers about the conversations I can remember and how the camps worked. "I'd probably recognize some of the sponsors," I eventually say.

"When I first looked into it, my interest was piqued because it all seemed off," Fabian says. "But I have to say that Mr. Lebedev is very careful. It's never discussed directly. Although I did find some slipups in what the sponsors said."

He produces a file from his bag and places it in front of me. "What's this?" I say, and he smiles.

"All the information I've gathered on his operations."

"Paper?" I ask.

"Bizarrely, it can be more secure than a laptop nowadays."

I flip open the first page, and Janus leans in to peer over my shoulder. There's a photograph and detailed notes of business interests for a series of men, quite a few of whom I recognize as people I saw or who talked to me at what they called social events. The next page is covered by a hand-drawn giant spider's web in neat sloping script.

"These are the interconnections between all the sponsors I could find involved with the Alliance Tennis Federation's academy. It will take me some time to piece together the money flows, but on here you've got company shareholders and directors," he says, tapping the pages with the pictures on. "Plus players they've 'sponsored,' who I've made some assumptions about given photographs I found and other cross-referenced information."

I stare at it in wonder, my hand shaking around the map he's drawn. "How did you put all this together?" I whisper.

"I've been working on it full-time since I came across his name, along with a couple of people from Janus's business. They've been tracking what's happened to all the young people." He makes a face. "We've discovered three so far who have died—by suicide or murder, it's hard to know—though whether we'd ever be able to prove that anyone else was responsible or get any real justice is another matter."

I close my eyes. "Oh, Jesus."

"Yeah, we need to do something," Jo growls.

"Are you saying it's difficult to go after Konstantin Lebedev, but we can go after these so-called sponsors?" Janus says.

"Yes. It depends on Anna really. As I'm uncovering more and more people who are connected to this in Russia, the more I think we should give it to a newspaper."

"Like you did with the Newssource papers?" Janus says.

I glance up from the file where I'm studying a picture of a man I recognize. "You were involved in the Newssource papers?" There was a huge fallout from that in Russia.

Fabian doesn't meet my eyes. "A bit," he huffs, and Janus looks up at the ceiling.

"This is extraordinary," I say. "But, Christ, releasing it, even Konstantin being aware that I've got something like this, would put a huge target on my back." Unease seethes under my skin.

"Yeah, I don't like that," Janus says.

"Perhaps we can play a cleverer game than that," Fabian says.

"What do you mean?" I say.

"I'd have to talk to some people, but if we set up other groups and people to do the investigating, we can get them to pull all this together. We can let them break the story." He waves his hand over the file. "There needn't be any connection to you, Anna."

"How could we do that, though?" Jo says. "They're bound to make the connection to Anna, given everything that's happened."

Fabian purses his lips and stares fixedly at the far wall.

"Yeah, I don't see any way out of that," Janus adds. "And as you said, they also know you were in his systems."

"Well, he knows some hackers were in his system, but not who," Fabian says, shaking his head. "I'm just a voice on a phone. When you hack into somewhere, there are thousands of systems obscuring the identity of where that comes from, and there's almost no way of knowing who originated a hack or even if you can stop it."

"Onion routing," Jo murmurs.

"But yeah, taking down his systems came through Anna, and you," Fabian adds, nodding at Janus. "They're likely to come after Anna or her family, possibly you too, Janus." He gets up and starts pacing around the room. "The good news is Konstantin's not the FSB, resource and skills-wise. And I'm in his systems now, and he won't be able to get me out of there, so we have enough leverage, even if the threat hasn't gone away." He waves his hand over the file. "We don't have to make this information public just because I've put it together. Maybe it would be safer to let sleeping dogs lie." He chews his lip as he stops walking. "Believe you me, there's a lot of people out there getting away with all sorts of shit."

Ugh. I hate that expression, *let sleeping dogs lie*. If I don't expose Konstantin, he'll continue to be a shadow over my life. He said as much. Maybe also my family, and Adam. Perhaps you can never escape your Russian roots, but you can always fight. I turn and look at Adam lying on the bed, face pale. Who's to say Konstantin wouldn't do something like this again? I'm in this now. *Never back down from a fight: If they know you are scared, they will take advantage.* What's more, I owe it to Adam and everyone else to do what I can. Mila is wrong: It's not about us or our tennis legacy. It's about everyone who comes after, about all those young people. I want every sentence after my name to be how I brought down this terrible system in Russia, about how hard I fought for that.

"Fabian, let's do it," I say.

His eyes jerk to mine.

"Let's give it to a newspaper," I add. "If he comes after me, we'll just have to deal with it. You can help us, yes?"

"More than help. Short-term at least, I can keep you safe. It's more difficult with your family because they're in Russia, but not impossible. I'm involved in some networks there."

And when I look at him again I find him staring at the same spot on the wall somewhere over my head and tapping his fingers on his legs, like he's deep in thought.

CHAPTER 40

Adam

Everything is welling up inside me like water rising behind a dam. Just when my life was turning a corner and the business was picking up and I felt something for the first time when I looked at a woman that wasn't fear, I end up in hospital. I groan and shift in the bed.

"Adam?"

The room is dark, a dim light coming from a bank of machines monitoring something. Anna appears at my bedside.

"Anna?" Her dark hair is spilling over her shoulders, and she has never looked lovelier or more out of reach. "What time is it? What are you doing here?"

My eyes meet hers and something shimmers between us, some warmth and understanding that feels like a lifeline. She takes my hand and squeezes my fingers.

"It's 9 p.m. I've been waiting for you to wake up." Her eyes fill with tears. "I'm so glad you're okay."

I swallow down the sandpaper that has taken over my throat. "You went to Russia. What happened?"

She closes her eyes. "Not my best decision. I didn't want to drag you and

Fabian into Konstantin's orbit. It seemed sensible at the time."

"I was going to come after you. I was booking a flight and then … I started to feel ill. Food poisoning, I think."

"It wasn't food poisoning. It looks as though you were somehow given a shot of insulin."

I stare at her. "*What?* By who?"

"Konstantin, or rather someone he employed."

"But how? … Fucking hell. Is insulin dangerous?"

"It can kill you if you're given enough, according to Kate."

"They tried to *kill* me?" I blink down at my hand resting on the bedclothes, the catheter going into the back of it, and turn my head to study the machines next to me. People don't do this kind of thing to me: I'm Mr. Quiet Life. Maybe not so much anymore.

"If Janus and Fabian hadn't got to you …" She rolls her lips together, and I reach out and squeeze her hand. "The doctors have no idea how it got into your system, though. We wondered if it might have been the delivery driver if you ordered takeout."

"No, I went out to the grocery store. Chelsea Market." I close my eyes. "What the hell happened?" Oh shit, the man who reeled into me. My sore arm! "That guy. In the corridor." Oh, fuck.

"What guy?"

"Someone bumped into me. I thought it was odd at the time. But there were a lot of people around, celebrating. He lurched into me and hurt my arm. I thought he was just some drunk. He could have followed me from the apartment, I guess."

Anna chews her lip. "Perhaps that explains it."

"How the hell did I get here?"

"I was at a breakfast with Konstantin in St. Petersburg and he said some strange, loaded things about you enjoying your evening that worried me. I phoned Janus and he enlisted Fabian. They came to your place and called an ambulance. They've been here by your bedside ever since."

All the times I waded in for them in college, and only once did Fabian have to rescue me, and that was from Celine. I mean the fact that I was injected with something is awful, but I've really lived the most risk-averse life. "Where are they now?"

"I persuaded them to go home and grab some sleep while I took a shift this evening. They were up with you all last night. They're coming back in the morning."

I groan. "They don't need to be doing that. They've got work to do."

She squeezes my fingers. "They were very happy to do it."

"What happened with Konstantin?"

"He threatened me. Pietr was there, saying I should be back in Russia at his side, and then Fabian took down their systems, and they let me go. I mean, I don't know what they were thinking I'd do given I'm playing tennis in Australia in less than two weeks."

I close my eyes. I can't believe she went to Russia. Willingly stepped back into the orbit of men she knows are dangerous criminals. I've seen flashes of this kind of steely determination in Anna, but the contrast between her and Celine, the strange role I took trying to rescue her, makes my eyes tighten and tears leak out of the corners of my eyes and down my cheeks.

"Oh shit, Adam. I didn't mean …"

Anna bends down and kisses my forehead. "I'm sorry. So sorry, Adam," she whispers. "I know I'm not the person you need. I'm amazed you're even talking to me after everything that's happened and the trouble I brought to your door and your peaceful life."

I grab her hand, pull it to my mouth, and kiss it. "You're just the person I need."

She makes a face at me like she doesn't believe me, but I've never been gladder to find someone at my bedside in a hospital.

"Anna, I'm so sorry."

"*What?* What are *you* apologizing for?"

"Being in here. You don't have to stay. You have a tournament to prepare for and food to eat that's not from a vending machine and …"

"Quit worrying, Miller. I've canceled my practices for the next couple of days. Jo and Janus took Pepper home with them."

"You can't do that! You've got a Grand Slam tournament coming up and …"

Her eyes narrow on mine. "Just watch me. I'm staying here with you until they let you out. They're bringing a cot for me. I can come and go if I need to. It's all organized."

"It's Christmas in four days. I'm supposed to be going home."

"You're not going anywhere. If you're out of hospital by then, you can have Christmas with me."

I nod as my head sags back on the pillow, too tired to even think about it.

*

Later, Anna pulls a nutritionist's meal out of her bag, and the hospital starts to quiet down for the night. It's like being at Janus's all over again, except the nurse comes to make me comfortable and records some vital signs for the evening. Anna settles down in the bed beside mine studying something or other on her phone, though I'd bet it's a competitor's playing statistics or something else tennis related.

The next thing I know I'm watching a truck barreling down a street behind Anna and she's walking along, oblivious, talking on her phone. I wave my arms over my head, screaming, "Anna! Behind you! Move!" and I keep yelling at her to shift out of the way, but she's just talking and talking, and I can't get her to hear, to look up, to do *anything*. So, I race across the road and dive for her, and thank Christ I make it in time. But I'm under the truck and being crushed by this huge tire, a searing pain in my stomach, so bad that I want to die. *Please let it stop!* But it goes on and on and it's the end … This is how my life ends. Then my eyes pop open to dim green lights and a hospital ceiling.

I gasp as a shadowy figure leans over me.

"Adam, are you all right?"

Anna. She's okay, she's okay. *Oh my God.* "I'm okay. I'm okay," I gulp out. "What happened?"

My heart rate recedes from the red zone.

"You were talking in your sleep."

"Yeah. Yeah. Fuck. It was a dream. Just a dream."

"Want to talk about it?"

"No. Fuck no."

She climbs onto the bed beside me and, careful to avoid my tubes and wires, she shuffles down and rests her head on my chest. "Is this all right?" she whispers.

I put my hand on her head. It's silky under my palm and my throat tightens in gratitude. I could lose her. Tomorrow or the next day, someone could get to her or me and she would be gone. They've said that I'm okay, but who really knows? We've been friends for such a short time. I've been cautious all my life and look where I am now—in no different a place than Fabian. He ended up in a hospital, too. Something else put him here, but it was no more or less self-inflicted. All this caution … for what? If nothing ever comes of this, what we're doing here, I want her to know.

"I love you, Anna."

She goes still under my hand. Then her face pops up next to me.

"What did you say?" she whispers.

My throat tightens unbearably. "I said I love you. I don't want us to just be friends. I know this is a crazy time to say it, and I know you want a better man than me, especially now, but in case I don't get another chance to tell you, I want you to know."

Even in the dim green light, I can see her frown as she glowers at me. "A better man than you?"

"You said you wanted to be friends, and you told me that at the start, too. I understand, Anna, I do. But it hasn't happened that way for me and …"

She presses a finger over my lips. "I said just friends in the beginning because being with a tennis player is a problem. I'm not here for ten months of the year. My focus has always been on my sport, not something or someone else. My relationship history, what I had to do … I've never met a good man, always dangerous manipulators. But then I found you, and you were a million miles away from that, and I realized that was what a man was supposed to be. That the best men look after you in all the right ways. The way that's best for you."

"But I was a distraction, too."

"No, you weren't. I lied about that. You were anything but. But with all the stuff with Arty, my history in Russia, I got worried that I was putting you in danger … I didn't want them to come after you." She grins suddenly, and her teeth look green in the strange light. "Rather ironic now, don't you think?"

She's so perfectly capable of looking after herself. I'm so relieved she's here: warm, alive, and so unbelievably okay. I start to cough as my throat closes up and she starts to climb off me, muttering, "I shouldn't be on the bed with you."

"I'm fine," I gasp, tightening my arm around her.

She gazes up at me. "I love you, too."

Now I really can't breathe. "What?"

She squeezes my hand and stretches up to place her lips on mine, mumbling, "I love you, too."

"You don't have to …"

But she squeezes my hand again. "I nearly had a heart attack when Konstantin implied he'd done something to you … I just … I've never felt anything like that before. Like an express train was rushing toward me and I couldn't get out of the way."

It's so like my dream, I want to laugh.

In fact, I want to swing from the rafters and dive off a high cliff, so I slide my hand into her hair and kiss her senseless.

EPILOGUE

Adam – Five Months Later

The crowd is completely silent as I watch Anna for the first time in a big match—the French Open final. I glance at the scoreboard for what must be the two thousandth time. This game is going down to the wire. It's 12–12 in the tiebreaker and, honestly, she must have nerves of steel. But boy, she has needed them today. Katarina Yenko has fought every point and come back time and time again when Anna's been in the lead. After Anna lost the first set, I thought it was all over.

She serves, but even I can see without the call or the electronic beep that it's out. *Fuck, Anna, don't double-fault now. Come on!* Ilov's face next to me is impassive—how is he so calm? Anna bounces the ball a couple of times on the court, then throws it up and smashes it over the net and Yenko stretches to get to it, but it's too fast and too near the center line. An ace! Fuck. I try not to gnaw on my hand like I want to. There are cameras all over this thing, and I've already had one or two Slack messages from my team saying, *You look cute on TV.*

We've got two months in Europe, starting with the French Open, then Wimbledon, and we've left Pepper with Janus and Jo, given she's now best friends with the cats. Susie's been running things in the business like a pro in my absence. I'm still online with people in the office every day. In fact, it couldn't be easier. The guys have been amazing, and I've done loads since coming here, even with attending all of Anna's matches. I've gone to a few hackerspaces in Paris, taking the suitcase full of electronic kit I brought with me, and I love the freedom and the peace I get while Anna's off practicing.

Katarina bounces the ball ready to serve on the switch. If Anna breaks Yenko's serve here, this could win her the tournament, but she's had these kinds of nail-biting battles with Yenko throughout this match. She's one point ahead now. *Make it two.* The ball whizzes down, and Anna stretches all out, managing to fire it back over the net, and it clips the top, but Katarina gets to it and top slices the ball as she closes in on the net, eager to make the kill. Anna is off-balance, her weight on the wrong foot, but even with my limited knowledge of tennis—though I'm getting better each day, I swear—I can see the opportunity it's opened up for Anna to put one past her opponent. She does, somehow twisting her body, not quite steady, and belting a ball almost too fast to see, straight down the line. It misses the end of Yenko's outstretched racket by millimeters, and the whole stadium erupts as Anna goes down on her knees, forehead pressed into the red clay of the court.

And I'm on my feet, eyes damp. Ever since I met Anna I've turned into a sap, but God, it's so fucking amazing being with this woman.

Then she's up and climbing up to the stands where I'm sitting with her parents, whom she flew in to be here, alongside her coach, Ilov, and her public relations guy, Damian.

The crowd is going wild, cheering and clapping as Anna arrives with us, tearful and sweaty, hugging everyone in turn. When she reaches me at the end of the line, her eyes are red and full of tears.

"I couldn't have done it without you," she says, as I pull her into a tight hug.

I laugh through my own tears. "I think you could." I kiss her temple. "Watching that was the highlight of my life. I love you."

She squeezes me tighter. "Me too. I'll see you later," she says, and then she's gone with a wave to the crowd as she heads back down to the court and her trophy presentation. No doubt she'll have to work through a whole round of questions at the press conference and everything else she needs to do. A hot, welling sensation takes hold of my chest. If I feel like this, what on earth must her mom and dad be feeling?

I glance over at her dad, and his eyes are full of tears. When I met him earlier, he was gruff and monosyllabic, but I've realized that's just his way. They both speak a little English. In the halting Russian I've been learning, I apologized to her mom for not being Arty Maroz and she grinned a grin that was so like Anna's it almost stopped my heart. Then she slapped my arm and went into a long diatribe in Russian, and I caught the words Maroz, his father, and something about wanting a son-in-law and grandchildren. *Maybe one day.* Understanding Russian is a long slog. With a lot of gesturing, I managed to communicate that the grandchildren were dependent on them—Anna's parents—living in the US. Anna's managed to persuade them and her sister to move to Latvia so they're in a much safer place, but I don't think she'll be truly happy until they're in the US. Fortunately, for now, Fabian is keeping an eye on everything. He has enough leverage and he keeps me briefed. It's not a long-term solution, but it's good enough for now.

Eventually, we're led behind the scenes for a drink and to chat with people, and everyone wants to speak to someone connected to Anna. We see Anna again briefly, but there are loads of interviews lined up for her, so I manage to extract myself and her parents and we head back to the hotel together. Ilov and Damian stick around to organize things and talk to the media. When I leave her parents at the door to their room, both of them are quiet but beaming, and I promise in broken Russian to let them know when Anna returns. There's a dinner being held tonight which we'll all be attending.

I settle back on the cushions at the head of the bed in our suite and pull my laptop onto my knees. I've got several hours of peace to work on a few things on the website for Susie and some designs Sean and I discussed yesterday.

But the next thing I feel is my laptop moving, and as my arms shoot out to save it from falling, my eyes fly open to find Anna smiling down at me, her hands wrapped around my computer.

"Long day?" she says with a wink.

"I watched a very exciting tennis match and it wore me out," I say, grinning up at her. "Ms. French Open Champion."

She places my laptop on the floor and climbs over my lap, eyes latching onto mine as she runs her thumb along my lower lip.

"I'm in the mood to celebrate," she whispers, sliding her ass down my legs and pressing in.

My relationship with Anna is warm and close and solid, but this aspect of being together is like some unstoppable force.

"Winning's a big turn-on, huh?" I say.

She smiles. "I think it is."

"What time is it?" I start to lift my wrist, but she pins it down to the bed and all my fighting instincts roar to life.

"We have time," she says.

So, I slide my hand through her hair and move forward as if I'm going to kiss her, but twist at the last moment, pinning her on her back instead. "I like a worn-out opponent," I say, rubbing my nose along hers and kissing her eyelids.

She smiles. "Who says I'm worn out? I've had a few energy drinks."

"I like the way you pick up on the fact that I said you were worn out but let the fact that I describe you as my *opponent* go by." I prop myself on my hands. "Congratulations, by the way. How does it feel to win your first French Open championship?"

She blows out a long breath. "God, I've been asked that question a thousand times over the last two hours. There's no greater feeling in the world. One of those special feelings that happen so rarely, when all your hard work pays off. Because so often it doesn't."

"I see." If there's one thing I've learned from watching Anna, it's that failure is far more common than success, and the only choice to make is to carry on, to fight another day, and another one and another one.

"A better man would have had some champagne on tap to celebrate," I add.

"I'd die if I had any alcohol." She makes a face. "I bet there'll be a lot flowing tonight, though."

She's got me hard by sitting on me, so I flex my hips forward and she gasps, hooking a leg over my hip and rolling me over. Then she sits up and tosses her ponytail over her shoulder. She's out of her sweaty tennis gear and in some soft-looking post-game pants and a top, no doubt provided by her sponsors.

"Do I have to wear anything particular this evening?" I say.

Her agent, Barb, has persuaded me to be involved in some of Anna's deals, and we now have an agreement about how that works and how much money I'm paid from it. I told Anna it didn't matter, but she was very insistent that I was treated fairly, which amused me greatly given that no one would be at all interested in me if I wasn't with her. Barb's chomping at the bit to sign me up to all manner of people who want to provide sponsorship, particularly in fashion, but honestly, the way I look most of the time, no one should want me as a style icon. Anna got Rolex to give me some super-fancy wristwatch after that first event we attended, and it's beautiful, but it's so unimportant compared to everything else. Barb has also been whispering about some big deal that's in the works. If it's good for Anna, I'll do it.

"Damian and June are turning up in about an hour to do some behind-the-scenes stuff."

"We're not doing pictures of me in my boxers!"

Anna snapped a picture of me in the bathroom yesterday and told me she lived with the hottest man alive. Which, given all the amazing male models she could be with, is patently ridiculous. Okay, I'm wiry from all the jujitsu, but I'm not built, and my body hair doesn't fit the mold for male hotness currently in vogue. But she studied the photo and a small secret smile curled over her lips. When she waltzed out of the bathroom saying it was the best picture to have on her phone, I shouted after her, "No posting!"

I'm looking a little thin. I lost weight in the hospital and afterward because I didn't want to eat, and if it wasn't for Anna, I don't know where I'd be now. She had to leave to play in the Australian Open, but she bullied me into going to live with Janus and Jo and gave me Pepper to look after for three months. She got her nutritionist to make me food and FaceTimed with me every night, no matter where she was. Janus got me up each day, cooked me breakfast, and walked Pepper with me. And after a couple of weeks of working with him at his apartment, I went back to the office. Between the pair of them, it stopped me brooding. Jujitsu always made me feel strong, but someone got to me so easily and I started to get this creeping sensation on the back of my neck if I was outside. Not something I've ever felt in New York. And the best thing was? Anna understood all of it. She's had people tracking her and exploiting her all her life. Having her talk me through the mentality and fear was everything.

Anna pushes her hips into me, and I'm fully hard now just from having her sitting over me. She leans forward and rubs her nose against mine.

"I'd like some naked pictures for my phone," she whispers into my skin.

"So would I. But imagine if someone hacked into it," I say.

She sits back. "Yes, Fabian has given me a whole new perspective on that."

"There's not many people who can do what he does, though."

"Not many isn't zero."

I squeeze her thigh. "No nude photographs then," I whisper back, my hands coming up to unzip her sports jacket, and she shrugs out of it, revealing a vest and bra. So, I whip the vest over her head and her hands go back, unhooking the bra.

When she's naked from the waist up, I slide my palms up her torso to cup her breasts, rubbing my thumb across her smooth skin and watching her face as her eyes drift closed.

"You're my reward," she says, eyes popping open. "Better than any title I could win."

My throat closes up. "What? No, Anna."

She nods, cupping my face. "Of course, Adam! All my history, how could you not be? I'm so glad you're okay now. I was so worried for a while."

"Thank you for everything you did," I say.

I've thanked her every time we've talked about it, but I can't help saying it over and over because it means so much having someone in my corner. In totally different ways, Fabian and I never had that kind of unflinching support. His father expressed himself with his fists and ended up killing his mother. My mother is just condemning, and my father never managed to offset that, despite his soft, dry humor.

"I don't think you felt like thanking me at the time."

I laugh. Sometimes when we FaceTimed, I was a grumpy old bear and as miserable as sin.

She pushes at my T-shirt with questing fingers, and I sit up so she can drag it over my head as she runs greedy hands over the curls on my chest. My mouth finds hers, her hips shifting over my erection. Sliding my fingers inside her tracksuit pants, I find the edge of her panties and snug her pelvis up to mine. Shivers run through my crotch and up my body as the friction against my length starts to register.

She tilts down to kiss me, and I bring one hand up into her hair, pulling it out of the tight ponytail and combing through its softness. I spin her over again, and I'd swear my cock has a mind of its own because before I know what I'm doing I'm grinding all over her. Her hands roam down my back and around my sides to the waistband of my jeans, trying to get between us to undo them, so I lift my hips to give her access as I tangle my tongue with hers. I swear every time I try and take it easy with her, something sets me on fire and I lose my head.

Then her hand grasps me, she runs a thumb over my tip, and it makes my breath wheeze out.

"Oh yes," she mumbles against my lips. "That's the sound I wanted."

"Slow down. Slow down."

"No, Adam, I …"

"Can't we savor this, just for once?" I gasp as she slides long fingers down to my base, feeling me, exploring me, and making me shake with need. My hand on her torso maps the curve of her breast, and I get a shiver in return.

"Not if you keep doing that," she chokes out.

It's like a house that's burning down, timbers falling down like dominos, both of us powerless to stop the impending inferno.

"I want to be on top," she says, so I roll onto my back and she sits up, pushing a cascade of dark hair out of her face. When the strands brush across her breasts, I can hardly restrain my groan. This is like the hottest fantasy. It's *always* the hottest fantasy.

Anna shoves down the waistband of her tracksuit, and I help her peel it off. A pair of sports boy shorts match the bra she was wearing earlier. Somehow, it's the sexiest thing on the planet that she never wears anything else and that only I get to see the woman underneath. But she pushes the shorts off, too, and I wiggle my jeans down my thighs as she scoots backward to wrestle them down my legs. But I leave my boxers on—perhaps a barrier will give me the illusion of control.

As if she can read my thoughts, she says, "Control is overrated."

"But very necessary, I find." My lips quirk as I take in her flushed face, sliding my hand between her legs and then up to rest my palm on her flat stomach.

It's my favorite thing to see the pink build on her chest as she gets close, so I feather my thumb over the smooth skin between her legs. She shakes her head and snaps at the elastic of my boxers, so I lift my ass up and she pulls them down and off.

Anna's so controlled and patient in everything she does, it's fucking wild how she loses the plot when we're together. Running her hands up my pecs, she grinds down on me, trapping my fingers as she falls forward and nips my lip.

Her hand steals between us to stroke my erection. Then before I can clock what she's doing, in one fast movement she lifts up on her knees, holds me up, and sinks down. *The wet. The heat.* My eyes stutter closed as my hips come off the bed. We stopped using condoms a while ago, and I swear I will never get used to how sensitive this feels. My cock twitches. *Holy shit. I'm going to shoot like a teenager.* I clamp my hand on her hip to keep her stationary and her lips curl against mine, the minx.

"Behave," I mumble.

"When have I ever behaved?"

And that's true, and Lord, I also love how she pushes.

Her tongue steals out to touch my mouth, and I open up to tangle my tongue with hers.

"I can't stop touching and feeling and …" Her short nails dig into my chest as she tries to shift her hips.

"Stop. Let me get some control here."

"I don't want control," she says. "I want power and …"

Cutting her off with my lips on hers, I roll her again, pulling out and thrusting back in, using anything to help me last, even the board design for a little electronic car that I was looking at before I fell asleep. *Fuck.* The grip and the wet slide. I'd give this woman anything she wanted, and she deserves it all. My time, my commitment, my generosity. Fast sex if she wants it.

I grind all over her, and she arches and gasps. "Oh … oh … oh …"

Her hands come up as if to scrabble at me, so I pin her with my arm across her collarbone, and she lifts her hips as I push down into her. She's strong, Anna. So often the sex we have is like fighting, and fuck, I do not need to be thinking about how hot that is.

As I pull out and press back in, rubbing all over her, she explodes around me like she was on a hair trigger, her muscles clamping down on my cock. My eyes roll into the back of my head, grinding my teeth as I thrust through it. Flutters of pleasure race down my length and coalesce in my balls, making them tighten painfully. *Don't come, don't come.*

I prop myself on my hands, looking down at where I'm moving, and Anna uses the opportunity, now I've freed her arms, to run her nails down my back, stroking over my ass. Goddammit, she's worked out that that's one of my favorite things.

The tingling moves up my legs and my pelvis cramps sharply. "Oh shit …" I shake my head. "No … no … no … I want one more, Anna."

She bites her lip as air whooshes out of her, my hand between us playing with her clit as she tries to bat my hand away, sensitive, but I know her tells now. She can give me another one.

I laugh. "You're a champion now—you can do anything."

"Goddammit, man. That is the first and last time you're using that line." Her breath halts as I swipe my thumb over her nub. "No, no, no. Fuck, Adam." She bucks her hips. "Stop!"

Her second orgasm is often better than her first. *Come on, sweetheart, where is it?* I want to make this fantastic for her, so I keep softly pressing and rolling and she lifts her head and sinks her teeth into my neck.

"You want me to bite you back? Show you how good it feels?" I whisper, and she groans, head thunking back onto the pillow. I can see the moment where it starts to feel good, where she's reaching for it.

I rub my nose against hers. "There you go, sweetheart. There. You. Go."

The way she's tightening around my length is causing serious pain. I've been inside her wet heat for too long. A sharp ache has taken over my pelvis and is now traveling down my legs, and every time I move in and out it only gets worse. I let out a groan as her eyes fix on my face.

"Yes, Adam. Yes," she says.

"Are you close?" I say, closing my eyes. I can't take her flushed face and soft brown eyes any longer.

Her nails dig into my butt, pulling me farther into her, and it's not helping. She bites my ear. "Such a sexy man," she says.

"*Anna. V* equals *ir. C* equals *q* over *v*."

"What the hell?"

"Basic electrical formulae," I say, and she laughs with a hiccup as I swipe my thumb over her hard nub again.

"Oh, oh, Adam. It's … I'm …"

Just as I think I might die this way, die happy buried deep inside her, she starts contracting around me, sweeping me along with her, her second orgasm triggering mine. Burning up my length so fast, the pain shoots through the whole of my lower body, and I gasp at the relief and the starbursts making my vision blur. A rap on the door echoes through the suite as I shudder and shudder, spilling myself into her.

I blink at the beads of sweat rising up on her skin and listen to our panting breaths and the silence behind them. *Did I imagine that knock?*

Again, tap, tap, tap.

Shit.

I collapse down onto her.

"Now," she whispers in my ear, "now I'm worn out."

"There are people at the door," I whisper back.

She smiles, eyes closed. "They'll go away."

"Just a minute!" I shout out, and she tries to keep a hold of me, with her strong thighs locked around my hips, but I shake my head, pulling out as she pouts. I think she lied about the time we had, the troublemaker. But then again she just won the French Open so she deserves any damn thing she wants.

I pull on a hotel robe from the heap on the chair and shut the bedroom door as I head to the door of the suite. No doubt flushed and sweaty. Well, whoever is here, they're just going to have to suck it up.

The makeup people and clothes people are standing in the corridor, gaping when they catch sight of me, but I wave them in and tell them to make themselves comfortable and set up in the living room, and that Anna is resting and I will be through in five minutes. Then another tap at the door reveals June and Damian and a cameraman, and after I've let them in too, I shoot off to shower and get into something more respectable as Anna lies in our bed with a pillow over her face.

We chat and are styled and primped while they get their background shots, and then I look at the strapless number that Anna's wearing and run my thumb over the top of it where it covers her chest.

"Can I take this off you later?" I whisper in her ear, and she smiles down at where my finger is exploring.

"You expect me to stay awake beyond 8 p.m.?"

"Are you going to face-plant in your soup?"

"What are you two whispering about?" June says.

"How fast Anna is going to fall asleep," I say, meeting Anna's eyes and smirking.

*

As we're standing in a corridor waiting to go into the hotel ballroom with a member of staff up ahead with a walkie-talkie because Anna's got to be announced, Anna squeezes my hand.

I need to talk to her. I didn't say anything earlier. She deserved to enjoy her win, but it can't wait.

"I had a message from Fabian while you were on court today," I say.

Gold silk shimmers around her legs as she turns toward me. The way it moves around her body reminds me of the dress she wore that first night I met her, and the idea that I might get to take this one off her makes my neck grow hot.

"Oh yes?"

"I didn't want to tell you just after your win, but Konstantin was arrested today."

"Are you *serious*? Oh my God!" She's already pulling her phone out of her bag.

"For pedophilia. Apparently, the Russian Tennis Federation is in uproar."

"How did that happen? I thought Fabian said the group of newspapers weren't ready yet, and …" She stares down at her screen. "Oh my God!"

"What is it?"

"All the messages on my phone! I didn't look at it because I just wanted to celebrate. I thought I could deal with all the congratulations tomorrow, but there's so many messages about the academy!"

I step forward and slide her phone out of her hand, pulling her back into me and wrapping my arms around her. "Perhaps we should look at it later, hmm? I wasn't sure whether I should tell you now but then I thought someone might say something tonight, or ask you for a comment, and I didn't want you to be blindsided. I don't want to spoil tonight with …"

She squeezes my waist. "Spoil it? This is amazing!" Her eyes are bright when she looks at me. "Perhaps I really will get out from under it."

And I laugh. If I could give Anna this … this freedom, it would be everything.

"Goddammit, nothing could make this day better. Except …" She tips her head back and looks at me. "I want to ask you something."

I grin at her. "What is it?"

She goes up on her toes so her mouth is next to my ear. "Will you do this with me?" she whispers.

"Do what?"

She sinks back down, biting her lip as a shot of vulnerability crosses her face.

"What, Anna?" I say, frowning.

"Travel with me? Come to tournaments? I mean not all of them, of course. I know you've got a business to run and ..."

We talked about me coming out to Europe with her for these two months, but not how this would work longer-term.

"Try and stop me," I growl.

Her lips part as her eyes roam from one of mine to the other. Then, as I watch, her eyes fill with tears and my throat tightens as I shake my head. "No, no, no," I say, stretching out to pull her back into me. "Don't spoil that amazing makeup."

"I never thought I'd find this," she whispers, pressing her mouth into my neck.

"Find what?"

She hiccups through a laugh. "Find *you*."

"I'm all in with this. You know that, right?" I whisper into the hair by her ear. She smells of the sea and pinecones.

"Oh God," she says, wiping a finger under her eye and tipping her head back.

"You won't be traveling and competing forever, Anna. It's not a downside. I have an amazing opportunity to do this very special thing, to sit in a competitor's box and watch you play. I wouldn't miss it for the world. Maybe I can't come every time, but the guys are competent, and the business is doing well now. They like being in charge of it, and I can work happily from anywhere."

"I've been on my own for so long," she says quietly.

And I think back to my silent father and my condemning mother and how I escaped my lonely life with them to a solitary life in New York. I had Fabian and Janus, and they're great friends, but it was never like this. I've always wanted somebody to share my life with. Dinner on our knees in front of a TV show about dogs. A set of shared goals. I think that's what cut me up so much about Celine: I got a taste of what it was like having someone on your side, and it was all a mirage. It turned into dust in my hands, and then I didn't trust myself.

Anna lowers her head and nods and nods. "I'm all in, too, Adam."

I tip her chin up as my gaze roams across hers. "I love you."

"I love you, too," she says, then she laughs, "and now I want to take you back to bed."

Over her shoulder, the usher is waving at us to come forward, and I can hear the MC announcing Anna's name.

Maybe you never know. Maybe you just have to keep getting up off the floor. Maybe the only risk you take is staying down for too long.

THE END

BONUS CHAPTERS!

Thank you for reading *The Game*. I hope you enjoyed it!

Want to read more about Jo and Janus, or learn what happened to Adam, Fabian and Janus at college? Sign up for bonus chapters from The *Techboys* Series here:

www.evemriley.com/techboys-bonus-content

THE TECHBOYS SERIES

THE REFUSAL

THE OUTCAST

THE SECRET

THE PHOTOGRAPH

THE GAME

REVIEWS AND MORE

I really hope you've enjoyed *The Game*, the fifth book in my *Techboys* series! If you have, please consider leaving a review on either the book's Amazon page or any review sites that you frequent. Your feedback and support is greatly appreciated.

There are more books to come in The *Techboys* Series and I'd be super-excited to share them with you. If you'd like to be the first to hear about the new releases, pre-orders, bonus chapters and special freebies, please join my VIP mailing list:

evemriley.com/signup

Thanks so much!

ACKNOWLEDGMENTS

The *Techboys* Series began with a simple but powerful vision: three young men—Janus, Fabian, and Adam—meeting in their first computer science lecture and forging an unbreakable bond. Janus was the ambitious go-getter, Fabian the wild experimenter, and Adam the calm, grounded force who kept them all together. Originally, Adam's story was set to be the second book after Janus's, but I wasn't happy with how it turned out, so I moved on to Fabian's story and then the adventures of Liss and Dan.

But Adam's story kept calling me back. This year, I returned to his character determined to make it work—and that's when Anna and her Papillon, Pepper, sprang to life, bringing a whole new depth to Adam's journey. He transformed into the sweetest guy with a hint of steel, and I fell for him all over again. I hope you've enjoyed reading Adam's story as much as I've loved writing it! And thank you for bearing with me through this slight leap backward in the timeline.

I've had such fun drifting along red carpets and imagining having my hair and makeup done alongside Adam and Anna. We're now five books in and, with 84 book awards for the series so far, it's amazing to see readers coming into the series at different points and then looping back to read earlier books. Readers' enthusiasm has surpassed all my expectations, and I can't thank you enough for all the amazing messages. I am so happy with where The *Techboys* Series has got to and very excited about the stories to come.

Each book brings its own challenges, from medical emergencies to tech issues and Russian transliteration. In this book, I wanted the glitz, the tennis, and Adam's struggling hardware business to feel real. So, I couldn't be more grateful to all the people who helped me to get *The Game* into shape. My lovely New York editor, Heather Demetrios, who read this first and questioned everything about Adam and Anna. This is an immeasurably better book with your input. A big thank you to my very own Techboy, Rob, who now reads the books at each stage and tears into the story logic, gives me tech advice, and encourages me at every point along the way. To Robert Tuesley Anderson, you've edited all my books so far, and I couldn't be more grateful for all your input. Your attention to detail and constant questioning have been unsurpassed.

Thank you so much to my amazing beta readers: Caroline, Donna and Kelsey. I am eternally grateful for your uplifting and thoughtful feedback. My apologies to you all if what I have written doesn't match up to all the brilliant advice you gave. Millie, what can I say? You've given me great ideas for all the medical emergencies in my books and opened my eyes to a whole new world. I can't thank you enough.

To the villages that are BookTok and Bookstagram—thank you for your patience and all your support. The kindness you've shown this indie author is more than I could ever hope for. To all the bloggers, influencers, and book fanatics who helped me spread the word about *The Refusal*, *The Outcast*, *The Secret*, and *The Photograph*—thank you. A lot of you have been with me for five books now, so a big thanks to: Alejandra, Alise, Amanda, Andrea, Anneke, Annie, Ashley, Azalea, Cassandra, Christina, Cindy, Deb, Dem, Em, Emma, Erika, Fabi, Felicia, Jade, Jessica, Kat, Kathrin, Kerri, Kristen, Latasha, Lena, Linda, Lisa, Maddie, Natasa, Nichole, Nicole, Rochelle, Rudra, Sue, Tammy, Virginia Lee, and Zsuzsi. But I am also looking forward to getting to know *all* of you who read these stories, so wherever you have joined on this journey, thank you for signing up for The *Techboys*.

Mark Thomas, you have produced a wonderful design for this series. I love it, and I love even more how it stands out in romance. Thank you for all your hard work on the cover and the interior of this book, and for always turning things around so fast and with such enthusiasm.

To everyone who reads this book or recommends it to a friend—thank you from the bottom of my heart. It means so much to me when you've enjoyed reading a story as much as I have enjoyed writing it. I'm excited about the characters and the stories that are to come!

ABOUT THE AUTHOR

I have worked for many years in the tech startup scene writing screeds of notes* that have percolated through my brain for years and have now weaved their way into The *Techboys* Series. *The Game* is the fifth novel in this series, and in total eight books are planned.

I love helping people escape their daily lives for a short while with the help of a steamy romance, some fun, and gorgeous fictional boyfriends. The *Techboys* Series revolves around the tech scene and the people that work for technology companies in New York City, something I became familiar with through my work and regular annual visits to close friends who live there.

I am a Scottish author based in Edinburgh with my husband, and I have two grown-up children. When I'm not reading or writing, I love running and can often be found tapping away on my laptop in local cafés or out enjoying the beautiful wild landscapes of Scotland.

Thanks so much for buying this book. It's a joy when people reach out to me, so please feel free to contact me as follows:

Website: www.everiley.com
Instagram: @evemriley

* I'm not a techy by background, but, fortunately, my techboy husband is on hand to advise. This also explains why all the tech references in the books are suitable for people whose level of understanding may be limited to plugging a connector into their phone to charge it up.

Printed in Great Britain
by Amazon

58174926R00182